NO PERFECT HERO

NICOLE SNOW

ICE LIPS PRESS

ABOUT THE BOOK

**Bossy. Heart of stone. Snarly mess next door.
Send help before I'm prick-matized...**

My next big mistake has a name.

Warren Ford. Best kept secret in this weird little town.

An alpha's alpha. Spartan abs. Too blunt for everybody's good.

Moody, broody, mysterious, and totally up in my business.

I thought Heart's Edge would be safe.

No two timing exes. No pink slips. No hulking, loud, inked up –

Oh. *Right.*

Leave it to a badass to bring the drama piping *hot*.

Then he goes and saves a cat who means the world to my little niece.

Making me a mushy little puddle of wishes.

Wishing I didn't know his savage kiss like my own reflection.

Or how erasing tears must be his superpower.
Wishing I'd never poked his scary past.
Or heard him growl when he swears it's not our future.

There's no way this works.
He's no white knight. I'm no princess.
I need to go. He says stay.
Even our sheet-ripping nights can't work miracles.
Only an answer as the danger closes in.
Is Warren my perfect slice of hero?

I: DROP DOWN WITH THE TOP DOWN (HALEY)

*T*here's nothing like a drive across the Pacific Northwest with the top down and the summer wind in your hair to make a girl feel human again.

Sure, it's a little bit of a cliché.

The typical girls' road trip, me and my niece in a convertible sipping strawberry smoothies every hundred miles, the sun beaming down on us like Zeus blowing a kiss. It's too perfect.

You'd almost think I'm totally not running away from my problems, darting off to the middle of nowhere to *find myself* after a colossal heartbreak.

But when you walk in on your ex-fiancé with your ex-best-friend-ex-bridesmaid in a fitting room with the ugly bridesmaid's dress *you paid for* hiked up around her hips and his untailored tux down around his ankles...

You earn the right to be a cliché.

I'd say I've earned a lot more than that.

Especially after I found my layoff notice sitting in my inbox.

Right-sizing. That's what they called the terminations at

1

the massive faceless mega-corporation I called my day job. I was out the door with an awkward hug and a mumbled half apology from my supervisor.

Then – oh, but then – everything really went to hell in a handbasket.

My side gig – my true passion – got tanked when the gallery I'd been working with practically pitched my paintings in a dumpster.

Low sales, they said. Lack of interest.

They might as well have pulled an Angela Bassett.

Get your shit, get your shit, *and get out.*

So I got my shit.

I packed it in the back of my sister's borrowed classic convertible – a pretty midnight blue shimmer 1988 Ford Mustang. I kidnapped my sister's ten-year-old daughter, Tara, because she's better company than some backstabbing, fiancé-stealing best friend anyway.

And now that I'm knee-deep into being a cliché, I wish we were leaving Vegas.

But we're actually leaving Seattle so I can start a new life in Chicago. We'll steal a spare room at my old college friend Julie's house for a month or two until I can get a new job and pay the rent on a place of my own.

I'll give the kid back eventually, I guess.

In a few weeks, when her parents get home from Hawaii.

I'll care about responsibility later.

Right now, I've got the mountains on the horizon, tall trees all around, the wind in my hair, the sun on my back, and enough of a grudge against life that I'm good with not making big decisions for a while.

I'll figure out what to do after I get to Chicago and see what the local job ads serve up. It's a big city. Lots of opportunities.

Until then, I'll enjoy the drive. The open road.

Sweet freedom I've prepaid for with a savage bee sting to the heart.

Tara snoozes half asleep in the passenger seat, her dark brown hair whipping across her face. She's a sun baby, dozing in the heat, curled up like a cat perched on a summer stone.

The radio shifts as we pass out of one zone into another, and she stirs at the crackle, yawning and scrubbing at one eye. "Auntie Hay?" she mumbles.

I hate when she calls me that. Mostly because it makes me feel old when my first instinct is to say *hay is for horses, baby* – and twenty-five is way too young to be throwing out that spinster crap.

But she's too adorable for me to twig her about it, so I glance over from watching the road, offering her a smile. "Morning."

She blinks at me drowsily. "It's afternoon...isn't it?"

"Not to you, apparently." I check the GPS.

We're just past Lolo National Forest and Missoula after a quick pit stop in Glacier National Park for Tara's sake. We swung up to Whitefish to take in the scenery. Next stop should be Billings. There's maybe a day or two of driving to Chicago after that, but it's not time to look for a hotel for the night just yet.

Tara's little hand goes over her yawning mouth.

"You hungry? There might be a place to stop in the next hour or so."

Tara scrunches up her nose. "Maybe. I kinda need to pee," she complains, and I bite back a laugh.

There's just something about kids and their shameless honesty.

I could use a little honesty in my life again.

I glance back at the GPS. There's a town up ahead, not

3

even named, just a little dot on the map and an off-ramp marker in about five minutes.

They'll have a gas station, at least. Hopefully a sanitary one – or some kind of restaurant.

I squint through the windshield, picking out the reflective green sign in the distance, and merge over into the right lane to take the off-ramp that leads down through a dense, tree-lined slope of land.

But just as we're cruising onto the ramp, the Ford starts to sputter.

My stomach sinks.

Uh-oh. That's *never* a good sign.

This beast is still moving, though.

I manage to get to the bottom of the off-ramp where the road curves around toward a little town in the distance, picturesque and dusty and a little too Norman Rockwell. Almost like it's been plucked out of those ubiquitous paintings in hotel rooms by artists you've never heard of but who've probably made a killing selling enough prints for every last Motel 6 down every stretch of Highway Americana.

I'm just not sure we're going to make that Rockwellian little town.

Not when the Mustang keeps coughing and slowing and when I curse, mashing my foot against the gas pedal, all I get is Tara gasping and whispering, "Swear jar!" and not an ounce more juice.

At least we make the turn.

And manage to coast forward about another hundred feet before the last little bit of *oomph* I get out of the Mustang sends us floating over onto the shoulder like an oversized yacht caught in a current.

That's what it feels like, trying to maneuver this long, bulky car after its get-up-and-go just got-up-and-went.

Exactly like trying to steer a big, heavy boat against the current, but that boat doesn't want to go anywhere but down.

The Mustang sputters out with a little grunt, like it's settling in and telling me it's giving up.

I try the key in the ignition, but the engine only makes a wheezing, rattling sound without turning over. Well, crap.

Craaaaaaaaap.

My sister's going to kill me if I killed her car. It was a gift from her husband on her thirtieth birthday.

She's one of the lucky ones who found a guy who gets her. Instead of *sleeping with her best friend*, John buys her gifts that suit her tastes.

She must've snagged the last good one. Because I swear every man I've met in the last five years – including the one I'd planned to marry – is trash.

Okay. Whew.

I'm bitter. I'm angry. Breathe in, breathe out.

Life goes on.

That's what I keep telling myself, a daily mantra.

And surely my brother-in-law can't really be the last decent man on Earth.

I have bigger worries right now, anyway.

Clenching my fists on the steering wheel, I stare between them. "Well, kiddo," I say. "Hope you don't mind peeing on the side of the road."

"Why can't I go there?" she asks. "I bet they have a bathroom."

She's leaning over the passenger side door and squinting across the field to the right of the car. I follow her gaze, squinting through the light.

I hadn't even noticed where we'd pulled off, too focused on trying to make the damn car move.

But there's some kind of...hotel? Inn?

5

I'm not sure what it is, but it looks like a vacation lodger's dream. There's a tall three-story house set far back in the field, lined with columns in the front. It's surrounded by well-tended greenery. Pretty shade trees are scattered across the manicured lawn, precisely spaced along little cobbled paths leading between a cluster of cottages, some singles, some duplexes.

The entire portrait is set against the backdrop of distant, smoky-looking mountain ranges beyond a steep cliff, and that Rockwellian feeling gets even stronger as I catch the sign hanging from a post up ahead.

Charming Inn.

Huh.

Well, maybe the name fits because it *is* charming.

Even if a city slicker girl like me probably sticks out like a sore thumb here, I hope the locals will be friendly. At least hospitable enough to let a kid use their bathroom.

I can't let Tara suffer much longer. She's squirming around, thighs pressed together, and I flash her a smile and get out of the car, slamming the door and reaching in the back for my overnight bag and her backpack.

"Come on," I say and offer her my hand. "Let's go meet the locals."

We push the quaint little white picket fence open and quick-time it up the central walk to the main house. It's an old plantation-style building, really strange to see here in Middle America, but it's been fitted out to be a hotel, it looks like.

There's a little bronze plaque to one side of the door, listing the lobby hours. When we step inside the carpeted, Victorian-furnished lobby, a small bell over the door rings. Behind the broad, glossy front desk, a faint snort sounds.

Followed by a crash, as the sleeping occupant of a tipped-back chair jerks and goes tumbling down to the floor.

Tara gasps with surprise – then squeaks, whimpering, dancing from foot to foot and clutching my hand tighter. "Auntie Hay..."

I glance around quickly, then notice the sign on the far wall with the little male and female symbols and an arrow. "There, sweetie," I urge, pointing. "Down the hall. Go."

Tara takes off at a crab-legged trot. I watch her for a moment, then lean over the front desk, peeking in tentatively. "Um, hello? Sir? Are you okay?"

A rheumy-eyed older man pushes himself up off the burgundy-carpeted floor, using the toppled wing chair to haul himself upright before grunting and flipping it over to stand properly again.

He spikes his short-cropped silvering hair with one hand, leaning on the chair with the other, eyeballing me as if he's not quite sure what to make of me before grunting and offering a reluctant smile.

"I'm fine, ma'am. Takes more than a tumble to kill this old ticker." He thumps his narrow, reedy chest. "Something I can help you with?"

"I hope so." I flash a smile. "My niece needed to use your restroom, sorry. But we're in a little trouble. Our car broke down right outside your inn, and I'm afraid we're stuck."

"Well, now..."

He rubs his stubbled chin. He's very jowly for such a thin, willowy man, like his face is melting. I know that look and try not to let my own frown show. He's a heavy drinker, and it's aging him fast.

I'll never forget that look for anything after Dad...

I don't know if it makes me feel softer toward the old man. Or just more bitter toward the first man who taught me people would always find a way to destroy themselves, and usually they don't have to look real hard to find it.

7

Dad grabbed the first opportunity when life went sour, one bottle at a time.

But the stranger smiles again, disarming and almost self-deprecating, as if he knows the picture he presents and how people judge. He shrugs. "We've got a mechanic here in town. Good 'un, too. It's late in the day, and you might get a tow, but you're not getting a fix to get out of here by sundown. We're all booked up on short stay rooms...but we've got a half-duplex available in one of the extended stay vacation rentals. It's even got a mountain view."

I frown. As nice as it sounds, I know it means money.

I'm operating on a limited budget since I basically tossed most of what I own and took off on my last paycheck, plus what I could sell back from the wedding that never happened and ate my entire savings.

I'll have to pay for the car repair, too. I'm crunching numbers in my head, and it doesn't look good. "I don't know if I can afford something like that."

"It's all I've got, and we're the only hotel in town." He folds his arms on the counter and leans toward me. I catch a faint whiff of rum, but not enough to drive me back. "Listen. I'm not about to let a lady in distress and a little girl sleep in their dang car in a strange town. I'll give you a discounted rate. Only charge you what I would for a single room. How's that sound?"

I twist my lips. "Name your rate."

"Sixty-five per night. How's that sound?"

I whistle softly. That's really not bad at all.

Back in Seattle, sixty-five dollars a night wouldn't even get you one of those cheap motels with the anonymously painted prints. More like the kind of place where people pay to live there by the week and police are in the parking lot every night. A place like this – half an entire duplex?

Yeah. I'd say we just lucked out when it comes to places to break down.

I look out the window, pretending to mull it over a little longer.

What do I have to lose?

The scenery's nice, the atmosphere's pretty, the lodgings are cheap...and I could use a little downtime somewhere quiet and relaxing to get past my Bitter Betty stage and move on with life.

Maybe it's meant to be.

I nod, imagining the next week. We'll stay until the Mustang's fixed, then onward to Billings.

"All right. Sold," I say, digging in my purse for my wallet and my credit card. "Who's in the other side of the duplex, by the way? Just so I won't bother them."

"Oh—*him*." The way he says it is a half snort. Almost ominous, but he waves it off with a shake of his head. "Don't worry, miss. He'll keep to himself. He's just a harmless grouch. Minds his own business 'cause that's all he ever minds. You probably won't even see him."

I arch a brow but pass my credit card across with a shrug.

Everybody's got their own way of doing things, and I'm not one to judge. I'll likely want to be left alone myself, minus the always entertaining company of my pint-sized sidekick.

"Is it too late to call the mechanic to at least get a quote?" I ask, watching him punch in my information on the keyboard behind the desk.

"Nah. I'll ring him up for you while y'all get settled. I need your number anyway for the register."

"Thanks." I rattle off my number quickly, along with my old home address and billing zip code.

Technically, I guess right now I'm homeless. I wasted no time walking the hell out and breaking our lease after Eddy's two-timing escapades, but the old Seattle digits will do for now.

While my trusty attendant hums to himself, I turn around, taking in the room around me.

This place has a soft touch to it, little vases full of fresh-cut pink peonies everywhere, gauzy white curtains draped over the windows so the sunlight makes them glow as it streams in. The light gives the room a sort of quiet, muted radiance.

It's nice. I'd like to paint the special way the light beams in, turning almost misty as it slants across the carpet. Whoever owns this place has an eye for comfort, and I throw a glance back at the front desk, suspecting it's not him.

Perfect timing. The old man's done, printing out my receipt to sign, and pushing a key across the desk just as Tara comes out of the bathroom, moving in that prim, princess-like way that says she's got her groove back with her bladder weighing a pound less, thank you very much.

I toss her a grin and turn to thank the old man, swiping the key and my card in exchange for a pen scribble.

"Thanks," I say. "What's your name?"

"Flynn," he answers. "Flynn Bitters. At your service anytime."

"Thanks, Mr. Bitters," I say, lifting my hand in a wave. "Just have the mechanic give me a call. No need to rush, we can probably stay a few days."

Tara looks up at me with wide eyes as we step outside into the brisk, warm summer afternoon. "We're...staying here?"

"Just for a little while," I answer. "Call it a mini-vacay until the car's straightened out. We'll soak up the sun, kick up our feet, maybe take in the sights and try some local food. This place looks fun."

She wrinkles her nose. "I dunno, Auntie Hay. It's so tiny...there wasn't even a name on Google."

"There was a name on the sign we passed," I point out and grin. "My darling tagalong, welcome to the illustrious town of Heart's Edge."

* * *

THE NUMBERED DUPLEX cabin we've been assigned to is actually around the back of the main plantation house, almost toward the far edge of the property.

Good. Plenty of privacy.

It's one of the larger cottages, made of unfinished dark wood, maybe cedar or fir. Just looking at it screams it's modernly simplistic and sweetly rustic with its wooden siding and wraparound porch and tall floor-to-ceiling windows to the sides and back.

But what really gives it soul is the *view.* The whole unit looks out on a long slope leading down to a cliff with a stunning valley view rolling right up the foot of the mountains.

My heart does a somersault when I'm really able to stop and breathe and take it in.

There's even a hot tub out back. I find it while we're scouting around the little porch, which is settled right in the middle. So, no question that the occupants of both sides either have to share or come up with some kind of scheduling agreement. There's no one around, though, so once we're tucked away and settled in, I might just take a little dip to get rid of the soreness from driving.

Once we've finished snooping around outside, we step back up the porch stairs and try the key in the lock on the left side. It jiggles and...doesn't do anything.

No go. Weird.

Bitters must've told us the wrong number. He told us we were Cabin 31-A, not 31-B.

No big deal. I slip the key into the lock for 31-B on the right side, and it twists open immediately.

We step into a cozy space, full of light shining off soft wood tones, with furniture in dark, earthy, welcoming shades. It's a little like Martha Stewart meets Mountain Home Magazine, and I'm loving the vibe.

My niece creeps in shyly behind me, peering around.

"We're fine. Looks newer in here than I would've guessed." I flash Tara a disarming smile and dump my bag on the sofa. "Let's check out the beds. This place looks big enough that we might even get separate bedrooms."

"If we don't," she says chirpily, already heading toward the hall, "we can just act like it's a sleepover!"

I can't help watching her fondly as I follow.

She's so resilient, so adaptable, putting the best face on everything. I miss when I was still that bright and optimistic and easily excited. But heck, maybe I can take a life lesson or two from a ten-year-old bumblebee.

Find the bright side to everything, appreciate new, and just *move on.*

But I'm too busy moving into the first bedroom off the hall to guess what's coming.

A big, rough hand grips my shoulder, spins me around, and the wall thumps hard against my back.

Holy –

Before I even have time to blink, there's a behemoth on me, a charging bull, appearing out of nowhere, walling me off in muscle and pine scent and dark, wily ink.

I'm too shocked to even scream.

So I yelp instead, my heart rocketing up the back of my throat, my pulse spiking.

Half a second later, I'm staring up into a grim, tight-locked, sharply handsome face and livid, hard blue eyes that bore into me as this giant of a man bears down.

He tightens his grip. Pins me to the wall with enough strength to make me feel like a gnat and enough body heat to make me feel like I've stepped into a furnace, burning off him in waves that touch me from head to toe.

"How the fuck did you get in here?" he demands, snarling low, a vibrating growl I can practically feel slamming into me. "Who sent you? Does Bress know? Is he coming?"

Holy hell.

This is new, and I'm frozen.

I'm not used to oversized men grabbing me and barking questions.

My brain can't decide between panic and anger or whether this asshole is getting handsy with me.

It settles on deer in headlights. Or maybe possum. Yep, that's me.

Trigger my fight or flight instinct, and I don't do either.

I just lock up.

Don't ever ask me to have your back in a bar fight. I'm useless.

Tara's more useful, though, because as she comes out of the other bedroom and gets one look at us, she belts out a shriek that could lift roofs for the next mile.

The giant whips back, letting go of one of my shoulders and whirling toward her.

Then I guess I'm not so useless after all.

Because the very *second* it looks like he's even *thinking* about going near Tara, everything in me fires up and I shove his other hand away roughly, glowering.

"Get your hands off me, you prick!" I snap.

He just blinks, dumbfounded, his massive fists suddenly hanging at his sides.

He's tall – Redwood tall, to the point where I'm not quite

sure how he fits in the hallway when his head is almost brushing the ceiling, his black hair a tangle just an inch away from the stucco.

His t-shirt looks more like something he painted on over thick, corded muscle with not an ounce of softness over chisels hard enough to cut someone. The blue fabric seems only subtly different from the texture of the tattoos snaking down his thick, bulging arms – a maze of patterns, stylized letters, and one simple one with the name *Jenna* etched in tiny script.

He drags a hand over his bearded face, the calluses on his palms audibly scraping against his stubble, still staring at Tara.

"Fuck. That," he growls, "is a kid."

"No shit, Sherlock," I bite off. "And she's with me. Stay away from her."

He jerks back toward me.

Big mistake.

Without waiting around for another opportunity, I smash my purse across his bluntly handsome jaw, whipping it across his face hard enough to hopefully leave fucking alligator hide imprints in his swarthy skin.

He staggers back with a grunt. I dash past him, grabbing Tara's hand and bolting for the door. "Come on!"

I should've known I wouldn't get far. Goliath may be huge, but he moves like a cobra – lightning quick and lethal. We make it three steps back to the living room before he's dodging around us, cutting us off, blocking the exit. Tara and I both draw up short, stumbling back.

"Move," I growl, hefting my purse again threateningly.

Sure, it can't do much damage, but I doubt it's fun eating a face full of leather.

Goliath folds his arms over his chest, squaring himself up

and looking down at me sternly. "Not till I get some answers, lady," he snarls.

"Answers to *what*? I just walked in here, and you started throwing me around like a freaking ping pong ball!"

"Yeah. You walked into *my* suite so—"

"Correction: it's our suite," I fling back, my face hot with frustration, brandishing the key like a tiny dagger. "Bought and paid for. I don't know what the hell *you're* doing in here. Maybe you should be the one giving some answers."

Before I can even pull back, he yanks the key out of my hand.

Son of a—

"God *damn*." He swears, peering at the key, then scrubs one hand over his face with a tired groan. When he looks at me again, he actually looks apologetic, his sky-blue eyes darkening to a simmering liquid cobalt. "Flynn gave you the wrong key. Sorry." His jaw tightens. "Move along. I'll get this straightened out."

I bite my lip. I really don't like being ordered around like this.

But I also don't want to be standing in the middle of the Incredibly Pissed Off Hulk's living space.

Reluctantly, I drag myself outside as he throws the door open for us, Tara trailing in my wake.

God. I *really* hope he prefers keeping to himself. Because the thought of spending a few days bumping into this jackass again just put a major damper on my idea of a relaxing mini-vacation.

But as he steps out onto the porch, slams the door, and locks it, I can't help lingering on the tight taper of his body as he walks away.

Why is it *always* the hot ones with personalities like an acid bath?

Even if he's a jackass, he's nice to look at.

Those jeans love his hips too much, and they seem pretty fond of his thighs, too.

His shoulders roll as he lopes with that kind of powerful strength that says half of it comes from learning to carry and manage his own massive bulk.

And his ink...Lord have mercy. We're talking tattoos so wild, so intense, so intricate they call to my artist's soul like a raging fire lures every moth.

I only got a few good looks at his scowling face, and it wasn't half bad either.

Midnight-blue eyes. Trimmed beard. Hair just a little too dark and thick, joining with his beard to form a rough halo of explosive testosterone around his face.

So there's something about that.

Something I like.

Maybe it's because Eddy was nothing like him, skinny and refined and boy pretty.

Maybe it's because Eddy hid his rotten personality too well, while Mr. Goliath wears his asshole badge on his sleeve.

Maybe it's because I'm still just trying to decipher what the hell even happened.

See? I *am* picking up Tara's habits, looking at the bright side.

Tara frowns, draping herself against the porch railing, watching him go. "He was kind of a butt, wasn't he, Auntie Hay?"

"Swear jar," I remind her and sigh, leaning next to her. "I think he's our new neighbor for the next few days."

"Where's he going?"

"I guess," I say, "he's going to swap our key."

I can't shake that gnawing feeling as we stand around a little longer.

Please, just this once, let something go right.

Please just let the key swap be the end of my drama with this caveman and his temper tantrums.

* * *

TURNS OUT, he wasn't going to swap our key.

Tara and I have relocated to the back patio for now and sprawled ourselves out across a couple of very nice, plush patio chairs to wait for our new key.

I'm not going anywhere, anyway.

My bag's still on the couch in that jerk's place, and he's locked us out. It's just the right temperature outside to bask in the sun, anyway, with late afternoon trending toward evening – still warm enough to enjoy the bake without sweltering or worrying about sunscreen.

I'm close to dozing off when I'm snapped awake by the feeling of my bag landing on my stomach.

"Oof!"

I open my eyes, clutching at it and curling forward a little.

Asshole Extraordinaire stands over me, huge arms folded over his chest again like he's making a bulwark out of himself, those hard blue eyes raking over me. I didn't even hear him come back, he's quiet like a lion.

Glowering up at him, I set my bag on the floor between the lounge chairs. "Was that really necessary?" I ask but don't give him a chance to answer. I just hold out my hand, thinning my lips. "So where's the key?"

"No key," he answers firmly. "I just bought out your side of the cabin. So you and your munchkin can be on your way somewhere else. I need my privacy."

"I'm no munchkin," Tara huffs. "I'm ten!"

"She's ten," I repeat, scowling at him. "And you don't get to kick us out. We're paying customers. Last I checked, you don't own this place."

"If money's what you're worried about, I'll pay you back *double* the room rate you paid Flynn."

I eye him. *What?*

This is just getting...weird. And suspicious.

Why does he need to be alone so desperately that he'll not only buy out the room rate, but spend even more to pay me back? Does this guy have a criminal background or something?

I shake my head. "Well, even if I wanted to take you up on your offer, I'm not going anywhere. I *can't*."

He arches one thick brow. "And why the hell not?"

"Our car broke down. Not that it's any of your business, and not that I should have to justify myself to you," I throw back. "And since this is the only game in town and the only room left, I'm not going anywhere unless *you* want to push my car all the way to the next town over."

An odd transformation passes over the jerk's face.

He actually looks worried for a moment. At least, I think that's worry and not heartburn.

Then he scowls like he's annoyed with himself for daring to feel a pang of guilt. There's worry again, then just grim resignation.

Goliath sighs, the sharp crags of his brows drawing together as he closes his eyes and rubs a thick, coarsely shaped hand over his face.

"I'm guessing Flynn called Stewart up at the garage about your car."

"I wouldn't know since the only thing I've been able to deal with since getting here is *you*. Guess I wouldn't be surprised if Flynn didn't bother calling about my car since you told him I'm leaving."

There's that worried look again. He reaches up, pinches between his brows, almost pained, before he closes his eyes again and presses his thumb and forefinger against his eyelids. "You're not going anywhere."

I blink. "Excuse me?"

"I said," he growls, "forget it. I'm not gonna dump you out on the street in a busted car with nowhere to go and a mun —" He darts a look at Tara. "A *young lady* with you."

I stare at him.

Wow. Is this porcupine lunk actually trying to be *chivalrous?* It's almost too easy.

I'm not ready to buy it. Or accept it.

Folding my arms over my chest, I look away from him.

"I'll believe that when I actually have a room key."

He heaves a massive sigh, raking a hand back through his hair until the thick, dark mass spikes up in a boyish mess, softening the chiseled harshness of his features. "Yeah. About that. Give me a minute."

This time I hear him walking swiftly. Instead of that silent cat-like tread, his step is heavy, weary, and even without looking, I can imagine the heaving sway of those massive shoulders.

This man is just officially *too much.*

And I don't even know his name.

* * *

IT's another twenty minutes before he returns.

A whole twenty minutes I spend soothing Tara's ruffled feathers, promising her we'll go find something fun to do tomorrow to make up for this crap circus.

I won't repeat the things she calls Goliath. They might not be swear jar worthy, but they're pretty playground-level mean.

Even if we both started giggling when she proclaimed him a doody-head.

Maybe that'll be his name until we leave.

When he returns, he just hands me a new key without a word – then turns around, walks through his back patio door, slams it, and firmly locks it without looking back. Not even a proper apology, and that *sorry* earlier didn't count.

Well. Let him sulk and grump alone if he wants.

I, on the other hand, have the best company in the world, and I think we've earned ourselves a movie marathon.

Key in hand, I marshal us both inside what's going to be home, sweet home for the next few days. We spend a little time getting settled into our rooms, putting our things away before I poke at the hotel phone directory.

Looks like Heart's Edge isn't so small that it doesn't have a pizza joint.

Within half an hour, Tara and I are curled up on the couch, sharing a pepperoni and pineapple while browsing for anything that might have Hugh Grant in it.

She's a little girl, but she's got good taste.

Still, as we flick through the pay-per-view offerings on TV...I can't help thinking back to that brooding, blue-eyed beast who hasn't made a sound from his side since the door slammed shut.

Who the hell *is* he?

What's his deal?

And why does he have me doubting not just the wisdom of staying here in Heart's Edge...but the entire massive upset I've just made of my life?

Am I really looking for a new beginning? I turn the question over in my head, literally chewing my thoughts in the pizza crust.

Or am I just running away from one problem and into another?

II: THOSE FLAMES KEEP RISING (WARREN)

*H*aley West.

That was the name Flynn gave me when I'd cornered him over the room fuckups and stared him down.

He started stammering, flinching like my glare could actually hurt him. Nothing new.

Flynn's got no backbone, just a hollowed-out tube for a spine full of Jack or whatever else he's guzzling today. It's amazing why the hell Grandma keeps him on payroll. The boy rolled over pretty fast after I said I wanted her out.

I should've known there was more to the story than he was telling me.

There always is with girls like *her.*

There's always trouble, too.

Damn if I could let that hotheaded little spitfire go wandering around Heart's Edge with nowhere to stay and not even a working car.

But I've got to get her out of here.

She almost blew my cover. As long as everyone thinks I'm the reclusive small town boy returning home for a hello, nobody blinks my way. Or even thinks twice about me staying at Grandma's inn.

Naturally, I picked one of the cottages rather than the basement in Grandma's house. A grown man needs his privacy, after all, and rumor has it I'm just staying here till I buy my own place in town.

Sometimes rumors are useful.

Say as little as possible, and usually people will invent the most plausible cover story without you having to speak a word.

The truth is, I can't let my dirty business touch my grandmother or all the hard work she's done keeping Charming up and running.

So I've got my business squirreled away behind lock and key – but leave it to that green-eyed little vixen to almost walk right into my war room.

Fuck.

If she'd seen my whiteboards, my newspaper clippings, my pin maps tracking movement...there's no telling what she'd have thought. I'd probably be in handcuffs right now, answering Sheriff Langley's questions.

I know what I thought about her.

That she'd been sent by Dennis Bress.

That he'd figured out I was hot on his trail and figured I wouldn't react ugly to a beautiful woman casually strolling in to find out what I know. I'm still not totally convinced.

But the broken-down Ford Mustang just outside the fence is pretty plausible.

Still. I've got to get her gone.

She's a liability and a distraction. The *worst* kind, when she's petite, curvy, tight-bodied, and from what I saw last night, far too fond of tight jeans and short, loose shirts that bare the tanned, toned curve of her waist every time she so much as breathes.

And the way that tumble of dark brown hair falls down, framing her face, lashing and swaying with her sharp, high-energy gestures...a man couldn't ask for a better way to make his dick like diamond.

Not something I need to be focusing on right now.

Not something I need at all.

She's hardly the only problem. Fuck, that poor kid with her came about a foot away from stumbling into my weapons cache.

Cases of guns, and I haven't had a chance to unpack everything and separate the ammo from the firearms yet. That could've been disastrous.

Ms. Haley may be annoying as hell, but I couldn't live with myself if I let her or the kid get hurt.

I knew setting up shop back home wouldn't be easy. Cornering Bress, even harder.

I just didn't expect this kind of complication.

But there's one way to get rid of her. And that's why I'm out here in the dead of night, on the cement floor of Flynn's dirty garage in the barn he lives in on the edge of the property, after we hooked up the old man's truck hitch and dragged Haley's Mustang inside.

It's a pretty car, that's for sure.

Well-loved, but someone's been putting used parts in it and while that'll keep it going for a while, they'll break down faster.

Looks like she's got a busted carburetor, but I might be able to work up a temporary fix that'll last her another hundred miles or so. Long enough to get her to a bigger city with a chain or a custom shop that carries Mustang parts.

It doesn't take me long to root around and realize she's got a stuck float valve.

A little shake, a little tap, and it comes loose.

It's just going to get stuck again – once a carburetor starts going downhill, it goes fast – but she'll be all right for another day or two of driving. Just have to make sure she knows to get it replaced in the next city she hits, whenever she hauls ass out of here – and out of my life – in the morning.

"Hey now, War," a familiar voice says from the doorway. "Keep right at it, and you're going to put me out of a job."

I roll myself from under the car, picking up a rag and swiping at the grease on my fingers.

Stewart Saxbe stands in the open garage, leaning one shoulder against the frame with an easy smile, his brown eyes glittering and his mechanic's fatigues straining against his blocky, muscular frame.

He's like me, ex-military, and can't let go of those old habits that say stay in shape and combat-ready at all times. We weren't deployed on the same team, even if we shared the same base camp many times, but you might say we served together in Afghanistan.

Jenna got to work alongside Stew and a few others I'd trust with my life.

Or hers.

But Jenna was the one who didn't come back.

No time to let myself linger on those memories, though.

I offer Stewart a smile as I stand, reaching out to clasp his hand firmly. "Just taking care of a nuisance. Nosy neighbor who'll be gone as soon as her car's fixed."

"I heard. Flynn gave me the rundown." He lifts his brows. "Figured I'd come take a look on the way home. What's wrong with it? Sweet lookin' ride."

"Bad carburetor." I shrug, leaning my hip against one of the work tables. "I popped the float valve loose. It'll hold till she can get it done up right."

He gives the car a measuring look, then pops the hood and leans in to peer. "Looks all right," he says, reaching a hand in and fiddling around. "Hm, the choke needs adjusting, too. You sure you want to send her on her way with this?"

"Not much choice," I say.

I can't really tell Stewart the real reason I want her gone quickly. I can't tell anyone.

I trust him more than anything, but he's friendly with everyone, and he might let something slip. News travels too easy in a small town, and it's too easy for it to reach somebody connected to Dennis Bress. "I doubt you stock a carburetor for this particular model of Ford. Unless you just happen to have one on hand?"

"Nah, but I could get a custom order in a few days. Fix her up good as new. Then she won't have to worry about breaking down before she gets somewhere safe."

I grimace. *A few days.*

He's right, and I can't think of any reason to argue that wouldn't draw suspicion and make him wonder why I'm so adamant about getting this girl out of here. "Won't that be expensive, for a classic like this?"

"That's what eBay's for." Chuckling, he pats the hood, straightening and giving the car an appreciative once-over. "Besides, having a pretty girl like that around? Should keep you plenty busy while you're back in town – and that's just what you need."

It's exactly what I *don't* need.

And exactly what I'm afraid of.

Too bad I'm out of excuses, for now. I'll take it.

It's not like my stay in Heart's Edge is finite. I have time. I can wait until Haley West and that adorable kid – her daughter, I'm guessing, the *young lady* who isn't a munchkin – get their need for a little rustic mountain life out of their system after a few days and head on down the road.

Dennis Bress isn't going anywhere.

Neither am I.

Not until I get what I'm after.

Stewart gives me a long look, measuring, knowing. He's a good friend, always seems to know what's on my mind, even when I don't say anything – or maybe because I'm not saying anything.

Thoughtful, quiet, he leans against the driver's side of the Mustang and folds his arms over his chest, studying me.

"You're not upset about the girl," he says softly. "It's something else eating you, isn't it? And if I know you as well as I think I do, War, it's the same something you've been upset about for thirteen years."

I tense, looking away, grinding my teeth. "I don't want to talk about it."

"No, you never do. Listen, Warren..." He sighs. "I thought maybe you'd come back to Heart's Edge to get some closure, but you're still as raw-edged as a razor, ready to cut shit to pieces. Why are you really here?"

"It's home. Don't think I ever need an excuse to come home."

"If it was home," he points out quietly, "you wouldn't be paying to stay in a room."

I smile, faint and humorless. "Come on, man. Haven't you heard the rumors? I'm in the market for a house and a wife. Eligible ladies beware."

Stew chuckles, then sends another worried look my way. "Well, your business ain't mine. Maybe you should just pick up Miss Mustang and head on out of town? Talk about easy."

"Bull. Don't even think about playing matchmaker. And no trying to run me off." I push away from the work table, straightening, and toss the greasy rag at him. "You just want me gone because you owe me...what, six beers now?"

He raises both brows with a deliberately blank look. "No earthly clue what you're talking about."

"Uh-huh. That shitty poker face of yours is *why* you owe

26

me six beers." Snorting, I elbow him. "Help me do one last check and close this thing up."

It's comforting, having Stew with me.

A reminder of better days, maybe. For a little bit, as we give the Mustang one last once-over and make sure everything's tight, it almost feels like old times.

Before that fateful day.

Before the news that made me beat my knuckles bloody. Before the folded flag, the sorrowful salute, the fucking obituary.

Before I knew Jenna wasn't coming home ever again.

For a little while, it's just me and Stewart swapping old stories, giving each other shit. And when he leaves to head home...

I feel a little more grounded. A little more centered, ready to get to work.

Sure, it might be past the town's bedtime, but I'm just getting started.

And I only spare one glance for the darkened windows on the other side of the duplex before I shut myself in my war room and get to work on counterintelligence.

* * *

IT'S ALMOST DAWN before I finally give up chasing ghosts for the night and fall into bed.

I barely bother to strip out of my shirt and jeans, down to boxers, before I pass out face-first across the mattress. I'm used to keeping long hours, but the past twenty-four have thrown enough curve balls my way to completely wear me out. So I'm really hoping to get some solid shut-eye.

Unfortunately, my new next door neighbor has other plans.

I think I've only been asleep for ten minutes before someone starts tap dancing on my skull.

Or at least, that's what I'm dreaming. Someone standing over my bed with a little hammer like the kind doctors use to test your reflexes, tapping on my skull, and in my sleeping imagination, the sound is tinny and rhythmic and flat, more like my head is a ball of glass.

It's actually a little wildfire standing on my doorstep, tapping away at the glass of my front door.

I groan, rolling over, letting one arm fall to the floor as I peer through the bedroom door and down the hall. Fuck.

I can just glimpse the front door from here, a fuzzy mess of too-bright sun glowing through the glass and turning the small, curving shape on the other side into a blur.

I don't need to see her clearly to know she's pissed. It's in her stance, hip cocked, her arms folded over her chest in between every round of impatient knocking that could give a woodpecker a good run for its money.

Grumbling, I turn my face into the pillow and muffle a curse into the cotton case.

What the fuck now?

Maybe if I stay put, she'll go away. Just get in her nice pretty working car and *go*.

"I know you're in there!" Haley calls, the glass paneling hollowing her voice. "I can see your ass."

Then you can kiss it, darlin', I almost throw back, before forcing myself to clamp my jaw shut, shove myself up on both arms, and slog march out of bed.

She'll probably think I'm hung over – shirtless, pantless, hair sticking up everywhere, bleary-eyed – but I don't care.

It's Come As You Are in Chateau Ford when you drag my sorry ass out of bed. Staggering to the door, I drag it open, leaning an arm against the frame over my head and eyeing her sourly.

"*What.*"

It's not a question.

She doesn't say anything. Just blinks at me, staring blankly, her gaze starting at my head and dropping to my feet before yanking back up again as if pulled on a leash, her pretty high cheekbones coloring – and I don't think that's blush.

"What the hell's the matter? See something you like?" As pissed as I am, I might as well have a little fun with this.

A guilty sound sticks in her throat. She looks away too quickly, clearing her throat and scowling at the distant, sunny horizon.

"Do you not understand the concept of clothing, you—you—"

"Warren," I say with a touch of dry amusement. "Name's Warren Ford, since you didn't bother asking last night."

"You *Warren.*" She says my name like it's the name of a particularly filthy breed of wild animal, and I almost smile. Her scowl deepens. "And you didn't exactly give me a chance for polite introductions. Not like you asked my name, either."

"I know who you are, Haley West."

She blinks, snaps a look back at me, then immediately looks away again. "How do you know my name?"

"Relax. Flynn told me when I went to sort out the rooms." I sigh, shifting to lean fully in the doorway, folding my arms over my chest and crossing my ankles. "So what do you want, Haley? I'm a busy person, and I'm guessing you are too."

My question seems to strike the fury back into her.

Little Ms. Nosey turns her glare back on me, planting her hands on her tight, curvy hips.

Damn if my eyes don't go there.

She's in cutoff shorts today, barely long enough to qualify as pants, tight-fitting enough to cut into the soft flesh of her thighs. The oversized baseball tee over them has been sawed off ragged, so it hangs loosely from her sweet pair, exposing hints of her midriff every time she moves.

Consider me completely screwed – or wishing I'd be. So distracted by the teasing glimpses of her navel that I almost miss her biting off her next question.

"What did you do to my car?"

"Car? The 'stang?" I frown, diverting my attention back to her face and those snapping green eyes, framed by a few ribbons of brown hair escaping in delicate little wisps from a messy clipped-up twist. "I fixed it for you."

"Without my permission?"

"You were going to get it fixed anyway. Does it matter who did the job?" I shrug. "Hell, I saved you a little time and money. Sue me."

Her rosy little cheeks fold in like she's just picked up a lemon with her teeth.

"You need a new carburetor, by the way, but I got the old one working. Well, enough to get you to Billings or the general vicinity." I arch a brow. "Unless you really want to stay in this little Podunk town long enough for the local shop to order you a new one?"

I don't tell her Stewart said he could.

Her eyes narrow. There's something stubborn in the set of her mouth. Something that tells me she just might take that as a challenge. "Really? I'm supposed to take some random stranger's word that he fixed my car and it's safe enough for me and a minor over open highway?" She sniffs as if she's holding in a *how dumb do you think I am?* "I'll wait for a professional opinion, thanks."

Goddammit.

She has a point, but I just – I can't *function* with her here. Separated from me and my grand plan by a wall that's too thin. Sure as hell can't make the kind of moves I need to corner Bress if she's over my shoulder all the time. I growl in the back of my throat, glaring at her.

"Fine. Suit yourse—"

Suddenly, I'm staring at her back.

She tosses a middle finger at me and stalks away, slamming the door to her half of the duplex.

I drag a hand over my face, groaning.

God *damn* it.

Whatever.

She'll get bored and move on soon enough. I can tell a city girl when I see one.

There's not much in Heart's Edge for people who are used to metropolitan night life. The mosquitoes get old real fast. Not to mention the constant call of the crickets and the lack of any high-end entertainment venues beyond a single pub with a dartboard that's got more holes than a cork.

It's everything that gives Heart's Edge its charm.

I'm sure it'll send her running for more civilized pastures by dawn with her kid in tow.

Sighing, I push myself back inside and close the door. I'm awake now.

I'll have to make do on a few hours of sleep. Maybe catch a nap after sundown before I need to be up after dark again, playing secret agent around town, digging for more intel.

Rubbing the sleep out of my eyes, I stumble into the shower, shocking myself awake with a cold, sharp rush of water right to the face. Old habit from the Army Rangers.

We'd be deployed too often in places where we'd be lucky to have running water at all. I learned to be mighty grateful for those cold showers to slap us back to our senses and keep us sharp.

That saying, *water is life,* never took on more meaning than with Uncle Sam.

I'm feeling more brisk by the time I towel off, dress, and

head into the kitchen to whip together a quick breakfast scramble and coffee. I glance up, though, as I catch motion through the window over the sink.

Haley's pulled the Mustang out of Flynn's garage. It's parked off the little dirt lane running along the side of the house, just outside the fence, her and the girl rummaging in the back with several bags.

Packing it in and leaving.

Thank fuck.

The sharp relief lets me actually enjoy my coffee while I sink down on the couch, planning my day.

The gossip about me looking for a house to settle down in will help. Considering the extent that Bress' business holdings have grown since he's worked his way into Heart's Edge like a bad infection, I'll take any excuse.

This one's perfect cover for cruising around town. I'll pretend I'm looking at *For Sale* signs on lawns to case his investments in broad daylight. I want to know every time Dennis Bress sneezes.

Where he spends his time. With who. What his weaknesses are.

And just what Jenna discovered about that asshole that made him kill her.

I've got a good idea where to start scouting from public records.

A few addresses, a route, a few more stops planned to make things look casual, then it's on.

I'm climbing in my pickup truck and heading up the highway into town.

No more sign of that pretty blue Mustang. The girls must've hotfooted it out without even saying goodbye.

If I didn't have a murderer's bug up my ass, I might feel sorry.

I'm completely distracted from any thought of the girls,

though, when I round a corner off Main and catch sight of none other than Bress himself.

Shit!

He's getting out of his old work-worn camper truck, parked right in front of the tack and feed store. It's the closest thing we have to a mall in Heart's Edge, if only because the owner, Tandy Thatcher, let her daughter have a little addition with a craft supply store, while her son runs a gardening shop out back.

Bress hauls himself out of the truck like a snake. Dripping with his trademark mix of weariness and quiet authority, this mask of a calm, thoughtful man laid over the demon underneath. He rakes a hand back through ash-blond hair, sighing heavily like he's carrying some great weight, and then trudges inside the main barn-like shop.

There's no one else around this early in the morning.

Perfect opportunity.

I park my truck on the curb, then steal a quick glance around.

There's no traffic and a barn wall between me and any line of sight from inside. Quickly, I rummage in the duffel bag I keep under the seat, until I find one of my GPS trackers.

It's magnetic, small, easy to hide inside a wheel well.

I slip around the far side of Bress' truck, letting its bulk conceal me, and bend in to tuck the tracker just above the right rear wheel.

"Playing mechanic again?" a tart voice asks from behind me.

I almost leap out of my skin.

I'm rewarded with a smack of my head against the camper of Bress' truck.

Hissing, swearing, I stand, rubbing at my throbbing

temple and whirling to see who's caught me – even though I already know.

Who the fuck else?

It's irritating that I already know her *voice* so well, this mix of saucy sweetness with a soft burr at the edge, always on the verge of laughter. And Haley West looks like she's laughing at me right now, leaning her elbow over the driver's side door of the convertible, watching with glittery eyes as she eases it in to park.

"You okay, mister?" the kid asks.

"I'm dandy," I answer, but fuck – *fuck,* did she see what I was doing? "What're you two doing here?" I demand, before she can ask what *I'm* doing here. "I thought you were heading out?"

"Oh? When did I ever say that?" Haley arches both brows with a prim little pursing of her lips, and I can see the resemblance between her and the kid. "Mr. Bitters was kind enough to point me to the craft supply store so I can stock up."

I stare at her blankly. "Stock up?"

There's something almost triumphant about her smile as she hauls herself out of the car.

She's such a lithe, spry young thing, she doesn't even bother with the door. Just pulls herself up on her arms and vaults over the top of it to land lightly.

The kid tries to imitate her, clearly a bit of hero worship, but ends up just clambering over the top and tumbling down before clearing her throat and straightening her sundress primly. Almost like a cat daring anyone to notice it tumbled off a windowsill.

Haley's more like the cat that got the cream, though, as she looks up at me with her green eyes blazing and her hands posted firmly on her hips.

"Turns out, I kinda like it here," she says with a smile so sweet, it can only be poison.

Absinthe, like the color of her eyes. Intoxicating and venomous.

My fists tighten, but I'm quiet as a stone, staring her down.

"Think we'll stay a bit, neighbor. Chicago will be there when I'm good and ready. What kind of artist would I be if I didn't follow my muse? And Heart's Edge is so *lovely*." Her smile takes on a razor's edge. "Besides. My little Tara's never really been camping in the boonies, so it's a great opportunity. But really, Warren. I appreciate all the hard work you did fixing my car and trying to run me out of town. I already feel like I've had the authentic small-town welcome."

I don't know what to say when it hits me like a brickbat to the face.

When I thought she was packing up this morning, she was actually *unpacking*.

Settling in halfway to damn well spite me.

I'm torn.

Torn between wanting to argue that I'm not some closed-minded mountain townie trying to run the fancy city girl off like it's a bad comedy flick...and wanting to drag her closer. Wanting to kiss that insufferable, satisfied smirk off her wicked little lips. Wanting to find out if she tastes like sugar and booze, just like the absinthe in her eyes.

Instead, I'm left frozen while she turns and walks into the shop with a little flip of her hair, her hand tangled in the little girl's.

Fuck. Me.

I've got to talk to Flynn.

One way or another, I need to get this distracting, ornery, entirely maddening woman away from me ASAP.

III: TALK ABOUT NOTHING (HALEY)

*I*t shouldn't have been so satisfying to walk away from that asshole, leaving him flabbergasted and wordless.

But c'mon. He *deserved* it.

Especially after he answered the door this morning, all broad, tattoo-swirled chest, and thickly toned thighs, and a pair of boxers so small I wouldn't even use them for a hand-kerchief.

I mean, wowza, if the crotch hadn't been cupping his bulge so snug, something just might've peeked out to give me a free show. And one more problem I really don't need.

Honestly, he could've had a little decency.

Or at least not opened his jerk-mouth, so I could've quietly enjoyed a little *in*decency.

Leave it to the gorgeous ones to talk too much.

I can't stand Warren.

He's surly. He's authoritative. He's presumptuous. He's rude. He's –

Taking up far too much of my headspace, apparently.

Because I should be thinking about the shades of blue

gouache paint I need to capture the colors of hazy sky around a distant mountain peak. Not about the particular shade of blue Warren's eyes were this morning when he'd been half asleep, his gaze dark and smoky.

Definitely not about the tousled hair falling into his eyes and the morning sun licking tawny gleams over the hard chisels of his bare chest.

God.

Settle down, girl.

There's a minor in the room.

And Tara's busy tugging at my shirt, pointing at a box of nearly two hundred Prismacolor pencils in a rainbow palette of bright shades.

I eye her with a sigh. She's too much like me at that age.

At ten years old, I picked up lots of things and tried them once and put them down before moving to the next – but I'm still crunching the numbers in my bank account. We're running on a tight budget.

But it's not fair to stock up on art supplies for myself just because I'm staying here out of some spiteful whim, and then tell Tara she can't have this one little thing.

Besides.

When I was a little girl, the thing that made me finally sit still and stop bouncing from hobby to hobby was a box of pencils. They came in various lead hardnesses and textures, a gift from a fourth grade teacher who admired the little doodles I left down the margins of my assignments.

Ms. Brandy hadn't been able to get me to pay attention in class, but when she put those pencils in my hand? Suddenly, I found something that could keep my complete and utter focus like nothing else.

Maybe the Prismacolors will be that for Tara.

And if not, she deserves the same chance I got to try

things again and again until she finds her one true love in a pencil.

I offer her a smile, shifting my load of canvases, paint tubes, and brushes to one arm so I can squeeze her hand. "You're sure that's the one you want? Not the markers or the pen sets?"

She shakes her head. "I like the way the pencils look soft when you color with them," she says. "I want to try that."

"Okay, baby." I grip her hand a little tighter, encouraging her. "You'll need a sketchbook to go with them, then. The kind that binds at the top. Spiral rings are easiest for pencil drawing. Go pick out one you like."

Her face brightens, her eyes widening, and she hugs me tight enough to almost make me drop everything. "Thanks, Auntie Hay!" she cries before racing off, leaving me watching her with a fond sigh.

I really do love that girl.

I don't see enough of her, living so far away from my sister, but maybe once I settle in Chicago, I'll make a point to take more time off to see family.

And she'll grow out of the nickname one day.

One day.

I turn to look for a few more things – a paint scraper, a little blending toner. But I can't seem to find the register when Tara comes bouncing back with her box of colored pencils and a large spiral bound sketchbook clutched to her chest.

Then I see the wooden sign over the open doorway. It's hand-painted, pointing to the attached barn that looks to be some kind of...horse shop? Farm shop?

They have bags of seed and bales of hay, at least. It smells warm and earthy and just dusty enough to tickle my nose.

Pay inside, the sign proclaims, so I rearrange my armful

and head through the door to do just that, stepping from the tile over the threshold onto a packed dirt floor.

That's how I bump right into a broad barrel chest, hard enough to send me rocking back with a squeak, clutching at my things.

Bad move. It just makes them go flying out of my arms like I'd squeezed a water balloon and sent it popping everywhere.

"Oops," a kindly, thoughtful male voice says, catching me by the shoulders and steadying me. "Here. Let me help."

I look up into blue eyes and for a moment think it's Warren – but Warren's eyes are a darker, stormier blue. More passionate and hot and wild.

These eyes are paler, softer, haunted by a quiet exhaustion that strikes me before I even fully take him in. He's tall, older but not quite *old*, with the same hard-cut ex-military build that makes me think of Warren as well. His ash-blond hair dips with a reserved smile he offers me as he drops down to one knee to start gathering my things.

"Sorry," I manage, sinking down to help, while Tara stands over us, watching curiously. "I should've been looking where I was going."

"Kinda hard to with all that piled in front of your face, I'd say." There's a soft drawl to his voice.

I wouldn't quite call it Southern, more like that particular flavor of Pacific mountain country you find in Oregon or California. With a chuckle, he helps me gather my spilled paints and supplies into the back side of a canvas, then frowns at the canvas itself. "Aw, looks like I got this one dirty. I'll pay for it with the owner if you want to grab a fresh one."

"Oh, no, it's okay." I shake my head, rising to my feet and smiling. "Canvases aren't hard to clean. I'll just buy this one, but thank you so much Mr...?"

"Bress," he says, offering me a hand, then chuckling and

dropping it when I eye it wryly, my own hands overflowing. "Dennis Bress. You look like a new face around here."

Bress.

Wasn't that the name Warren snarled at me when he caught me in his side of the duplex?

I don't understand. This man seems so *nice*.

Why would he be sending anyone after Warren, especially a hapless artist and occasional corporate slave?

I keep my thoughts to myself, though, and wiggle my fingers in a little wave in lieu of a handshake. "I'm just passing through for a few days while my car gets fixed. Staying over at Charming Inn. I'm Haley West, and this is my niece, Tara Brenley."

Tara pipes up with a chirpy little "Hi!" and lets go of her death grip on her prizes long enough to shake Bress' hand like the delicate little lady she likes to be. He bows over her hand, mimicking touching his forehead to it like a proper gentleman, and she giggles.

"Charmed," he drawls, then straightens and flashes me another smile. "If you're ready to check out, I'll help you get all that into your car."

I'm grateful for his help. Especially after I meet the owner of this strange little conglomeration of shops and find out that the rumors about small-town hostility aren't at all true.

Not when Ms. Thatcher is all smiles, offering a few suggestions for getting the dirt out of the canvas with rubbing alcohol. She even gives me a discount, though it's my fault the canvas was damaged.

Tara gets a few warm, inquisitive questions about her artistic talents without being patronizing, and then Bress helps us pile our shopping bags in the back of the car.

"Have you been to see the mechanic yet?" he asks as I climb behind the driver's seat.

"Not yet, which is a little ironic," I answer dryly. "He's the one person I need to see most, but I haven't had a chance to get into the shop yet and find out about the part I need."

"Well..." Bress' sigh is long and slow as he folds his elbows over the door of the Mustang and leans on them. He's not looking at me, but instead somewhere in the distance past me, but there's a troubled knit to his brow. "If he can't help you, look me up. I'll make sure you're taken care of."

That's an odd thing to say. Or maybe I'm projecting because of Warren?

I frown, but then his gaze drops back to me, and I quickly shift into a smile, hoping I don't look as uncomfortable as I feel. "Thanks, Mr. Bress. I appreciate it."

He doesn't answer my smile. Just looks at me for a long, wandering moment, his gaze strange, before he straightens, pulling back with one last light tap against the car door.

"You take care, Ms. West," he says. "And welcome to Heart's Edge."

* * *

I'M BROODING over our conversation on the entire drive back to Charming Inn.

Something's not right here. I feel like I just stepped into an Agatha Christie novel.

Small town that looks picturesque on the surface, but the people are all just a little too weird in ways you can't quite nail down. Not until you find out there's a dead freaking body under the floorboards of your cabin or something.

It's just strange. Warren's shady as hell, intent on getting me away from him – as if he's hiding something in his side of the duplex, and he's afraid I'll find out.

So maybe a few of the things he's done for me would be considered nice, if he wasn't clearly just doing them to get me as far away from him as possible. And then this guy he

41

mentioned, Dennis Bress, just happens to bump into me in the craft store and starts speaking cryptic, although when I compare him to Warren...

Bress seems like an angel.

At least *he* has manners.

He knows how to dress himself, and he doesn't give that hell-look like some kind of chest-thumping Tarzan. The look that makes me think Warren either wants me in flames or wants to throw me against the wall and kindle something far more wicked than another cursing, spitting fight.

So what's going on here?

Is there some kind of grudge between Warren and Bress? Like a small town blood feud?

Is Bress a criminal? Hell, is Warren? A gangster, a thug, squeezing poor Bress for something he's owed – or just for the sport of it?

My lips twist sourly, none of the options seeming quite right.

Bress is too nice. And Warren...

Well, he's not nice. Not at all.

But there's some kind of core of honor and morality there, or he'd have insisted on having me hauled off the property even after he'd found out Tara and I had nowhere else to go.

Or maybe I'm just dickmatized.

Maybe I'm losing my mind.

And I don't want to believe a man who could put every LA underwear model to shame when he's in his boxers could be so awful.

I haven't forgotten Warren at his finest.

This lion of a man standing in the doorway like Hercules himself came back to earth and stopped by a tattoo shop, bed-tousled hair, the elastic band of his boxer briefs hugging up snug against that dip of flesh just below his crest.

God.

Somebody stop me.

I'm still turning it over, chewing my lower lip, completely wrapped up inside my own head when I turn off onto the little side lane leading to the back of the Charming Inn's sprawling property and our own little private corner. I'm so preoccupied unloading the bags and closing up the Mustang that I don't even take in the cabin as I'm mounting the steps, sorting through my keys for the new one on the ring.

Then Tara screams.

High, shrill, scary.

My blood instantly chills to ice water as I jerk my head up, racing to grab her, to protect her.

But then I stop, my brows knit together, as I finally see what frightened her.

"What in the world?" It just falls off my lips, suddenly as numb as the rest of me.

And the first cold fingers of real, dense fear prick my skin. I can't stop staring at the mess smeared over my front door.

Blood.

Stark, fresh blood, dripping crimson, outlining letters written in a hasty, angry hand.

LEAVE NOW OF YOUR OWN ACCORD
BEFORE YOU CAN'T LEAVE AT ALL
THIS IS YOUR ONLY WARNING

I CLAP a hand over my mouth to stifle a panicked scream trying to claw its way up from my lungs.

Stuck in the blood are soft, curling brown feathers, giving

43

me a terrible idea of exactly where the blood came from. The kind of person who'd do this to an innocent animal just to send a message.

They're getting their meaning across, loud and clear.

And if they'd do this to a bird on a whim...

What would they do to a woman and a little girl?

"Tara, get back in the car," I gasp, reaching out blindly for her hand, backing down the steps, pulling my petrified, sniffling niece with me. "Get in the car, baby, and we'll leave. We'll get settled and call the police from somewhere sa—"

"No need to call the police." A voice like thunder rises behind me, all grim growl.

I freeze, my knees locking up, my breaths seizing up at the sound of Warren coming closer.

The first thing flashing through my head is *holy shit, he's the one who wants me gone!*

I can't breathe. I can't think. I can't decide.

My legs are stiff like cement as I turn slowly, instinctively pushing my niece behind me so I can shield her. I remember Warren's truck is parked behind my Mustang, bumper to bumper – *blocking us in* – and he stares over my head with hard eyes, looking past me at the cabin.

Suddenly, I'm far too aware how large he is, intimidating and massive and powerful. This deadly bulwark of a man who looks like he's made to be a human wall.

I'm just not sure if he's designed to protect or hurt.

It's too easy for people like him to turn their strength into something worse. And if he's lost his mind, if he's gone completely crazy...

But he brushes past me without a second glance, his face set in dark, brooding lines as he rakes the door over with a glance.

"This wasn't meant for you," he says softly. "Don't worry. You're safe."

I glance at Tara first. Her little eyes are wide and wet, and she's trembling.

I'm not scared anymore when I see my baby girl scared. *I'm pissed.*

"Go, kit," I whisper, giving her shoulder a soft stroke, then a gentle push. "In the car. I'll be right behind you."

And I will. But first, a few words with Mr. W.T.F.

Tara turns and scrambles away, safely out of reach. I watch her climb in the back seat of the Mustang, before ducking down out of sight like a scared puppy finding a hidey-hole.

Good girl. If this gets uglier than I think and we have to run, she'll be ready to go.

I take a few more steps back, putting a little more distance between myself and the cabin – and Warren. I'm tense, ready...but even if I'm scared, with every second that passes, I'm angrier.

I want answers. *Now.*

"How can I be safe if someone's writing messages on my door?" I bite off. "What do you mean, it wasn't meant for me?"

He's focused, silent, assessing the message scrawled on the door with penetrating eyes. He reminds me of a cop, all of a sudden. Solemn and intense, dissecting a crime scene for clues.

The idea shouldn't make me feel better, a little less ready to bolt. For all I know, he's the reason we just stepped into some seriously bad juju.

But I just can't feel any menace vibrating off him.

And I want to trust my intuition. But then, my intuition got me engaged to Eddy.

Still, I relax a little as he glances at me.

His gaze flicks over me, softening, brilliant blue eyes darkening with concern, cutting through me faster than any steely glance. "Whoever did this made the same mistake you did. Asshole didn't know which side of the place was mine. You hurt?" There's a fierceness in his voice when he says those last two words.

Something dark. Something sweet. Something territorial.

"I...no. I just...I'm fine." I'm thrown off, stammering at yet another reason to be shaken.

Did this jerk just crawl out of his cave long enough to be worried about me?

"You sure?" he rumbles again, eyeing me up and down, assessing.

"Still in one piece." I nod more firmly this time.

"Good." He nods back, decisively, then fixes his burning blue gaze back on the door. "This was left by someone who knows me. It's a coded message. *Sua sponte.* 'Of their own accord.'" His mouth creases into a hard line. "It's the motto of the Army Rangers. They're saying they're onto me."

"You're a Ranger?"

"Former." He sinks down in a crouch with his thighs bunching hard and taut against his jeans, narrowing his eyes at a clump of bloodied, matted feathers on the mat.

Then he straightens, turning to face me. His movements are heavier somehow, as if he's suddenly tired and his massive bulk is weighing him down.

"Warren?" His name is just a question on my lips.

Sighing, he descends the steps, drawing closer to me. "Now do you get why I want you gone? You have a *kid*, Haley. You and your daughter don't need to get caught in the crossfire."

"Niece," I correct, folding my arms over my chest. "And I don't exactly know what we're in the crossfire *of.*"

His expression hardens. "That part's none of your business. Trust me."

"Um, kinda hard to trust when people are defacing the cabin I paid good money to rent."

"Technically," he points out, "I paid for it."

"Technically, you're an asshole." I'm snappish, but I can't help it.

We just passed Agatha Christie turf and went right to Stephen King. Next thing you know, there'll be a serial killer monster peeking in the window with bloody knife in hand.

Sweet Jesus.

I take a few shaky breaths, ripping the clip out of my hair and running my fingers through it to ease the tension headache starting to pull on my scalp. "So let me guess. I'm not supposed to call the cops over someone murdering a bird and smearing my windows with pigeon blood—"

"Paint," he interrupts softly. "It's tempera paint and craft feathers. Probably from the same store you were at today."

I go still, my eyes widening. *What?*

The art store...where I met Bress? The man Warren's somehow involved with?

The man Warren clearly doesn't trust, when he thought I'd somehow been sent to spy for him.

The man whose truck Warren was tampering with when I pulled up to the shop.

I'm not blind. I saw him doing *something,* even if I couldn't quite figure out what.

Was there more than I'd realized behind that tired, gentlemanly façade?

Had Dennis Bress gotten here ahead of me somehow, left this mess to scare Warren, and then taken off before anyone could catch him?

Why?

What the hell is going on underneath the portrait-pretty surface of this weird little town?

"Hay."

Suddenly, Warren's in front of me, his broad hands on my shoulders – and they're gentler than I ever expected them to be, gripping just firmly enough to ground me and hold me steady with his warmth, his solidity.

For the next few seconds I'm in his thrall. I'm not even bothered when he calls me *Hay,* maybe because there's no *Auntie* tacked on at the front.

He bends toward me, enveloping me in the fire of his body heat as he leans in to catch my eye.

"You're scared, aren't you?" he asks softly.

I swallow hard and jerk my gaze to his. "Wouldn't you be, stranded in a strange town when something like this happens?"

"You're not stranded. You can leave any time." He smiles slightly. Not one of the smirky, cynical smiles I've seen before, but a wry, almost self-deprecating smile. Almost reassuring. "Hell, just go stay somewhere else. I know a few real nice folks around here who wouldn't mind being an on-call AirBnB. They'll keep you safe. Anywhere but here is safe." He touches my cheek, then strokes his thumb along it, his callused skin rough against mine. "You'll be fine as long as you stay away from me, Haley. I promise."

His word shouldn't mean anything.

I stare up at him anyway, my breaths trembling. "Who the hell are you?" I whisper. "What is all this?"

"That's not something you want to find out." He looks at me a while longer, flame-blue eyes searching deep before his hands fall away and he straightens, pulling back. "Let me take photos for evidence in case we need them. Then I'll get Flynn to clean this mess up. You and Tara can sleep at my place tonight, and I'll make some phone calls tomorrow."

I stare after him, biting my lip, while he trudges back up the steps. "Why do we need *evidence* if we're not calling the cops?"

"No need to involve the police. Not yet," he says, and that alone makes me worry even more.

Because even if he might not be the one who did this, it's not hard to see he doesn't want the law sniffing after whatever he's doing in Heart's Edge to bring this kind of warning to our doorsteps.

He turns, looking back at me. "It's my problem, not yours. I want to be prepared just in case."

Just in case?

Just in case of *what?*

The question hovers on my tongue...but I'm too afraid to ask.

What the hell have I walked into?

* * *

IT'S MUTED and strange as Tara and I retreat to our side of the cabin to get what we need together to stay with Warren.

Part of me can't believe I'm taking him up on his offer.

But a bigger part worries what'll happen to us if I don't.

If whatever psycho who left fake blood and feathers hits the wrong side of the duplex again – our side.

Meanwhile, on the other side of the wall, I can hear Warren moving things. *Hiding things,* I instantly think, when he'd been so snarly over finding us in his place at all yesterday. He confuses me so much.

First, he says I have to stay away for my own protection.

But then he says *stay with me, so I can protect you.*

I mean, it makes sense. We can't just up and leave right now, and he needs to make arrangements for us to go somewhere. But until then, he wants to make sure he's standing between us and whatever wave of mess is crashing down, floodwaters threatening to drown us in his mess.

That's not why I feel strange.

Maybe it's not the situation.

Maybe it's *him*, making me feel like I'm dealing with two completely different men.

One dangerous and cold and grim, this wary animal raising hackles and baring teeth to defend his territory.

And one worried, tired, withdrawn, sad...the beast wounded, yet still shoving himself between me and danger to protect me because that's what's in his nature.

Both men, both beasts, twist me up inside and make me remember how his hands felt gripping my shoulders, that light touch against my cheek, skimming to rough.

I don't know how to reconcile the two whenever I look at Warren.

But I don't know how to separate them, either.

By the time I'm done putting together my overnight bag and making sure we haven't left any valuables among the things we'll be loading back in the car tomorrow, Warren's taken his photos of the mess and left Flynn to clean it as best he can, the old man grumbling the entire time.

The paint won't come off easy, not completely, not with the soap and water he's using. So now there's a red-tinted film over the glass, turning the light that streams through it pink.

But the feathers are gone. So I can stop letting my imagination run away with brutal possibilities when it's just a fifty-cent bag of craft feathers smattered in paint.

Still.

I'm almost relieved when Warren opens his door and stands there with his arm stretched out holding it, ushering us inside. Forcing me to squeeze past him.

My body brushes his, sensing muscles so hard-cut I can feel every ridge of his abs as my chest and belly glide against it. There's all kinds of *uh-oh* chiseled in this mountain man.

For a moment I look up and wish I hadn't.

Because I catch a burning stare scorching me, raking me, grinding every point where flesh presses together and my body molds to conform to his.

I thought the term *eye-fuck* only existed in movies and romance novels but this...this is pure heat lightning. The most animal kind.

Our eyes linger far too long.

One of us has to give before Tara starts staring like we've lost our marbles, so it's me. I flinch away, my belly twisted in hot little knots, and suddenly I can't breathe.

Not until he clenches his jaw and looks away sharply, turning his glare into the cabin.

The broken chain of eye contact slaps me back to my senses, and I suck in a breath, duck my head, and dart inside. Before those blue fires in his eyes can hold me hostage again.

Holy hell, what's wrong with me?

I suddenly wish I could trade what's coming next for every bad roomie experience I left behind in Seattle combined.

Somehow, I'm going to have to survive more than stalker creeps with bad intentions and cheap craft supplies.

I have to survive the storm named Warren Ford.

IV: GAME, SET (WARREN)

I think I just made one of the dumbest damned decisions of my adult life.

I don't know what the hell I was thinking, telling that wildfire girl and her niece to stay with me tonight. Sure, I managed to get all my shit packed away in a walk-in closet that's been closed with a chain and a padlock so they can't get at anything – not my evidence, not my damn guns – so that's not the problem.

The real problem's those searching looks Haley keeps giving me.

Like she can't believe what she's staring at.

Like she's desperately trying to find out who I really am.

Then the way her body felt up against mine, tighter than a drum – fuck!

Her tits were soft, lush, almost swollen against my stomach. Those sparking, fiery eyes of hers went liquid, downright melty as she looked up at me like she wanted to ask a question but wasn't sure what.

I can't afford questions.

Much less this broad who's too hot for her own good

figuring out who I am or what I'm after, or the distraction she provides.

Which is why, while her and Tara curl up on my couch to pick at leftover pizza and watch me in veiled sidelong looks, I make so many phone calls I feel like I'm lighting up the small-town phone tree with gossip.

There's got to be somebody to throw me a damn lifeline.

My friends, Blake and Doc, have nowhere for the girls to sleep. They both live like consummate bachelors in as little space as possible.

My old grade school teacher, Ms. Petty, *would* put them up in her spare room, but her niece is in for summer break from college, so it's *sorry, dear, why can't the girls stay at Charming Inn again?*

And then I don't have an answer for that.

Nor do I have an answer for my Aunt Gracie – not really an aunt by blood, just an older neighbor who'd babysit when I was a kid – whose guest room is undergoing renovation after a water pipe burst. Or Jenna's old friend, Shana, and her husband. He's happy to let them crash while Shana herself vetoes it with a bitter *why should I let your new girlfriend shack up at my house rent-free again? You've got plenty of people who owe you favors, War.*

That's what I get for a bad late night bar hookup with Shana years ago before she tied the knot.

Fucking karma.

I don't get the chance to even protest *she's not my girlfriend* before Shana hangs up on me.

Stewart's my last option, but there's some snarly territorial part of me that doesn't want to turn Haley over to him. Good man or not, he's too charming, too good-looking, and a hell of a lot nicer than I can afford to be right now.

Am I afraid my good friend's gonna steal a girl I don't even know and can't risk being interested in right now?

Maybe.

Fuck.

I rub the bridge of my nose, sighing and pitching my phone on the kitchen island, leaning forward to rest my elbows on the wood. "I got nothing, Hay. I'll make a few more calls in the morning," I tell her.

What I really mean is, I'll find the nerve to get over my shit by morning and ask Stewart.

I can *trust* him to protect her, more than anyone else. He's ex-military like me. He had Jenna's back. He's tuned up damn near every vehicle I've ever owned like it was his own kid, even when I had to drive them in from Spokane before they went kaput.

There's no sane reason for shutting him out when he can help.

Too bad there's nothing sane about the ridiculous ego between my ears.

"You should probably try to get some rest. Bedroom's all yours," I say, trying not to bite my tongue.

Haley looks up from toying with a pizza crust without really eating it. "Where will you sleep?"

I half-smile. "Couch is good enough for me. Spent plenty of years sleeping on worse."

She answers my smile with a wistful, tired one of her own. There's a softer side to her underneath the angry spit-fire. A side that makes this unexpected roommate dilemma even harder.

And I haven't even had a chance to see it yet in full because I've pissed her off from the moment we met. It's starting to peek out now.

Her guard comes down with how clearly exhausted she is, and the weariness and sadness in her smile wrench at me. *This is all my fault.*

I got her tangled up in my bull.

I'm the reason she's smiling so I won't see the fear in those darkly glimmering jade-green eyes.

She sets the crust down in the empty box and stands. I watch her reach over to ruffle Tara's hair as the little girl yawns, then bend to kiss the top of her head before straightening and glancing at me. "Mind if I use your shower before I turn in?"

"Knock yourself out."

She flashes me that wrenching smile again and tucks her knuckles under Tara's chin. "Go in the bedroom and get changed," she says. "I'll be in in a little bit."

The little girl is subdued, but she bounces off the couch with a nod, stretches up to kiss Haley's cheek, then skitters away and heads back to my bedroom. Haley lingers for a moment longer, fixing me with a long, thoughtful look.

I don't dare look back. Not the fuck again.

Finally, she ducks her head and leaves the room.

Air huffs out my nostrils, shrill relief. *Crisis averted.*

It feels like too big an accomplishment that I haven't pissed her off again, and she hasn't given me another hard-on savage enough to hit a home run with.

I sink down on the couch and crash my head against the back of it, closing my eyes with a groan. I hear water turning on in the bathroom. Nothing's going according to plan. *Nothing.*

But while I have my privacy, I drag my laptop over from the corner of the coffee table, flip it open, and pull up the tracker app connected to my GPS devices. I've only got one out now, the rest inactive, their labels in the offline list in the left-hand menu. I tap the active one and relabel it *Target B,* then zoom in on the map to see where Bress might be right now.

Then frown, pulling out for a broader view.

His camper's on the way out of town.

Heading north along the main road, toward the highway.

It's odd, but not surprising, either.

If he's into what I think he is, it's par for the course.

He's probably heading out to meet contacts in Missoula.

I rub at my chin, frowning as I follow the dot up the highway. Missoula's not that far. He could be there and back by morning.

I should put myself somewhere tomorrow where I can bump into him.

See how tired he is – and if he's tired enough to slip. Say something incriminating.

I'm starting to hate this fucking waiting game. I'm only after Bress for one thing, and his dirty dealings may be a window to get to him and take him down.

All I need is hard evidence he was responsible for Jenna's death.

Evidence, and license to do whatever it takes to bring him in.

I won't lie.

If I had my way, I'd skin the fuck alive.

I'll settle for slugging him in the face, breaking teeth, if he gets hostile and resists a lawful citizen's arrest.

I'm so preoccupied I don't hear the water shutting off in the bathroom or realize I'm not alone till a soft throat-clearing catches my attention. I jerk up almost guiltily, slamming the lid of the laptop shut.

God *damn* am I glad for the computer across my lap.

Because the nanosecond I see Hay, my cock swells, hardens every moment she stands there dripping in the living room doorway.

She's wearing nothing but a tight-fitting grey cotton spaghetti strap tank top, molded to her like it's sucking on her body. It's matched by skimpy grey cotton sleep shorts that crease between her thighs, riding up so high they're practically panties.

No bra, of fucking course.

I can tell far too easy from the heavy sway of her chest, the way those sweet tits strain against the tank top.

Even worse, she's soaking wet.

Her hair is a dripping tangle swept to one side, droplets pouring down her hairline over her cheeks, kissing her lips. Her shoulders are beaded damp, but it's her little pajama set that's distracting me.

A few soaked patches, dark against the cotton, cling to her body so close I can make out everything from the dip of her navel to the size of her nipples, looming hard against the thin material. She's...fuck.

Fuck!

She's not wearing any panties underneath those shorts.

Ask me how I know.

I'm staring like some animal in rut.

It hasn't been *that* long since I last got laid. A flirty glance is all it takes, brushing hands and trading drinks in a bar with someone who'll call herself an Uber in the morning. The usual.

But it's been a long damn time since I had an *immediate* reaction this explosive to a woman just at the sight of her. Maybe it's not all looks, but how much she pisses me off, and all that anger has to go somewhere, channeling into this sudden hot surge of desire.

I've got to get myself under control.

She's not helping.

Especially when she looks at me through the damp spikes of her lashes, green eyes luminous and shadowed, drawing her wet, gleaming lower lip into her mouth, toying at it with her teeth as she sways on one foot. It's as innocent as a succubus.

Her other foot crosses behind her ankle as she watches me uncertainly.

Hell. *Did she just say something?*

"What?" I tear my gaze from her mouth, her breasts, to her eyes. My entire body feels too damn hot. "Sorry, what did you say?"

She arches a brow, eyeing me skeptically.

"I said you're out of bath towels." She shrugs, and it's almost shy, like she doesn't know what to do without her defensive armor. "I don't know if you're supposed to like, wash them yourself or the staff takes care of that, but I thought I'd better let you know."

"Oh." I clear my throat and force myself to look away from this torture. My face must be as red as a forest fire. "Fine. I'll ring the front desk for service and turnover in the morning. Sorry. You going to be okay going to bed wet?"

Horrid choice of words.

The second I say *wet*...my brain goes every damn which way but where it's supposed to. Mostly heading south.

Every sense I've got goes to the creases of soft fabric between her thighs, the splash of water on her skin, to the fabric molding it against her flesh, giving form to something more, mouthwatering, *luscious*...

Her laugh sounds dry – so completely clueless where my brain is right now. "I'll live. It's the middle of summer. I'll steam dry before I even have much of a chance to soak your sheets. But don't blame me if my hair looks like Frankenstein's bride in the morning."

Soak your sheets.

Christ, does this girl even *hear* herself?

My mouth is cotton, my tongue tied, and I'm staring off somewhere in the kitchen to keep from looking at her. If she meets my eyes, she'll *know*.

Know real fast I'm thinking about shoving her up against the wall.

Thinking about kissing her.

Thinking about licking every stray drop off her skin and then sucking at her nipples through her tank top till the fabric is drenched and they're pert as little red cherries in my mouth.

I'm not saying anything.

The silence stretches on, long and awkward, until finally she clears her throat again and says, "Well...good night, Warren."

"Yeah," I mumble, barely finding my voice, hoarse and raspy. "Good night, Hay."

There's a pause, then the faint noise of her bare feet on the wood floor, moving away.

I don't relax until I hear the bedroom door open, and then the distant sound of her voice and Tara's. *Thank God.*

Groaning, I lift my laptop up, looking down at the hard rise straining against my jeans.

"You," I mutter, "are really damn annoying sometimes."

My cock doesn't answer.

I'd really have to be crazy if that happened, but I'm starting to think I'm losing it.

Something about this woman gets to me like no other.

And I wonder if it's because she needs me right now, because all this is *still* my own damn fault.

So here I am. Back in my hometown, playing host to two strangers, trying to hunt a killer, and wanting like hell to fuck a woman I can't stand who shouldn't be dragged into *any* of this.

Smooth.

I force myself to focus, parsing more work on my laptop, ignoring the wayward thoughts racing through me and praying my cock calms the fuck down. Other thoughts help.

Thoughts of Bress, of Jenna, help to pull me back on track.

I stay up for hours digging through old files, tracing movements, locations, timelines, trying to find anything that'll open a crack in Bress' carefully crafted persona. He's hardly the hometown boy turned savior, who's supposedly breathing life back into the town's stagnant economy.

People wouldn't love him nearly as much if they knew where that influx of dirty money was coming from.

By the time midnight rolls past, I need to admit I'm human and get some rest.

I'm calmer now, but not in the best place, either.

Just to make sure everything's fine, I slip into the bedroom to peek in at the girls. I doubt anyone could've gotten into the cabin without me hearing them climb through the window.

Still, I need to see for myself that there's no bedbugs around to bite.

They're sound asleep, tangled up under the covers. Hay's shifted to hold on to Tara protectively, cuddling her like a little doll, curling around to shield her with her body. They're both a tangled mess wrapped up in the sheets, a few damp spots from Haley's hair on the pillow.

My pillow. It does something odd to see them in my bed.

If I'd had a normal life, if I was a normal man, maybe I'd be here on vacation with my wife and kid.

Some boring-ass job in the big city, but in the summer we'd pack up the 'stang and drive to my hometown and stay at Grandma's inn for a sweet month.

Instead of a stranger, the little girl would be my daughter, riding on my shoulders while I take her hiking and show her all the places where I grew up. I'd tell her all the stories of Heart's Edge, and maybe when she's thirteen or fourteen, she'd meet a local boy and get a crush.

Then I'll tell her the story about throwing flowers over the cliff, and why the town's called Heart's Edge. All the local lore based on love, the sappy shit every local boy pretends doesn't count, but really keeps it close because it's part of hometown pride.

And if I had a normal life, that woman in my bed would be my wife, my love, my lover for the taking.

Not this strange wildfire who came tearing into my life, fucking me up every which way.

But my life *isn't* normal. Bress made sure of that.

And this dream we're pantomiming, as they sleep so sound, secure in the knowledge that I'll keep them safe...

It's not for me.

It's not meant for Warren Ford.

My chest aches, this dark, heavy weight inside me. It shouldn't be there at all.

I don't know what I'm thinking right now, but it's far more distracting than Haley's tight body in that skimpy little sleep set.

But I know one damned thing.

There's no way in hell I'm letting her stay at Stew's.

The very idea of her walking around his place dressed like *that*, wet and lush, curves falling out everywhere? That's a big screaming *NO*.

Go ahead. Judge.

I've got no right to be territorial. Hay's nothing to me, just a stranger who shouldn't be here. We're not even friends.

But the beast inside me says it's my job to protect her because I'm the asshole who put her in danger. I can't let her out of my sight for the last few days she's here.

It's my fault she's in this mess, so it's my job to fix it.

I'll figure something out in the morning.

Maybe after some sleep, I'll get my head screwed on straight.

And maybe by the light of day, I'll have answers.

I'll know what the hell I'm supposed to do with Haley West in my life.

* * *

THE SMELL of frying bacon wakes me up.

I don't even remember falling asleep, but I know I did with the sun beating down on my eyelids in hot orange bursts. My back sticks to the couch cushion under it, the support bar below the upholstery digging into my spine. Soft, feminine voices are murmuring somewhere nearby, animated but muted, as if trying not to wake me.

That's not what woke me.

It was my stomach growling like a damn bear, slamming against my abdomen like it wants to crawl out of me and go on the prowl for the tantalizing smell of cooking meat.

Groaning, I open one eye, squinting against the sunlight.

It must be almost ten o'clock, judging by how bright it is. Guess I wore myself out yesterday, but even if I'm still tired, my houseguests are bright and chipper.

Haley and Tara are moving about the kitchen like they live here, putting together breakfast. Two skillets sizzle away on the stove. The girls are up to their elbows in flour as they shape biscuits on the counter. While I watch sleepily past the forearm draped over my face, Tara reaches up and dots Haley's nose with a fingertip of flour, only for Haley to cross her eyes comically, making the little girl laugh.

I'm not sure when I started smiling like this.

This isn't me.

And what the hell is this ache?

I force myself to stop grinning like a fool and push myself up, wincing as my vertebrae all realign like someone picked my spine up and snapped it like a whip. The girls look up, watching me as I stand, before Haley grins and wipes her nose free of flour.

"Morning, Rip Van Winkle," she says.

"Very funny." I stretch wide, rolling my shoulders, and risk letting myself look at her fully.

Today she's in jeans and a coral-pink shirt. It's loose, almost see-through, hinting at a tank top underneath. Pretty and feminine but much less distracting. I shouldn't feel a pang of disappointment.

"Looks like you got over your scare mighty fast," I say.

She shrugs merrily, rolling another biscuit between her palms before placing it on a cookie sheet with rows of others. "When you think about it, it's pretty childish. Paint and craft feathers? I mean...hard to be afraid of someone who'd do something so silly."

You should be, I think, but hold my tongue.

I don't want to spook her more.

Instead, I join them in the kitchen, working around them in a way that feels far too natural as I put coffee on and then check the bacon to make sure it isn't burning. "It's mostly petty vandalism. But I'll make a few more phone calls after breakfast and see about finding you somewhere safer to stay."

Haley makes a soft sound under her breath, her gaze fixed somewhere out the windows, contemplative. "It's a shame, really. This is such a nice little inn. I'd love to have spent some time painting on the back deck."

"You can see the mountains from town."

"Yeah, but it's not the same." She glances at me. Her smile is so warm. I'm not even sure what I did to earn it considering just yesterday we were hissing and spitting at each other like wet cats in a bag. "This really is a lovely place. Even if it's got its share of small town secrets."

You have no idea.

"Listen, Hay..."

"Hm?"

I work my jaw, searching for words.

I must still be off my head after last night. Don't know why I'm offering an olive branch like this otherwise. "Since you're staying a few days, maybe I could give you the grand tour."

She looks at me like I've lost my mind.

Fuck.

So much for bad ideas, like offering to show her around town. Stupid ideas that sure won't make this any easier.

Still, I thought it'd do her good to see all the little charms, the sweet spots around Heart's Edge everybody loves. Sure, it'd give me fresh cover to get out and do some snooping without being Captain Fucking Obvious, too.

But maybe some part of me wants to show her what there is to really love about my hometown beyond the views and the imminent sense of danger hanging over our heads like a guillotine waiting to drop.

Or maybe I've gone as crazy as her look says.

Before I claw back my words, her phone starts trilling in her back pocket. With a sheepish smile, she drops the ball of dough she'd been kneading, lifts a floury hand, and says, "Hold that thought. Really."

Then she's off with a damp dish towel, hastily scrubbing her fingers, fishing her phone from her pocket.

I shouldn't be so interested in who can make her face light up like she's expecting Santa Claus on the other end of the line. For all I know she's married, or has a boyfriend, or a girlfriend, and – fuck.

Is that why she gave me the deer-in-headlights look? Is it because she's taken?

Not my business. Shame it's so damn hard to believe it when I realize how hard I'm clenching my fist.

"Hey, Jules," she says into the phone with a warm smile. "What's up?"

I try not to be obvious about eavesdropping as I check the coffee pot, pulling down mugs from the cabinet, but it's kind of hard not to overhear when we're all bumping elbows in the kitchen.

I glance back at Haley – then catch little Tara watching me. She gives me a pointed look and clucks her tongue, shaking her head.

"It's bad manners to eavesdrop, Mister," she whispers harshly.

I can't help but grin. Striding over, I lean down so we're face to face.

"Don't tattle on me, okay? Might be a Snickers in it for you later," I whisper back, watching as she breaks into a brilliant smile.

Hay's not smiling, though.

She's frowning.

Starting to pace around while she runs a still-messy hand through her hair, leaving floury streaks against the dark, glossy brown. "No...no, that's okay. I understand. No, really, it's just fine. Jules, you have to take care of *you*. I'll be okay here." She pauses, her smile tired and sad. "I know. I know that feeling, trust me. I'm just sorry it had to end with a twist of the knife."

It's my turn to frown. Whatever's upsetting her, I don't like it one bit.

Another pause, then her listening look. "We're in this little place called Heart's Edge way up in the mountains. It's *purty.* You should come visit some time! Lovely place to relax and take your mind off cheaters."

I can't help but be curious.

Cheaters. The bitter note in her voice says she speaks from far too much experience.

Is that what sent her out this way with the kid? She'd mentioned Chicago once, but I didn't know what her point of origin was or why she tossed a munchkin in the car and decided to hit the road with, from what I saw, damn near everything she owns stuffed in the trunk of the Mustang.

Did some man hurt her? Drive her off on this trip?

Did some selfish piece of shit take a hammer to her heart?

My blood steams more than it should just thinking about it. *Hay, in tears, face down in a pillow, hiding how bad the world's latest prick just kicked her up and down.*

I glance at Tara again and force a smile. They say if you do it enough, you'll feel happier.

Doesn't work here, but it does help my anger from dialing up to ten.

But I turn back to the coffee quickly when she hangs up and glances at me, making eye contact before I clear my throat and look away like I hadn't just been listening.

"You know, I thought you were some kind of super spy, maybe, but after that awful eavesdropping act...I don't think so. You've got no skills, Warren." Her voice is tired and amused at my back.

"You don't know anything about my spy skills, woman." I look over my shoulder. "How do you like your coffee?"

"Twenty percent cream, fifty percent sugar. Thanks." She hoists herself up to sit on the counter next to the baking sheet while Tara watches curiously, the little girl still rolling biscuits between her palms.

"So..." Haley sighs. "Looks like I'm not leaving Heart's Edge for a while."

I jerk so abruptly I splash hot coffee over my hand and hiss, yanking it back and setting the carafe down before reaching for the paper towels. "*What?*"

"Sorry to disappoint. I know you were kinda dead set on

getting rid of me." There's that hint of acid again, corroding the momentary ease that had settled over us. "I was going to stay with my friend Julie in Chicago until I could get a job and find an apartment of my own, but..." Her voice is tight, thick. "Her shitty husband has been cheating with his secretary. Just told her he wants a divorce and her out of the house by the weekend. I don't really think couch surfing with her is an option anymore."

"Swear jar!" Tara cuts in.

Hay shoots her a withering look. "Not now, hun."

"Then how 'bout going *home?*" It's out of me before I can stop it as I whip around to face her. "Just go back where you came from, Hay."

"Don't you get it? I *can't!*" Her eyes are wet, her face screwing up in a way that tells me she's too proud to cry in front of me, but the stress and upset are eating her alive. "I don't have a home to go back to, Warren. I lost my job. My fiancé slept with my best friend and bridesmaid. Weeks before the stupid wedding. Which ate most of my savings...I don't have enough money to just shove off to Chicago and start over like it's nothing. I needed Jules. I needed Missoula." She takes a rough, shaky breath and scrubs her knuckles against her eyes, glaring at me.

Damn fool, if only you'd kept your mouth shut!

I didn't. Now I've got to find some way to un-fuck the damage.

"Hay, listen to me –"

"Listen to *what?* I'm stuck here for now. Good thing I won't be your problem anymore once you find a friend to pass me off to, right?"

I don't know what to say.

She never should've been my problem to start with.

That's when I realize it's hard to think of her as a *problem* at all.

Not when she's here, in front of me, cut to pieces, trying to hold her waterworks for the sake of her niece.

Problem? No.

Just someone I need to take care of. Do right by. Even if her staying here in Heart's Edge for more than a few more days *will* cause ripples I don't know what to do with.

And I don't know what to do with her, either, when that proud, fierce expression cracks. The tremble of her lips, the stiffness of her shoulders, they make me want to pull her into my arms.

Make me want to comfort her. Tell her it'll be okay, even if it's not. Even when that's not a promise I can make right now, and I'm pretty sure she'd punch me if I tried.

Tara wipes her hands off carefully, then lays her head against Haley's thigh, curling a hand over her knee. "Don't cry, Auntie Hay. I'll stay with you."

Haley smiles, watery but brave, and strokes her hand through her niece's hair. "Then I'm gonna be A-okay, kit," she murmurs. "I'm always okay as long as I've got you."

I lean my hip against the counter, folding my arms over my chest, watching her. "So what're you going to do?"

"What else can I do?" she retorts bitterly, then drops the bombshell so hard I feel the explosion rock through me. "I guess I'll get a job."

V: MATCH (HALEY)

J'm starting to feel like some kind of bad luck charm.

Except the only person I'm charming into disaster is *myself.*

First, I lose my job. Then my gallery show. Then my fiancé, my best friend, all the money I spent on the wedding – which should've tipped me off, coming out of my own pocket – and my faith in humanity.

All in one fell swoop.

When I try to shake it off and leave the crap factory behind me on the open road, I wind up breaking down in a cute little town that should've been a vacation dream.

It's been nightmare territory since the minute I walked in on this gorgeous prick of a man who's currently staring at me like I insulted his mother.

All because fate dumped another load of bitter and I'm trying to make the best of what I can.

"You're going to do *what?*" Warren demands, his expression thunderous. "A job? In town? Absolutely not."

I push myself off the counter and stand, glaring up at him.

"Last I checked, you don't get to tell me what to do, Warren. And unless you're going to call every business in town and tell them not to hire me..."

"What if I am?"

I snort. *Is he for real?*

"Then I'm pretty sure they'll tell you to go screw yourself, unless everyone in Heart's Edge is just as crazy as you," I throw back. "I don't think they are. People here seem pretty nice. With *one* big, notable exception."

"Swear jar," Tara whispers quietly.

Great timing. This whole conversation is so surreal I have to hold my breath to keep from laughing out a lung.

"You have no *clue* what people here are like, Hay," he growls. "Or what's hiding under that niceness."

"So?" I fold my arms over my chest, eyeing him up and down. "Guess I'm supposed to just appreciate *you* because at least you're honest about being a jackass?"

"*Swear jar,*" Tara insists again, rubbing her nose.

"I'm not—" Warren huffs out a frustrated sound, muttering, and looks away, raking one hand back through his hair and spiking it up into fluffy tufts of black that only fall back into seething blue eyes. "Look, how much do you need to start over?"

I blink. "Excuse me?"

"How much, darlin'?" He scowls. "I'll cover it. Transportation, repairs on the car, first and last month's rent. Hell, I'll even make sure you have enough to eat breakfast, lunch, and din—"

Enough.

I step forward, plant my palms against his chest, and *shove* like my life depends on it.

Nothing happens.

Not that I ever had a prayer of budging a human mountain, but it makes him shut up. Warren just stares down at me, hands held out helplessly at his sides, as if he'd wanted to grab me to stop me but thought better of it.

"You asshole," I bite off, struggling against my closing throat, my welling eyes. "You *asshole!*"

"Auntie Hay..." Tara interjects one more time, another *swear jar* at the tip of her tongue.

But I'm well into losing it, snapping, about to blow up on the launch pad. And not even her ill-timed favorite quip can pull me out of laying into Mr. Popularity.

"I don't *know* you," I bite off. "You're just the dick renting the other half of this cabin, but you come charging in like you get to decide my fate, my life. Like you can order me around, tell me what I can and can't do, and I'm just over here trying to get my life back together! I don't owe you anything, least of all a say in what I do or how I handle my problems. I sure as *hell* don't want your—"

Every word in my mouth dries to nothing and crumbles to dust as he moves.

Warren hooks a powerful arm around my waist and drags me close, jerking me against his body and crushing me into the sleek, deadly shield that's all him.

Seething, sparking blue eyes glare down at me hotly.

Twisting me inside out as I instinctively clutch at his shoulders.

His bare shoulders, tattoos writhing under my palms, his skin as hot as a furnace, tanned and taut and pressed against me so close I feel like he'll burn me to ash without breaking a sweat.

His hand is so *huge* against the small of my back. It spans my entire waist, branding into me, and I can't breathe.

My lungs stall, and my lips part on words that won't come as he leans down, those stern, almost cruelly beautiful lips parted as if he'll...

Oh. My. God.

At first, I can't tell if there's a pounding at the door or it's just my heart. But the noise makes Warren stiffen, stop, and let me go, the two of us bouncing apart like magnets with the wrong polarity, charged force shoving us away from each other.

Breathing hard, I press my hands to my overheated cheeks, staring blankly at nothing.

Way too freaking close.

With a growl like he knows it too, Warren pulls away, moving with that slow, animalistic lope as he strides toward the door.

Tara stares at me. I stare right back, sucking in a shallow breath, trying to make my stomach calm itself down.

What the hell *was* that, anyway?

For a second, I thought he was about to kiss me.

I lift my head at the sound of a stern but warm feminine voice from the door. Warren opens it to a trim, tall, older woman with a no-nonsense look about her, from the tidy bun of her silvered hair to the neatness of her pencil skirt and cardigan.

She's practically dressed for tea even on this hot summer morning. Her blue eyes strike me immediately. They're the same shade as Warren's. They've got to be family, considering how confidently she reaches up to cup the back of his neck, pulling him down so she can lightly brush her lips to both of his cheeks, Parisian-style, before pulling back with a disapproving look.

"Really," she says, a touch of amusement in her tone. "This is how you answer the door?"

"Wasn't exactly expecting you, Grandma," he says dryly, sounding for all the world like a chastised little boy.

I arch a brow. *Grandma, huh?*

Suddenly, I'm glad I decided to put on some clothing before taking over Warren's kitchen to make breakfast.

Speaking of breakfast, if I'm not careful, I'm going to burn everything. *Crap.*

Turning, I quickly lower the burners on the stove and run the spatula through the bacon and the eggs, making sure they're not stuck and ruined. As I dip to put the biscuits in the oven, though, I sense someone behind me.

Without warning, I'm face to face with Grandma herself. *Jesus!*

I stumble back with a yelp, bumping the stove closed with my butt accidentally.

Yet another family trait with Warren, moving like a damned cat and creeping up on people.

At least I manage not to burst out swearing. Grandma has a kind face, seamed into lines of laughter.

She looks me over with a measured gaze, though her pleasant smile never fades. I clutch a hand to my chest, taking a few steadying breaths, then offer a smile and tuck my hair back uncertainly.

"Sorry," I manage. "You just startled me." I offer her my hand – then take it back, wiping it on my thigh once I realize it's still got flour on it. "Haley West."

"Yes, dear. I know who you are. You've become quite the hot topic since the wind blew you into our little town." She takes my hand, a light, ladylike grip, but still warm as she squeezes and lets go. "I'm Wilma Ford. Warren's grandmother and owner of Charming Inn."

"Oh! Of course. I hadn't realized." I hope she's not upset with me over the vandalism, even if it wasn't my fault.

But it's weird, I think, that Warren is related to the owner but renting the most remote cabin on the property, paying for it and everything. I keep my smile on anyway, wrapping my arms around myself. "It's a lovely place, Mrs. Ford. I love the view."

"Yes, I'd hoped to provide a touch of atmosphere for vacationing couples." The look she casts Warren is loaded, and my cheeks burn while he ducks his head with a fierce, almost petulant scowl. "Perhaps my grandson will entertain you with the story of the cliff that gives the town its name. For now, though...are you all right, darling Haley?" She cocks her head at Tara. "And who's this delightful young lady?"

Tara beams. "I'm Tara! Auntie Hay's sidekick."

"So your niece, I see." She bends toward Tara in a prim little curtsey, and I already know Tara's about to have a new idol when this woman reminds me of Meryl Streep in *The Devil Wears Prada.*

Tara, God bless her, spent two weeks practicing her sassy little *that's all* and haughty little turn the first time my sister Marie let her watch that film. "It's lovely to meet you, Tara. I hope nothing's frightened you too much since you came here."

Tara shakes her head quickly. "I'm not scared. And neither is Auntie Hay."

"It was just a little paint," I say. "We're fine, I promise. I'm sorry about the damage to the cabin, though."

"Nonsense." Wilma waves a hand. "You're the one who deserves an apology, dear. This sort of thing is entirely abnormal around here. Your stay will be completely compensated for as long as you'd like. You're welcome here in Heart's Edge, even if that terribly childish prank may have indicated otherwise."

"Oh, um...thank you."

Wow. So maybe the rush to step in and fix things is in the family genes too. If only Warren had his grandmother's finesse.

It's not hard to tell he's simmering, standing behind this woman with his jaw clenched so hard the thick muscles in his neck bunch and strain. He's also suspiciously silent, and I'm starting to get an idea of who rules the roost in this family. I offer a small smile. "I really don't want to impose or take advantage of your hospitality. I might be here just a little while. Turns out my end goal just turned into a fumble, and...well, I don't have anywhere to go. So I'm looking for a job to save up until I can move on with some cash. That might take a few weeks, if you don't mind—"

"Nonsense. It'll take as long as it's meant to, and you're still welcome," Wilma says firmly. "In fact, I just might have a lead for you."

Warren makes a garbled sound, starts to bite off a curse, then stops himself as Wilma's sharp eyes cut to him. I almost grin, barely holding it back.

It's kinda magical. Watching this big, tattooed, blue-eyed badass of a man brought to heel by a woman half his size and three times older and wiser.

It makes him seem less frightening. More like a big grizzly bear who still loves his granny.

And it makes me feel a bit warmer inside. A little less alone and bereft and dripping with bad luck, to have this woman treating me so firmly like I'm family and she just wants to *help*.

Not even my own sister does that.

It's not that our relationship is bad. Growing up with our dad hooked to the bottle, we both learned to be self-sufficient and closed off, maybe a little too distant.

It's hard for Marie and me to lean on each other. Or to offer to open up when it was every girl for herself when he came home smelling like vodka and rye.

I pull myself from those memories, from their darkness, and back to the brightness of the living room and Grandma's job offer. "Whatever it is, I'd be happy to help. I've done a lot of everything. Back in Seattle I was a claims adjuster, but I've got customer service experience, call center experience, and I'm an artist..."

"So I've heard. You'll have to show me your paintings some time. Perhaps I could commission a piece or two for the house." Wilma hooks her arm in mine, leaning on me almost companionably, her eyes gleaming with a wickedness that belies her age. "But for now...how do you feel about college boys and short skirts?"

Uh, oh.

Whatever I expected to come out of her mouth, it wasn't that.

And the soft, slightly amused quirk in her lips tells me I'm in for trouble.

* * *

So I GUESS I'm staying in Heart's Edge.

As a waitress.

In the only pub in town.

Remember to breathe, I keep telling myself.

It's a job. And with Wilma letting me stay rent-free – and promising I can come up to the main house to see her any time, when part of the large building is private family quarters – I've got this.

This being the most crazy, humbling position I've had since...ever.

But I'll be able to put my tips and wages aside for my Chicago fund. I don't know how long it'll take. Maybe a month or two, if I'm lucky.

Of course, I'll have to ship Tara back home to her mother in a couple of weeks, as school draws nearer, but until then we'll just have a little fun. I can make sure she's bedded down and safe before I leave for work every day. Wilma told me that although Tara would be perfectly fine in the cabin, really she'd feel better if my niece spent the nights with her, and I could pick her up when I got off shift.

I don't know why it's so much easier to accept Wilma's assistance than it is to take Warren's handouts.

Maybe because Wilma's just giving me the hand up I need to do this on my own, while Warren keeps trying to buy me off like money is all that matters and I'm perfectly okay with letting other people pay my way.

I'm so not.

Right now, though, I'm not thinking about that.

I'm not thinking about the stilted phone call with Marie, which I hadn't even wanted to make when I'm interrupting the first vacation she's had in years, and it's awkward.

We don't talk about our feelings or our misfortunes if we can help it. Dad's ghost still makes us stop just short of acting like real sisters.

I know she's hurting over something. I hear it in her voice. She talks up Maui and its beauty and beaches, how her and John fell in love years ago the first time they went down the Road to Hana with its wicked, pinprick turns. But when I asked her if it felt like old times, there's something missing from her voice.

No spark. No soul. And no freaking clue what it means for her or her rocky marriage.

Poor Marie. Poor, closed off, confused Marie.

And poor John, too. If these two can't make it, I don't know who can anymore.

Feelings were one reason I fell for Eddy, snake that he was. He had a way of getting me to open up with this effortless charm, giving me this outlet, this relief. But now I can see how superficial and self-serving that charm was.

He only wanted me to talk to *him* because it made him feel good about himself. A shitty, psycho savior complex if there ever was one.

The fact that he was so good with women even the defensive, temperamental Haley West melted for him.

I guess once the conquest was over, the challenge wasn't so interesting.

No.

I'm not going down that path right now. I'm in my zen place.

Packed up, moved back to my side of the duplex and away from that asshole Warren. Tara happily watches rom-coms in the living room with an orange cat in her lap.

Whose cat, I don't know. He kind of wandered up while I was bringing our stuff over from Warren's, and I guess he's ours now.

I can't mind it much while I'm out on the back deck with an easel, a canvas, paints, and a stunning view of clouds lit up from beneath in neon peach-pink colors until they glow like bioluminescent creatures swimming across the dusky ocean sky.

I'm happy, in this moment, as I look over the horizon and let my mind wander along idle thoughts of scene composition and color blends.

Until I hear the door creak open behind me.

My shoulders tense.

I already know, from the bristling cloud of stormy tension at my back, it's not Tara.

Sighing, I pray for patience, but don't look up from the horizon.

A faint groan of porch boards is my only warning before Warren shifts to lean on the deck railing next to me, propping himself on his elbows and folding his thick hands together.

Do I *dare*?

I do, risking a glance from the corner of my eye.

There's a pensive knit to his brow, dark and heavy, adding somber lines to his handsome face. The shadow of stubble says either he doesn't give a damn or he's too tired to bother, and I have a sneaking feeling it's the latter.

"Congratulations, Hay," he says slowly, "you got your way."

"It's not *about* getting my way," I bite off – then stop, setting my brush and palette down on the little folding table I'd set up, turning to glare at him. "You know what? You're right. It *is* about getting my way. Because I still don't understand why my life or what I do with it has to be any of your business just because you're from this town and I'm passing through. Renting the room next door doesn't grant you authority in my life decisions, and I'm pretty damn confused why you think it *does*."

Somehow, his silence is worse than any quip I could imagine.

I fold my arms over my chest. "So yeah. I *got my way*, no thanks to your grandma, who seems to understand personal autonomy a little more than you do."

"Grandma doesn't understand that the person who did this won't stop at red paint and fake feathers," he growls, his eyes flashing as he straightens, glowering at me like he's going to stare me into submission. "I don't give a good goddamn what you do with your life, as long as you don't get killed on my watch."

"But *I'm not on your watch*. It's not your job to watch over me," I fire back. This tension between us bristles, but it's a *hot* thing, charged and sparking and making the air around me feel too warm. "Why do you think Dennis Bress would kill me, anyway?"

"Because you're flinging his name around as a potential suspect, for starters," he growls, eyes narrowing. "Why the hell do you think it was Bress?"

"I don't. *You* do. He's the one you were snapping about when you grabbed me the first day." I eye him. "Mr. Bress is nice. I don't think he did shit, or if he was after you then you must've done something."

"I didn't—" He breaks off with a thunder-hiss under his breath, tilting his head back like he's asking for patience, breathing slow as he drags a hand over his face. "Look. Hay. You really have no idea what's going on or what you're talking about. But if you need a job this bad, I can make a few phone calls in Spokane. Missoula. Coeur d'Alene. *Anywhere but here.*"

"Right. You seem to be making phone calls everywhere." I smirk. "How's that working out for you?"

"Dammit, Haley!" Suddenly he's close again, before I can even blink.

Clasping my shoulders, his heat and power everywhere. Even if he's all fierce mountain wild, his touch is so gentle, like he's trying to keep me from breaking in his grip as he stares down with smoldering eyes.

"Warren..."

"No. Don't you get it? I'm not trying to be some kind of controlling asshole for the fun of it. I can't tell you what's going on here. I *can't*. Plain can't tell you why you need to be far, far away from me. But if there were any other way, I'd leave you alone. Live and let live. Trust me when I say I can't, and it's for your own good."

I'm shaking my head, anger flicking through my stomach again. I pinch my eyes shut.

"What *good* is that?"

"Everybody's. I couldn't stand it if you or Tara end up hurt or dead thanks to my bad business."

Hurt? Dead? My tongue ties itself in knots.

I don't get how he does this to me every single time he's near. It's like this scent – this rough raw scent of aftershave and something like hot metal and pure male sex – just crawls inside me and smothers my thoughts.

Until all I can think of is the feeling of his heat prickling on my skin, making words meaningless.

Holy hell.

If this is an attraction, a crush, then I must not have ever known it before, because *no one* ever made me feel like this.

Not Eddy. Not my college boyfriends. Not even the too-perfect-for-life men you find in movies and books.

And the worst part is, Warren isn't even trying to deliver these torrid, ridiculous feels.

He's just too intense. It radiates from him in this aura, this energy field of crackling lightning.

Stand too close, and he'll catch you up in it and consume you.

As he stares down at me, something in his expression changes. Something tense, something hot, and then I can feel it in the charge pulsing through me, starting in my lips and centering lower. I feel it in every tiny hint of space vanishing between us as he leans closer.

Only for the sound of a stomping foot to cut us off as Tara shrieks from the open back door of our duplex.

"You leave her alone!" she shouts, rocketing out, all pint-sized fury, her little fists clenched and beating ineffectively against Warren's thigh. "Don't you hurt my auntie!"

That's our cue to break apart, end whatever weird, layered thing keeps almost happening but doesn't.

Warren holds both hands up, breathing shallowly, looking down at Tara with wide blue eyes. "Whoa. Hey. Hey, now. Slow down, kitten. I wasn't hurting nobody."

Tara glares at him, shoulders scrunched up, her face twisted in a mask of protective ferocity. I'd hug her if I wasn't so shaken, trembling, pressing my hands over my face and trying to calm the racing of my heart.

"Liar!" she accuses. "She's gonna cry."

I shake my head quickly, dropping my hands and forcing

a smile. "No tears here, Tara. I'm okay. Just a little startled. Warren surprised me, that's all."

Warren stares between us, hands still held up like he's facing down the cops.

"For the record, munchkin..." He licks his lips, then says, "I wasn't gonna hurt your aunt. I was gonna kiss her."

What?! I'm physically rocked back by his words.

He slowly lowers his arms, and darts me an uncertain glance before looking back at Tara, offering a reassuring smile. "I just wanted to hold her because I wanted to kiss her."

Instead of slowing down, my heart nearly does a full somersault. I stare at him, my mouth dry.

He's joking, right? Just trying to calm Tara down and explain without frightening her?

But after that charged moment where our eyes locked, Warren leaning closer...

I'm not sure of anything.

And I'm not sure what I would've actually done, if that domineering, stubborn jackass *had* kissed me.

Tara frowns, tilting her head, her scowl easing as she looks at Warren, puzzled. "You...you like Auntie Hay?"

Warren grins, easy and warm. "Yeah."

"Like...boy-girl like?" she whispers.

"Like boy-girl like."

"Oh," Tara says, before her face lights up and she blushes, giggling and covering her mouth. "*Ohhh*. Wow."

Nope.

Oh, *God*.

I have to end this.

It's bad enough that I'm sitting here, wondering how much hot blood can flow into my cheeks before I either pass out or burst into flames.

It keeps getting better.

Now my ten-year-old niece thinks the dick next door has a crush on me. Stifling my groan, I run my fingers through my hair, glancing back at the horizon and the beautiful sunset I'm missing, when I'd wanted to at least capture the general feel of the color palette on canvas.

"Go back inside so Warren and I can talk, kit," I say, managing a smile for Tara. "I'll be in soon to make dinner."

Tara bites her lip, bouncing on her heels. I just know I'm going to have to field a thousand questions over dinner about whether I like Warren and if we're going to kiss and be boyfriend-girlfriend.

No. No way. Abso-freaking-lutely not.

Damn that munchkin for even putting the thought in my head.

But she smiles too brightly to stay mad at, tumbles over, and tackles me with a quick hug, before pulling back and, with another little giggle, darting inside.

She's humming under her breath. It's thirty seconds before I recognize the tune. It's *Haley and Warren, sitting in a tree, K-I-S-S-I-N-G.*

Meanwhile, Warren just stares, scratching at his neck like it's the most natural thing in the world to have my kid niece thinking we're a thing. And to have him standing here, as beast-like as ever, a storm in his eyes hinting at a conversation that might be the last thing on earth either of us need.

Somebody, please.

End me.

* * *

As the door slams shut, I slump back against the deck railing, furiously rubbing my temples. "Boy-girl like, huh? Thanks for that. Thanks *a lot.* Her mother's going to kill me for speeding up *that* conversation by a couple years."

"Sorry. My bad," Warren says sheepishly, and he actually seems like he means it. "Had to think fast, Hay. So she wouldn't be upset."

But his lips are twitching, and so are mine. We can't hold it in forever.

Then we're laughing.

Tired, rough, broken laughter, but laughter nonetheless, a thing so sharp it's like a pin popping the balloon of tension between us, weary but oh-so-necessary.

I need it so bad. I need it to unravel the knots in my chest, to ease the prickling in my skin, the confusion in my brain.

And he just seems like he hasn't laughed at all in a very long time.

As the hysterical little giggle fit passes, Warren slumps, leaning next to me on the railing, crossing his ankles and folding his arms over his chest, his biceps bulging hard against the sleeves of his t-shirt.

He's not laughing anymore, but there's still a warmth around his eyes, a curl at the corners of his mouth, as he sighs.

"Really," he says, "I'm sorry, Hay. I didn't mean to scare her. Or you. I just...fuck."

He trails off. I watch him sidelong, then half-smile. "You're really passionate about things when you care, aren't you?" I lean over and bump his arm. "Even keeping people you don't know safe. And then you get all worked up and explosive."

He clears his throat, ducking his head. "Something like that."

I grin. "You embarrassed, Warren?"

A sullen look darts toward me. "Shut it."

"Nah." I turn to the view, bending over to cross my arms on the railing. "What *do* you do, anyway?"

"Don't think I need to tell you that."

"What's going to happen if you do?"

"Maybe nothing. Maybe you get hurt." He looks past me at the canvas. "You were going to paint the mountains?"

"Maybe," I muse, watching the brilliant blaze of colors as the sun disappears completely behind the distant peaks, making a corona around the mountaintop. "More like I want to paint how everything shifts and changes, right where that cliff drops off." I prop my chin in my hand. "Have you ever heard of ukiyo-e?"

"Not much of an art critic here. I know I like looking at it. It's pretty, and I admire people who can make something imaginary come alive. I sure as hell can't."

I smile to myself.

It's a better answer than I expected.

Most people just dismiss the fine arts as a frivolous thing, scribbling for fun. "It's a style of Japanese art. Most people recognize it when they see it even if they don't know what it is. It borrowed a lot from Chinese art before it evolved to become its own thing. But one thing that's universal to both is how perspective gets created. There's a layering of foreground, midground, and background. The smaller objects become large in the foreground. Big ones turn smaller in the distance." I nod toward the view beyond, where the dramatic curving cutoff of the cliff drops down to the valley, then the distant line of the mountains. "See? Just like that."

"So the view here, Heart's Edge..." He looks over his shoulder, across the field to the cliff. "It's *ooh-kee-yo-ee?*"

I can't help laughing. "It could be inspiration."

"Damn. Think I'd like to see it, Hay. You painting Heart's Edge up real pretty in that style." He turns to face the view as well, bracing his hands against the railing, his broad shoulders pushing stark and hard as he leans on his arms. "Since you and Grandma got on so well...did she tell you the story about why this town's called Heart's Edge?"

85

"No. She mostly told me you're all bark and no bite."

He smiles dryly. I give it back.

"Don't believe her. I bite plenty." But he chuckles, shaking his head. "So this is just an urban legend, but it's one everybody here knows. You learn it when you grow up in these parts. See the way the cliff's shaped? How it comes around this big, round part down to a taper?"

I tilt my head, trailing my gaze along the edge of the cliff, only to suck in a breath. "It's like...half a heart, isn't it?" I realize I'm right, a smile dawning.

"Yeah. And there's this story that way back in settler days, there was this poor farm boy who was in love with the mayor's daughter. The mayor was another farmer just like him. Everybody out here worked like hell to make their own way and make this a real town, a real place where people could live, but the old man still thought this dirty boy was born too low for his little girl."

There's a nostalgic edge to his rough, growling voice, softening it, making it husky enough to thrill like a velvet touch over the skin, and I catch myself watching him. I'm listening intently, watching him smile slightly.

"Go on," I whisper softly.

"But they were in love. So naturally they decided they were gonna run away. They had a marriage in secret right there on the edge of the cliff, just them and God, pledging before the sky when no priest would have them. Then they threw her flowers over the edge and ran off into the mountains to live together. Made their own happy ending with nothing but the big sky country approving."

I smile, tilting my head. "That's a nice story. Maybe they're still out there. Happy in a little cabin somewhere with all their kids and grandkids gathered around."

"They'd be some hundred and fifty years old. But it's a nice thought." He laughs, low and rumbling, then trails into a sigh. "Everybody goes up there at night in the summer, in junior high and high school. You go with the boy or girl you like, and you throw flowers over 'cause you want to be together forever. Or you go by yourself, thinking about the person you long for most, and toss your flowers with a little hope those petals will make their way into their heart."

Like a wishing well, then.

It's such a gentle story, such a sweet legend, that I hardly expect it from *him*, or the way he seems to go soft at the memory.

This place really is home to him, I realize, even if he's acting strange, and he's clearly up to something. He cares about Heart's Edge, and I'd like to think that whatever else he's involved in wouldn't lead him to hurting anyone.

Maybe not even Mr. Bress.

He wouldn't do anything to harm the town he loves so much. Or that stern yet sweet woman he calls Grandma.

I turn to face him, leaning my elbow on the railing. "So, Warren...did *you* ever stand there on the cliff and throw flowers over and whisper a girl's name?"

"Nah," he rumbles, then looks down at me, his blue eyes nearly glowing in the deepening dark, the same color as the descending night sky. "Not yet. I threw some flowers once, but there wasn't no love in the equation."

There's a darkness in his tone. And a sweetness when he says *not yet*.

Something clutches up in my chest as I look up at him, warmth flushing through me, burning in my cheeks down my throat, over my whole body and –

Hold up. No, this is Tara putting those thoughts in my head – and I look away quickly, tucking my hair behind my ear and clearing my throat, taking a step back.

"I have to go feed Tara and drop her off with your grand-

87

mother," I murmur. "Then it's time to report for my first night at work. Good night, Warren. Wish me luck?"

He doesn't say anything as I turn and walk quickly away. Not until the door is almost closed, and that low growl chases after me like a hunter in the night.

"Good night. Good luck, Hay."

VI: WAITING GAME (WARREN)

*L*ooks like I'm not chasing Hay off.

Hell, it feels like every time I try, it backfires. Just ends up with her more firmly embedded in my life, deeper entrenched in Heart's Edge.

It's time to make the best of a bad situation.

With her next door, I can keep an eye on her.

That's another double-edged sword. With Haley this close, someone coming after me could hurt her and Tara. But I can also keep myself between her and Bress, make damn sure he can't lay a hand on her or that little girl.

Still, with Haley that close...I can't fucking focus.

This magnetic pull between us keeps getting stronger, making it hard for me to think about my mission at all.

Call it what it is – a heaping slice of *absurd*.

I don't *know* her.

I don't know this chick at all, but that's part of what's driving this wolf craving.

Something fierce and crazy and overprotective makes me want to know her from the inside out.

Every damn thing about her, from those pretty green eyes to the soft blue paints she uses to smear the sky on canvas.

I'd love to know what drove her out here, really, besides an asshole fiancé. She mentioned a job and a gallery going bust. A familiar hard luck story she doesn't deserve.

Hay's a sweet mystery wrapped in *want.*

I want to know what she's trying to prove.

I want to know what ignited that crackling blaze inside her.

I want to know what makes her so maddeningly stubborn, so maddeningly beautiful.

I want to know what makes her gasp, makes her sigh, what kindles those glassy sparks in her eyes into desire.

And I really want to know how she whimpers when she comes, rocking so hard under me while I etch her little outline into the mattress.

Yeah. I'm moonstruck.

I'm fucking foolish.

All because Hay went and stood up to me. Told me repeatedly to shove it where the sun don't shine, instead of simpering after me and trying to cozy up with bedroom eyes like most girls her age.

Maybe that's why I've never gotten serious about anyone.

Nobody ever showed me fire.

Didn't catch my interest, even if avenging Jenna's the real reason there's no place for any woman in my life, spitfire or not.

Goddamn. I shouldn't be thinking this.

I've stopped focusing on my laptop screen and the GPS tracker dot following Bress' movements. He's back in town. It looks like he's been...at Stewart's shop?

Shit. I wonder if he found the tracker and went to Stew to have it looked at.

What's bothering me even more, right now, is that the tracker shows Bress' camper parked at Brody's.

The pub.

Where Hay's working tonight.

I swear under my breath, look away, look back, start getting up, then make myself sit back down.

Wait. No.

There's nothing to worry about since they're in public. I don't need to go charging in like a damned bull. Bress has no reason to think she suspects him of threatening me and vandalizing the cabin.

Hell, she doesn't even think it herself – she thinks I'm the asshole here, and Bress is Mr. Rogers.

'Course, he doesn't know that.

He might be checking her out for a good chance to get her alone, out of the way. My fingers curl into a fist.

Fuck. I can't stay here.

I just want to check out the lay of the land. And if Bress is onto me already, then he'd damn well better know I'm watching him, and forget the letter of the law if he goes anywhere near Haley.

If he touches her or the girl, the gloves are coming off. I'll send him straight to hell myself without giving him a chance to rot behind bars.

I'm dressed and in my truck before I even realize it, cursing at myself the whole time. I'm doing the right thing, I tell myself.

Taking it slow, real cautious, just like Jenna would've wanted.

But it sure as hell feels like more than that, with the tight knot of agitation coiling in the pit of my stomach.

When I pull up outside Brody's, I don't see Bress' car in the lot.

I *do* see Stewart's old souped-up muscle truck, a fucking

monster on high wheels with flames down the side of the cab. I know nearly every car in town.

When Heart's Edge has a population under two thousand, you get to know your people and their rides even when you've been away for a while.

The pub is pretty lively. While it's not exactly a college town, it's a magnet for college kids to come out on a drive with their bros or their dates for a secluded spot. A twenty-something-year-old kid's dream place to get drunk, make out, and fall asleep under the stars.

The lights are bright, familiar, when I step inside. The jukebox plays some old nineties grunge band. There's people milling around the grey, weathered floors and tucked in clusters at the tables, booths, and against the walls. Old classic neon signs glow overhead next to road signs scavenged from diners and highways across the States. It smells like beer, onion rings, and hormones.

Home, sweet home. Brings back a lot of memories of my younger days.

Brody's mostly hires pretty girls looking for their first job. It's like a small-town Hooters, and the uniform is pretty loose: cutoff denim mini that shows everything but the goods and a sports team jersey knotted below the midriff.

Only one rule: that jersey better not belong to the Cardinals, the Patriots, or the Rams.

Most of the girls here are college-aged themselves. I don't feel quite right looking at those midriffs and naked thighs when I'm almost thirty-damned-five – save for one.

The moment I walk in the door, I zero in on Haley.

Don't know if she went shopping or someone let her raid their locker, but I think that girl's trying to fucking kill me.

She's got on a swatch of denim, frayed edges that barely lick against the lower curves of her ass.

Everything rides down so low on her hips I can see the

V of creased flesh to either side of the lower swell of her smooth, toned belly. Right where it starts delving down toward panties she can't be wearing, or I'd see them when there's only enough skirt to keep those smooth thighs and tight curves from being a full-on pornographic peep show.

The chunky leather belt she's wearing is almost bigger than the skirt, anchoring it in place. Only thing keeping her breasts from spilling out everywhere is a tight-drawn knot right below and between them, pulling an oversized men's jersey down until the V-neck shows cleavage.

Fuck.

Cleavage that's currently in Stewart's line of sight as she leans over his table and drops a foaming mug of beer in front of him, along with a tray of fries. Her unbound hair tumbles everywhere, this loose mess of windswept waves I just want to wind my fist in as I drag her against my body.

I shouldn't be steaming inside, but damn she's giving him a flirtatious little smile from under her lashes. Stewart's all charm, easy and calm and affable with his lazy, pleasant smile.

My vision tints red.

They're murmuring to each other. I *must* be out of my goddamn mind because I'm thinking all kinds of nasty things I shouldn't be. I've got no claim.

Stewart's my best friend.

Hay's a stranger, and if she's going to work at Brody's, flirting is practically in the job description.

Head on straight, Ford, I tell myself. *Get over the damn girl.*

Then figure out why your tracker says Bress is here when he sure as hell isn't anywhere in this crowd.

Stewart gives me an excuse to stop standing in the door like a block of wood, though, when he catches sight of me over the top of his booth and raises a hand.

"War!" he calls, beckoning me over. "Hey, man. C'mon. I didn't expect to see you here tonight."

Reluctantly, I make my way over.

Real reluctantly, at least, because the second Stewart says my name, Haley goes stiff. She flashes me a sharp, accusing look, her flirty smile turning to poison again.

Damn. She must think I came to check up on her.

Maybe she's a little right, but I can't stand to let myself look at her, or I won't look away.

Hay's all suntanned smoothness and tempting, lickable skin. Another second of watching the gap between her thighs or the shadows that hint at *more* under that skirt and my cock's going to have trouble fitting in my jeans.

As I slide into the booth, Hay leans over me, bending just a little closer with her arms folded under her breasts, plumping them till they're suckable mounds threatening to drag my attention away from my friend's knowing smile.

"So what'll it be?" she asks, almost too phony sugary-sweet.

"Just draft," I say, mouth dry. "And the charbroiled mushroom swiss burger."

"Don't need a menu?"

"I've had the menu memorized since I was twelve," I point out. "Only out-of-towners use menus at Brody's. But it helps that Grandma owns the place."

"And he always gets the same thing," Stewart says, his grin sly. "Don't tell anyone, but he helped create the menu when he was a kid. That's his signature burger. Me, I like to change it up a little. Tell the cook to surprise me, sugar."

Hay's eyes flash. I'm almost satisfied by that spark of irritation as she retorts, scathingly nice, "You got it, 'sugar.'"

I have a feeling if she didn't need the paycheck, she'd probably have told Stewart to shove his *sugar* up his ass. He'd deserve it, too, for telling her that little bit about me and the menus.

Still, I can't help but grin as I watch her turn around and walk away with those pretty hips swaying, those soft thighs sliding together.

"Enjoying the view?" Stew asks, his brown eyes glittering with unvoiced laughter.

"I'm not dead yet." I drag my gaze back to him. "What're you doing here?"

"Didn't feel like cooking tonight. Bachelor life gets boring. Plus, I was on my way out to see you, after."

My brows furrow. "See me?"

His expression sobers, and he glances over his shoulder, sweeping his gaze around the pub, lingering on a cluster of older men playing darts on the decaying dartboard before he fixes on me again and leans across the table. Then his hand disappears for a moment and emerges with something familiar.

My GPS tracker.

Shit.

He passes it over with a covered hand. I swipe it before anybody can see it, glancing around myself and whisper, "What the fuck, man?"

"I saw you this morning," he mutters. "You're lucky no one else did. What the hell are you doing, War? You know what kind of trouble this can get you in? Could be a felony. I'm saving your ass, man."

"It's *business.* I have my reasons," I bite off, tucking the tracker into my back pocket. "Fuck. That explains why I saw his car parked at your shop all day."

"You have to be more careful." He watches me closely, gaze concerned, brows knitting together. "I pulled your ass out of a fire this time – you know what Bress can do to you for this? – but I don't even know what you're up to. I can only cover for you so long if you're keepin' me in the dark."

"I can't tell you. Trust me, Stew." I shake my head. "It's safer for everyone if you don't know."

"Safer for everyone but you, you mean." Stewart studies me sourly for a minute, then turns his head to watch Haley sail from calling orders over the bar into the kitchen to make the rounds of a few more tables. His gaze tracks her curiously. "So what's up with that? You gonna keep your lips sewn shut with her, too?"

"You already know. About the breakdown, the car, and whatever." I shrug. "She was supposed to go stay with a friend after blowing town, I guess. She's trying to start over, but that fell through, so she's staying here a while longer. Grandma felt bad for her, so she's more houseguest than paying patron. Stubborn thing's determined to work her way out of town, saving up till she can relocate."

Stewart keeps eyeballing her, something that brings a growl up my throat.

My jealous eyes can't help watching her, too. The way she moves with quick grace and confidence, you'd never know this was her first day on the job. The way she smiles, a flash of sass in every grin, in the glitter of her eyes, while teasing boys reach out with flirtatious hands...

They're mighty disappointed when she dances deftly out of the way and warns them with a half-playful, mock-serious look.

Fuck. The sheer wild *heart* in this woman, after the crap it seems like she's been through? Anyone else would be crying at their own pity bash.

Not Hay.

First thing she did was start looking for ways to fix her dilemma.

"War? You still with me?" Stew's teasing tone causes me to whip my head around. "Do I detect a touch of admiration?"

"She's a babe," I admit with a shrug. "I'll give her that. Same thing I'll give plenty of girls."

That's a half lie.

"Yeah, cute," Stewart echoes. "Young 'un, too. Barely older than those college brats. What is she, twenty-five, twenty-six?"

"Not sure." I try to keep my tone bland. "You interested?"

"Nah, you know me, man. I keep my hands to myself when a brother's already staked a claim," Stewart answers slyly.

Goddamn.

My fist coils against my knee.

This boy knows how to push my buttons too damn well. My hackles are rising and I don't even know why.

Stew's my *friend*, someone I've always trusted. I know he's good to women, but something about the way he talks about Hay sets my teeth on edge. I clench my jaw, forcing my tone to remain even, calm, friendly.

"I haven't staked nothing," I say. "No need to yack about her like that."

He arches a slow brow. "Like what?"

"Like she's an object to be passed around."

Stewart blinks, then breaks into a broad grin. "So you *do* like her."

My blood's about to boil over.

"I like treating her like a human being, Stew. That's it," I growl. "Don't much think she likes being called 'sugar,' FYI."

He spreads his hands apologetically. "Ms. West it is, then." He turns his head to watch her for a bit longer. "It is *Miss* West, right? I didn't see no ring."

Why are you so curious? I want to roar but keep it to

myself. Under the table, now I've got both hands forming fists.

Christ. *Easy.*

Why's this *getting* to me so much?

"Yeah," I mutter. "She said something about a cheating dickwad fiancé, so I don't think she's feeling too charitable toward men right now."

"You sure it's not just toward *you,* Mr. Sunshine?"

I glower at Stewart's wide, companionable grin. "Bite me."

Anything else we might say gets cut off as Haley comes swinging toward us, balancing a tray effortlessly. She slides a plate in front of me with a thick, steaming burger dripping with swiss cheese and a side of onion rings.

Thank God for the distraction.

"Here's your beer and burger," she says tartly, her venom-smile back, and damn if I don't want to kiss it right off her as she bends over us, sliding a frothing mug of beer toward me. "And your surprise," she adds, spinning another plate down deftly in front of Stewart. Looks like fried shrimp tails arranged in a spiral and a little plastic cup of red sauce.

Stewart picks up a shrimp and swirls it in the sauce, taking a crunchy bite, then swallows with an appreciative grunt.

"Shrimp and spicy cocktail sauce!" he says, licking his lips. "My favorite."

Hay smiles, tucking her tray against her stomach, flicking us both with penetrating looks. "Anything else you boys need?"

"We're good," I say, while Stewart just locks eyes with me and grins.

"What he said," he tells her, never taking his gaze away from me, although he pitches his voice to Haley. "Don't forget to call me tomorrow, though!"

"Call him?" I snap without thinking, even though I know damn well he's baiting me just to get a rise over a girl.

But it's too late. Hay's smile is gone, and she flashes me a sharp, irritated look. "Mind your own business."

Then she pivots and practically flounces away, the lash of her hair like a whip threatening to cut me open if I push too far.

Stewart watches me knowingly, toying a piece of shrimp against his mouth. "About the new carburetor," he clarifies. "That's why I need her on the horn. We were talking about the make and model before I order the part. Should be able to get it for her in a couple days, before that little duct-tape job you did goes *pop!*" His grin widens. "What'd you think she was calling me for, War?"

I swallow another growl.

I'm not gonna let him do this. Not the fuck tonight.

He's always teased me, ever since high school. One of his favorite tricks was to get me flustered over a girl. After Jenna, he backed off, but fuck if you can keep the class clown down forever.

But this isn't senior year, or that time I had a crush on Tammy Preacher so bad my eyes crossed every time I saw her.

This thing with Hay's different.

I'm not into her. I don't have time.

I just need to keep my crap with Bress away from her, and that's all I care about. It's all I'm allowed to care about.

And I refuse to look at her as she sails across the room. So instead I pick up my burger and take a big bite, digging my teeth in fiercely.

"War? We okay?" Stewart nudges me again. "You know I was just yankin' your –"

"It doesn't matter," I snort around the burger. "Just eat your damn food."

Stewart doesn't say anything.

He doesn't have to.

His smile speaks a thousand words as he just shrugs and tucks into his shrimp, thoughtful brown eyes tracking Haley the whole time.

* * *

I GET out of Brody's as soon as I've finished my food. There's no reason for me to stay, and if I do, I'll be tempted to...

I don't even know.

I'd say I won't think about it, but certain ideas are getting...interesting.

An Advil and my bed sound better, though, by the time I get home. I'm hounded the entire drive by a client's voice nattering over speakerphone, demanding I get my ass over to Boise next week and do a little skip tracing on some loser who ducked out on his child support and went off-grid, supposedly untraceable.

Supposedly.

No one's untraceable for me.

I'm a born tracker just like Jenna was. Hell, we had ourselves a bet in the war, racing each other to see who could pull more high-level terrorist fuckwits out of caves and spider holes first. Whoever lost owed the winner a year's supply of smokes.

It was looking like I'd have to pay out the nose with her ahead of me by two, before...

Fuck.

Bad bets and cheap tobacco were another thing we shared.

Two more habits I gave up after she was taken away.

But I'll worry about it in the morning.

Heart's Edge is my home base for now, but I tend to work

nationwide. I usually don't keep a static address, but right now I need to focus my attention here and then make up my mind about where to go next, after I've dealt with Bress.

I've waited thirteen damn years for my moment to shine, watching from afar until he tripped up enough to bring me back. Once he started expanding his operations out of town, I knew it was time.

A friend and local tipped me off that he'd started buying up properties in plenty of small towns in a fifty-mile radius. The thing with underground businesses is they don't stay under wraps for long the bigger they get.

And it's too easy to get sloppy.

Get caught.

Bress isn't going anywhere, though. He's established in Heart's Edge, so deeply rooted in the local economy that if he cut and run, he'd ruin himself.

I've been keeping an eye on his financials through some less-than-official channels. He's got so much sunk into real estate and business investments that he has almost no liquid assets.

If he runs, he'll be running damn near penniless with nowhere to go. In essence, I've got him trapped, cornered.

Right where I want him.

Which means I can probably afford a brief detour to Boise to pick up a quick contract to keep *my* liquid assets flowing.

I turn that over, settling into the hot tub out back on the cabin porch to let the steaming jets of water – plus a few beers, chilling in a bucket of ice – soothe away my tension and hopefully take my headache with it.

Should be an easy paycheck. I could be in Boise in five or six hours, probably have that asshole collared and turned in to the law in less than twenty-four, and be back before my bed's even gone cold. Two days, tops.

So why does the idea of leaving make me so uneasy?

It's not Bress. Not really. I know what it is. I just won't say it.

It's Hay.

It's this damnable need to keep her in my sights at all times. Because some fucked up part of me is convinced if I leave her alone too long, the next time it won't be red paint smeared all over.

Because I wasn't here to stop it.

It's a morbid train of thought I can't linger on.

Bress isn't completely insane. He won't do a big, gory hit on a stranger in town because that'd bring in the Feds.

Nothing's going to happen to Haley if I take off for two days, except she'll rest a bit easier without us butting heads. God, she's a pain in my ass.

Always has to challenge everything until we're locking horns.

I've never met anyone so stubborn, but that's what makes those little moments of softness stand out even more.

The way she is with her niece.

The lost, rapt look on her face as she studies a sunset with an eye for what's pretty, brush in hand.

The occasional way she looks at me as if I'm a beast with a thorn in its paw, and she's torn between gently prying it out – or jamming it in deeper just to watch me wince.

Goddamn little sadist.

Even if she only seems to be that way with *me*.

I'm not all sunshine and roses, but damn.

I'm not even sure how long I sit there thinking about Hay while trying *not* to think about her, letting the beer cloud my mind as I stare up at the stars. For a little while, it's working.

Then there's a rustle in the bushes. I damn near jump out of the water, but what scurries out is too small for any person.

"Damn it, Mozart. That you again?"

A loud, frayed *meow* answers back. When he speaks up, there's no mistaking the high-pitched, deafening music that's his namesake.

He's a big Tom, a stray Grandma's been feeding since winter. I've taken to the habit, too, seeing how he started hanging around this cabin more ever since I came back.

He calls at me again, his orange tail swishing in the darkness.

"No vittles tonight. I'm trying to relax. Go on, git!' I sink back in the tub, slapping the water as I hear him dart away.

I'm rewarded by a few minutes of peaceful bliss. *Finally.*

I halfway drift off with my eyes open, watching how the Milky Way explodes across the night out here. That's one of my favorite parts of Heart's Edge, hardly any lights to drown out the sky.

I'm so focused I don't hear Haley come home. Or even realize she's here until the creak of the back door opening snaps me out of a waking dream.

She steps out, her head bowed as she folds a towel over her arms. Then I see what she's wearing – or not wearing – and my jaw nearly makes a splash.

Hay's all slim and pretty with that tight, curvy body nearly naked in a pale teal bikini. One with the kind of little ribbons that tie over the hips and make you want to pull 'em loose with your goddamn teeth, licking your way down paths of bare flesh with every slip of fabric falling away.

There's another one tying the top closed over her tits, a little bow between, and all that soft suntanned flesh straining against little stretchy triangles of fabric that can't quite hold them in.

Fuck.

I don't know what's worse.

Seeing Hay like this...or the fact that I'm *fucking buff*

underneath the swirling, barely-concealing froth of hot tub bubbles. I've suddenly got a lot to hide.

I grunt as I shift to adjust myself, hoping a little pressure will coax my surging cock to sit the fuck back down.

The sound makes her jerk, sucking in a breath, looking up just in time for me to look away before I get caught staring.

There's a moment of silence. Then a low, "Oh."

Just that *oh* and nothing else. I think it'd be easier if it was disgusted or angry, annoyed that I'm in the place she wants to be.

There's no way we can both relax in this hot tub together, not when the moment we're in each other's presence, the air crackles with a sizzling, wild tension that seems to turn the night into a silent storm. After a few laden seconds of silence, her quiet footsteps pad closer, soft against the wood of the deck. Then there's a low splash, and I risk a glance from the corner of my eye.

She's sitting on the edge of the hot tub, her legs dangling in the water, her hands braced to either side of her naked thighs while she swirls her feet in the bubbles. Her vivid green eyes watch me idly, turning into glowing stars by the reflections of the lights under the water.

Her gaze is curious, thoughtful, and very obviously staying above the water's surface, her cheeks a touch pink.

"Rough night?" she asks softly.

It feels like a white flag. A truce. Like she's saying *I come in peace, let's not trade shots right now.*

"Should be asking you that, feels like," I venture. "Haven't seen Brody's that busy in a good long while."

"So that wasn't normal? Thank *God.* My feet are killing me." She laughs, kicking said feet a little in the water, splashing me gently.

"Bad first night?"

"Not bad. Just been a long time since I was a waitress, and last time, I was at least on wheels."

I blink, tilting my head. "Wheels?"

"Sonic." She grins. "You know, the cute little waitresses that spin around on roller skates in tiny shorts and Sonic hats? That was me in college. Had to pay for textbooks somehow."

There's another image I don't need.

I'm trying like hell not to picture her gliding around a parking lot in shorts almost as tiny as that tempting bikini bottom, and I distract myself from thinking about it by reaching into the ice bucket and fishing out a fresh beer.

"Here," I say, nicking the cap off with the edge of the bucket and then offering her the bottle. "You earned it."

Grinning, she takes the bottle and raises it in a salute. "Damn right. I didn't bite anyone the entire night."

I snort back a laugh and swig my own beer. "Didn't think that was part of the job description."

"It should be." She rolls her eyes. "Employee-customer relations sub-clause 12A: any college boy who calls me 'sugar tits' gets bitten. Then I dump his beer in his lap."

"Not sure the kids these days say 'sugar tits.'"

"They do when they're drunk and messing around with their frat brothers. Ask me how I know." With a sigh, Hay slips down, easing herself into the water with a low, sensuous groan that makes goosebumps stand up on my skin.

Her lithe movement reminds me very pointedly of the throb in my cock I'm trying to ignore.

Settling on the seat opposite me, the water bubbling up around her shoulders, she leans her head back against the edge of the hot tub and taps her beer bottle against her lips.

"That bad, huh? Shit. I'm sorry Grandma sent you in there without waders."

"It's not all bad. Good tips. Should make *you* happy. The

105

more money I make shaking my ass for minimum wage and a few little gratuities, the faster I can get out of your precious town."

There it is. The first shot fired.

I clench my jaw, looking away, swearing I won't give in. "Thought you were so charmed by Heart's Edge you wanted to put down roots?"

"Nah. This isn't somewhere I'll stay, even if it's pretty. I need bigger digs for art." She quirks her lips. "Though I don't know where the hell I'm going now. I guess Chicago's still the goal...but I've got to make contingency plans for what'll happen when I get there."

"You taking the kid all the way out there with you?"

"Don't know. Depends on how long I'm here." With a grim smile, she takes a deep swig of her beer. "For all I know, it'll take me years to save up enough to get out. Rent isn't cheap in the Windy City. Maybe I'll grow into the walls. Then even if I don't mean to put down roots, I'll be stuck here long before you run away again."

I growl. "What makes you think I'm gonna cut and run?"

"Call it a hunch," she says. "People who try to chase others off are usually doing it to save themselves the trouble."

"Bullshit. I think you're projecting," I mutter against the mouth of my bottle. "If anyone's running, it's you. You really think dropping everything and taking off across the country will fix all your problems?"

"Considering my biggest problem was a man who can't keep his dick in his pants, yeah," she flings back. "What Eddy did isn't my fault. And you can't blame me for wanting as much space between me and him as possible. Won't fix my issues because moving can't make *him* a better man, but a fresh start never hurt anyone."

I sigh, pressing my cold beer against my forehead. The hot tub is starting to feel too warm, and I can't tell if it's my rising temper or just the heat of having her close. She turns me all around, and I keep saying the wrong thing.

"Look, I didn't mean—" I break off, cursing. "Your fiancé was shit-scum, okay? That's not your fault. Not in the slightest. I didn't mean to imply it was. Sorry, Hay."

She doesn't say anything.

It's unnerving, the silence, this screaming empty thing that says something's *wrong*, but I almost don't want to look when Haley has her pride. If I look at her right now, it might just gouge her in all the wrong ways.

But after a couple more wordless minutes, I risk a glance, suddenly wishing this fucking feeling I get around her would be strong enough so she'd let me reach out, touch her, comfort her.

She's staring out across the deck toward the cliff and the mountains. Her hair is damp at the tips and clinging to her shoulders, beads of splashed water on her cheeks and her lips, but it's not water gleaming in her eyes.

It's the beginning beads of tears, her mouth trembling, her expression taut and pensive. Barely hard to tell she's not seeing anything.

Not me, not seeing the starry skyline, not the water.

Nothing but the memory of a selfish pissant who made her cry because he couldn't treat her like a human being.

"You know, that's one thing he never said," she whispers, finally. "He was all slick, easy charm and friendly smiles, got along with everyone. And I can't think of a *single* time he ever apologized. You're the biggest fucking prick I've ever met – no offense – but at least you know how to say you're sorry. You even sound like you mean it sometimes."

"I do." I smile faintly. "I gotta have one or two redeeming qualities, right? I'd rather be an honest prick than a lying nice guy."

"Seems like any guy who claims to be nice is lying." She

sniffles roughly, then lets out a shaky laugh and scrubs an arm across her nose. "Ugh, the steam's making my eyes water."

Sure. The steam.

I may be a swinging prick and a half, but I'm not going to embarrass a woman in distress. Let her have her pride.

"Hey," I say, searching for a distraction. "Truth or dare."

She blinks at me quizzically, wiping at the wet beads spiking her lashes. "Truth or what?"

"It's a thing. When I was a kid, me and my friends would steal Grandma's beers and hang out in the hot tubs in the empty cabins during the slow seasons. We'd watch the stars and play truth or dare. So I'm inaugurating you into a Heart's Edge tradition, but that means you have to pick. Truth or dare?"

Another blink, before a slow, almost shy smile dawns on her lips. "Truth. I don't know if I trust you with dares. You've got too much practice at this, apparently."

"Aw, like I'd make you do anything terrible on a dare."

No. Never.

Just maybe ask her to slip that top down, those little bikini straps grazing down her shoulders, just enough to tease my – *nah.*

I'm not going to be that kind of guy. And I tear myself from tracing my gaze over the curve of her shoulder, focusing myself on my beer. "All right. Truth. Did you slash your ex's tires before you left?"

Her sudden burst of laughter comes out startled, delighted. "No!"

"Did you *want* to?"

"Oh, no, you don't." Grinning, she points at me. "That's two questions, Warren. Save that one for your next round. Your turn. Truth or dare?"

"Truth."

Her eyes sparkle wickedly. "No dare? Don't trust me?"

"*No.*"

That prompts another laugh, and I grin back.

Hot damn, she's gorgeous when she laughs, the way her eyes crease at the corners and shine, the way her lips part, how she throws her head back and gives herself to it fully. I'd rather see her laughing than crying, though I get needing to get those feelings out, cry them dry, until they're not so hard to carry anymore.

Right now, she's distracted and eyeballing me, tapping her beer bottle against her lush, rosy lower lip while she thinks.

"What's up with you and Stewart?"

I blink. That's a weird question. "Stew?"

"I can't tell if you're friends or enemies. You were kind of circling each other like wolves over a bone at Brody's tonight."

Shit. Was it really that obvious?

At least I can blame the hot flush in my face and neck on the steam, just like her. Because I can't tell her we were circling each other over *her*, and Stewart tried to goad me into admitting some attraction to her. So even if I picked truth, I'm going to have to lie.

"He's one of my closest friends," I say. "We're just like that. Ballbusters. We show affection by jabbing. Doesn't really mean anything."

"Are you like that with everyone?"

"Define 'everyone.'"

She shrugs. "Your grandmother, your other friends, coworkers...girlfriend?"

I snort. "Grandma would skin me alive if I ever took that tone with her. The rest of my friends are complete cases of arrested development, more problems than you can shake a therapy stick at. I don't have coworkers, and if you're asking if I have a girlfriend, that's two questions."

Fuck, why does she care if I have a girlfriend?

Her grin shines back, triumphant. "Actually, three. You answered if you were like that with everyone, so I got an extra in."

I steal another swig of beer. "Does that mean I get two this time?"

"I shouldn't since you were the one who missed it, but..." She sticks the tip of her tongue out at me merrily. "I'll let you. But how do you know I was going to pick truth?"

I can't help myself. My gaze dips over her, trailing down to where the water turns her body into nothing but swirls of color. I know what she looks like now and can only imagine the wet slick glistening on her skin, making it gleam like caramel, waiting to be licked and licked and *licked* until she writhes. And as I raise my eyes again, hers are a little too wide, heart-shaped lips parted as she meets my gaze, beer bottle clutched in both hands.

"You want to pick dare?" I ask softly.

Haley swallows, tucking a strand of damp hair behind her ear, lowering her eyes. "Truth. I'll stick with truth."

Tell me the truth. Are you attracted to me?

I can't ask that.

Can't have those kinds of complications and entanglements right now.

Truly, my mind's on one thing and one thing only – but I've got to divert myself before one of those downswept glances dips below the water and notices something I can't really hide without being too obvious. It's only the refracting light dancing on the water making me decent.

So I search for something else, anything, and finally settle on it.

"You said you did claims adjustments...but you were painting. I thought you were an artist?"

"A wannabe," she retorts bitterly before tacking on, "Oh, wait. We're supposed to call ourselves 'aspiring.' Or 'struggling' if we want to be really edgy. Sounds better than 'starving,' I guess." She shakes her head. "I keep trying. Have been for years. But...I thought I had a break when a local gallery did a showing for me. No one bought a damned thing, though. Not after a *month*. So the gallery tossed me out on my ass. Which was already sore from the spanking fate gave it with my day job firing me and my fiancé fucking my best friend."

"Doesn't seem like she was much of a friend," I say. "Assuming the friend was a she."

She lets out another laugh, but it's not the same as before. It's harsh and self-mocking. "I'd be less upset if it was a guy. If Eddy had just like...needed to find himself or some shit. I'd rather realize my fiancé was gay than *know* he just doesn't respect me enough to keep his hands off other women."

"I'd say doesn't matter who it was. If you're with someone, you honor that agreement. And if you can't, you have the decency, the integrity, to break it the fuck off. Before fucking around with other people."

"Yeah, well, asshole missed that lesson." She shakes herself, taking a deep breath. "You're supposed to get another question."

And that's her way of saying she doesn't want to talk about this anymore.

Okay. I can take a hint. "All right. You want truth for this one, or dare?"

"You know what? Screw it." She shrugs defiantly. "Dare. Hit me with your worst."

"Show me one of your paintings," I say.

She goes so frozen it's like she's been captured in still life

111

herself, the brush strokes of a woman. She just stares at me, those wide green eyes pure liquid crystal, parted lips so swollen and pink. "I...what? Why?"

I shrug. "I want to see how damn stupid that gallery owner had to be."

Haley smiles wanly. "They're not that great."

"Beauty, eye of the beholder, you know the saying."

"Do I?"

She sets her beer down on the edge of the jacuzzi and folds her arms in tight, and in that moment, she's so small and vulnerable I have to remind myself I'm *naked* to keep from going to her, taking her in my arms, comforting her.

It's like those paintings cut her deeper than even her ex, and I don't think she realizes it – and I won't be stupid enough to point it out – but she's probably got a hell of a lot more heart for her passion than she ever did for a man who was clearly all wrong for her every which way.

With a shaky breath, she says, "I'll think about it. What are the stakes if I won't?"

"None," I answer. "It's just a game, Hay. We're just relaxing over a couple beers."

"Maybe...yeah. Yeah, okay." She forces a smile, then snatches up her beer and downs the entire thing in a few gulps, her throat working roughly before she slams it down on the edge with a deep breath. "Okay!"

I arch a brow. "Okay? Are you?"

"No, silly, okayyy. Now I get to ask *you*." She reaches toward the bucket with grabby hands, flexing her fingers playfully even though it's out of her range. "Truth or dare?"

I roll my eyes. I get the hint and fish out another beer, pop the cap, and pass it to her.

She grasps it in both hands, nursing it like a little chipmunk, bright-eyed and too cheerful. I watch her with a sigh, wondering at this fond feeling of warmth in my chest, then shake my head.

"Truth. I still don't trust you with a dare."

"Relax. It's not like I'm going to ask you to streak through town."

If only she knew.

Hay takes another sip, musing, then asks, "What do you do? You're so weird. All cloak and dagger, and I know you're ex-Army, but I don't think deployment sent you on a mission back to your spooky little hometown to uncover all its dirty secrets in the name of some special government operation." She wiggles her fingers with a little *ooo-OOO-ooo* sound, then smirks. "So spill it. What is it you do that's got you acting like Agent Mulder?"

I don't even know what that means, but I also know I can't even fucking answer her question.

It's not even that she'll figure out I'm here after a mark. Or worse, figure out I'm *not* here after a mark, that this thing with Bress is entirely personal.

It's that I know she'll wonder things about me.

Wonder what I've done.

Who I've hurt.

Who I've killed.

And it bothers me to have her think worse of me than she already does.

"Can't tell you that," I say, and smile. It feels like too much, heavy and sad, a smile I'm not used to. "Top secret. Guess it'll have to be dare."

"Aw, fine," she retorts. "I dare you to tell me what you do."

"Then I guess I'm gonna have to lose the game." I lean over and clink the neck of my bottle to hers with a faint smile. "Since we didn't ante up any stakes...let's go another round."

For a few seconds her eyes meet mine, mischief gleaming.

I wonder if she understands what I'm offering her. A distraction, mostly.

For both of us.

One sweet moment to forget who we are, our worries, and why we're here. That she ran out here after a man hurt her in a way she never should've been hurt and cut her off at the knees after life had already kicked her down, while I'm here chasing down the demon who took what I loved.

Haley tips her head, a faint, wistful smile crossing her lips.

Yeah.

She knows.

She knows, and with a tired little shrug and a *hell-with-it* smile, clinks her bottle right back. "Hit me, then. Truth."

This time, I play it safe with my questions.

Less because I'm worried about her prying out my secrets, and more because I'm worried about hurting her with hers.

So it's the little things, this time.

Most embarrassing high school memory. Favorite color. Dare you to beat me in a foot fight.

I find out that she once stood on the roof of her high school in a prom dress, declaring her love for the high school football team's star quarterback. All because he'd said he'd date her if she did.

Turns out, it was just a cruel fucking prank to see if she'd really go that far.

Hay tells me her colors like an artist.

How she loves the slate-blue color of a Seattle horizon in the morning, when the sun's up but the city doesn't seem to have figured it out yet.

Then this chick shows me she knows how to win a foot fight.

Before I know it, we're kicking and splashing at each

other, and she gets me right on the sole of my foot and tickles me with her toes till I damn near surrender, laughing and sweeping a wave of water at her to make her stop.

She's also a real lightweight.

After her fourth beer, when I ask her what she dreamed about being as a little girl...

"Happy," is the one word she whispers, right before her face caves in, and she bursts into tears.

Fuck.

That's it. Game over.

Hay's clearly had too much to drink. She's too raw for this, for this playact of forgetting and pushing everything aside to be light, free, careless.

She doesn't need to be wallowing in a hot tub, chewing on her feelings in front of a secretly naked guy she can't even stand. She needs rest.

Carefully, I pry her beer bottle from lax fingers and set it aside, then shut the jacuzzi off.

While she's still scrubbing at her eyes, I hoist myself out and steal her towel to wrap around my waist. Then I kneel at the edge next to her, catching her gently under the arms, lifting her.

"Here," I coax. "C'mon. Let's get you to bed."

"I'm a big girl, Warren. I can walk. Let me –"

"Hay. I've got this. Got *you.*"

Then she just gives me a look that says *okay*, her lips tremble, and her body softens.

She doesn't protest, even leaning into me as I lift her out and into my arms, hefting her up against my chest. I can't even notice the slick skin, the exposed flesh, the plushness of her body right now.

Before she'd tempted me like a siren. Now she's tugging at my heartstrings.

I'm more worried about that forlorn sniffle and the redness in her eyes than I am about my own runaway dick.

Quietly, I slip through the door for her side of the duplex. Tara's not there, she must've fallen asleep at Grandma's. I carry a quiet Haley into the bedroom and set her down on the bed, still soaking wet and dripping.

"Wait here," I say, holding up a finger.

Then I dart into the bathroom to retrieve another towel before raiding the bedroom drawer. There's an oversized Pittsburgh Steelers shirt – no time for good taste – and a fresh pair of panties.

Sinking to my knees in front of her, I wrap the towel around her shoulders, scrubbing it lightly over her body and hair, looking up at her with a small smile. "There you go. I'll turn around for a minute so you can change."

There's ten words I never wanted to say.

She looks at me miserably, clutching the edges of the towel in her fingers, trying clumsily to help me dry her off, though she's getting in the way more than anything. I just maneuver around her hands, letting her do as she pleases. So long as she's not hurting herself.

"What's gotten into you? Why are you being so nice to me?" she asks.

I arch both brows. "You're drunk, Hay. And I'm not *quite* as huge an asshole as you think I am."

"But you're always meaner when you're trying to be...protective. Like you always say you're trying to save me, but you won't say from what."

My jaw tightens. *No, darlin', and I never will.*

"Because not telling you is part of protecting you," I tell her instead, nudging my knuckle under her jaw gently. "Right now, I'm just protecting you from waking up sick as a dog with a hangover. So get yourself changed, and I'll grab you some water."

She shakes her head. "Not thirsty."

"Best way to prevent a hangover, sweetheart."

Haley scowls at me. "Don't call me sweetheart. Eddy called me sweetheart."

Cringe. You know some people are colossal assholes when they can ruin entire words for life.

"Got it. No more of that shit, I promise." It shouldn't burn me to be compared to that scumbag, even when she's out of sorts, but I'll be damned if I'll sound a thing like him. Standing, I squeeze her shoulder reassuringly. "Change. I'll be right back."

I head into the kitchen, keeping one ear perked up just in case Haley manages to nearly kill herself struggling with a t-shirt. She belts out a few frustrated grunts, but nothing life-threatening, so I fish a few cold water bottles from the fridge, taking my time to give her a chance to get herself decent before I duck back into the bedroom.

When I do, she's sitting on the edge of the bed in a sulky bundle, her knees pulled up to her chest, safely away from the damp mark she's left on the sheets.

I line two bottles up on the nightstand and offer her the third. "One for now, two for the morning. Drink it all."

She wrinkles her nose up and pokes her tongue at me. "You're so bossy."

"I know."

"And stupid."

"Stupid is as stupid does." I chuckle, folding my arms over my chest. "Anything else you want to call me?"

"A really bad liar," she mumbles, then plugs her mouth with the water bottle and gulps it down.

Just a few drunk words chill me, leave me disquieted.

What the fuck does she think I'm lying about?

I've been trying to avoid dishonesty with careful diversions, but if I've left a trail a stranger like Hay can pick up, then it's no wonder Bress figured me out. Enough to start sending misdirected threats.

Damn.

Sobering, I hunker down in front of her. "Think you can sleep?"

With a muffled grunt and a shrug, Haley flops over and buries her face in the pillow. "Nope."

"You're a crappier liar than me." Smiling faintly, I catch the rumpled covers and pull them up over her. "Sleep well, you little wildcat."

She shoots up immediately, damp hair flying everywhere, eyes wide. "Wait. The cat!"

I glance around the room. "What cat—oh. Mozart adopted you?"

Her brows wrinkle. "Is that his name?"

"Yeah. He's kind of become the mascot around here. He'll adopt a new family in our cabins, but mostly he hangs around me and Grandma." I nudge her shoulder. "Don't worry about him. That boy knows his way around. He'll be back when he's ready. Get some rest, Hay. Tomorrow it's another night of beer and frat boys."

"Fuck. My. *Life.*" Groaning, she flops back into the pillow. "One of them slapped my ass, you know."

Who? I'll take his hand off at the wrist, I think immediately, but bite it back for her sake, clenching my teeth. "*Good night, Hay*," I say pointedly.

Her only answer is a listless, noodly arm flopping toward me. I sigh, watching her for a few moments longer before turning to let myself out.

She's a cute drunk, but God *damn* is she a handful.

I only hope, for her sake, that she doesn't remember this in the morning.

She doesn't strike me as a woman who likes being fragile.

Then again, a few hours ago, I didn't strike myself as

someone who gave a damn about her feelings when she's been about five ticks away from clawing my eyes out ever since she showed up here.

Too bad I can't ignore what she's hiding underneath her sharp tongue and sharper wit.

Even if she's taking her pain out on me for being a bit of a dick, I wasn't the asshole who caused it, and apparently, it turns out I don't mind being a punching bag for a pair of big green eyes as long as it makes her feel better.

I linger at the door, looking in through the glass at the glimpse of the bedroom, and her prone, quiet form – then make myself pull away.

Feels wrong inside. I don't know what the hell I'm thinking anymore.

I only know this is a distraction I can't afford.

Not when every delay just has Jenna turning restlessly in her grave another day.

Not when every misstep pulls Dennis Bress further from my reach.

* * *

GODDAMMIT, I love my Grandma, but I *really* didn't come back to Heart's Edge for this.

Socializing. Yeah, it's as shitty as it sounds.

I'd planned to spend my Sunday evening on the prowl. I still don't know where Bress was going when he was heading out of town the other night before Stew stole the GPS tracker and screwed everything up. Or saved my ass, I'm not even sure which.

Still, just when I was getting myself together to head out – and avoiding Haley after that Friday night of strange confessions – Grandma came sailing into my side of the duplex and practically hauled me out in a full Nelson hold.

Sunday dinner, she said, was *exactly* what I needed. And I wouldn't dream of disappointing her and possibly agitate her aging ticker by turning her down, now would I?

Aging ticker, my ass. I swear that woman has a heart of steel.

And she uses it effectively to bludgeon me into doing her bidding with a smile on my face.

That's how I find myself up at the main house in the area sectioned off for private living quarters, sitting in the kitchen where I grew up while Grandma ladles out her famous pot roast and gravy.

And while Flynn Bitters eyes me uneasily across the table.

I don't know why he's even here, other than Grandma's hospitality.

This is family space, the kitchen lined with framed photos of my grandparents, my parents, me, my sister. Flynn isn't family, and he looks just as uncomfortable as I feel.

"You know," Grandma says, "the two of you could try speaking. 'Thank you, Wilma, for such a lovely dinner.'"

"Thanks, Wilma," Flynn mumbles. "Good eats."

"Thanks," I add dryly. Her and those old-fashioned manners. "Not like I had much choice coming to din—"

All it takes is one razor-sharp look to shut my yap, keen as a dagger, before she smiles pleasantly. "Now, now, I don't like the idea of anyone eating by their lonesome. Flynn's been coming up to the house for dinner lately, and I know if I leave you out in that cabin, you'll just microwave some dreadful packaged thing barely a step above your Army rations." She arches her brows mildly as she takes her place at the head of the table. "Unless that nice Haley girl is cooking for you again?"

Oh, fuck. Here we go...

"Nah. Haley's too busy slinging drinks at *your* pub to cook for anyone," I point out, instinctively folding my napkin in my lap.

It's old habit around her. I'm used to eating rough by myself, living raw. Hell, she's barely joking about the rations, I've gone months longer on just bacon and eggs than I ever did on deployment.

But around Grandma Wilma, the respectable boy she raised comes out. "I don't even know how she manages for Tara," I say, shaking my head.

"She has a little help," Grandma answers, tapping her collar. "Tara's such a delight! I've been teaching her a few little kitchen tricks myself. But you'd be surprised how resourceful your Haley is. She's so lovely with her niece. I can only imagine what a delight she'll be with her own children one day."

Your Haley? She's not my anything.

And it shouldn't feel so strange knowing she isn't.

Worse, I'd started to take a bite of pot roast just as Grandma dropped that a-bomb about kids.

I start choking on it a second later, the meat turning into a knot in my throat until I force it painfully down. Wiping at my mouth, I stare at her. "That was...about as subtle as a sledgehammer."

She watches me cannily across the floral arrangement in the center of the lace-doilied table. "I have no idea what you're talking about, dear. What's the trouble with pondering young Haley's future?"

"She's a stranger, Grandma. Her future isn't really our business."

My grandmother smiles sheepishly. An award winning act if I ever saw one.

"No, I suppose it's not," she says, blotting the corner of her mouth with a napkin. "But it could be."

"Ah, hell. That was less sledgehammer and more *wrecking ball between the eyes.*"

Grandma lets out a soft, ladylike laugh. "Really, Warren? Is it so awful of me to notice that the two of you do seem to have quite the spark?"

"Sparks start forest fires around these parts, Grandma. Lucky we're in the dry season right now, so let's not tempt fate."

Flynn snorts a laugh – then my grandmother pins him with another of her flinty looks.

Suddenly, he's diving into his plate, hunching over it and stuffing his face with mashed potatoes and peas swirled in gravy. But after a few bites, he mumbles, "Warren tried to run the poor thing off."

Traitor-fuck.

Now Grandma's scorching gaze lands on me, and I feel like a little boy squirming as she says mildly, "Did you now? And why would you run off a paying customer with a little girl?"

I don't have a good answer.

Not one that'd satisfy her without drawing her into my mess, and I damn sure can't afford to do that.

This family's lost enough. Grandma couldn't breathe the day two men in uniform showed up at Charming, a *'ma'am, we regret to inform you...'* on their lips.

I was overseas, still on a mission. I heard about it later from the same backstabbing drunk who's sitting next to me. He had to rush her to the ER just to keep her from joining Jenna with the Reaper.

Fuck.

I don't say anything, just lower my eyes to my plate. After several long moments, Grandma continues, "You know, I can't help wondering where she finds the energy, but then again...I'm low on that myself these days. I fear I may be slowing down, closer to retirement than I'd care to admit."

I smile faintly. "C'mon. You're not going to quit on us till you've goaded me into something, are you?"

She looks at me innocently. "Isn't that a grandmother's job?"

"Yeah. And it's why I love you. But if you're thinking about passing the torch...do you really think you can trust me to manage this place *and* the pub *and* the half-dozen other properties you own and that I don't even know about?"

"That's why you need a good woman to ground you," she replies promptly, and I groan.

I set myself up for that one.

She's not done. "And yet you seem set on ignoring common sense—and ignoring the obvious fact that there's no ring on her finger."

"Just because she's single doesn't mean..."

Shit. I can't.

Not just because of Bress, but because of *last night*.

Because I can't be another man who breaks Hay's heart, and sometimes I think that's all I know how to do.

Break hearts and lose people.

* * *

Thirteen Years Ago

"DAMN IT, WAR." Jenna flops down next to me, leaning just a little too hard on my shoulder in that way she has, until she starts to subtly shove me over. I laugh and push her back.

"What're you complaining about now, sis?"

"We're not being sent on this run together! I know,

different units, but they want you on the border, damn near in Pakistan?" She pouts. It's a strange thing to see, this woman in her desert fatigues with her dark hair pulled back in a tight bun, no makeup on, the perfect image of the soldier...pouting. "Why'd you have to go with the Rangers? They send you all the good places. I thought this was my break, not being stuck in a bunker somewhere crunching numbers on logistics sheets. Borrring."

"Those numbers are the only reason people stay alive," I tell her. "You're keeping me safe, even when we're not near each other."

"Yeah?" Her pout turns into a smile, and she hooks her arm in mine, resting her head on my shoulder. "That's some consolation. But it's also my job to protect you."

I lean into her. "That's funny, I thought it was my job to protect you."

"It can't be both?" Eyes bright, she pulls back and offers me her pinky.

"You be careful," I say more seriously. "The mine runs are pretty quiet, but shit happens when you least expect it in the field."

"Yeah, yeah. I think I can walk with the guys to escort that big-ass lumbering thinga-ma-jiggie while it pulls up old mines. Easy work."

More dangerous than it sounds, I think without telling her.

"C'mon, bro. Let's promise we'll come back together."

Snorting, I flash her a sideways look. "Pinky swear? Shouldn't you be doing that with your new boyfriend?"

Her crooked smile sinks. Too damn fast for my liking.

"What's up? Don't tell me he isn't treating you well?"

"Nah, not that. Dennis is lovely. It's him and this other guy, really. Causing some real drama with the unit."

"Drama?" Folding my arms, I look her up and down. "What the hell kind of drama? Listen, Jenna, if it's putting anybody in danger, that's something you've gotta bring to command. Or you tell me his name and I'll –"

"No." She stands up, tall and straight, eyes like daggers. "We're not in Heart's Edge no more, War. I can handle myself and I'll handle this too. Probably just my own mind playing tricks on me..."

My lips twist sourly. I wonder what the hell she's getting at, wonder if this 'drama' involves anybody I know. Too bad I know she won't back down and tell when she's looking at me like that.

"So about that pinky promise..."

I eye her crooked pinky and then break into a laugh. "Jesus, girl. We're not in grade school anymore. Something about it feels like jinxing shit."

"Don't be silly! A pinky swear's a pinky swear, and you've *never* broken one before." She stares at me challengingly, that finger held out. "Promise me."

I look around, embarrassment flushing through me. There's no one in the bunks but me and her. After a moment, I hiss and hook my pinky in hers. "Fine. I promise. Happy?"

She laughs, shaking her head. "You're such a porcupine sometimes. But that's why we all love you."

When I start pulling back, she only curls her pinky tighter and holds mine, grinning at me fiercely. "Hey, you didn't promise me. You have to say something to make it work."

I stop cold, tongue pressed against the roof of my mouth.

I can't explain why this suddenly feels too real, the playful air dissolving to leave me chilled, prickling with premonition. But I decide she's right. I'm being stupid.

So I hook my finger tighter in hers and whisper, "I promise, Jenna. Promise I'll always come back for you."

I have three days left.

Three days before that promise becomes a lie.

VII: STRAY CAT STRUT (HALEY)

*S*urprise! It turns out telling college boys they can look, but not touch, leads to some pretty great tips. It's like edging.

Except the final gratification is all mine at the end of the night. That's when I fish out the dollar bills tucked in my bra and stuff a little extra in the shared tip jar for the bartender and the other servers.

My starving artist soul doesn't put me above my pride if it means more dollars to blow this town.

This morning I count out the bills over brunch, stacking them by denomination on the kitchen island and swinging my heels against the barstool. It's mostly ones and fives, a couple of tens and twenties, one very generous Benjamin that I'd thought was a mistake until a rather nice older man told me no, keep it, I remind him of his daughter.

Um, I kinda hope not.

No one needs to see their daughter with her ass hanging out of that postage stamp of a skirt I wear to work every night.

But after five nights working at Brody's, I'm up to four

hundred and twenty-seven dollars in tips. More than enough to tide me over until my first paycheck deposits.

I'm not doing half bad.

It'll definitely help keep me afloat in Heart's Edge while I save up for the last big jump to Chicago. I may even put out some online job applications in a couple of weeks, so I have some prospects and interviews waiting for me when I hit the Windy City.

Today, though, I think I'll splurge on a little treat for me and Tara.

It's my day off, with Wilma informing me that Wednesdays are the slowest and I should get some rest and take in the town. I'd like to spend a little time with my niece, especially when I know what's coming.

I'm going to have to send her home soon.

I may be stuck here, but her parents will be back from Hawaii in about a week and then she'll be heading home for summer camp, and then back into school. Leaving me and my problems behind.

It's a little scary to think I might *still* be in Heart's Edge by the time Tara's school year starts up again.

Still in Heart's Edge. Still half broke. Still dancing around Warren freaking Ford.

I still can't believe I got drunk in the hot tub with him – and he was *naked!*

Did he really think I wouldn't notice?

Then he'd put me to bed. I'm not sure if I'm glad or mortified that he's apparently been avoiding me ever since.

I mean...who would want to talk to the girl who started blubbering over her ex in front of a smolderingly hot, tattooed, *naked* brute of a man?

If this was a rom-com flick, I'd be eyeing that smolderingly hot tattooed brute and thinking about the many, many ways he could help me forget my ex before I move on with life and forget them both.

Instead, I'm busy trying to figure out how to ask him if I said anything really embarrassing. I can't wholly remember the night.

I just remember him carrying me inside and how *warm* he was.

Like that burn when you lean against sun-warmed wood or leather, and it's just a little too hot but it's absolutely perfect, too, and you just want to soak it all in. I didn't realize he could be so amazing.

So gentle.

He was so sweet with me that night. Tucking me into bed, fetching me clothing, letting me keep my decency and my dignity, making sure I wouldn't wake up with a crappy hangover.

I still feel his arms around me, how thick and strong they were, how he made me feel like I was floating and lifting away, and it had *nothing* to do with the beer.

Oh, God.

I can't actually be letting that dick get under my skin.

Can I?

He was just being a decent human being. Nothing more. He did what anyone would do with some drunk stranger lolling all over them.

It doesn't mean anything. It doesn't mean we're friends. It surely doesn't mean he's not a complete and utter jerkface.

"Auntie Hay!"

Tara's shrill voice rips over the duplex, tearing me from silly thoughts.

My heart drops out and practically goes bouncing across the floor.

I don't remember standing.

I barely register the barstool nearly toppling over. I just

know I'm on my feet, racing out the door like my heels have wings, terror turning my blood into something thin and cold as I race toward the sound of my niece's screams.

"Tara?! What happened? Baby, what's wrong–"

I draw up short as I see her standing on the edge of the front porch.

She's fine, I realize with a quick once-over. No bruises, no blood, not even dirtied, but she's crying over something that's moving in her arms.

Whatever I expect, it isn't her holding that orange tabby like her dear life depends on it, while the cat makes disgruntled, deep *rrrr*ing sounds that may mean anything from *I'm not feeling so well* to *I'm about to claw your face off and wear it as a jacket.*

Breathlessly, I stumble to a halt, clutching at my chest. "What happened? Tara, what's wrong?"

Tara sniffles, then rubs her face dry on Mozart's fur.

"Mozart's hurt," she mumbles. "I found him and he was limping!"

Oh, God. She nearly gave me a heart attack, but I can't help my worry shooting to the poor cat, too.

"Here," I say, reaching for him. "Let me have a look."

Reluctantly, Tara hands the beast over.

He's almost bobcat-sized, far too big for her little grip, but I'm able to cradle him a bit more carefully in my arms. The fact that he lets me is worrisome...

He's always been rather prideful, coming in as if he rules the roost and only deigns to let us humans occupy his space. That he's so docile today is troubling.

But I figure out why pretty fast. I'm checking his paws, murmuring to him and scratching his belly in between, when I see it.

One paw looks bloodied, like something bit down on it.

Frowning, my heart aches as I gently try to peek at the

damage to his paw pad while he makes pained, terribly sad little mewls and flinches away.

"Come on, little guy," I murmur, coaxing him with nuzzles between his pointed ears. "I just want to look so I can help you."

"Did...did someone hurt him?" Tara asks, her eyes streaming. "Auntie Hay, who would do that to him?"

A chill runs up my spine because I just don't know.

Whatever did this – person, animal, accident – it isn't good.

"I don't know, sweetie, but there's got to be a vet in town. We can ask Ms. Wilma if—"

"You don't need to ask Wilma anything," comes a gruff voice at my back. Warren.

I haven't heard him in days. It's so sudden and startling that the deep rumble of his voice seems to shake through me like an earthquake. I glance back, and he's leaning out of his doorway, half asleep and rumpled, and it's not hard to tell he slept in his clothes. Just raising nagging questions like who he is and what he's doing and what secrets he's keeping today.

"We have to do something," I say through clenched teeth. "He's really hurt and I don't know if–"

"Hay."

For a second, we share a glare. A gaze that says too much. Mostly, it's the same stark plea turning over and over in his midnight-blue pools.

Trust me.

Trust me this time.

Trust me to fix this like I fixed you that night.

I want to. But right now, I can't think about all the trust issues with this whirlwind mountain man.

Not when there's a big mewling baby bawling in my arms and Warren steps out on the porch to tug his boots on. "I know just the man. Grab a blanket, wrap the cat up, and let's go."

* * *

ONCE AGAIN, Warren comes to my rescue.

Well, technically this time it's Mozart's rescue, but once again I get to see another side to him.

After a breakneck drive through town with Tara sandwiched between us in the front seat of his truck and Mozart swaddled in her lap like a baby, Warren gently takes the cat from her. I watch him hold the furball in the crook of his arm, murmuring a soothing word or two under his breath as he scratches under the cat's chin and then elbows open the door to a small, nondescript building.

I'd never have known this was the vet's office, tucked away between a deli and an abandoned shoe shop with the windows boarded up.

There's no sign over the door. No decals on the windows. No emergency drop-off marker.

But the instant we step inside, I'm hit with that warm smell of fur that always seems to permeate vet offices, and the sound of various pets barking and mewling and cawing in the back room.

There's only one other person in the waiting room, a reedy older blonde woman with a golden retriever resting with his head on his paws and the cone of shame around his neck.

She's texting one-handed, her other hand wrapped around the retriever's leash. She glances up and offers a sympathetic smile as we come bursting in like a tangled cannonball of human and cat, with Tara practically clinging to Warren's leg, never taking her eyes off Mozart.

The receptionist starts to lift her head with a chirpy

greeting stuck on her lips. She never gets the chance to speak when Warren, without looking up from the cat he's coddling, belts out, "Doc! Get your ass out here."

"I see someone's forgotten the chain of command yet again." A dry, cool, smoky masculine voice drifts from the back.

A second later that voice's owner emerges, a tall man with an elegance that seems out of place somewhere as earthy as Heart's Edge. Dark haired, oddly chiseled, sharp and straight as a scalpel in his lab coat.

Adjusting his glasses, green eyes glinting, "Doc" leans over the counter, peering at Mozart, before sighing and thinning his lips. "Again, Warren? This cat must be on the thirtieth of his nine lives by now. Let's bring him back, let me get a better look at him."

Warren starts to step around the counter – only to stop and look down at Tara, who's on him like a burr.

"Hey," he says softly, bending down toward her. "Give Mozart a kiss for luck."

Tara nods solemnly, then leans in and presses her lips to Mozart's fuzzy little forehead. The cat looks entirely annoyed, while Warren's gentle smile is warmly approving as he nods to my niece. "There we go. Now we know he'll be fine."

Then he straightens, looking at me, and I realize I've been staring at him too long.

Just gawking in flipping *awe,* trying to figure out who the heck I'm seeing and why he looks so much like Warren Ford, Super Asshole.

My legs won't move. They're petrified in the middle of the room, caught between fear for the cat and this bizarrely tight, warm, wonderful feeling in my chest watching this 'other' Warren.

How gently he handles the cat.

How gently he handles my *niece*, and that sweet way he smiled for her.

And how he gives me that same smile, stealing my breath, as he nods firmly. His thick dark hair is still a boyishly bed-rumpled mess, falling into those devastatingly blue eyes and shadowing them until it's like someone cut two pieces of the night from the sky.

"Don't worry," he says. "Doc's the best in the state, even if he's...an odd bird. He'll get Mozart on his feet in no time. Sit tight."

"Right," I murmur, still dazedly. "Thanks."

Then I shake myself, reaching for Tara's hand. "C'mon, baby. Let's wait for the doctor to take care of Mozart. Sounds like he's used to it."

"You have no damn idea," Doc retorts dryly – but for all his personality quirks, his hands are gentle as he nudges under Mozart's jaw. "This little beast and I have a special relationship."

Tara giggles as Doc looks up and flashes her a quick wink.

That makes me feel better as I watch the two men disappear into the back with the cat.

It seems to soothe Tara, too. But of course it doesn't stop her from climbing into my lap.

The little lady's only *ten whole years old* when she wants to assert her independence, but when she needs comfort and reassurance, suddenly she's every bit a little girl again, clinging to me and burying her face in my chest.

I hold her close, stroking my hands over her back, calming us both.

It's silly to get attached to a cat in just a few days, but how can I blame her? He's kind of turned into my morning wake-up call every time he bounces on the windowsill and starts yowling to be let in and fed the scraps from a brunch I haven't even made yet.

Honestly, he's a bit of a nuisance, but he's become *our* nuisance.

Not unlike the asshole next door.

God.

I'm so *not* falling for that jerk.

Especially not because he was nice to a cat and a kid.

That's the oldest trick in the book. *Me and Warren Ford?*

Never, ever happening.

* * *

The wait feels eternal.

And when Warren finally emerges alone, his face black and stormy with fury, my gut somersaults with dread of the *worst* kind.

Tara jerks in my lap, looking up at him, then whimpers, flinching and ducking her head, peering at him with wide, apprehension-filled eyes.

"Warren?" I ask tentatively as he stalks across the waiting room toward us. "What happened? Is...is Mozart okay?"

He stops in his tracks, blinking as if he's not quite sure what words mean, before sighing and dropping his heavy bulk down into the chair next to us. He's all powerful, compact muscle as he leans forward, draping his elbows over his knees.

"Yeah," he says, dragging a hand over his face. "He'll be fine. Doc's putting stitches in now. Worst hit he'll take is to his dignity when he's gotta wear a cone for a week or so. He's gonna have to be an indoor cat for a while just to make sure he recovers."

"That's okay," I say quickly. "We'll take care of him, right?"

Tara nods emphatically. "I'll make him a bed and give him his pills and everything!"

Tara's voice seems to pull Warren out of himself. He gives

her a tired smile. "He'll love it. The boy already acts like a king."

I frown. "Then...why are you so angry, if Mozart's okay?"

"I'm not–" He starts to bite off a curse, but stops himself, glancing at Tara. "It's nothing. Looks like he got caught in a trap. There's supposed to be no goddamn hunting in Heart's Edge city limits. All the forest around here is protected land. People out here messing around aren't just breaking the law. They could hurt people, kids, pets. Frankly, it pisses me off. And if they're putting traps on Grandma's property..."

I wince. "Maybe a camera could catch them?"

He gives me a wearily, amused look. "We're not that modern, darlin'."

We all look up as one then as Doc emerges with Mozart cradled in his arms. The tomcat's clearly drugged, sluggish and slow with glazed eyes.

His mouth hangs partly open, but his bloodied paw is clean and neatly bandaged, and a small cone now hugs his neck. Tara goes rocketing toward him, only to stop and pull back, watching fearfully as Doc draws closer.

"Can I...may I hold him, doctor?" she whispers. "Or will it hurt him?"

Doc looks down at her, his eyes softening, sinking down to one knee. "Here," he says, carefully guiding the cat into Tara's arms. "Just like this. Like a baby. Don't let him slip, but don't hold him too tight. Let him breathe."

Tara's eyes well, and she nods shakily, biting her lip. She shifts Mozart to the crook of her arm.

"Better," Doc whispers, his quiet warmth breaking into a thin smile.

"He'll really be okay?" Tara pleads again.

"Really and truly. I assure you he'll be right as rain in two weeks or so," he vows, still holding his faint smile.

The news only makes Tara burst into a wail, cuddling Mozart closer, the cat stirring with a muffled purr.

"I'm going home next week...and I don't wanna!" Tara sobs, and suddenly both me and Warren are there, kneeling to either side of her, both of us reaching to comfort her.

We almost bump into each other. I blink, locking eyes over my niece's head before another sniffle and sob from Tara pulls us back to her.

"Hey now, munchkin," Warren says. "I've been taking care of Mozart a long time. Don't you worry. He's my little buddy, and even when I go away, he's always fine. Promise you he'll be okay. Me and your Aunt Hay are gonna take real good care of him."

"And I'll send you photos," I add, pulling her into a hug until it's just a bundle of me, little girl, and dazed, confused cat. "He'll be in the best hands."

"Mmph." With a sulky sound, Tara buries her face into the cat and leans hard into me. "I don't want to go home."

It's a little unnerving to realize it, all of a sudden. This crazy urge to stay.

I don't want to leave either, even if it's not like I've got much choice in it right now. I'm stuck here, but now I have a reason to stay a little longer.

Maybe it's something I needed.

There's really nothing else for me here. Heart's Edge has been nothing but trouble.

But my eyes drift to Warren, who's staring down at the three of us, smiling in his faint, secret way. A lot like the same way Doc smiles, and while the vet really is a handsome man, he's *nothing* like this burly, loud mountain badass.

Nothing here, I said. *Or is there?*

* * *

THE DRIVE back to Charming Inn is quiet. Sort of.

It's as quiet as anything ever is with Tara around, when she's alternating between singing Mozart to sleep in little melodies and looking at Warren with shining, adoring eyes.

I think she has a new hero.

She thanks him again and again for saving the cat.

I might as well not have been there, honestly, except for moral support. But I'm just glad the rusty little furball's going to be all right.

If Warren hadn't been there, *I'd* probably have started crying along with Tara.

I'm soft on small things, okay? My niece. Cute, fluffy animals. The usual.

What I can't do, though, is go soft on the very large thing behind the wheel of the truck.

The thing that's ripped, loud, mysterious, and inked.

The thing, the man, the storm that's Warren Ford.

Tara's eyes aren't the only ones wandering, but mine do for very different reasons.

I'm watching him on the drive back.

He seems preoccupied, pensive, completely exhausted. I wonder if maybe he wasn't avoiding me at all. Maybe he was just busy?

Busy with whatever strange yet oh-so-important stuff he does.

He's still so confusing. Just when I think I've got a handle on him, he goes and does something like comforting Tara, reacting as instinctively as I did when she's not even related to him.

It's almost like they made him extra big to hold this extra big heart. But he had to go and bury it under a spiky layer of asshole just to make sure no one could ever get to it.

I'm still turning that over when we pull up to the inn and our duplex.

Somehow, I manage to help Tara out without her ever letting go of the cat. I'll have to go into town later to fill his prescription and get the special food the vet says he needs to have.

That's going to take a chunk out of my tips, but I don't care.

I can spare it if it'll help Mozart get better faster. The poor thing looks so bedraggled and lost it just makes me feel heartsore, and I can't help nuzzling at him before shooing Tara toward the house.

"Go get him settled, love," I say. "Remember to set him down gently and don't let him walk too far. He'll be woozy for a day or so, and he might hurt himself."

She nods firmly, her pigtails bobbing. "Got it!" she says firmly, marching toward the porch with her precious burden —but then she stops, giving Warren a shy glance. "Thanks again, Mister." Prim, but almost whispered. "Mozart says thank you, too."

Warren looks awkward, raking a burly hand through his hair, but then he smiles. "It's nothing, little lady."

Tara only beams at him and bounds up the steps and inside.

Hell, we'd left the door unlocked after such a messy rush over the cat. *Ugh.*

My mind drifts back to the incident with the feathers. It's been all quiet on the stalker front, but I need to be more careful. Still, I won't let it ruin our little victory today.

So I let out a soft, rueful laugh that trails into a sigh, curling my hand against the back of my neck.

"What she said. Thanks, Warren. I'd never have found the vet." I pause. "Oh, crap. I just realized...we didn't settle the bill—"

"On the house," Warren growls. "Doc's an old friend. Owes me a few."

His voice is distant, and he's looking over my head, like he's trying not to see me.

He's letting me off the hook.

God.

I should hold onto my silly tongue and the sudden tempo in my heart. But I guess I can only manage one.

Stealing another quick glance at him, I look down, scratching at my aching chest.

It's only a favor. For an animal. Not even for you so...

So.

He's just some asshole, I tell myself again.

None of this matters. None of this counts.

I'm totally not getting wrapped up in some ridiculous crush on Mr. Snarlypants Mountain Man after two freaking favors...right?

"Look, just be careful around here for a while," he says gruffly, as if he senses the stars in my eyes. "I'm going to walk the grounds. Make sure there aren't any more of those damn traps anywhere. Can't have you or Tara stepping on one and getting hurt. Nearest clinic's damn near thirty miles away, and Doc doesn't do house calls."

"House calls? For people or...?"

Warren looks at me, his eyes bugged out for a second, and then he shakes his head fiercely. "Forget it. Just a bad joke."

Is it? I really wonder, but I know when to pick my battles.

Whatever's up with that strange small town vet, now's not the time.

I smile weakly. "It's been a long day. And it seems like you're always looking out for us. We do appreciate it, you know. Me, Tara...Mozart."

He almost flinches, and I'm not sure why.

"Warren?"

"Yeah, well..." He shrugs, shoulders tight. "It's not over yet. If I catch anyone leaving traps on this property, there'll be *hell* to pay." He turns away, lifting a hand in something that's not quite a wave. More like half dismissal. "Gotta go, Hay. Let me know if you need anything else for Mozart."

For Mozart.

Lovely.

Am I actually *stung* that he cares more about a cat than he does about me?

He took care of you, too, I remind myself.

Damn right he did. And here I am watching him walk away with my *thank you* frozen on my tongue, the words refusing to come out.

I'm not shy. Not really. I've never had trouble speaking my mind.

Yet Warren gets me tied in knots, until I can't untangle my thoughts, my feelings, my words to know what to say to him.

If there's anything to say at all.

Because now, for what has to be the millionth time, I tell myself the cold truth.

We're nothing.

Not friends. Not lovers. Not even long-term neighbors.

We're two people lost in the ruins of our lives. That's not love or hate or even silly, desperate infatuation.

That's pure delusion.

* * *

DELUSION DOESN'T MEAN I can't express my gratitude.

And they *do* say actions speak louder than words.

Which is why, this evening, after Tara's fully calmed down in one last stress-relief tearburst, and she's cuddling the cat to the point that I can almost see the patient endurance in his eyes, I *try.*

I'm standing on Warren's doorstep. Knocking. I shouldn't feel this nervous, but...

No buts.

I'm just trying to say *thank you* in my own way, and I'm better at showing it than I am with words. That's all it is.

That, and I really hate losing a dare.

But I'm still a mess of flutters and erratic breaths.

Jesus, I must look so weird standing here, fidgeting and breathing in rapid little pants and clutching a gift bag. Maybe that's why he gives me an odd look when he comes to the door and balks.

It's just a moment's hesitation, him looking through the glass, staring at me like he's debating whether or not he wants to open up. My cheeks bloom with heat.

Oh boy.

He's probably wondering if I'm drunk again. And I can't blame him.

I still can't *believe* I let myself go that bad, and he had to take care of me, even if it was sweet of him. That's the other thing I'm thanking him for.

Even if like *hell* I'll say that part out loud.

I'd rather never mention it again.

After a few skeptical moments, he opens the door and braces one brawny forearm against the frame, stretching his long, tight body out in a near slouch of chiseled muscle, that shirt doing obscene – and I mean *ob-fricking-scene* – things to his chest.

I think it's *licking* him. Can a shirt lick someone?

"Need something, Hay?" he drawls lazily.

Um. Oh, crap.

Dragging my gaze back to his face, taking a deep breath, I reach down and find my courage.

Then I thrust the bag at his chest.

"Thank you!" I blurt out like a nervous kid, and the

second he has a handle on the bag, grabbing it with his blue eyes wide and thick fingers fumbling not to drop it...

I'm off.

I turn tail and *run*, escaping the few steps to my door and slamming it sharply behind me, only to collapse against it and *pray* he won't follow. My legs hurt. My chest hurts more, and my head is just chaos.

I need to clear my mind. Stop letting it wander.

Because I can't look at Warren Ford that way. Or any way.

He's a dick, remember?

I'm not staying here, and he's up to something shady.

I'm done with shady men, supposedly, and I can't let him rope me in just because he's been nice to me a few times, and my niece adores him. Just because he looks like a small town Samson put on Earth to make me wet and angry.

Tara's not the only one who adores him, some dirty traitor voice inside me whispers.

"Shut up," I hiss.

Tara peeks over the arm of the couch where she's cuddling with Mozart. "Auntie Hay? Who're you talking to?"

I freeze, then plaster on a slightly manic smile.

"Nobody, sweetie," I say. "Just your crazy aunt talking to herself."

I wrinkle my nose. You *know* it's bad when a man has you talking third person.

Shoving Warren out of my head, I rise to my feet. "C'mon. Let's give Mozart his five minutes a day out of that torture device so he can eat."

VIII: SPINNING IN MY HEAD
(WARREN)

*S*ometimes, Haley West makes my head hurt even worse than my dick.

It's been a breakneck few days trying to track Bress when suddenly he's gone incognito. No one seems to know where he is, meaning long nights of stakeouts.

I spend half my time crouched in the trees near his secluded house in the woods, watching as he comes driving in at two or three in the morning. He steps out of the car with those weary hangdog motions that always make him look like he needs a friend's shoulder, versus a fist to the face.

It's part of how he keeps people fooled. No one wants to accuse a war veteran who looks so hung out to dry of being the reason why hard drugs are funneling into Heart's Edge, the gruesome price of the sudden cash influx into the economy.

I haven't had much time to think about Hay.

Hell, I won't *let* myself think about Hay.

Because if I think about her, I'm going to worry.

I've *been* worried since that night in the hot tub. This whole mess isn't right.

Her stuck here after some shitty guy chased her away from the crumbles of her old life. She shouldn't be in this situation. And while she's damn brave and stubborn, I'm worried the stress of it will push her to crack. But that's a distraction I can't afford right now, and up until the incident with Mozart, I'd managed to push her out of my mind.

Only now I've got a constant reminder of her, staring at me from across the coffee table where I've hung it up on the wall.

It's a painting.

Whatever I'd been expecting when she thrust that bag on me and bolted, it wasn't this.

It's small, just a little bit over a foot on each side, but it's full of *her.*

Bold, brilliant colors in tones that capture the sheer luminous wild of a sunset over the mountains in Heart's Edge. I don't even know when she found time to finish it, between her shifts at Brody's and looking after Tara.

No denying she's damn good. Beautifully talented.

And bold enough not to back down from a dare.

She makes a good coffee cake, too. I take another bite of the second half of her gift while I lean back on the couch, drumming my fingertips against the side of my coffee mug.

I don't even like sweet things, but this is just right. So's the painting, making this space feel different.

Human.

Sometimes, after Jenna, I think I've forgotten what that is. All those little human touches that make a life, versus every day lived with a militant sense of purpose.

I'd buried it deep, any need for it. It feels like Haley's digging it up again, unearthing a few too many things I'd rather keep hidden. I want to resent her for it.

But as I reread the note she left, *Now we're even*, all I can do is smile.

Spitfire. Minx. *Siren.*

I want to be angry at the thought, but it's getting harder to stay pissed over this little tangle of energy that came smashing into my life and threw it out of order.

She's out back right now. I can glimpse her through the blinds, working on another canvas, capturing the morning sun.

But I can glimpse more there, too. That girl likes to wear as little as possible. Those cutoff shorts and the ripped basketball jersey leave her thighs and midriff exposed in tantalizing glimpses.

When I realized how drunk and hurt she was the other night, her body and my libido were the farthest things from my mind. Today I can't help but linger, feeling that tight heat growing in the pit of my stomach.

Fuck, there's just something about her.

I've had women writhe in my lap, pleading, and it has less effect on my dick than Hay with just the smallest glimpse of the tight swell of her stomach.

Or the way her thighs rub together as she moves, angling herself around the canvas.

I remember those thighs slick and wet from the tub. It'd be a thing of beauty to see her inner thighs dripping and beaded with her own—

God damn it, Warren.

Focus.

I'm putting not just myself, but Haley and Tara, in danger by letting myself get distracted by this woman. I can't get attached. I *can't.*

Not when all I'd be doing is painting a target on Hay's sweet forehead.

* * *

BACK ON THE HUNT.

I need my mind where it belongs, and tonight it's on Bress. I don't know how a man who does what he does can be so oblivious.

Amazingly, he's missed me tailing him across town, even if sometimes I had at least a little sense and turned down parallel streets so he'd only glimpse me now and then on cross streets. I've long suspected that not all of Bress' nightly trips have to do with his illegal business, and tonight I'm proven right.

He's got a mistress.

I can't help but think of how disgusted Jenna would be.

As it is, I feel terrible for Bress' wife and kid. Newborn baby, happy young mother, and this piece of shit's stepping out to meet a side piece on the other side of town.

I even know who she is – Felicity Randall. Last Randall in town, ever since her drug addict dad finally kicked off and left her the sole owner of a little coffee shop and bakery that'll go under any day now when she's out here struggling on her own.

Guess I can't blame her for turning to someone like Bress, if he can help her out. Desperate fucking times call for desperate measures.

I can blame him, though.

I blame him for a lot of things.

But this is the first time since I came back that he's been to see her – that I know of – so if Bress isn't taking these long nightly road trips to see his other woman regularly...

Where's he going?

There are a dozen satellite towns between here and Missoula, each larger than the last, increasingly under his thumb as he buys up property after property. He could have a network of associates anywhere, and untangling that web takes some damn time.

I'm not sure it's even what I want.

There are faster ways to take Bress down. I could start with his business dealings, unravel them, leave the right evidence with the right agencies, then watch his life fall apart as a prison sentence comes crashing toward him like an out of control Mack Truck.

But that doesn't feel personal enough.

That's not good enough. Not for Jenna.

And tonight, it looks like he's not coming out of Felicity's place. *Damn.*

I can't stay here any longer, or someone might spot me.

Heart's Edge is your typical small town. Everyone notices what everybody else is doing, and you can bet it'll get back to so-and-so until next thing I know, I'll have Bress himself in my face. Asking if I'm jealous, if I don't have a life of my own.

It's funny how we used to *know* each other.

And now we somehow always manage to avoid actually speaking to each other, two ships passing in the night.

It's better that way.

If I have to talk to him face to face, my risk explodes.

I can't keep a lid on what I might do to him, especially armed.

But tonight, I'm striking the hell out.

It's time for me to pull out and head home. I need to try to get some actual sleep on a normal schedule, or people will notice that, too.

They'll realize I'm never around, that I sleep all day and drive around acting shady all night.

It's a delicate balance, trying to scope out a criminal without getting pegged as one myself.

So tonight, I'll be a good boy. I drive home, making it back to Charming Inn just in time to catch the sounds of laughter drifting out the open window next door, along with the tantalizing scents of dinner.

Hay and Tara must be amusing themselves while they wait for their food. It could feel like coming home, if this was my home to come to.

It's not.

And I ignore the pull toward the other side of the duplex as I head to my own door. Then I catch a glimpse of orange fur through the glass of the front door, groan, and drag my hand over my face.

Do I really have to? Yeah.

I want to check on that damn cat. Mozart is a Charming Inn institution, and he might as well be my pet, even if he's adopted Hay and the munchkin for now.

That's all this is.

A wellness call for the *cat*.

That's why I drag myself over to her door and knock. Sure.

But at least it's Tara who answers. I don't know what the hell I'd say to Hay without stuttering like a fool.

The kid, I can deal with. She's a bright little spot of sunshine, and she lights up with a smile when she sees me.

"Warren!"

Next thing I know she's got my hand, dragging me inside with a dozen *come-sees* and *Mozart missed yous* and a few other chirpy things. At least she's happy, which means the cat's gotta be fine.

A minute later I see for myself. He doesn't look much more than stoned out of his mind.

Tara hauls me over to the little bed she's made for him in the corner of the couch. Mozart lolls on his back with his head hanging half upside down, his paws twitching lazily in the air, big gold eyes half closed and tail languidly switching.

"Nice job, Tara. You've got him on the mend."

While I eye the cat in amusement and reach out to scratch his belly, Hay emerges from the back, oddly distracted.

There's something stormy pinched on her face, something dark and angry that warns lightning could strike at any moment, and I'm caught by how vividly her eyes crackle. I barely notice the slip of paper clutched in her hand for a second.

She stops on the threshold of the living room, pulling up short and looking at me.

"Oh," she says faintly. "Warren?"

What the hell?

She's in that bad a mood? Not ripping my head off for intruding? Something's definitely wrong.

I bite my tongue and shrug. "Tara invited me in." More like dragged me in, but I leave that part off and look down at the cat moving sluggishly under my hand, a rusty purr vibrating through him. "No more shame collar?"

Hay smiles faintly. "We found out if we keep him high on catnip, he's too lazy to bother biting his bandages or stitches. Plus, he can eat whenever he's hungry, instead of waiting." At my incredulous look, she flushes, narrowing her eyes. "Hey, it *works*."

"I've got no comment about you getting our cat stoned," I retort dryly, which earns me a smile.

"Wow. That's the first smart thing you've said since I met you."

"Everybody's got Einstein potential."

"Maybe." Hay's subdued as she crosses the room to the table and tucks that slip of paper into a notebook, then turns a warm smile on Tara. "Baby, go wash up for dinner."

"Okay! Hey, Auntie Hay..." Tara looks up from playing with Mozart's ears and bounces to her feet. "Could maybe Warren stay?"

Damn.

Hay and I must be wearing identical *oh, shit* expressions

on our faces, her eyes wide and stricken. I protest first, "Nah, Tara, I've got to—"

"*Pleeeaaase,*" Tara insists, clasping her hands together and begging. "He got his friend to fix Mozart for free. We owe him some dinner, don't we?"

Gotta hand it to the kid.

She's good.

And Hay and I exchange rueful looks over Tara's head before Haley shrugs and mouths, *Hungry?*

Sure, I mouth back, wondering why it feels like an apology, then reach over to ruffle Tara's hair. "So what's for dinner?"

* * *

IF NOT FOR TARA, this would probably be the most awkward meal ever.

Hay's real subdued, toying with her food with no appetite.

I'm downright uncomfortable. Feels like I don't belong here, and even if I don't think I'm the one who upset her this time...I'll bet my presence is just making it worse.

Whatever the hell *it* is.

I know one thing: if I give in to this ridiculous urge to wrap my arms around her, pull her in until she goes soft and spills what's eating her alive, she'll probably slug me instead.

So I let myself be Tara's willing conversation partner over steak and onions with caramelized asparagus tips. She chatters on like a magpie about her parents going to Hawaii without her.

About how she wanted to see the volcanoes, and how unfair that is.

About not wanting to go back to school but kind-of-maybe-wanting-to because her friends are there and she misses them.

I counter with stories of the time I hiked the Yellowstone Caldera, and the sleeping supervolcano that makes the geysers the area is so famous for, and the hot springs.

When I catch Hay actually looking interested, watching from the corner of her eye, I gush out a few more details about the landscape. That's what makes Yellowstone worth the memory.

The riptide sunsets, crags of ocher stone, the serrated cliffs, the way the whole sky looks like a billion scattershots of light reaching out to us across eons and time.

That's the kind of big question shit I like.

Except for the times it reminds me of Jenna. Wondering where she is now, if she's anywhere.

Hay cocks her head, then says, "You...you went hiking? I don't even know what you do, and I know you're not the type to quit work for a camping vacation."

"Work, Hay. That's why I went," I say without thinking. Talking to Tara has relaxed me too much, made my tongue loose. "Following a mark."

Haley's brows knit. "A mark?"

Fuck. Make that *too loose.*

I hiss under my breath, keeping the curse words on my lips from curious listening little ears, but the truth's out now. "Had a suspect who skipped bail before going to trial. I had to hunt him down and bring him back."

I can see the wheels turning behind her sweet eyes, the moment it *clicks.* They widen, and she sucks in a breath, just staring at me. "Wait. You're a bounty hunter?"

"What's a bounty hunter?" Tara pipes up.

"Nothing you need to know about, love," Haley answers quickly, firmly, and her sharp stare says I'd better *not* enlighten the girl, either.

I sigh and shrug. "So what if I am?"

"Well, it explains a lot." Her gaze narrows. "So instead of spending your life chasing people off, you just spend your life chasing? That's no way to live."

"Newsflash, darlin' – not everybody wants to stay in one place for ten hours at a time just to capture the perfect shade of a cloud."

Hay snorts, but some of the tension eases from the air as she looks away. "Oh, please. Is that what you think I do? Anyone who *needs* ten hours to capture one shade either isn't a very good artist...or might just be the best in the world and really devoted to their craft."

"Which one are you?"

She shrugs, her smile fading. "A talentless hack who's less worried about accuracy and more worried about how it feels."

"Not talentless," I growl, wondering why she'd even think it. "You captured the feeling of Heart's Edge damn well."

No lie. No exaggeration. It's hanging on my wall, isn't it? But I don't tell her that.

I just wonder how she'd capture the feeling sitting heavy in my chest, or what's rattling around in her, betrayed by the startled way she looks at me.

Then she twists away with a blush, turning her suddenly soft, a hellion tamed into something sweet and silent and grateful for my words.

* * *

THE REST of dinner goes down quiet. Less tense.

I don't even feel like I've worn out my welcome, but I also think maybe I should give Hay some space. Something's clearly pressing on her mind, and she brushes off my offer to do dishes to pay for my meal.

"Already paid with free vet care, remember?" she points out with the same faint, troubled smile.

Fuck my life.

I can't just walk away when she looks so miserable. "Doc fixed up Mozart, not me," I say, and start gathering up dirty dishes into a stack. "So you'll have to make one more complimentary dinner. I was just the wheels. Speaking of...how's your car?"

"Running. For now," she says, following me into the kitchen with a handful of utensils. "Stewart says if I keep driving it around, it's going to pop again. And then my sister will kill me."

For some reason, Stewart's name on her lips makes me bristle. I force it down and carefully set the stack of dishes in the sink, then turn the water on. "What were you doing with your sister's car, anyway?"

"I don't have one," she says. We're working side by side as if it comes natural, her pouring in dish soap, me stealing the utensils from her and dropping them in a rapidly filling pot to soak. "I lived in Seattle. It's one of the best public transit systems in the world. And crazy expensive to park anywhere." Her lips twist bitterly. "If I needed to go somewhere fast, I'd just borrow Eddy's car or hop a ride."

"Fuckface fiancé Eddy?" It's out before I can stop it.

"*Ex*-fiancé," she bites back.

I hold up one soapy hand in surrender.

"Ex. Damn right."

"Yeah." She throws a subtle glance over her shoulder, toward the notebook, before she snorts and steals the faucet, swinging it around to her side and turning it on cold. "You wash, I dry?"

"Deal." Grabbing the sponge, I start swiping down plates, but can't help following that quick glance. "You heard from him recently?"

There's a long second of silence.

"He *wrote me*," she bites off, seething, and I'm half afraid she'll crack the next plate I hand her with that fierce grip. "Like email or text messages aren't a thing."

"You can delete those unread. Block his email and number," I tell her. "You can't block a piece of paper."

"I don't even know how he found out we were here. My sister didn't say anything. That's Eddy, though. Sneaky. And oblivious. If I'm not answering the phone or email, he could be a decent human and get the message...but that's asking too much. Instead, he's forcing his bullshit on me!" she flares. "I wish I'd just ripped it up."

I steal a look over my shoulder at Tara, but she's distracted, watching something on TV and snuggling up with Mozart, her cheek pillowed on the cat's flank. But I keep my voice low as I ask, "You want to tell me what he said?"

She eyes me warily and sighs. "What do cheating bastards always say when they realize they tossed away the best thing in their lives?"

"Can't imagine."

I really can't.

Because if a woman like Hay let down her defenses and blunted her thorns enough to let me in, what happened with Eddy McFuck was tragic.

I can't even picture fucking up like that.

Not the way this douchebag did her.

"How about the crib notes?" She's scrubbing a paper towel over the plate till it shines. "He's sorry, can he come visit, he just wants to rescue me from this horrible little place and...make things right. *Idiot.*"

I frown. "How'd he even get the address here?"

"Oh, *get this*," she bites off with a bitterly sardonic smile. "He works at my bank. Weren't we so exciting? A bank loan associate and an insurance adjuster."

"For reality TV, you'd be the starving but glamorous artist. He'd be the loan shark." My brows furrow, a sense of unease eating at me. "Wait. He looked at your debit card transactions to find out where you were?"

"*Yes.*"

"That's fucking illegal, Hay. I don't care if he works at the bank and has access. Just because he *can* look doesn't mean he's *allowed*. That's stalking, and the prick should be reported."

She throws me that hard, hurting smile, the one that makes me want to hold her together before she breaks. "How much would you charge to haul him off, Mr. Bounty Hunter?"

"For you?" I bump her arm with my elbow and start on the next plate. "Free. Got a summer special on dumbass cheaters."

"So generous." There's an amused crack in her voice, and she subsides, falling quiet as we work through a few more dishes, before she murmurs, "And sorry for earlier. I was just surprised, you know."

"Yeah?"

"About...what you do, I mean. I don't know. I'd been trying to guess. Figured all this weird stuff like private investigator, undercover cop, maybe even covert ops or CIA. You said you were a Ranger." She shrugs one shoulder. "Bounty hunter's a little less dashing and noble. It caught me off guard."

"Hey, I'll have you know I'm plenty dashing, and I can pull off noble in a pinch."

She laughs, soft and startled, shaking her head. "It's just, you know, you think about it, and you think about Dog the Bounty Hunter and all this trash TV stuff that makes it look scuzzy. When really, you're doing a good thing. You're finding people trying to escape the law, making a little less work for police by bringing in the bad guys." She lifts her head, looking up at me with clear, warm green eyes. "So. You know. Sorry if I made you think I was freaked out or anything."

"I think it'd take more than one bounty hunter to freak you out, Haley."

Her lips twitch up at the corners. "That almost sounds like a compliment."

"Might've just been." Chuckling, I plunge my hands in for a handful of forks and knives. "C'mon. Let's finish this up so you can put Tara to bed."

She just hums a soft sound. Acquiescence.

And I wonder what the hell I'm doing again, acting like I'm in any way part of this odd little family.

IX: I DON'T DANCE (HALEY)

I don't know why I haven't ripped this letter into pieces.

Ripped it up, set it on fire, then flushed the ashes down the toilet.

I sit on the couch, reading over the crumpled pages again in the rising morning light. Tara's still asleep, all the shuttling back and forth between here and Wilma's is wearing her out.

Poor baby. She keeps trying to keep my hours to have more time with me.

I feel guilty, but I've got to look at this as making a paycheck, keeping a roof over both our heads and a full fridge, even if Wilma's got us covered on the rent. I have to pretend I'm a responsible adult until it's time for her to go home to Marie and John.

Part of me knows, if I really wanted to, I could go with her.

My sister wouldn't be awful about me staying for a while, but...

There'd be something between us. Something hard and

ugly and wrong, and I'd feel like a failure, and she wouldn't mean to judge me, but she would.

I love my sister, but life around our dad broke us in different ways. We both prefer to keep our problems as *ours* and nobody else's. Hating to rely on anyone, completely self-contained.

But I'd like to think I'd help someone who needs it. Marie's more of an 'every woman for herself' kind of person.

I can't even be angry at her for that or think there's anything wrong with it. Not when we learned to hide, to be small, to be silent at such a young age while Dad had his drunken fits. Not when sometimes it was so terrifying all there was to do was *run* and not look back.

Not even for the sister you were leaving behind and just *hoping* she found her own way out.

That's been our relationship for our whole adult lives.

We hope for each other, but we never reach for each other. We're so used to feeling unsteady, unstable, that we're terrified reaching out for someone else will just tip us back down into the dark.

Is that the real reason I won't respond to Eddy?

Because I'm afraid of reaching out and getting dragged into a nightmare again, not being able to pull myself back out?

No.

Hell no.

I crumple the letter in my fist, hissing as I stand and stalk toward the trash can.

I won't respond to Eddy because he's a cheating piece of crap, and he stole not one, but *two* relationships from me. My best friend stole my fiancé...but my fiancé stole my best friend, too.

I hope they rot in hell together. Though judging by the

way Eddy's already trying to slither back, their fun together didn't last long.

Deep breath. I'm going to be *fine.*

I toss the crumpled note in the trash and peer into the fridge to see what I'm going to whip together for Tara's breakfast and my dinner before I leave her with her sketch-book and her stoned cat while I catch some sleep.

But before I can pull out the carton of eggs, the sound of a roaring engine and churning tires jerks me from my thoughts. I blink, straightening and peering out the window just in time to see Warren's truck come tearing down the front lane before slewing to a halt in front of the main house.

I can't see much of him as he gets out and stalks across the lawn to vanish into the house.

But what I see looks *pissed.*

I'm not worried about that asshole. I'm *not.*

But I am curious, and I slip my feet into my sandals, tug my pajama shorts down enough to be decent, and head outside. I'll just casually drop in with something about needing fresh towels.

I'm sure no one will believe I'm not being nosy, but, well...

Any thoughts of curiosity vanish as I make my way down the path and hear the sounds of angry, raised voices.

Two of them. Male. One of them Warren's.

My heart skips a beat just as my stride skips a step. I surge ahead, jogging down the path to the front step. When I mount the porch and push the door open, I freeze in place as I stare at the insanity before me.

Warren's got Flynn Bitters up against the wall, grasping the front of his shirt in both hands and dangling the man off the ground like a scarecrow. Flynn's red-faced and wheezing while Warren...holy *hell.*

I've never seen him like this.

I'd thought I'd seen him angry, but apparently all I'd experienced was his grumpy scowling and sulking. This is different. Chilling.

Warren so completely stock-still it's like raw fury has complete control over his body and won't let him move an inch, his face a cold mask as he stares the old man down.

"You expect me to believe," Warren says, slow and menacing, his voice a lion's growl, "that you didn't know shit?"

Flynn spits, aiming for Warren's face, but it ends up dribbling down his own chin as he thrashes and glares. "Let go, asshole! It ain't my business, so I didn't make it my goddamn business!" he flares. "Get the fuck off me, boy."

"*Boy*." Slowly, Warren tilts his head, eyes narrowing. "I'd rather be a boy than a miserable, broken coward."

Anything else they might say is cut off by the involuntary squeak in the back of my throat. *What the hell is going on here?*

My hand flies to my mouth. *Oops.*

They both go stiff, Flynn's head jerking toward me while Warren keeps his gaze locked on Flynn.

Yet he's speaking to me when he calmly says my name.

"Hay."

Just like he's greeting me over eggs at my kitchen table.

Slowly he steps back, letting Flynn drop with a clear look of contempt, a simmering promise in those dark blue eyes. I think if he wasn't so calm, I'd almost be afraid when Warren is an imposing man, one made for brute violence. But that calm says he's in total control.

Flynn isn't even bruised. Just indignant as he drops down to the floor with a grumble, brushing himself off.

For just a moment, those stormy blue eyes lock on mine, and Warren sweeps past me and out the door. It's not rage anymore in that stark, heavy gaze.

It's pain.

Something almost like...betrayal?

I stay frozen in the doorway for a few moments longer, torn between following Warren and minding my own business. But a baleful look from Flynn sends me scurrying out.

I feel like Warren has me on a tether, drawing me after him when I can't stand that aching look on his face, that hidden agony in his eyes, whatever deep-buried wound drove him to such animal fury.

I don't know what I can do to ease it. I don't even know why I *want* to.

I just know I can't let him go right now.

Not like this.

He's already halfway across the yard to the cabin before I even get close enough to call his name, but he doesn't slow down as I say "Warren!"

Nothing. He just takes the front porch steps two at a time, and he's half a second away from slamming the door before I catch up with a quick-burst sprint and insert myself against the jamb.

He stops, barely catching the door before it hits me. A mute simmering look flashes toward me before he grunts and Incredible Hulks his way inside.

"Warren!"

No response to his name, but he doesn't stop me from following. After a breathless moment, I slip through the door and close it more gently behind me.

"What happened? What was that?" I ask, watching as he just stands in the middle of the room, breathing deep and slow, hands curling into fists. "You could've hurt him. He's just an old man."

"He's a lying asshole, and he's holding his tongue so hard I hope he chokes on it," Warren growls, broad shoulders heaving in tight waves of muscle, handsome jaw locked tight, muscles ticking against weathered, tanned skin. His entire body's so tense his tattoos writhe over the cut chisels of his arms as if they're alive, these wild beasts mirroring their master's outrage. "If he gets someone hurt, nothing I could do would be enough."

I'm so confused. Flynn Bitters? That old drunk? He's more likely to hurt himself than anyone else. One day the drink's going to be too much, and something's going to go wrong. I shake my head, curling my hand against my chest.

"I don't get it," I say again. "How could Flynn hurt someone at the inn?"

"Don't," Warren grinds out. "Don't, Hay. You're not in this circus."

"Warren..."

Heart beating hard, I take a risk, stepping closer, reaching out to rest my hand lightly against his arm. It's rock hard underneath my palm, hot as forge-fire.

He turns his head just enough for one burning-bright slit of blue to look down at me, scoring into me. It's a terrifying, exhilarating feeling to have him looking at me that way, because even though I don't know him, even though we're nothing, I just sense something.

I *feel* him.

Feel the man I know he is.

And the man I know would never turn the bristling violence his body is capable of on someone like me.

So the thrill that rushes through me when he hooks his arm around my waist is only part fear. The rest is charged adrenaline.

Climbing a man like Warren is like climbing Mount Everest, a rush to the senses and a high to the soul. My heart slams against my chest like it's trying to rip out to reach him, and he comes right in to meet it as he crushes us together.

There's no breath. No space between us, only thin fabric

and body heat, and I realize I'm still in my thin pajama shorts and they don't do a *thing* to keep the fire of his flesh from whispering between my thighs.

Suddenly I'm too warm and wet. Too hot everywhere, this fire surging in my blood.

Part of me wonders if all of this anger and animosity has just been a vicious, futile struggle against raw animal attraction.

The rest of me can't wonder anything at all. I can't think when he's looking down at me that way, suddenly leaning in to capture my lips.

One moment I'm aching to soothe that wounded look in his eyes.

The next, I'm caught up as if I've been captured by a wild creature and devoured.

Holy fricking hell.

His kiss comes hard. All savage teeth and claws and hell-fire. Utterly consuming, leaving me bleeding desire from my pores.

Instead of pain, he gives me pleasure as he shreds my senses with dominating, captivating caresses of lips to lips, and a searching tongue that asks, and yet seems so very sure I'll give in.

For once, he's so right.

I'm trembling, clutching his arms, a confused and smoldering mess of heat and longing and igniting *need*.

He tastes like the forgetfulness I need. He tastes like everything that'll leave my run of crappy luck behind and just feel something *good*, and I want to find amnesia with my legs wrapped around his thick, powerful body, muscle moving against my inner thighs while he plunges against me with all that raw power channeled into every thrust.

I need it. I want it. I want *him*.

Every last bit of Warren Ford and that blue-eyed wild he calls a soul.

With a low moan, I push myself up on my toes, leaning into him hotly. My lips part for his tongue, letting him *have* me. Claim me.

Letting him stroke inside my mouth and taste me in ways that I feel all over my body.

Letting him explore me so intimately it feels like we're doing something wrong.

Oh, and damn right we are.

I shiver with the delicious thrill of it.

He's so tall I can barely reach, but then those thick, strong hands cup my ass, lift me up, dig into my flesh so hard it's a wonder I don't come right then and there.

I'm honest-to-God melting. Slick. Squirming.

And as I push my fingers into his lush black hair and drug myself on the scrape of stubble against my skin, I can't help a begging whisper, "*Warren.*"

But it's like I threw cold water over him.

He stiffens with a shudder, growling as he rears back, his hands still hot and hard, sending conflicting messages when he's looking down at me like I did something wrong, accusatory and sharp and...guilty?

Then there's this plunging feeling in the pit of my stomach.

I hate that I'm putting myself in a position, yet again, to let a man jerk me around.

And I'm already closing off, bracing myself for the sting when he lets me go with a curse, not quite dropping me on my feet.

He gives me a second to steady myself before he pulls back completely. Pacing back and forth, all prowling tension, he rakes his rough hands through his hair, spiking it into an inky mess.

"Fuck," he swears. "Fuck, Hay."

I tried, idiot, I think to myself. *I wanted to.*

But of course I don't say it.

I don't say anything. I'm just trying to take deep breaths, calm myself down, and still my whirling thoughts when that kiss practically threw my brain in a blender.

Maybe he's right to prevent another huge clusterfrick neither of us need in our lives.

He flings me another of those tiger looks. I swear, if he does it again, he's going to get *punched.*

But he stops my little fist dead in its tracks when he bites off, "Get what you wanted?"

I blink. Did I...what?

Now I'm just confused. Second-guessing.

I know I followed him in here, but he's the one who dragged me in, who kissed me like the war just ended. I have no idea what's going on. Only that every bit of heat inside me goes cold and sick.

I want to lash back at him, fight him, tell him to shove his accusations you-know-where, but I can't find the words.

Because this actually *hurts.*

God damn it.

It hurts so bad because I'm past even lying.

I think I have a rebound crush on this asshole.

When I don't answer, he glares at me. "What the fuck are you trying to do to me? Are you happy now? Will you just go *away?*"

I don't know how to answer that. I don't know what I'm doing, when now that the dizzying, simmering desire between us just exploded on the launch pad, I can't ignore the tension clouding the air as thick as mist.

I can't lie to myself about what I'm feeling every time he pisses me off.

That magnetic energy builds violently between us,

drawing me in like gravity. If I'm not careful, I could let this man swallow me up in his intensity. All thanks to my desperation to *feel* something besides frustration, hopelessness, the shadows of the past.

And I don't have words for that, or for what that seething, sparking blue glare of his does to me right now.

Parting my lips, I try to say something, but Warren only sighs, and I fall silent again.

He looks away, glaring across the room – at my painting, I realize.

He's glaring at the painting I gave him on an impulsive whim, but some of the fury seems to bleed out of him to leave his shoulders sagging, his hands hanging helplessly at his sides.

"I'm sorry," he grinds out, deep and gravelly and scorched at the edges. "I shouldn't have said that. Any of it. Fuck. It's not you I'm mad at, Hay. It's Flynn for hiding shit. It's my grandmother. It's Dennis Bress. It's this whole clusterfuck situation, and you shouldn't be stuck in the middle of it, dealing with me being Captain Asshole."

That actually gets me to smile a little, though it's not easing this crack in my chest. "You could try not being an asshole," I venture. "Then you wouldn't have to apologize. Funny how that works."

"You might as well ask me to change my genetics." But his lips crease slightly, a rueful grin before it fades. "I'm just trying to keep people safe. You. Grandma. She's getting mixed up in business with people who could hurt her, and Flynn knew and didn't tell me."

"What business, Warren?" I ask, knowing I'll probably get some evasive half answer or he'll just completely shut down.

It's not his job that makes Warren like this, I realize. He's evasive because it's who he is.

So stubbornly determined to handle everything himself.

166

And I wonder if there's someone he relied on once, who betrayed him.

Or someone else relied who on *him?* Maybe he feels like he let them down and has been carrying that around for so long it's molded the shape of his burden into armor.

But before he can cut me off, shut me down, there's a knock at the door. We both tense, glancing up sharply, but it's just Tara on the other side of the door, peeking in drowsily.

"Auntie Hay?" she calls softly. "I'm hungry."

"Just a minute, baby. I'll be there," I say, forcing a smile for her sake. "I'll make eggs."

"I have a better idea," Warren says. "Let me take you both into town for breakfast. You must be tired from your shifts. You shouldn't have to cook when you're exhausted."

It takes me back a little that he's noticed. I don't want to get hung up on little details.

I'm not the type to jump into reckless flings on the rebound after a major breakup.

If I'm honest, I'm scared.

I'm scared if I give in to the strange feelings I get around him, I might start feeling something that seems real.

Way too real, when I'm still licking my wounds from Eddy, only for it to all go south when my temper and Warren's temper turn what could be an easy comfort thing into bitter fights until I snap out of it and walk away from him once his purpose is served. I don't even like *thinking* that, like it's okay to just use him to ease my own hurt and distract myself, so I just won't let myself do it.

But he's making a peace offering, waiting for my answer. And I *am* hungry.

"Sure," I say, with lips that still throb with the taste of him, the heat of him. "Let me put some clothes on."

* * *

I THINK it's for Tara's sake that we're pretending everything is normal.

As normal as it can be when I don't know what normal even *is* for us. That hot, grasping kiss sure didn't help define it, either.

It's just another reminder that Warren and I don't know each other. Not really. And maybe we shouldn't.

We're barely what you'd call friends. Still we're trying to be friendly over breakfast at a sunny little fifties-style diner twenty minutes later. It looks like the last nice, wholesome place people stop before they drive on to get murdered in a bad thriller novel.

Or maybe the fact that I think it does just says more about my state of mind.

We're so freaking strained, but managing. There's even a few smiles, this gentle teasing mostly centered around Tara being picky over the kinds of napkins she'll use. Funny, because I know her mom taught her something weird about textured paper and chapped lips.

Marie was so obsessed with her lipstick smearing when we were girls. And it looks like her obsession might've rubbed off on her daughter before Tara's even applied her first test color.

She's really such a little princess, but I love her that way.

So I can't help pulling her away from her pancakes to give her a squeeze, just holding her tight.

This is what matters. Whatever else happens to me in Heart's Edge, at least we'll have our memories.

She's family, important, *real*, and once I get past this dumb quarter-life crisis and dead engagement, she'll still be there. And so will all my love for her and Marie.

"Auntie Hay?" she asks, still clutching her syrup-beaded fork. "Are you okay?"

Jeez. Is it that obvious?

"Fine, kit," I say with a forced laugh, resting my chin to the top of her head. "Everything's just fine."

As I let her go, though, Warren looks up from his plate of steak and hash browns as the bell over the door swings open. I crane to look over my shoulder at who he's staring at.

Stewart leans inside, tall and sun-washed, his brows pinched together. He lifts his chin to Warren, beckoning him in a tight, sharp movement.

That's odd. Almost ominous.

Same with Warren's total silence as he meets Stewart's eyes grimly.

A second later, his gaze snaps back to me, and he dips his head in a nod. "Sorry. I'll just be a minute. Order anything else you want and throw it on my tab."

Then he slides his tall bulk out of the booth, moving with lion grace and strength, joining Stewart outside. Through the window, I watch as they lean against Stewart's giant penis-envy truck in the parking lot, huddled close and speaking urgently.

Warren looks agitated. Stewart seems displeased over something.

Whatever it is, they're both completely absorbed in their chatter, their motions...and it seems serious.

Oh, God.

Much more serious than whatever bounty hunting job brought Warren back here and that he's being so secretive about.

There's something about his posture, about the intensity shrouding him.

A chill cuts right through me, chasing away the summer heat. I shouldn't judge.

I really, *really* don't know him.

I don't know what's going on, and I have no right to demand not to be left in the dark. I have no right to anything.

Again, I remind myself he's a *stranger*.

Such an awful shame he kisses like sheer madness, and I can still taste him on my lips.

X: READY TO BLOW (WARREN)

*G*od, I'm such a fuckup.

I can't believe I kissed Haley.

Kissed her, then snapped at her like she'd somehow made me do it when that was all me, giving in to the heat of the moment and acting on it the only way I knew how.

Right after all the fury inside turned into an inferno. My only outlet was giving in to the simmering attraction, the need, the *hunger* that damn infuriating woman rouses with just a saucy glance or a stubborn little smile.

I've got to remind myself that her stay in Heart's Edge and mine are only temporary.

We're gonna forget that kiss ever happened and then go our separate ways.

"Hey. *War*."

Shit.

I've zoned out, thinking about Haley instead of listening to Stewart. I lift my head, blinking at him. "Sorry. What'd you say?"

"I said, what the fuck is going on between you and Dennis Bress?"

I frown. "Nothing. I've hardly even spoken to him since I've been back in town. We're not tight anymore. Not since..."

I can't fucking say her name. Not today.

"Yeah, man. I know it. I know." He claps me on the shoulder. "Listen, I haven't wanted to say this—"

"Then *don't*," I grind out.

Good friend or not, I wish he'd mind his damn biz.

He gives me a searching look. I already know what he'll say because it's the same thing *everyone* says.

"Warren, sometimes things happen out there on deployment," he murmurs. "It's war. And it's not anyone's fault. I know it's easy to blame Bress as Jenna's commanding officer—"

"*Stop.*" I knock his hand away, glowering.

He knows.

He was the one that saw it, who told me. Told me that Bress set her up, left her behind. And he did it to cover his own money-grubbing ass.

Thanks to Stewart, I know there's more to Bress than anyone in this town might suspect, except a few people who work for him. It's only later that Stew questioned his own memory, questioned what he saw in the heat of battle, but fuck, I know. The stone-cold truth.

I work my jaw, glowering at him, trying to stay civil. "Concern noted. You need to stay out of this."

"Then you need to be less obvious about stalking, dammit," he points out. "He dropped by for a tune-up this morning. Asked if I'd talked to you. If I'd noticed you acting funny."

My jaw tightens. "What did you say?"

"That you're in town on a job and it's stressing you out,

having a mark this close to home." He gives me a long look. "That *is* why you're in town, isn't it? And why you're staying in the cabins? Is one of Wilma's summer guests who you're after?"

It's an easy lie. It's the most sensible, and he's practically feeding it to me.

So I grunt, nodding. I can't make myself say *yes* out loud, not when I don't like deceiving people, much less a friend. A silent lie by omission will have to do.

Stew frowns. "You think your mark's the one who threatened Little Ms. Mustang with that messy Halloween paint trick?"

"Yeah. Gotta be." That, at least, is the truth.

Considering Bress *is* my mark.

Looking past me and through the window of the diner, Stewart arches a brow. "I see you've got a bit of company, on that subject. How're things getting on with her, man?"

"They're not because there's nothing *to* get on," I growl, and he smirks.

"So you're just stepping in as a surrogate daddy figure for fun?"

"*I'm not.*" I smack his arm lightly. "Look, I'm just worried the mark will target her to get to me. It's easier to keep her safe if she's in my sights, since she's putting down roots here for a bit."

"She's really popular at Brody's. All the boys are howling like wolves after her."

I eye him. "You've been seeing her at work?"

"A man's gotta eat, and Brody's is the best game in town. Me and the crew go over there a few times a week for lunch."

"We have a grocery store. Use it." Sighing, I know I'm being crazy. So I settle myself more heavily against his truck, folding my arms over my chest. "So your advice is to get over my shit with Bress, finish the job I came here to do, and get out of town again?"

"It's what you do best." He settles companionably next to me, tucking his hands into the pockets of his jeans. "Face it, War. You're a drifter at heart. You don't just settle down nowhere. Hell, I'm half afraid to goad you to take your shot with Little Ms. Mustang, when you're probably just going to break her poor heart when you run off again."

"Already done. And it wasn't fucking me," I snarl. "Don't worry. I doubt she'd give me enough of the pieces to break them more."

"So you *have* thought about it."

Goddamn. This isn't getting better.

"I can't think about it," I admit. "Too much on my plate. Grandma's thinking about going into a business deal with Bress. Says she needs someone to take over Charming Inn when she's ready to retire, and Flynn's not even half the man."

Stewart chuckles. "You know that was a hint for you. Probably about as subtle as a damn baseball bat to the face. I know your granny."

"Yeah, but...like you said, I'm a drifter. Can't stay in one place. Spokane's the closest I've got to home."

It is. Even though I've never bothered to even hook more than a month-to-month rental there, ever since I left Heart's Edge after my honorable discharge.

Though I'm really starting to wonder if this restlessness is choice. Or if Hay's right about me.

Maybe I move from town to town because I'm running from something I can't face.

Jenna.

I glance over my shoulder. Her and Tara are watching us through the diner's window, and when I catch their eyes, Hay immediately looks away while Tara grins and waves. I manage a smile for the girl and raise a hand, only to turn back to find Stew watching me knowingly.

"*What*," I bite off.

"Nothing. Just haven't seen you smile like that in a while."

"Enough with the hints." I push away from Stewart's truck, straightening. "Look, thanks for the heads up."

"Just tell me you'll listen this time," he says quietly. "Promise me you'll put this bullshit with Bress to bed before it gets messier than you can handle, War. Do the job you came to do and get out."

A slow, strained sigh hisses out of me. "I can't, Stew. Wish like hell I could promise you that."

I don't know why I can't tell him the job I came to do is Bress.

He's a smart man. He has to realize it, but maybe he's letting me have my safety lies.

"Well, you'll do some thinking, and I bet you'll come to your senses. With Bress and with Ms. Mustang." He gives me a nod.

We part with a clap of hands. A soldier's grasp, a warrior's hold, palms to wrists, gripped tight, before he lets go with a wave, and I head back inside.

Stew's right about one thing – if I don't do something this shitshow with Bress is going to eat me alive.

Hay watches me with a thousand questions in her eyes, but I just force a smile and slide back into the booth across from them.

"If you're done eating, feel like a hike?"

Tara erupts into crowing enthusiasm. Haley groans, bowing her head and sagging. "You want me to do this day-walker crap when I have to go to the bar tonight?"

"Promise I'll get you back in time for some solid sleep and a shower before your shift." I raise my hand, signaling for the check. "C'mon, Hay. Since you like painting Heart's

175

Edge so much, I want to show you the real beauty around here."

* * *

THE HIKING TRIP was an impulse to deflect questions and my own boiling rage.

But once we're geared up with proper boots, safety ropes, water bottles, a few other necessities and out on the trails, I'm surprised to find myself *enjoying* the walk.

The trails around here start off gentle on open terrain lined with tall waving grass and bits of scrub, then blend into thicker and thicker trees. Before you know it, you're up in the foothills toward the mountains and the nature preserves.

Everything looks so pristine and untouched. You can imagine yourself thousands of years in the past, before logging and farming reshaped the land and cut down so much of the old growth.

Out here, beneath the shadows of moss-faded trees, the rocky slopes cragged and ancient, it's downright primeval.

Breathtaking, too.

We climb higher toward a clear summer sky, looking down over the splendor of the huge cliff beyond the town and the valley sprawling on for ages beyond.

The tension broke somewhere along our hike.

Tara's enjoying herself the most, chasing pale spring-green butterflies around, picking up different kinds of leaves and flowers and bringing them back to identify. She's damn near running circles around us with more energy than one little girl should ever have.

Hay's quieter, save for when she laughs at Tara's antics, but it's a sort of rapt, reverent sound.

I can see the appreciation in every look as she takes in our surroundings with the eye of an artist. I can't help but wonder what she'll create from this trip. What that lovely passion and talent and ingenuity will bleed from the emotion the grand, awe-inspiring landscapes evoke.

Now and then she catches my eye. And *smiles.*

Damn! Here I thought the scenery was the prettiest thing up here.

It's a whole lot harder to keep walking with a hard-on as heavy as these trees.

It's not even her trying to be sexy. More like a small, strange smile, thoughtful, but *there.*

Like we're sharing some secret between us, acknowledging it in stolen glances that catch me off guard and make my heart thud harder in my chest.

When we reach the top of the trail and stop, breathing in the warm, woodsy scent around us and the crisp mountain air tinged with just the faintest far-off whiff of snow, we're there.

The *zone.*

We're speechless as we look out over the vista. Staring at this great, sprawling, beautiful thing that somehow makes us small, but not insignificant.

We're part of it. Part of this awesome natural wonder, part of the feeling of *immensity* that settles over us. And we're quiet for a long time, quiet together.

That's something I haven't had in a long time.

Together with anyone, part of something, belonging somewhere.

I'm not sure whose hand reaches for whose first.

Maybe we just brush in our daze, and somehow it sends an electric signal through us.

But then everything shifts. We're holding hands, our fingers twined real tight, and her touch is a spark going through me. Tara finds us and leans against us both.

Today we're not Hay and her fucked up ex. Or Tara and

her worries over heading home. Or me and my soul crushing memories.

We're three happy people, dammit.

And we stay like that – *happy* – as calm settles over us like the world at large is trying to send a message. Then I see Hay's smile, and there's no doubt whatsoever.

Life goes on, and one day I'll wake up and find out it's gone on without me.

Unless I manage to tear myself from this sick obsession to savor the present.

Savor times like this and grasp them tight when they come, because they may well be few and far between.

Same goes for a fine, gorgeous young woman with her soft hand in mine.

* * *

I DON'T GET to savor for long.

That client's still up my ass. If I want to keep a job and my reputation, I can't let my contracts lapse for the sake of my own personal projects.

I tend to work with district attorneys and bail bondsmen. Once they realize they can't rely on a bounty hunter, they stop calling for new hits.

So I set out for Boise, keeping that quiet day on the trails wrapped around me like a shield of armor. Thinking of Hay makes the miles on the road go by like nothing.

I circle back to that moment when the sun started dipping low and mellow in the afternoon, the color of the light changing to this burnished, bronze, tinting everything around us.

There'd been murmurs about needing to head back if she was going to survive her shift. We'd looked at each other, and for a moment I'd wanted it again. So fucking bad.

I wanted to kiss her.

Kiss her for real, a conscious choice rather than diving in on fury and impulse and adrenaline.

Kiss her the way she deserves to be kissed.

Show her I'm not an utter asshole, just maybe ninety percent.

I wanted to clear the air between us, cut away some of the nettles and barbs bound around us, and maybe lay the foundation for something that isn't quite so combative.

A friendship, at least.

A storm, certainly. One where I'd sweep my lips across hers like I owned her, cherished her, ready to call her *mine.*

Sure, she was driving me nuts with desire, and she's the most goddamn sexy woman I've seen in years. But it's not that wrong to want to be friends with her if we're going to keep bouncing off each other like pinballs.

It'd make both our last few days in Heart's Edge a lot calmer, at least. And less stressful, not just for us, but for Tara.

She's not my kid. She's not even Hay's, but she's grown on me, this adorable little munchkin with the most delicate and exaggerated mannerisms only kids have.

She really loves Mozart and chatters my ear off whenever she can about that hairball. Haley and I may not be her parents, but it's going to affect her if we keep circling each other like scorpions with stingers at the ready.

Once again, though, I force myself to put my thoughts aside. I check into my hotel in Boise and settle in to do the job proper.

It's almost laughably easy, honestly.

Most criminals stupid enough to skip on bail are too dumb to disappear convincingly, though now and then you get the occasional mastermind who vanishes without a trace.

NICOLE SNOW

The man I'm tracking, Thad Roshank, isn't a criminal mastermind.

And after all my time and prep work sniffing out the extent of Bress' operation, Roshank is a baby. A pup compared to a wolf.

He's left trails everywhere, with associates and debit card purchases, not even having the basic common sense to pay cash. Every transaction is like a heat map tracking his movements.

I know where he's been every twelve hours or so since he jumped bail and took off.

He'd been arraigned in Coeur d'Alene. Guess he at least had the sense to know trying to leave the state would make things worse if he got caught.

But while Boise's a big city, it's a *close* city. It barely takes a week of careful tracking and a little late-night surveillance to lead me to Roshank's doorstep.

He's staying in the kind of pay-by-the-hour motel you either book if you and a "guest" only need it for an hour. Or the kind you rent by the week because you don't intend to stay in town long enough to be detected.

It's dirty, dingy, and the alley across the street where I've taken up position smells like liquor, piss, and used latex. I've tracked Roshank multiple times returning back here, staggering in late with escorts on his arm and booze drifting off him. Someone like that shitstain, I really hope the woman he ducked out on doesn't actually want him back.

But if he can spend that much money on liquor and prostitutes, he can sure as hell afford to pay his child support and then some.

He's a spot of white in my vision as he comes reeling around from the front of the building, his button-down shirt untucked. His skin looks pasty, sucked dry. No girl on his arm tonight, thank fuck.

He's alone. Perfect.

That'll make this that much easier.

I wait until he disappears into room 117, the same room he's been slumming around in all week, drinking and fucking and probably getting up to a few actionable drug charges, too.

Just a little longer. Just enough time for him to get complacent, before I let myself out of my truck, check the Glock holstered against the small of my back, and saunter across the lot to pound on his door.

He doesn't answer at first.

I knock again, louder, and hear curses, banging.

I brace, just in case he isn't as alone as I think. But no, he's just drunk. Very, very drunk.

As he creaks the door open, he peeks up at me blearily, his narrow face twisted in irritation.

"Huh? I already paid for the week," he slurs. "Whaddya want?"

I smile grimly. "Thad Roshank? You're under arrest for bail hopping."

His eyes widen. He freezes, gaze darting about, but there's nowhere for him to go.

No other exits from the room, and I'm blocking the door.

He turns and bolts anyway, darting for the bathroom. *Idiot.*

I'm on him in a second, catching him up around the waist and lifting him off his feet with one arm. He kicks, struggles, hissing and snarling and cursing me over and over again, but he weighs practically nothing to me and inebriated, his arms are wet noodles.

I slam him face-first down on the bed, the mattress bouncing. I'm not trying to hurt him. Fun as that'd be, I just subdue the prick instead.

In seconds, I've got him in a tight hold, wrists wrenched

behind his back, his body pinned under my weight while I maneuver him into cuffs.

Just to be on the safe side, I cuff his ankles, too. He looks like a runner.

Someone who'd try to bolt for it even after hope's lost. I'm not having it.

There's a cell waiting for this asshole.

I can't imagine having a family and just dropping them like a bad habit.

But as I lean back, taking in the dingy, musty motel room, I sigh.

It's too fucking typical.

Drug accessories everywhere. Bent spoon, lighter, rubber hose. Little bags with clear rocks inside. Roshank went off haywire long before he skipped out on his family and his child support payments.

All this evidence is going to take forever to catalogue, if I want it done right.

To hell with it.

I hit the speed dial for the Boise Police Department, and have a little conversation with one of my contacts in the narcotics division. I'll stay here only long enough to hand him over, and make sure my client gets notified. It's not the way we usually do things, but as long as he's in custody somewhere, that's all that matters for the contract to be fulfilled so I can *leave*. Get back to Heart's Edge.

Back to Haley.

I can't tell myself that a second time. I can't let it mean that much.

Damn if I don't feel her, like she's pulling on something inside me, something hooked deep.

I'm restless while I wait for the cops.

When the patrol units show up, I brief them on my rights as a bounty hunter to make a citizen's arrest, notify them of his outstanding warrants and judgments in Kootenai County, and shove the wriggling, still-swearing bundle of Roshank into their arms.

I'm back to my truck in seconds. That bust was almost too easy. I didn't even need my gun. Hours of driving and a week of surveillance, all for it to be over with a quick tackle.

Just means I'm not too tired to make the drive back tonight.

I try not to question what feels so urgent as I head back to my own hotel, pack up, check out, and hit the road. I could've stayed, gotten a solid night's sleep, and then gone back in the morning.

No one's really *waiting* for me in Heart's Edge. I just have business there.

What if Haley's waiting for you, asshole?

What if she's watching for you to come back?

The questions keep coming, and I wonder.

One flaming hot kiss doesn't change the fact she's been hurt bad. She's still pretty raw, and I'm not exactly winning brownie points when the two of us are like fire and ice, clashing and burning and freezing, making a mess that'll just destroy us both.

Doesn't stop me from pressing down on the gas pedal a little harder, devouring the miles back to my hometown faster.

I get to watch the sunrise coming up over the mountains as I hit those more familiar interstate roads that tell me I'm almost home. But I'm not expecting my phone to start ringing in my bag.

Weird. People only call me on business, and at this time of morning?

I can't get to it fast enough, not driving one-handed, so I pull over for a minute to fish it out of my duffel bag before putting it on speaker and cruising forward again while my voicemail dials in.

Then I nearly crash the damn truck into a road sign.

Tara's little voice comes rushing over the line, playing back in urgent, upset little words.

"Warren?" She sounds so scared, so lost, and my heart jolts with a prickle of fear that makes the hair on my forearms stand up. My fingers clench the wheel tighter. "Everything's all wrong now. I...I wish you were here. I'm scared, I haven't seen Auntie Hay, and...she's usually home by now, and *he's* here. When are you coming back? Will you be home soon?"

Fuck.

Any bubble of warmth at hearing that sweet girl call Heart's Edge *home* is completely eclipsed by the sudden churning knots in my gut.

He's here. What had she meant? Who?

And why wasn't Haley home from her shift yet?

I've got one good guess.

Bress. Dennis fucking Bress must've realized I'm getting attached to her and decided she'd make good leverage.

If he's done anything to her, I'll...

I don't even know.

I can't trust myself right now. Can't put anything past him, though. Can't put anything past me if I find her hurt thanks to my shit.

Right now, it's her safety I'm scared for.

After what he did to Jenna, disposing of Haley probably wouldn't even ping on his moral compass. My hands hurt, palms grinding against the steering wheel, and it hits me that I'm going twenty over the speed limit, my eyes locked on the road. A hot mix of rage, endorphins, and relentless biting terror makes my shoulders tremble with the tension rushing through me.

I don't have time to care about cops or speed traps. Not when Hay might be a fucking hostage, or worse.

Dead.

Dead like your sister.

And I barely glance in the rear-view mirror before I slam my foot down on the accelerator, sending my truck leaping forward, synced with the beat of my racing pulse.

It's a tense twenty minutes as I cover the last miles to Heart's Edge with morning breaking over the sky, too bright for my black and dire mood. Dust clouds stream behind my tires as I rip around the last bend toward Charming Inn and the cottages.

Haley's Mustang is nowhere in sight when I pull in the back lane and vault out of the truck.

But there's another car I don't recognize, a newer Chrysler in slick black – what we used to call *city cars* when I was a kid. The kind of thing nobody in Heart's Edge would drive when it would probably drop the transmission in a heartbeat on the roads around here.

I don't trust that car.

It's not Bress', at least, but fuck.

I nearly jump out of my own skin as the front door of the duplex bursts open.

Tara flies out, still in her pajamas, and flings herself against my leg. "Warren!"

"Hey. Hey, munchkin." I try to keep my voice gentle for her when she's clearly upset, her eyes damp, her voice ragged, and she's trembling as she clings to me. I grip her shoulders and squeeze gently, as if that can stop her from sensing my worry. "What happened? Where's Hay? Did he hurt her?"

She shakes her head quickly and buries her face in my stomach. "N-no. No, but he was gross, and I didn't *like* him."

"Who's he?" My voice almost cracks. "Tara, *who?* Where'd he take Hay?"

"Stupid buttface Eddy," she mumbles against my stomach. "I don't *like* him. And they went to breakfast without me, and Auntie Hay made me stay here. I should've gone with them so I could *kick* him."

Eddy? Oh, for *fuck's sake*.

I'm not sure what's worse – the phone call from a frightened little girl where I built up all these abduction scenarios in my head, which always ended with me breaking a dozen laws to get back here in record time to save Hay.

Or the fact that she's just having breakfast with her shitheel of an ex.

Even as my fear eases, it raises my anger.

What the hell?

She'd made it clear she was done with him. Didn't want to see him again, and I'm already damn skeptical of anyone who'd abuse his position to stalk a woman after she'd justifiably dumped him for cheating.

I shouldn't stick my nose in. It's not my damned business.

But when Tara looks up at me with a plaintive pout, begging, "You'll make him go away, won't you?"

She doesn't have to ask twice.

I'm about to step in a minefield and get my leg blown off for it, but goddamn, I'm going to go check up on Hay.

"Sure, munchkin," I say. "Go put some proper clothes on, and I'll take you for breakfast, and we'll check and make sure that stupid buttface Eddy isn't upsetting your aunt."

She's dressed in a jiffy and bundled into my truck. I'm quiet, arguing with myself mentally that I don't have the right to be possessive. Too bad.

And good thing Tara talks enough for both of us.

She tells me how Eddy came cruising up this morning

and kept banging on the door until Hay opened it. She says he talked. A lot. Too damn much.

Haley couldn't even say anything until she finally said she'd listen to him, but not here.

So she told Tara to lock the door and not open up for anyone but Wilma, but Tara hadn't liked being alone. She just wanted the gross man to go away, and I was the best person to call for that.

"Who gave you my number?" I ask her.

I don't even remember giving it to Haley.

Tara beams.

"Grandma Wilma," she answers. "She stopped by to check on me. Said you'd wanna know about this Eddy stuff."

Of course.

Of frigging course Grandma's meddling, playing match-maker, pushing all my Neanderthal mating buttons in the worst way.

Fuck.

Mission accomplished. I've got a manic urge to throw Hay over my shoulder and drag her back to my cave, after I bust in Eddy Fuckface's nose.

Like I need Grandma of all people encouraging me.

I shouldn't be thinking these things in the first place. But we're past thinking and I've got to *act*.

* * *

HALEY'S MUSTANG is in the diner's parking lot.

As we pull up, I can see her through the window, seated across from a man. The little idiot has ordered, poking at a plate of hearty diner food in front of him.

Haley hasn't got anything except a coffee. She's curled in tight on herself, closed and tucked in, as if she can hold herself in this defensive ball that won't let anything vulnerable out. Not where he can reach it.

Who could blame her? He looks like a smarmy-ass salesman, all superficial charm. Not all my instant dislike is because of how he treated Haley. There's just something too slick about him, from his swept-back sandy-brown hair to smiles that don't quite reach his beady eyes, even as he offers her one so ingratiating, so fake, I want to punch his teeth out.

Down, boy, I snarl to myself.

Thankfully, the conversation doesn't look like it's going well. He's talking a lot, probably too much, while her mouth is pinched shut. She shakes her head again and again.

I've seen enough.

As Tara and I step inside, I catch her low, urgent words, cutting Eddy off.

"No," she says firmly. "No, Eddy. You messed us up and you have to live with that now. I don't."

"But baby—" oh, hell, do I want to slap that *baby* right out of his damned mouth, "—everyone fucks up. Everybody has a lapse in judgment. Cold feet happen, and I just...I just needed to work it out of my system. I went a little crazy. I'm over it now, and I miss you. Miss you so damn much."

Haley's lips tremble, her eyes shining so bright it's like she could call down lightning with her drilling stare. "What you're saying under all that is, you were so scared to be with me that you tripped and your dick landed in my best friend."

"What? No, I...I just want you home. C'mon, babe. We had a good thing. Let me bring you back, away from this bumpkin town where half the people look like they can't tie their own shoelaces."

I'm not sure who wrinkles up faster at his shitty dig at the town – me or Hay.

"See, the thing is, I don't think it was cold feet," Hay interjects. She hasn't even noticed us, locked on her target, eviscerating him one word at a time. "I don't even think it was me. It's you, Eddy. This is who you really are, and I can't *believe* I wasted years and money and effort and *love* on you."

"Haley..."

"No." Her voice is thick, her eyes glimmering wet. "You need to leave now. Don't ever contact me again. I'm changing banks. And if I see you anywhere near me, no matter where I go, I'm calling the cops."

Her voice breaks on the last word, and that's when Tara pulls away from me and launches herself across the diner, tunneling into the booth seat with Haley and gluing to her side in a tight hug.

"Don't cry, Auntie Hay!" she pleads. "Me and Warren came to fix it!"

Haley goes pale, her head jerking up, and she locks on me past the self-righteous douche's shoulder. "Oh," she whispers. "Oh, crap."

"Don't worry," I say. "I'm not here to make it worse."

I saunter closer to the table, glaring. The way *Eddy* looks me up and down with a sneer, clearly annoyed by the unwanted interruption, I need to piss him off a little. It's either that or yank out his poor excuse for a spine.

So I completely ignore him as if he's not even important enough for me to acknowledge while I focus on Haley. "You okay, darlin'?"

She nods, a stiff and jerky thing. "I was just finishing here," she answers, slipping her arm around her niece's shoulders.

Eddy frowns. "We weren't done talking."

"*You* weren't done talking," she retorts, nudging Tara out of the booth so they can both stand. "I have nothing else to say, and I'm done listening."

Eddy stands quickly, his body between me and Hay. Then he starts to reach for her.

She jerks back, positioning herself between Eddy and Tara, and glares up at him. He freezes, holding his hands up.

"I still have more to say." Self-important, as if that's all that matters. "You love me, Haley. You wanted to spend the rest of your life with me."

"And now I don't want to spend another minute with you." She starts to shove around him, but he moves to block her with his body.

Enough of this shit.

Frowning, I step up close behind him. Close enough that he'll be able to feel me, feel it coming, know I've got at least sixty pounds of muscle on him, not to mention height.

"You deaf?" I growl. "She doesn't want to talk to you. The lady asked you to leave."

Eddy whirls on me, looking me over with disdain. Probably checking me for the ignorant country brute, or maybe checking me for how the hell I know a woman he considers his. "This is none of your business," he says icily. "Why are you bothering Haley?"

I lean in close. Closer. *Closerr*, until we're almost eye to eye, and when I smile it feels like baring my teeth. "Way I see it, I'm not the one bothering her. But you've got three options. You can walk out of here on your own. You can be carried out of here when I throw your ass over my shoulder and drag you out. Or you can leave in handcuffs when the cops come charge you with stalking."

Eddy makes an indignant sound. "Stalking? This is absolutely ridiculous!"

"No. That's you. Since I'm sure Hay didn't give you a forwarding address, you had to get the information somehow." I fold my arms over my chest, forming a wall. "So you can make your choice: walk away from my girl or get dragged away."

My girl. It comes out before I can stop it, and in clear earshot of the dozens of nosy patrons listening in avidly.

Fuck. It's just to get Eddy to back the fuck off and realize he's playing a losing game here, but goddamm, it feels *right*.

Eddy stares between me and Hay with something like scorn. Disgust. Disdain.

Then he lets out a scoffing laugh, eyeing her while gesturing at me. "Really? This is your rebound? What a downgrade."

Tara sticks her tongue out at him, scowling, and bites off, "Don't you say that about Warren, you buttface."

A second later, she promptly steps forward and kicks Eddy in the shin.

He yelps, stumbling back, and careens right into me.

I don't move, just grab his stupid ass. I'm not gonna let him fall, and I'm not gonna catch him, either.

He wavers before staggering away from me and regaining his balance. A wave of quiet laughter rolls through the diner.

Eddy straightens, smoothing his suit coat and looking around huffily, his cheeks bright red. I know his type.

Threaten him with violence and he'll treat you like an uncultured brute.

Publicly humiliate him and make a dent in that narcissistic ego, though, and he'll turn tail and run.

He proves me right, sniffing and adjusting his cufflinks. "Play with your Neanderthal if you want, Haley," he says coldly. "If that's how you feel you need to punish me, fine. Come home when you're ready to be an adult again."

There's a calculated viciousness to his words. I wonder if this is the first time Haley's seen this side of him, when she's pale and looks so exhausted, so hollow.

"Home was never where you are," Haley answers, soft but firm. "And it never will be."

Eddy's silent for a moment – all the time he gets. Then I

grab him by the shoulders and carry the fuck out, hurling him on the sidewalk as soon as we're through the door.

"You brute, that's ass–"

"Assault? Yeah. And it'll be a thrashing in self-defense if you don't take your chickenshit ass out of my town." I'm snarling, watching his lips twitch angrily, so I point back at the window "Don't even think about lawyers. I've got witnesses. Everybody in that diner will back me up."

Slowly, he stands with an awkward sniff. I wait until he moves away from the diner before I head back inside.

Through the window, I watch as he stands there clumsily like he just remembered he's left his car at the inn. Then with his back straight and his nose in the air, he turns to march down the side of the road in those Italian leather shoes that are going to raise up some blisters real quick. *Good.*

He's gone, and Haley goes loose, groaning as she leans hard on Tara. I cross to her quickly, starting to reach for her, then damning it all and resting a hand to the small of her back.

"Hey," I say. "You okay?"

"Yeah. Maybe," she says, then shakes her head quickly. "*No.*"

"Come on." It feels natural to curl my arm around her, gather her against me, and guide her toward the door. "Let's get you somewhere private where you can wind down."

She's stiff for a moment before she leans against me as if she needs me to hold her up, fitting herself into the crook of my arm. My chest warms. I feel almost satisfied right now, being able to do something for her.

To be her physical and metaphorical shield.

I'd do it for anyone stuck in a situation they don't want to be in, especially with a fuck like her ex, but it feels more right to do it for Hay.

After this, I'm sure we're technically friends. And that's when it hits me.

I've been lying to myself.

Never in a million years will I get off being nothing more than 'friends' with this chick.

I've got to make a move. One that's a lot more fun than throwing the bastard who broke her heart into the dirt.

One fine day, when she's in a better place for it, when her eyes don't look so hollow and shocked and she's got her fire back, it's gonna happen.

Haley and I need to have a talk.

XI: DISASTER ZONE (HALEY)

I so wasn't ready to see Eddy again.

That's what I keep thinking on the drive back to Charming Inn. Kicking myself the whole way.

Honestly, I wasn't ready to see him again because I never wanted to see him at *all*. And when he showed up outside the cabin with that shit-eating grin and the pleading started...I had to spare Tara from a *scene.*

She was half the reason I didn't punch him right then. And the other half was because just seeing his face brought that horrible, sick feeling back.

The same feeling I'd had in the bridal shop, in the fitting room, *in the dress I was going to wear to our freaking wedding.* I couldn't find either him or Britney anywhere. So I followed the hint of familiar voices and walked in on them fucking in a fitting room with her bridesmaid dress around her hips.

If they wanted to completely destroy me in three seconds flat, they'd found a good way to do it.

I've always prided myself on being strong. Practical and no-nonsense, to balance my creative flights of fancy.

But that day something fragile and emotional inside me shattered, some precious thing I'd trusted to Eddy to hold.

He'd crushed it like a playground bully swinging a baseball bat at a ladybug.

And then he'd shown up today and used the sharp jagged fragments to try to cut me *again*.

All because the selfish prick can't stand losing.

All because he never learned to take no for an answer.

All because it's too big a blow to his ego.

That had to be part of the thrill, for him, the day he was busted – playing this risky game of getting caught, convinced he could manage both Britney and me in the same building, with no one the wiser.

It's strange how clearly I can see him now.

I don't know why I *ever* fell for his flat, false, too-smooth face. Why I thought he was someone he wasn't. Why I believed I loved him, when I know now I can do so much better.

Not that the man sitting quietly behind the steering wheel is any sane option for *better*, but...I can't deny one thing.

If my heart sank at the sight of Eddy, it nearly floated to the moon when Warren called me *his girl*.

I'm not crazy. I know it was just a heat of the moment thing meant to scare Eddy off, but it made me realize my feelings are way more conflicted than I thought.

I can't dwell on them right now, though. I'm not going to lie, I'm down in a dark place, and when Warren pulls the truck up near our cabin and we get out, the first thing I do is tell Tara to go up to the main house and see if Ms. Wilma needs some help with her crocheting.

It's better right now. Better for everyone.

She keeps giving me these mournful little looks that tell me her ten-year-old head is too conscious about how I'm feeling. I don't want the awful way I feel to rub off on her and bring her down. She's too young, might end up imprinting something she'll carry forever and that's hardly fair.

Eddy already did enough damage to me.

I *won't* let that damage spill over onto her.

Tara's the happiest little girl I've ever known, and if I have anything to say about it, that's how it'll stay.

But Warren's almost *hovering* as we mount the steps. Rather than going for his door, he gives me a worried look.

"Can I come in, Hay?"

Honest to God, I don't know.

I frown, looking up at him. I still can't believe he did that, fighting like he did.

I don't even know how he knew where to find me, but I can hazard a guess, and that guess involves pigtails. "Why?"

"Because." He flexes his hands, shaking his head once, that wild crop of dark hair teasing across stern brows that just don't look as severe as usual. Not when he's looking at me like I might break. "Because there's no fucking way you should be alone right now."

"Keep thine enemies close," I murmur wryly, but right now...he doesn't feel like the enemy.

He hasn't for a while.

Feels more like a man who keeps trying to save me, over and over again.

Granted, sometimes I don't need saving.

But today? I think he may have just rescued me from more hurt than I can stand to deal with right now.

I toss my head to him and step inside. He follows, and when I sink on the couch, he settles down just close enough for me to feel his body heat and catch the dark, earthy comfort of his scent, reaching out as if he'd wrap me up again in comfort. Like that smell alone can create a wall of safety between me and the world.

I don't know what to say now that we're both sitting here like this, awkwardly silent. So I stare down at my hands, working them together in my lap before curling them over my kneecap.

"So," he says tentatively.

"So?" I answer.

"How you feeling?"

I smile bitterly. "Like roadkill. Even worse...like an idiot."

Warren watches me thoughtfully. The usual fierce crackle is gone from his eyes, replaced by a gentle, softer warmth I'd never expected to see. Not with the way we clash and crash and rip at each other.

"You're not an idiot, Hay," he promises. "An idiot's what a piece of shit like him deserves, and he's *not* having you."

The low, possessive growl in his throat makes me shudder.

"I just..." I shake my head, scrubbing the heel of my palm against one eye, *daring* it to start to water when it's already hot and burning dry. "That was him. That was the real Eddy. And I feel like I've never seen him until today. I don't know how I got pulled in by that mask so easily, but I should've been smarter. I really shouldn't have been so *stupid,* building this fantasy life and imaginary future like it was real, when he was just playing all along."

Warren says nothing, at first.

I risk glancing at him.

He's holding one broad, weathered hand out, just offering it to me quietly.

Oh, God. I wonder how many times my heart can break in one day.

Once, from betrayal. Twice, from kindness.

I bite my lip, then slip my hand into his, enjoying that calloused warmth enveloping my fingers in sheltering closeness, making the chambers of my heart contract. It's like every door leading into my vulnerable place tries to slam shut on what these feelings mean.

"Hay, listen to me good," Warren says firmly. "Nothing that happened with that prick is your fault. If he played you, it's because he made a choice to play you. Not because you did something wrong by not preventing it. He's a con man of the worst kind. Sold you a fucked up lie he wanted you to believe, and it's his fault that the lie turned into a game."

"But..." It's too much, and I try to cut him off. Before the tears come.

"Listen, darlin'. There's no crime in loving someone. Never, ever. You loved who you thought he was, the idea of Eddy. It's not your fault he spat on that and turned your love into a lie."

My throat goes horribly, painfully tight. I swallow hard, clutching at his hand, an anchor, something to ground me. *Don't cry, don't cry...*

"Did I really love *him?*" I whisper with a sniff. "Or was it an ideal? All the stuff I'm supposed to want out of life? A husband. A home. Kids..."

My lips are trembling. It's a hard, horrible realization to deal with.

Not just that my fiancé never loved me. Maybe I didn't love him, either.

I accepted him, or who I thought he was, because he was what good sense said I should want in a man.

Someone stable and charming and from a good family. Someone who'd marry an insurance adjuster but who wouldn't look twice at a full-time artist, and who'd just laugh off his wife's 'harmless little hobby.'" Just as long as I kept painting in between pumping out babies after my inevitable career retirement. Just as long as I took care of our family, our home, while he was off screwing his eighth secretary.

That's what I'd been headed toward. Suicide by a love that wasn't even real.

Killing the only part of me that feels real. Killing my dreams for a mirage. All because I was too focused on the destination and not who I'd been about to take the journey with.

The art, the creation inside me is a tempest, a firestorm, a hurricane of colors and emotion.

And I was going to hang that up to marry a man who'd fuck my best friend in a fitting room.

That's the real shame I'm feeling.

And suddenly that dam inside me shatters. I try to hold in the keening sound in the back of my throat, but it's just not working.

I curl forward with a harsh sob, my eyes bursting, running over with hot tears. Pulling my hand back from Warren's, I just want to wrap up in myself until I can make this *stop*.

Only trouble is, he's not having it.

I don't expect the hard body that envelops me, shielding me in *Warren Ford*, as if he can use his massive bulk to shield me from my own feelings.

"Haley." He says my name so softly, so fiercely, a sand-paper growl grinding through my bones.

With soft, coaxing, soothing sounds, he draws me into him, and I let him.

He feels *good*, and not just because he's ripped and gorgeous and all this slinking sinew under my palms as I press in and clutch at his shoulders.

It's because he's warm. Because he's human. Because underneath that constant grouch-cloud following him around everywhere is a decent man.

A kind, thoughtful man who may wear the mask of an

asshole, who may be into craziness I can't even wrap my head around, but who uses it to hide his own gentleness.

That's what makes him gather me into his lap now and hold on while I cry myself out.

"Warren, I..."

I don't even know. Because it's on me like a force of nature.

I never really had that big fuck-you cry over the dead engagement and the betrayal.

This hits me like that – the catharsis I need to set this aside to become a memory so I can truly pick up and move *forward.*

"You're good," he rumbles, pulling me even deeper into his grip. "Long as I've got you, you're safe. You're good. You're free."

Oh, sweet Jesus, he has no idea.

I fall to pieces. It feels like I cry for an hour. The whole time, Warren holds me patiently, keeping me close, saying soft things I can't quite understand. But the steady murmur of his voice lulls me until I no longer feel like I'm shaking apart with every deep, rasping sob.

And as I gradually fall silent, huddled against him, scrubbing at my eyes, he asks, "Better?"

"Better," I answer hesitantly, pillowing my head to his shoulder. "I'm sorry. This must seem ridiculous."

"No apologies, Hay. You heard me the first time." He gives me a warm, gentle squeeze. "You get to feel whatever the fuck you want right now, and it's okay."

Maybe he's right, I realize.

He's not just saying it. Actions speak louder than words, or so they always say.

He's *here* for me. Here, in all his big, inked, rock hard flesh.

So I tilt my head back, looking up at him, studying the

stark line of his jaw and the clean cut of his bearded profile, that hint of mountain roughness that makes him seem like a wild animal.

I bite my lip. "Thanks, Warren. I won't forget this."

He turns his head, looking down at me with a small smile.

"No thanking me, either," he teases softly. "I'm only doing this to get rid of my karmic debt."

"Nice try, Mister. I forgive you, but I think you'd have to save ten more orphans to smooth things over with the gods," I throw back, feeling a smile peeking past my own dreary clouds.

He answers with a grin that lights up his eyes. "I saved a stray. Make that nine more orphans, Hay."

"What worries me is, I'm not sure if you're talking about Mozart, or me."

"Considering half the time you're madder than a wet cat in a bag–"

"*Hey.*" Chuckling, I shove lightly at his chest. "...you're not wrong, though. I've just...I've been trying not to be so angry, but it's *hard*. It's like the whole world decided to take a dump on me all at once, so yeah, I'm pissed. At Eddy, at ex-bestie, at the suits who gave me my pink slip, at the gallery owner, at the people who looked at my paintings and just never cared." I make a frustrated sound in the back of my throat, knowing I sound way too much like the entitled artist. God. "But...none of them care if I'm angry at them. They barely remember I exist. So it feels pointless, and yeah, I wind up being mad at *everyone*. And it's useless. It's all so pointless."

"Not pointless." Warren squeezes me again. His big, strong arm around me makes me feel safer, more secure, after I've felt adrift for days. "We get pissed for good reason, Hay. A lot of times, anger is the thing we need most to keep us moving forward in the face of shit that'd make us shut down, give up, and freeze. It's just important to know when your anger's useful, and when it's hurting you so much that it's time to let go."

He makes sense. Far more sense than I want to admit.

If everything hadn't made me so angry, I might not even be here in Heart's Edge.

I might've just gone slumming over to my sister's and curled up in her guest room and refused to function for a few months. Instead, I decided to pack up and hit reset on my life.

And sure, everything's gone catastrophically wrong since then, and I'm semi-stranded in some backwater mountain town flashing cleavage for enough tips to truly start my new life in Chicago, but it's not all bad.

I'm not stagnating. I'm in control. And I'm kinda having fun.

Looking up at Warren, I know something else – the scenery here in Heart's Edge isn't close to half bad.

So maybe, just maybe...I'm ready to stop being angry, too.

"So if it's time to let go of being mad," I ask carefully, "what then?"

"Then?" He exhales slowly. "You figure out what you want to feel. What needs to happen for that to be real."

I don't know what that is. Mostly, I think what I want to feel is just happy. Hopeful.

Like if I keep forging on, there's something good waiting for me on the other side.

It's not so hard to believe it right now with Warren holding me and a bit of the ache in my heart soothed. Even if I despised seeing Eddy today, it was the closure I needed.

Deep down, some part of me was convinced I'd done something wrong to drive Eddy into Britney's arms. That maybe I'd deserved both of them being such two-faced shits.

But I can feel it in my heart now.

I didn't do anything wrong. I didn't deserve it.

I don't have to carry the pain they gave me because that's just letting them win.

And the reason I know is thanks to this huge, handsome complication staring down at me.

I can't help smiling at him. Warren cocks his head. "I like this look better, Hay. That smile you're wearing?"

Suddenly, he puts his fingers to his lips and lets out a wolf whistle. I burst out laughing, slapping playfully at his chest.

"Mama, lock your boys up –"

"C'mon!" I whack his pecs again, this time a little harder. "You're being ridiculous."

"Nah. We've got a live one here. She's beautiful and *happy*."

I shake my head. "Just thinking through some things. Working my way to a better place."

"Good," he rumbles warmly, giving me another squeeze.

I can't help leaning into him. He makes everything stable just now.

"Hey," I murmur.

"Hm?"

"You know, I really didn't give you a fair shake from the start. I just want to say I'm sorry for that."

He lets out an easy, warm chuckle, gentle and not in the slightest bit mocking. "You serious, Hay? The first time we met, I grabbed you and started barking shit at you."

I crack a grin. "Okay, fair."

"And you hit me with a purse."

"You *earned* it," I squeal, poking a finger into his side.

"Yeah, maybe I did." He shakes his head with an amused sound. "Point is, we got off on the wrong foot in all the wrong ways. We've had a few cease-fires since then, but–"

"Not a real truce," I finish.

"Right." He tilts his head, fixing those deep blue eyes on

me. "What do you say we change that today? If you're with me, if you're ready..."

His hold on me shifts, gathering me closer, my thigh sandwiched against the powerful bunch of muscle in his leg. *Oh, wow.*

My body fits against his hip, his side, all too well.

Fits in a way that curls warmth deep inside me and makes me think of far more than just waving the white flag of peace. And when he holds his free hand out to me, I nearly shudder.

Because the thought of touching him is *doing* things to me, giving me wicked and dark and crazy ideas.

"I'm calling truce," he says. "You game?"

I know what he's asking.

If we can start over. If we can try to be friends. If we can see each other as people, but I think it's already too late for that.

I've stopped seeing him as a complete nuclear asshole for some time and started seeing him as someone who makes my days here in Heart's Edge worth it.

Someone who only makes me so angry because it frustrates me how strongly I react to him, how easy it is for this strange man to make me laugh or hurt. How being so *vulnerable* to someone again terrifies me.

Terrifies me, but deep down, I kinda like the thrill.

And it's the thrill pushing me to do something crazy. Something wild.

Something I've wanted to do since he kissed me.

"Hay?" he whispers my name again, his eyes searching mine.

So I lean closer, slipping my hand into his. "I'm with you," I whisper. "I'm with you all the way, Warren."

Then I push myself up, sliding my body against his, and kiss him like the world just flipped upside down.

He's still for only a second, lost in a startled breath where I think he might push me away, laugh it off, tell me *no, that's not what I meant...*

Then suddenly he decides.

There's nothing but him and me and crashing together as he kisses me back, as he slants his mouth hard against mine with a groan that sounds almost pained, like a beast breaking off its leash.

Searing, wild, furious, he takes over my mouth and leaves no doubt who's in control here, even if I started it.

I'm breathless, swept away as he bruises my mouth with a kiss that's all violence and sweetness and everything I need to feel like myself again.

To feel like a living, breathing woman and not some grieving, tattered castaway on the shores of my own life.

I don't know how I end up straddling him, his body pushing my thighs apart until I'm open for him.

There's just his endless strength against me, under me, and then his hands clutching hard at my ass.

He pulls me down into him as he savages me with a deepening kiss. Every time his tongue chases mine, I feel it in the wettest depths of my pussy.

Like he's already slipped inside my depths when he's barely laid a hand on me.

It doesn't help that he's so damn hard against me.

His cock rubs between my thighs, dragging against my shorts, already throbbing.

That mad, mad pulse in his hard-on does some *wild* things to my bloodstream. Just knowing I can do that to him with one sharp, hungry kiss.

I can make him want me, as much as the heat in my blood craves him.

He breaks his kiss off, pressing his forehead to mine, snarling half breaths. "Fuck. Fuck, Hay."

Those thick fingers kneading my ass nearly make me come right there.

He digs in hard, pulls me down harder against him. His friction and rhythm move me head-to-toe, my breasts caught heavy between us and my nipples aching against my tank top as they drag against his chest.

It's like full-body foreplay with contact and caresses.

Every inch of his muscular frame stroking over me. Every curve of my body sliding against his until I feel sparks shooting everywhere. And those sparks rouse into flames as he nips my mouth, teases his way inside, curls his hands against the back of my neck and fists my hair and draws me in *deep*.

"Warren," I gasp, raking my hands down his chest, catching his shirt, tugging it.

God.

I want *skin*. I want his tempered bronze, writhing muscle and wild ink hot against my palms, and he shudders under me like some huge machine with its engines grinding into overdrive.

"Fuck," he whispers on my lips, settling his hands on my hips, holding me still when all I want to do is rock against his bulge until something inside me finally snaps. "You want me in you, Hay?"

My mouth goes dry, but I can't deny it.

I break back from his lips, looking down at him, then nod slowly, breathing out a shy but completely certain "*Yes*."

The way he looks at me then...holy hell.

It's like he's never seen me before, not fully, but what he sees now holds him spellbound.

I'm almost worried with the deep intensity of it, the way he seems to take me in.

But then I'm torn from that trembling moment when Warren abruptly heaves under me. And I squeak as his arms come around me, lifting me up against his chest as he stands, caging me inside all his broad muscle.

I'm safe and sheltered and burning apart as he carries me from the living room.

We barely make it into the bedroom before the frenzy comes.

Him tearing at my clothes. Ripping away my tank top.

My bare breasts spill free, aching to the touch, my skin so *sensitive* I cry out and toss my head to one side as he skims his fingers over their curves and traces patterns against my skin. He's so heavy over me, this dark thing blocking out the light and capturing me in his shadow, making me his prisoner.

Making me a prisoner, too, to the raw sensations rushing through me.

Warren slowly circles his fingertip over one nipple, then the other, the rough texture of his finger painting heat against my skin and making me writhe, sliding my thighs together.

I'm already so wet for him, so desperate, and I want to beg – but I can't find my voice to do anything but gasp, whimper, and moan as he gives me the barest taste of what I'm craving.

I'm almost too ready for it when he slides down my body.

My stomach quivers with the rasp of his beard on my skin and the sweet press of his lips below my navel. He's quick to strip my shorts away, even quicker to toss my panties aside – yet there's a moment as his fingers slide down, feeling how wet they are.

His eyes kindle bright, sparking and knowing, and he smiles slowly as he presses his mouth to the damp spot, breathes in, eyes narrowing, before he tosses the scrap of fabric aside to leave me naked for him.

Open to his every assault.

I've never felt so conquered by a gentle touch.

My body responds like lightning to the slightest graze of his fingers against my folds, the lightest trace of his thumb against the throbbing heat of my clit, the softest caress of a searching, knowing tongue.

I'm electric and he's the wire. Guiding, shaping, owning.

He torments me, rocks me, crashes me in waves of deep pleasure that strike me so hard it hurts.

They make me shake and quiver and roll.

I have no shame. None whatsoever as I spread my thighs and let him stroke me, taste me, lick and swirl and caress with the rough flat of his tongue.

Then I'm just gone, a mess of shaking legs and shallow breath.

His tongue comes faster, thrusting up inside me, giving that empty ache in my cunt some relief, that feeling that begs for something *more*.

I can't take much more.

I can't.

Between his tracing, relentless tongue and his slow-thrusting, thick, coarse fingers, I'm a mess, dripping, curling my toes against the sheets, digging my fingers in his hair.

I'm already lost to myself and the world as I arch my back, sucking in my stomach, trying not to spontaneously combust.

Is that a thing? Can sex be so powerful it turns a person into a little pile of ash?

With him, it's a big fat *maybe.*

And when he stops...when Warren stops as I'm *right-on-the-edge,* I almost break like never before and beg him to fuck me.

He's right there with me, watching with smoldering eyes as he unzips his jeans, baring his cock.

Soon there's a new reason to gasp.

Huge is a glaring understatement. What he's holding is thick, hard, dense. A line of pearl leaks out the tip onto his palm, and I only have a moment to glimpse it before he rubs the slick, flared head against my folds.

"Pill, darlin'?"

"Wh-what?" I can't even think, much less form sentences.

"You on the pill or something, or do I break out a damn rubber?" The *damn rubber* part sounds more like something he spat.

"Yeah. I'm good. We're good. Warren...*please.*"

Relief fills his eyes. He bends down, burying me in another sultry kiss, the heat of his cock returning to my labia, my wetness, my clit.

"Good. Now I'm gonna fuck you so hard you forget Eddy Fuckface ever existed." His growl is a promise.

A second later, his dick drives deeper, parting me, spreading me open, making me jerk with the sudden sharp feeling of heated flesh stroking me from the inside out.

Holyyy hell. Here we go.

I press my knuckles to my mouth, biting back a whimper.

It's nothing compared to the cry that builds in my throat as he nudges into me, slipping the very first inch of his cock inside, stretching me open in a way I've never been stretched before.

I'm coming unglued, floating in the sweet madness of this, and I reach for him.

He comes to me so willingly, enveloping me in his arms, making me *safe.*

Making me *his.*

There's no mistake as he captures my mouth again, kisses me deeper, draws me into him until there's Warren Ford and nothing else.

He slides deeper, reshaping my body to fit his, showing me pleasure unlike anything I've ever known.

It's not something he's doing to me.

It's not something I'm riding through alone.

It's *us*. Him and me.

Together, moving as one, as he surges slow and deep, kissing me with a rapt and wondering reverence, turning all the violence and wildness between us into something sacred and hot and so flipping *total*.

My body feels like an extension of his, and his like part of mine. And I give myself up to him completely as this beautiful, wild beast-man arches and gives me all of his strength, his back shuddering under my fingers.

It shouldn't feel like this with a near-stranger. Sparks shouldn't become entire galaxies. We shouldn't be gasping together, arms and legs entangled, my ass pressed deep into the mattress as his thrusts bury me alive.

But Warren's more to me than a stranger. More than a chain of crazy, incredible, pussy-claiming thrusts.

And as he pushes me harder, higher, deeper, I just know I'm going to fall so hard.

Eddy? Did he even exist?

I barely remember his name as I gasp out "Warren!"

Then I clutch around him, cracking apart in shotgun bursts of white light and hot tension and flooding sweetness.

His pubic bone grinds my clit as he sends me over the edge; a screaming, clutching, breathless mess too on fire to even call his name again.

Coming!

It's like a full body lick. It's like a pillow of fire, a bead in my brain, an electric hum that starts in my pussy and explodes up the long, singed fuses of my nerves.

I'm coming with a sweetness and an insanity I never even knew. And it doesn't stop as his hips pick up, thrusting even harder, testing the entire bed.

I halfway wonder if we'll go crashing right through the

floor as my thighs tense again. My nails dig into his back and my teeth hit my lip.

Holy hell doesn't work anymore. More like *holy freaking Warren.*

"Goddamn, darlin'. Don't you stop. Not till I fill that sweet little pussy up."

I'm clenching so hard I could break, hugging his thrusting, manic thickness. It brings us off together, a roar exploding up his throat, then a scorching wave of fire pumping in my depths.

All his seed. All his flame. All him, him, beautifully *him.*

God, this was reckless. This was impulsive. This was probably the worst thing I could've done when I'm so fragile, so confused, so vulnerable.

And I don't regret it one bit, even as he holds himself in me for what seems like forever, spilling every last bit until I overflow with our slick, steaming heat.

I take his slow, hungry tongue again and savor every second of him falling apart, trembling and snarling and stealing new moans from my lips with deep, thrusting kisses.

We're such broken, pent-up people, but this time is different.

This time we break *together.*

XII: TAKING OVER (WARREN)

*O*f all the bad decisions I've ever made in my life, this has to be the worst.

And I don't regret it in the slightest.

I definitely don't regret fucking her three more times till we have to stop before our hearts give out.

Hay comes so many times I've lost track, the last time with her bent over, her hair in my fist, my hand crashing against her ass as she engulfs my cock, sucking my balls damn near dry.

Fuck.

Now she's soft and warm against me, tucked against my body with her curves practically flowing into me to fill all the spaces and hollows in my body. I can still feel that throbbing warmth inside her, even though we've disentangled to curl into each other and my cock is spent and sore. Can't forget the way she shivered under me, held fast to me, the burn of her nails still in my back.

Hell, I haven't had sex like that in...*ever?*

It's a wild possibility.

And what's got me fucked up is how deep this feeling is

inside me. Like if I let it, this could turn into something. Me, her, I don't know what.

But goddamn does she make me feel *everything* in spades.

Anger, passion, possessiveness.

Desire. Warmth. Laughter.

Even when she's pissing me off, she just soothes something inside me, because she's *like* me. All temper and wildcat fury until she calms down and then it's just steadiness and strength.

That's what I admire so much about her, I think.

She's *strong*.

So damn determined to take care of Tara, herself, and everybody else.

And that just makes me want to protect her that much more.

From the world. From her past. From all the harsh bullshit life hacks up.

But most of all, from that chicken-necked weasel ex of hers.

I don't know how anyone could ever claim to love Haley and then treat her the way that jackhole did. It's proof enough he never loved her at all.

His loss.

And if I see him in Heart's Edge again, I'm going to show him some *love* by throwing him right off our namesake cliff. If flowers going over it will keep you together forever, who the hell knows what a blood offering might do?

I can't help chuckling to myself.

I'm being damn ridiculous, deep in full caveman mode, I know.

Against me, Hay stirs with a drowsy murmur. "Mm? What's so funny?"

"I was just thinking about your ex."

"Well...he is pretty laughable."

"Yeah. But I was picturing the look on his face when I toss him over the cliff and make a wish—and then I realized I'm being a chest-thumping ape."

She lets out a short, startled burst of laughter, and instead of me thumping my chest, it's her small hand that thuds down lightly between my pecs. "I think you scared him enough. You got his suit dirty, that's pretty much like a punch to the face for him. You don't need to go to jail for murder."

"No? Well, ma'am, if you insist..."

"Oh, don't even *pretend* to have noble intentions now. You're not some knight in shining armor, Warren. You may have screwed my brains out, but I didn't lose any IQ points." She lifts her head from my shoulder, propping her chin against it instead so she can look at me with her eyes glimmering bright through her soft tangle of dark brown sex hair. "We've got to be sensible. Even if you did come charging to the rescue..."

I shrug. "Tara was upset. Can't ignore a lady in distress."

"Oh, *I* get it now. You did that for my niece. Not for me. Totally."

Her saucy grin is irresistible, and I lean in to steal a taste, kissing her lightly. "I did it because if I tried to do it just for you, you'd take my balls off. Least Tara gives you a safe buffer that lets you accept help without *really* accepting it."

Haley blinks, going oddly quiet, her smile fading. "Am I that easy to figure out?"

"Maybe to someone who's just like you," I say. It's harder than I want to admit to get these words out. To just calmly package up these old pieces of myself into words and give them to someone else like it's nothing. "My sister and I grew up without parents. It was just us and Grandma...a single older woman with two kids on her hands, trying to start a business in a backwoods town. She would've given *anything* for us, but we didn't want to make her. So we tried to need as little as possible, so we wouldn't be a burden."

Eyes misting, Haley smiles slightly. "Sounds familiar. My sister and I are kinda like that too. But I don't think Wilma would ever consider you a burden."

"Maybe not. Still, so kind that we didn't want to take too much from her. Grandma was all we had."

"If it's okay to ask...what happened to your parents?"

"We don't know." I turn my head against the pillow to fully face her, until our words fill the small space between us to make this thread of whispers, connecting us. "They went on a road trip one day and never came back. No one ever found their car. Police never turned up a glimpse of them. Maybe they drove over a ravine. Maybe they started a new life somewhere else. Maybe they just vanished into nothing."

My chest aches. It's been more than a decade since I told anybody that story.

Damn.

I'd never really thought of myself as anybody with abandonment issues. My parents are just hazy figures. I can't even remember their faces. I was only four when they disappeared.

My mother, I remember as a tumble of black hair spilling down over me and a scent of lilacs.

My father, the scratch of his stubble and the way his hands were so strong. When he picked me up, he always held a little too tight without meaning to, but I didn't mind because it meant he had me.

Then Grandma eclipsed all of that. This flood of light and the yellow of the daffodils always in the vase in the front foyer, the silver of her hair and the kindness of her smile, the sharp wit in her eyes and the way she touches *everything* – from a simple curtain to a clinging, frightened grandchild – with such utter, pure love.

She's all I've ever needed for family. Her and Jenna.

Fuck, no wonder it hurts to think of my parents leaving after all this time. It's the same, really.

Jenna left, too.

And I won't have Grandma forever. Her thinking about retirement, getting the inn mixed up with asshole Bress, is one more reminder.

What'll happen then?

Who will I call family once she's gone?

Is a man like me even fit to have his own?

I'm pulled from my blank, circling thoughts by Haley's fingers. She brushes them gently to my temple, then slowly traces backward to my hairline, as if she's exploring me. Mapping me.

And as her fingers slip into my hair, her weaving it in soft, delicate touches and strokes down to the scalp, I close my eyes. That hard, fucked up knot in my chest loosens like she's taming the most savage of beasts with a sweetness I'd never have guessed underneath that hellion's fire.

"I'm sorry," she whispers. "Sorry you've had to live with so many unanswered questions your entire life."

"It's not the only one. Or even the worst. I've learned to deal, Hay." I turn my head to brush my cheek against her wrist, the faint flutter of her pulse moving against my skin. "Shit, sorry. This is a little heavy for pillow talk."

"It's okay. I get it." There's a smile in her voice that I don't need to open my eyes to see. "At least now I know we're really not that different."

"Yeah?"

"Yeah. My mom didn't exactly abandon me...but it felt like that when she died. Leukemia. I was so mad at her for leaving me and my sister alone with *him.* It took a long time to stop hating her for something that was out of her control."

That *him,* the soft crack in her voice, prompts me to open

one eye, watching how the hazed shadows of afternoon fall over her face through the blinds, dwelling in her eyes. "Him?"

"Our father," she answers bitterly. "The alcoholic."

"Oh." Then it clicks – *oh, shit.* "Is that why you seem so uncomfortable around Flynn?"

"Mr. Bitters?" She shrugs, her whole body moving soft and slow against me. "A little, maybe. I just can't look at him and feel much contempt like most people do with alcoholics. It's a disease, and it's one that hurts them so much...but it doesn't change the fact a lot of alcoholics hurt people, too. So, yeah, I get all mixed up. Sympathy and resentment and confusion. Whether I ever loved my dad or hated him."

That protective anger for her returns, bubbling in my blood, but I yank on its leash as hard as I can and try to keep my voice neutral. "Did he hurt you, Hay?"

She's quiet for a long time. Almost too long.

And then she bows her head, pressing her brow to my shoulder, her hair hiding hers, her voice small and muffled.

"Sometimes," is the only word she'll say. I can't stop myself.

Wrapping both arms around her tight, I sweep her into me, shifting my body like I can shield her from past demons if I just use my bulk to take the blow. Every dose of reckless pain she's ever felt.

"Sorry," I say. "No man should ever do that shit. Not to his daughter, not to anyone."

"It's fine," she whispers against me, still trembling. "I learned to survive. So did Marie. We...we learned to fend for ourselves, even if sometimes it meant leaving the other person to take care of herself. We *had* to. We couldn't both go down when one of us could be saved."

I inhale slowly, trying not to let my hands form fists. Not that they'd do any good on a dead man.

"Dad was a cop who knew people, so protective services

never showed up. No matter how many teachers we confessed to, or how many anonymous tips were called in. We just learned not to ask for help because it never seemed to come."

"Doesn't mean you didn't deserve help, Hay. That you don't deserve help now." I'm about to explode with the depth of feeling rushing through me right now. This wild, over-whelming need to just make everything perfect for her, give her everything she could ever need to be happy, safe, and alive.

I'm burning with it. Scared I'll scorch the woman in my arms into ash with the coarseness racing through my veins.

"Warren?" She looks up at me.

"It's all right to need help, Hay. That's why people have friends, lovers, families. So we can all lean on each other. Pull together when it's too damn hard to do the pulling alone."

"Yeah?" she whispers, and her small arms creep around me, her hands curling against my back, clutching for dear life. "Who do you lean on, then?"

"Don't really know," I admit. "I don't. Still trying to figure that out, maybe."

Hay lifts her head, looking up at me with red-rimmed, glimmering eyes, still too proud to let out those tears she'd spent earlier, holding her smile bravely. "I'd say you could lean on me...but you won't tell me why you need to, will you? I *know*. Because you're trying to protect me from the dangers of Heart's Edge."

It's not Heart's Edge that's dangerous.

It's Haley.

Because that smile, that soft and hinted plea for me to lean on her, to let her be something to me is too rare. Too precious.

Fuck, she could destroy me with the slightest touch.

Far more easily than Dennis Bress ever could.

I don't have answers for her. Not one that'll satisfy this ache in my heart that wants to let her in but won't endanger her. Not one that'll ease the pained look in her eyes.

So I give her one thing right now – the promise of forget-fulness. A sweet distraction that lets both of us stop thinking about old pains and just live in the now, the moment, the pleasure of her body with mine.

I kiss her like it's gonna be the last.

And as I slowly ease her back down to the bed, savoring how small and lush and supple her body is under mine, I try to show her with every touch that it's not *her* I'm shutting out.

Not by half.

I touch her like I'm engraving myself on her skin and branding her on me.

Like I can somehow ease the thorns, making this new thing between us both painful and wonderful, the agony of every prick bleeding with pleasure.

It's pure torture, watching how her glistening lips part as I kiss and bite and lick her jaw, her throat, trailing her pulse with my mouth.

I chase it right down her body to her smooth, curving shoulders, her delicate collarbones, her lush, full breasts.

The taste of her skin is better than any black label booze.

I drug myself on her, making myself dizzy sucking sweat off her skin, caressing the texture of her nipples with my lips, my tongue. It burns damn hot inside me.

Then she arches for me, threading her fingers in my hair, holding fast to me like I'm the only thing in the world anchoring her – and I can't hold back.

Can't hold back from *needing* her all over again so soon.

Even if my cock hurts from strain, I don't care, dammit.

Wanting Haley is pain, and I'll take every last stab aching

NICOLE SNOW

through me as my body throbs for her, craving that soft, pink sweetness inside her.

My face moves between her legs. I'm on her clit, this time no teasing, just raw focus on bringing her off.

Making her forget. Making us both fucking lost in our haze.

She whimpers pure sugar, dragging her nails through my hair. I pull her legs in, bringing her fully to my face, and then I'm all teeth and tongue and feasting madness.

I could eat this pussy for days.

Days.

Too damn bad she comes like a rocket in a couple minutes, her ass moving on the bed, flames hitched in her lungs, a breathless *scream* ripping out her ruby lips as I suck her clit to heaven.

Yeah, darlin', right the fuck like that.

Come for me.

I spend another minute savoring her taste after she's able to open her eyes and come back to me. All I can stand before I have to be in her.

Her legs part, and I take my sweet time aligning my dick to take her again. I've unloaded in her three times and I'm still hard as a brick. *Fuck.*

If that isn't something special, then I don't even know.

I love how she cries out as I slip into the welcoming heat of her pussy, gliding on a yielding wetness and gripping, pulsing flesh. Her heat sucks me off, right down to my balls, sending a vicious kiss up my spine.

"Shit, darlin'. You're gonna kill me with this pussy," I say, barely an understatement. Right before my words melt into growls as I start to move.

Then we go *hard.*

Yet when I stop, slowing my thrusts, trying to prolong this addictive hellfire, she pulls me down, kisses me fiercely, her mouth wet and sweet underneath mine, her breaths coming harsh, slender hands cradling my cheeks.

Her thighs wrap around my hips, taut flesh gliding against me, binding me to my own damn senses.

Maybe she's a witch, and I'm completely fucking beguiled. Maybe this pussy feels like perfect sin on my cock because it's enchanted.

Whatever it is, my shoulders tense, and I can't stop myself from driving into her again and again, throwing everything I've got against her body.

It's not just about the pleasure, the mesmerizing heat gripping me tight, wringing me from my own head with a gasp.

It's about wanting to sear myself on her from the inside.

Claim her real deep.

It's insane. This can't be permanent. Can't be real. Can't be anything more than an impulse and a fling.

But Hay's already deep inside me, making me feel every tender, broken place in my heart that's been craving a gentle touch for too long. Craving to be *with* someone the way I'm with her now, so completely locked in focus, sweat dripping between us as I bury deeper, hotter, faster.

Fuck, I need to see her face. Need to see her lose control – and it's like she knows.

She tosses her head back, crying out my name again and again with the most beautifully lax expression of raw, captive ecstasy etched in her pretty features. I want to see her make that face again and again, want to hold out just a little longer, but I need to come more.

She pulls me in, draws me deeper.

I've got no control with this one.

A feeling like rushing lava wells up in my balls, bringing my pleasure to a head and turning me wild, monstrous, driven to extremes by her smallest touch and the sound of her voice.

I come so fucking hard it turns me inside out. She takes every drop.

Takes all of me, and I'm only left wishing for one thing.

I wish I could truly give her everything.

* * *

I HADN'T MEANT to fall asleep.

But Haley and I crash into each other like wrecking balls past noon, and I've been through days of military training that didn't wear me out as much as sex with that little firestorm in there.

It's evening by the time I wake up.

There's a text on my cellphone saying to let Hay know that Tara's fine, and Grandma made her dinner but don't forget to wake Haley up on time for the pub. I can't help a faint smile.

Grandma's treating her like family already.

Looking out for every little detail, minding the p's and q's.

It's like she's goddamn psychic.

It's still a couple of hours before Hay needs to get moving, and she looks so peaceful curled up in her bed. At some point while we were unconscious, she turned away from me, snuggling her back into my side.

Her pert little ass nudged up against my thigh, and her entire body curled around one of the pillows while her hair spills across the sheets. I can't help a grin.

Maybe the pillow was easier to tackle than me, when she can't even fit one of her slim arms fully across my chest. But it makes it easier to ease out of bed without waking her. I slip carefully off the mattress, then pull a sheet up to cover her so she'll be tucked in without sweating to death in the lingering evening heat.

I step into my jeans and hitch them up around my hips, then slip out onto the back porch and rest my elbows on the railing, looking out over the view.

Times like this remind me of when I used to have a free moment during deployment. I'd always slip off guard duty and find a quiet place to lean against a portable camp, or maybe just a rock, and have a smoke.

I haven't smoked since Jenna, but the low clouds slipping across the sky serve the same purpose. Their winding, wind-driven patterns draw me in the same way the slow curls of smoke used to, letting me blank out and ease my mind.

Night back then was always silence over desert sand. An endless quiet, one that sucked me in deep and blanketed out everything else.

It could be frightening, if you'd let it – but I always found it soothing, having just a few moments where, for once, things weren't trying to crawl inside my head and lay down roots.

The sounds of night sinking over Heart's Edge are almost as soothing, too.

Charming Inn is far enough from the main town that I can't hear cars in the streets or the rowdies already getting started at Brody's. Won't take long before light and music will be spilling out of open windows and doors with the carefree mood of people who either want to forget their troubles or have very few of them to start with.

Here, though, it's just the sound of crickets. The whisper of the wind fingering the tops of the trees, the occasional frog that wandered off a little too far from the creek down in the valley.

Small sounds of people, too. The other vacationers in the cabins making dinner or putting a movie on or calling home to tell their loved ones how much fun they're having in such a rustic little place.

I'd never thought Grandma would be able to make a backwater like our town into a tourist attraction, but it makes sense.

There's nothing special to attract people to Heart's Edge. No monuments or history or legends besides our little romance tale about the cliff. But when you spend your life surrounded by city stress where everything moves at a million miles an hour and there's always this gnawing anxiety over the smallest thing, it can be a relief to get away somewhere.

A place time moves at the speed of honey-gold afternoon sunlight and the only thing to do is take in the beauty and the silence.

For people facing deadly hypertension before they're thirty, a place like this is a *dream.*

Yeah. Yeah, I get it now.

I felt that way when I finally came back, too. Never mind the fact that I originally came home to finally settle the score with Bress.

Didn't matter. I felt like I'd come home.

Maybe I should stop using the house hunt for a cover and think about finding somewhere real.

I'm so sunk in my thoughts I don't hear the door opening behind me, or the soft footsteps creeping up.

I just feel the warmth as Hay presses her body into my back, something thin that feels like a t-shirt between us. It separates our body heat by the thinnest tissue-fine layer, doing nothing to stop my guts from igniting when her tits yield in soft curves against my shoulder blades.

"Hi," she whispers almost tentatively, laying her cheek against my spine.

It aches to hear the uncertainty in her voice, to feel it in the subtle tension in her touch, waiting to pull away at a moment's rejection. Like she thinks once the passion's over, our temporary truce might break and I'll tell her not to touch me, to get out, get away from me.

Not anymore. I can't fucking do it, even if a part of me says I should.

That scares me a little, but not enough to thrust her away.

So instead, I turn in the circle of her arms, leaning my hips against the railing, and wrap her up tight to haul her more firmly against my body, smiling down at her.

She goes soft instantly, her smile warming as she rests her chin against the peak of my ribs.

She still looks half asleep, my t-shirt falling off her tanned, freckled shoulder and her eyes drowsy and glimmering liquid-dark like leaves. The best green shade of summer I've ever seen. "You didn't wake me?"

"Looked like you needed the beauty rest, darlin'. Especially since you're due on shift and on your feet for another eight hours soon."

Haley laughs. "So you're tracking my work hours now?"

"Nah." I grin. "Grandma texted me that I'd better not let you oversleep."

Her eyes round. "Oh my God. How did she know I was with you?"

"I didn't think of that." Choking back a laugh, I clear my throat. "Maybe she was just asking me to be neighborly. She raised me to have manners like that, you know."

"I'd never be able to tell." With a half laugh, half groan, Hay thuds her forehead to my chest. "I don't...I didn't mean to..."

"I know," I say. "I know. It's okay, Hay. We did something we both wanted to, and I'm all right with it if you are."

"Yeah," she says softly, sighing and turning her head to rest her cheek to my chest, her half-lidded gaze drifting out across the sea of grass and sky and gently swaying trees. "I think I'm *more* than all right with it."

"So?"

"So...?"

Fuck. Why do I feel like a nervous schoolboy all of a sudden instead of a grown-ass man?

This tiny firestorm of a woman has me all tangled up. "How do you feel about doing this some more until you leave?"

She's quiet, but she doesn't tense. Doesn't tell me with her body language that she's upset or angry or rejecting the idea, or even scared. She's just thoughtful, and after a minute she licks her lips and says, "And by a few more times, you mean?"

"Whatever we want it to mean. A thing. For now."

"For now."

"Since you're not staying, I mean."

"I'm not?" she says tentatively, and my chest tightens like that's the only way to keep my heart from slamming right through it.

My arms tighten on her, then relax, and I take a deep, steadying breath. "What're you saying, Haley? You've got Chicago waiting. Soon as you've got your cash reserve replenished, you'll–"

"I'm saying I like it here, Warren. And it'll be a good long while before I save up enough money to start over again in a city that expensive. I don't have a free place to crash there. Crazy cost of living and all, so..." Her words are casual, but her voice is anything but.

It's hitching and soft and nervous. I can feel her heartbeat slamming against me, twin to mine, like we're two stiff statues who can't quite say the right thing. If we'd just let them, our hearts would break away from all our problems and crash together into something simple and bright. "So, yeah. I'll probably stay. For a while. Maybe a long while." She swallows audibly. "So if we had 'a thing' as you so eloquently call it..."

"Have," I correct sharply.

"Have?"

"We *have* a thing, Hay," I whisper.

Fuck, everything is chapped inside me, and I cup her face to kiss her, drawing her up into words that I print against her mouth as I draw her toward the door, the bed, another round of this furious, needy thing between us.

"We have a thing, beautiful. And I'm okay with it not having an end date."

XIII: PREGNANT SILENCE (HALEY)

*D*uring my entire shift at Brody's, I can't help thinking about what Warren said.

We have *a thing. And I'm okay with it not having an end date.*

Sweet Jesus.

I'm not even sure what he means. 'A thing' without an end date might mean anything in strange, growly mountain man speak.

Honestly? I'm not sure I want clarity.

Because I'm not the only one who's only in town temporarily.

With him bounty hunting whoever he's after, he'll probably finish his job here and move on when he's ready. Hell, it'll be funny if he leaves before I do, when I don't even belong here.

Do I?

Waitressing at Brody's isn't exactly a dream job. But it's fun and mindless and the people here *like* me.

They give me the social fix my extrovert half needs, which makes me feel at home in this little town that's nothing like Seattle or Chicago or anywhere I'd ever imagined living.

Plus, it leaves me free to have my life on my own terms with my paints and canvases every morning, my feet tired but my mind on fire and my soul at ease. Here in Heart's Edge, everything is simpler, with the exception of one hulking man.

Work doesn't leave me with a dozen deadlines hanging over my head like the office did. I can just walk away from Brody's without more burdens following me home and crushing my creative drive.

And it's weird to think that right now, as I sling drinks and wipe down tables and laugh with the regulars, that I'm actually looking forward to going *home*.

I can't wait to see the cabin and find Warren and Tara and Mozart waiting for me.

It's near dawn by the time I finish helping with cleanup and shutdown and pile myself and my sore, aching feet into the Mustang.

It's a picturesque place by day, but in the early morning darkness, there's something sweet and magical about it.

Here, it's one more lovely little house settled among its neighboring cabins with the stars winking out one by one overhead. The only light is the faint glimmer of lamps through a window here and there, like fireflies in the dark.

One of those lights is on in my cabin, and it guides me home like a beacon.

It's hard to keep a Mustang quiet, but I try just in case I'm waking Warren up.

I shouldn't worry. Before I left, I told him it was okay to treat my half of the cabin like his, and maybe deep down after that conversation this evening, I hoped he'd wait for me.

I'm not disappointed.

But when I ease the door open on the darkened living room, it's not his voice I hear between the heavenly smell of scrambled eggs and bacon and brewing tea. It's Ms. Wilma's, and she's murmuring soft things to Tara as she eases my niece down on the sofa and covers her with a blanket.

I tilt my head, blinking. Warren's in the kitchen in a grey denim *apron* of all things, making a cartoon caricature out of himself as he cooks with *exaggeratedly* quiet gestures. I smile, knowing how focused those thick fingers of his can be.

He looks up as I step in and grins, holding a finger to his lips, nodding toward Tara. Ms. Wilma straightens and smooths her skirt with a quick, warm smile for me.

"She woke up and said she wanted to come home to wait for you," she whispers. "I couldn't say no, dearie, but the little turnip was unconscious before I even got her here."

I wince. "Sorry if she woke you."

"Oh, don't be silly. I'd been up for half an hour already. We Fords are born early risers."

I bite back a laugh so I don't wake Tara. As I look at my niece sleeping snugly on the couch in her little pajama set with her hair pulled down from the pigtails, I can't help how my heart goes soft.

She doesn't even stir as a wobbly, still quite catnip-high Mozart scrambles up onto the couch and snuggles against her. His purr says it all.

I want to protect her from everything. My lips twist, wondering how the hard 'talks' Marie and John are having in Maui are going.

Whatever happens with them, she has to know she'll always have a family. To give her the shelter I never had as a little girl, and that my sister didn't have either.

I know Marie wants to keep Tara safe just as bad as I do, or my niece wouldn't be with me right now.

What Tara doesn't know is that this Hawaii trip really is

her parents' last-ditch effort to save their marriage. John may be a good guy, and Marie's my sister and I love her...but sometimes two people just don't work.

No matter how much they love each other or their daughter. They've been trying so hard to hide it from Tara, but I wonder if it's why Tara tries to be so bright.

She knows. Kids always do.

She knows, but she's trying so hard to make her family happy anyway.

I swallow the lump in my throat and settle down on the couch next to her, gently brushing her hair back.

"Thank you, Wilma," I murmur. "Tara really adores you, you know. Every day she always wants to show me new sketches she draws of your flowers. And the new types of crochet stitches you taught her? I think she's died and gone to heaven sometimes."

"Oh, I adore her too," Ms. Wilma answers with the brightest, warmest smile that makes me miss my mother, miss *someone* who would smile at me that way. "It's good to have little voices and little laughter around the house again."

At that, she throws a pointed look at Warren. He coughs in the back of his throat, ducking his head and suddenly focusing very, very intently on the skillet and the spatula in his hand.

I cover my mouth with my hand to hold back a giggle. This looks like a familiar exchange, but it warms me so much to be included.

It's only now that I realize I'm not used to the feeling of a nuclear family, these people who wait up for you to come home and make breakfast for you and look after your niece when you're at work.

The Fords aren't my family. Not really. I'm not even sure if, after one night and an uncertain promise, I can even call him my lover.

But they make me feel at home.

They make me realize, wherever I start over, I know what I want out of life.

This feeling. This carefree, wonderful feeling, like my art isn't an afterthought and my job isn't a dull time sink, and the people around me aren't just placeholders in what my life is supposed to look like.

As chaotic as this is, as crazy, as completely accidental, I could see a life that looks something like this.

The kind of family I never had. But the kind I want with a husband and children and room for my art.

A family of people who support each other, who reach for each other, instead of hunkering back behind their defenses, leaving everyone to fend for themselves.

It's not something I'd ever thought of before. It's not something I even thought I knew how to create, but now?

I want to try.

And I know I *can*.

I realize I'm watching Warren as these thoughts circle through my head. He glances up from the stove, catching my eye with an amused head tilt. I twitch, jerking my gaze away and coughing quietly into my hand, face hot.

Whatever I'm thinking about is for later. *For Chicago.*

This, right now, is like a practice run.

A trial without an expiration date.

That's all it is.

Sure.

When I look up again, Ms. Wilma is watching, her eyes gentle, her smile warm and knowing, as if she's picked up on my thoughts.

I can't hold her gaze, and I look away, tucking my hair back and pulling up the plunging neckline of my jersey, suddenly feeling too exposed in this tiny skirt with my cleavage hanging all out.

Ms. Wilma chuckles, leaning over to pat my knee, then straightens and turns toward the door.

"I'll be off," she says quietly. "Should count out the register and check today's arrivals on that ghastly Kayak site Flynn insists I use. Do come up to the house for dinner some time, though, Haley dear. I promise my cooking is far less...*coarse* than my grandson's."

"Hey!" Warren protests, then darts a guilty look at Tara and lowers his voice. "I've been cooking for myself for years."

"Yes," Ms. Wilma says dryly, folding her hands primly, "and that puts you ahead of ninety percent of the male species. But it simply doesn't change the fact that you cook like a soldier and you always have."

"I *am* a soldier," Warren retorts.

"Are you?" Ms. Wilma asks, quiet and pointed and suddenly so serious.

Warren quiets, his motions subdued.

He jerks his gaze to look out the window. "Don't," he murmurs. "Not here, Grandma. Not now. You just—"

"Know my grandson?" she finishes for him. "Yes, I do."

"If you know me so well, you know why I'm not happy," he bites off grudgingly.

"If you're so interested in my business affairs, you can either choose to get involved, or you can stay out, but last I checked, I had no need for an advisory council," she retorts firmly.

Dang. Even if I have no idea what the hell is going on...

This woman's got a core of steel I admire more than anything else.

And she's certainly got Warren in hand, because he says nothing other than a murmured "I'm sorry, ma'am" that she accepts with a tart nod.

Her fierce expression gentles, though, as she flashes me another warm smile, then turns to let herself out.

I hold my tongue until the door closes, then whistle softly under my breath. "That was something."

"That's my grandmother," Warren answers with a touch of cynical fondness. "I never know if she'll show up to find out what's up with the gossip about us or rake me over the coals for sticking my nose where it doesn't belong."

I blink. "There's gossip about us?"

"I kind of went caveman on your ex in the middle of a crowded diner, Hay." Warren snorts. "Yeah. There's gossip."

I smile sheepishly. "I suppose. But...what was that about her business affairs?"

Warren's shoulders tighten. I expect him to shut down, tell me to mind my own business again.

I don't need to know, it's too dangerous, the usual.

But after a few more scrapes of the spatula against the skillet, he mutters, "It's nothing. I'm keeping an eye on some people. They've got their hands in some pretty shady business, and Grandma doesn't see it. She's thinking of investing with them to keep the business afloat when she's ready to retire, so she doesn't have to outright sell Charming Inn or Brody's."

I don't have to be a genius to know that the person he's talking about is Bress, after the way Warren went after Flynn over keeping secrets from him on that front. It's making more sense.

After a few weeks in town, I've picked up that they have history but they don't speak anymore, mostly from Stewart, who stops by almost every night for a different kind of burger and a quick chat.

I try to be nice to him, but there's something about him that leaves me uncomfortable. He's too quick to play diplomat, not-so-subtly trying to diffuse this...whatever it is between Warren and Dennis.

He's not flirting with me. Not really, and I think maybe that's it, too.

He *acts* like he's flirting, but there's something too fake about it that makes me wish he wouldn't bother, especially if neither of us are interested. I don't need more fake in my life.

Still, he does give me juicy tidbits here and there, about how Bress and Warren were in the military together. Once, he mentioned *her*, and I don't know who *she* is, and he wouldn't give me a name, but I guess there's more than one reason why Warren came back to Heart's Edge.

There's no denying something's brewing between him and Bress. I'm worried about what will happen when it finally comes to a head.

If I push any more, though, I know Warren will cut me off the same way Ms. Wilma cut him off, so I just sigh, looking down at Tara and settling the blanket more securely over her.

She must be worn out, if the smell of breakfast hasn't even started to wake her up. I still feel bad she got caught in the middle of my mess with Eddy.

"Sounds like a tough decision for Wilma to make at all," I answer neutrally.

"Yeah," he says. "I guess. But if she ends up in bed with the wrong people, it'll end in heartbreak, sooner or later."

If that isn't apt, I don't know what is.

I'm not even sure who's going to get her heart broken for ending up in bed with the wrong person.

Ms. Wilma...or me.

* * *

I DOZE on the couch for a bit, before I'm woken up by a suddenly energetic Tara just in time for food to be ready.

She's like one of those old Tamagotchi pets that were

popular when I was a kid. You have to take care of her 24/7, but she's really only perky and active when you're around and paying attention to her, and when you hit her *on* switch, it's *go go go*.

And her pep tells me it'll be afternoon before I get to steal a proper sleep before my shift tonight, when she's managed to fill up her sketchbook with drawings and hell, now I'm out of two different shades of blue from trying to capture the hues of the Heart's Edge sky.

So after breakfast – Warren really is a good cook, no matter how Ms. Wilma teases – I kick him out to go help around the inn with some long-neglected repairs, then get myself and Tara cleaned up so we can go do some shopping at the feed-slash-art-supply store.

It's a little weird, still, that when I go inside, Ms. Thatcher greets me by name and tells me her daughter got in a new stock of these oil paints from a different supplier, and I might want to try them.

It makes me feel like I belong here.

Small town hospitality can really mess you up, I guess.

As I'm talking to Tara about her first sketchbook and what she did and didn't like about the paper texture so we can pick a better one this time, she pauses, frowning and tapping her finger against her lower lip.

"I want to draw Warren," she proclaims firmly. "What kind of paper should I use for that?"

I blink. "Warren? I don't know. Do you want to draw him in color, or black and white?"

"Black and white!" she says without a moment of hesitation, and nods sharply. "I looked it up on my phone. I want it to be in *mon-o-chrome*." She sounds out the word carefully, like it's the first time she's saying it out loud. "Your boyfriend's really dramatic, Auntie Hay. So I want his picture to be dramatic!"

I'm choked off from laughing at Tara calling Warren dramatic when that other word sinks in.

Boyfriend.

I start to splutter that he's not, but I...

I don't know what he is.

It's been less than twenty-four hours since he left me gasping and raw and hurting inside so deliciously, so sore and full and aching like we'd just fought for a prize we both ended up winning in the end.

We said *no end date*, but what are we doing? Are we dating? Is this exclusive?

Do we both agree this can't go anywhere when one or both of us are leaving, or...do either of us think maybe, just maybe, plans could change? If this turns into *more* than just a few hot nights in tangled bedsheets?

God. Slow down.

Why am I even *thinking* about this after what was barely a one-night stand?

Maybe because one-night stands are strangers. And Warren's not a stranger anymore. A stranger wouldn't run my ex out of town like a raging grizzly.

I don't realize I'd stumbled back from Tara until I suddenly bump into a wall display and an entire stand of craft beads goes crashing to the ground.

"Crap!" I yell out.

"Swear jar!" Tara pipes up, but I'm too busy scrambling to pick up the beads to tease her back. At least they're all in bags. I'm still mortified and blushing and oh my *God,* what's wrong with me?

"Just help me," I tell Tara. At least this gives me a chance to change the subject. "Before any of the bags pop open and we have to buy them. I can't afford this whole rack and your sketchbook."

"Not fair!" she complains. "You knocked it over, not me!"

"Life isn't fair when your bank account's empty, munchkin," I point out. "C'mon."

Sulkily, she crouches to help me. We manage to get the display upright and the little plastic bags back on the racks. To thank her – and apologize – I buy her both a big, thick hardbound sketchbook with softly textured paper that takes well to pencil and also an entire case of graphite drawing pencils.

She's beaming as she lugs out a book that weighs almost as much as she does, and as we pile into the car, she opens the glossy faux-leather black cover and strokes the pages happily.

I'm content to take it slow through town with the top down.

We barely make it a few blocks before the Mustang gives a guttural little sputter and starts to slow down.

Not. The. Hell. Again.

Luckily, we're near Stewart's shop. I've been in a few times to check on that part, but it's been taking longer than he expected to get it in.

Maybe I'll get luckier today.

At the very least, my safety luck holds out long enough for me to send the Mustang coasting down the street on momentum and easing its giant land whale ass into the gravel of the parking lot of Pep-Pep-Go Auto.

I'm not really a big fan of the name, but the shop itself is understated and quiet and classy, stylized with the same lines as old classic fifties automobiles in muted colors.

Shining new parts gleam through the front windows, while the huge quadruple garage is open to the day, a few apprentices in greasy coveralls tinkering around with a beat-up Chevy and someone else's brand-new BMW.

"Auntie Hay?" Tara finally seems to notice something is wrong, looking up from her book. "What happened?"

"The car's just being silly again," I say. "We'll leave it with Mr. Stewart and call Warren to pick us up. Get your things together, okay, baby?"

"O-*kaaaay*."

Even as I'm getting out of the car, Stewart's already coming out to greet me, rubbing his brow.

He raises his hand and waves before brushing his messy, sandy-brown hair back with a dirty hand.

"Ms. West," he drawls, even though I've told him a thousand times to call me Haley. At least it's not *sugar* today. "Don't tell me this beaut's giving you trouble again?"

"I can't believe it either. Guess you were right about Warren's hack job," I say dryly. "She just tried to die on me in the middle of the street. Barely got her here. Hoping you've got that replacement carburetor in stock?"

"Not yet," he says ruefully. "Only person I could find with an actual factory-new one instead of a worn-out, half-used part is overseas. It's hung up in customs somewhere between Tokyo and Heart's Edge."

There it is again – that sense of fakeness.

I don't know why it bothers me, why it makes the things he says seem false when it's just perfectly ordinary conversation. He'd have no good reason to lie to me about a car part.

Maybe it's just that Stewart's guarded and closed off in his own way. He's got history with Bress and Warren, too. Something about their military past, and something about being in the military makes men secretive even when it's not necessary.

Maybe Stewart's been attempting to cope. To shake off wartime. And in his attempt to be brighter and warmer and friendlier than the shadow of whatever might be haunting him, he's made this slightly plastic façade that doesn't quite blend the way he wants it to.

I try to brush it off. He's Warren's friend and seems to be

the only person besides Ms. Wilma and a couple of other ex-military buddies Warren trusts.

So I offer my most genuine smile as I reach out to shake his extended hand as he draws within reach, not minding the oil and grease. "Think you could maybe pull the same trick for a short-term fix just so I can get around?"

He grips and shakes my hand gently but looks worried. "I could, maybe, but..."

"I promise, I'm just driving between Charming and Brody's, maybe running a few errands. No steep roads or cliffs. If I break down, it won't be anywhere dangerous."

Stewart frowns thoughtfully. "So you're not going anywhere for a while?"

"Nah." I smile wryly, tucking my hands in my pockets and rocking on my heels. "It'll take me a month of tips just to save up to pay you for this, let alone enough for me to make it to Chicago."

"Hey, this one's on the house," he says with a rumbling laugh. "My dumbass friend tinkered with your car, so it's my responsibility to fix it. That's what I do, look after War. You just keep on keeping him out of trouble. Leave the worries about the car to me."

I blink, leaning my hip against the car door and folding my arms over my chest. Tara is unusually quiet next to me, huddling in close against my side and just behind. "What kind of trouble is he in?"

"Oh," he says, looking at me strangely. "He still hasn't told you? Damn, I'd have thought with...you know."

"With what?" I ask a bit too sharply, and he winces, looking away and rubbing the back of his neck.

"Well, after that incident at the diner, it's no big secret you two are an item," he says. "I'd have thought he'd be more open with you, that's all."

I don't want to pry. If there's something Warren doesn't want me to know, Stewart shouldn't be telling me.

But I also have Tara to consider. While I've pretty much sorted out that Warren's not dangerous, I can't live with myself if I remain ignorant of a situation that could bring Tara harm.

So reluctantly, I ask, "Open about what?"

"This isn't a nostalgic trip back home for him," Stewart says, his expression drawn and heavy. "It's a memorial. Grief. It's almost thirteen years to the day since he lost Jenna."

Jenna. Where have I seen that name before?

Then it flashes to me: his tattoos.

They're so intricate and detailed, down to the smallest curls and patterns, it's easy to lose the little things in them. Little things like letters.

Little things like the name *Jenna* and a date, tiny and circled in the detailed, almost betta-like fins of a coiling, ferocious mermaid.

I don't want to know, do I?

I don't want to know who Jenna is, or why she mattered enough for Warren to ink her name on his body. To preserve her as this fierce, mythological effigy.

Because I don't want the feelings that might come with knowing Jenna was a girlfriend, a special friend, a wife, a sister.

I know that if I find out, I might turn selfish. I'm going to compare myself, I'm going to hurt for something that I can't have when it belongs to a woman who, according to Stewart, is probably dead.

You don't say words like *lost, memorial, grieving* for someone who just divorced your friend and moved away.

If Warren's here to hurt, if he's here to hold on to that memory, fine.

NICOLE SNOW

Let him hurt without my feelings in the way. That's his. That *belongs* to him.

Just like this weird shot of hurt, of fear, in my chest belongs to me.

And it's a weight no one else should have to bear.

But I can't talk, all of a sudden. I can't anything.

And I thank Stewart with noncommittal sounds while he promises to call me when the Mustang's ready, saying it shouldn't be more than two shakes, while I usher Tara down the street to the diner.

We'll have an early lunch. I decide I'll call Warren after I settle my nerves with a couple cups of coffee while Tara wolfs her way through a massive burger.

Jesus. I've *got* to get my head on straight.

I can't be that girl who gets *dickmatized* after one hot round in the sheets.

Well, five or six rounds in a few hours, but that doesn't somehow cement my place in Warren's life, or his in mine. I have to talk to him about what we're doing.

This free-floating insanity keeps raising questions I'm not ready to ask, and it's too soon to think about. I just need a name. Terms.

Something I can come to grips with as easy, simple boundaries for where we stand.

But first, I need a ride.

I manage to calm myself down enough to sound normal when I fish out my phone and dial his number. He sounds breathless, the sound of it making my heart flutter and flip when he picks up the line and answers, "Hey, Haley."

"Hey," I say. "I hope you're not messing up the inn the way you messed up my car?"

He snorts. "What're you talking about?"

"I mean the Mustang died in the middle of Main." I laugh. "I left it at Stewart's. The part's still not in, but he's going to

242

rig it so it'll hold a little longer until the new piece gets through customs."

Warren swears, then laughs. "Look, all I did was what Stewart's gonna do, and it'll last just as long. You're just going to have to hopscotch your way through temporary quick fixes until that new carburetor comes in."

"My sister better be grateful for me returning her car in better-than-new condition." I roll my eyes. "So, since we're currently stranded at the diner and people are eyeing me like they're waiting for another scene..."

"Are you asking me to join you for lunch, or just using me for my wheels?"

"You know that's not the *only* thing you're good for. But if you've got time to come eat with us, Tara's already gorged herself, but I haven't ordered yet."

"You know what? Sure." I can hear him moving on the other side of the line, setting something down. "I've got to head out for a job this afternoon and could use a little fuel in my stomach before I go."

"You won't be at the house tonight?" I ask. *The house*, like it's our home and not a vacation duplex. "I'd been thinking about getting Jenny to cover my shift tonight since I probably won't have wheels until tomorrow."

A rumbling growl enters his voice. "So you're saying you'll be home and in need of some company?"

I dart a glance at Tara, then bite my lip, lowering my voice. "I wouldn't mind."

"Then that's incentive for me to bag this scum up in record time and get myself back," he says huskily. "You cooking or me?"

"I'll cook. Spoil you for once, instead of the other way around."

"Hey." It comes out soft, earnest. "I like spoiling you."

Shit, Warren. Don't say things like that, you're just going to get me more confused.

"Don't get used to it. I like my independence."

"Yeah, yeah." He chuckles, then pauses, his voice turning hesitant. "You all right?"

"Sure," I lie breezily. "I'm dandy, why?"

"You just sound like you've got a lot on your mind."

"Financial planning," I answer weakly. "Funny how a few weeks off the job in Seattle and I've lost my knack for numbers. Just trying to sort everything in my head."

"Okay," he says. I can tell he doesn't believe me, but he doesn't push. "Let me grab a shower and I'll be there in a few minutes. You want to order for me?'

"Char-grilled burger with onions?"

"You noticed?"

"It's what you got last time."

"Yeah," he says warmly. "Thanks, Hay."

"Sure." I hang up quickly, taking a deep breath – and freeze when I see Tara watching me with a smug, knowing smile. *"What."*

"You *liiike* him." She kicks her legs under the table. "It's funny."

"Grounded."

"You're not my mother!"

"For *life.*"

"Hey!" She pouts. "Not fair, Auntie Hay."

"Grown-ups are usually unfair. Just wait, one day you'll get to be unfair too."

"Hmph." She sticks her tongue out at me. "I don't know why Mr. Warren likes you."

"Do you think he actually likes me?"

"You're silly. He *said* he did," she proclaims emphatically. "He even said *boy-girl like.*"

"My mistake," I reply with a fond smile, watching my niece huff over her ever-so-oblivious aunt. "I guess he did."

XIV: FINDING OUR GROOVE
(WARREN)

J don't think I've ever collared a bail jumper this fast in my life.

Wasn't far away, just one county over, a quick and dirty local job with a three-time DUI offender. He'd only made bail on bond and then jumped ship. Asshole tried to go dark before the police could pick him up again.

The cops lost him in less than twenty-four hours. I had him back in less than three in exchange for a tidy sum tucked away to keep paying rent for me and Hay both.

I know I don't have to. Grandma said it's on the house, and Hay would be furious if she knew.

But paying renters keeps Charming Inn afloat, and Grandma's losing out on not one, but two room rates with me and Hay shacking up in the duplex. I just can't let my grandmother's pride and joy take a hit because she's got a soft spot for strays and always tries to spoil me as her grandson.

I can't let her end up burned by Bress, either.

That's what's on my mind right now as I meet my friend Blake for a couple of beers at Brody's.

I need a little time to come down before I go back to Charming Inn to spend the evening with Hay.

Fuck, I'm always a keyed-up mess after a fast job. All the adrenaline builds up so fast, not having nearly enough time to expel itself by the time I'm done with the gig. Plus, Haley and I just found a truce, and I don't want to go back prickly and wind up stepping in something that'll turn into a fight.

Blake's late, though. I'm on my second brew before that wily bastard saunters in, walking with an exaggerated pseudo-cowboy lope. Something he developed to hide the limp where he took a chunk of shrapnel to the thigh and nearly severed his femoral artery, leaving the entire muscle in ribbons.

He's doing a lot better now, but some days you can tell it still hurts him.

Not today, though.

Today he's all swagger and bluster, and he grins real broad, his teeth bright against his rusty-brown beard, as he raises a hand. "Warren, you skinny ghost. Why the hell haven't I seen you in two weeks?"

Skinny bastard. I'm an inch taller than he is and just as broad. I roll my eyes as I stand to clasp his hand briefly in a tight grip before we both drop back down into the booth. "Been busy. Work."

"Work, huh?" He arches both brows skeptically and raises a hand to signal for a waitress. "So throwing down with pretty brunettes is your job now?"

"Don't even start on Haley," I chuckle. Word gets around at light-speed in this town. "Yeah, all right. I've been a bit distracted by a pretty girl. What about it?"

"Hey, no shade." He holds both hands up. "Honestly, it's good to see. I haven't seen you date in fucking years."

"Yeah, well, I had my reasons." I prop my chin in my hand,

scratching my beard. I'm not sure if I want to think about those reasons right now, or what changed.

When did I become ready to move on?

When did life on the other side of this grief seem real, possible?

Shaking my head, I say, "I'm not even sure what we're doing could be called dating."

"Yeah? What would you call it then?"

"More like a freelance fling. We're just consulting on a short-term contract for what a relationship could be like. Before she's gotta up and leave for Chicago."

"Ouch." He frowns. "So you don't think this thing with Haley could be real?"

"No fucking clue, man. We just had one night. It's like my brain's picking that up and charging full-speed ahead five or ten years in the future." I grumble. "I get that I've got a lot of lost time to make up for, but it's damn annoying I can't rein myself in."

"You're lonely. No shame there." Blake's usual jovial smile vanishes.

He's always all hotheaded emotion, everything from laughter to anger coming out as this intense fire, but underneath he can be deadly serious. And he's all solemn right now, looking at me with brotherly concern. "Look, bud, it hits all of us sooner or later. We get tired of fucking around and we just want someone to come home to. Someone we get. Someone who gets us. Someone who makes the rough days better just by being there."

"Shit, where's Violet? Bet she'd think her old man's the sweetest in the world."

He smiles sadly. "More like it'd go to her little head and send it halfway to goddamn Jupiter."

We both know his words could apply to his daughter or

that reckless, screwed up woman he loved. Before she left them both behind.

Is Haley *that* person? The one who evens out your days and makes you smile through the storms?

If you'd asked me a week ago, I'd have said she was the *cause* of half of my thunderheads.

Then something shifted. Then we found out our edges don't fit together half bad...and now it's almost comfortable.

Almost downright *comfortable* shuttling between her half of the cabin and mine like we're one big household.

Same kind of comfortable teasing Tara, lifting her up on my shoulders while Hay looks on too fondly. Same comfortable remembering her schedule so I can have breakfast ready when she gets off shift, and so I can work my own local gigs around being awake when she is.

It's comfortable as hell – or maybe heaven – feeling like she's always been a part of my life, instead of this shooting star that came crashing down to Earth to smash my world to pieces.

I start to answer Blake, but freeze as the door to Brody's swings open and I catch, in the reflection on the glass, a familiar head of ash-blond hair before the reflection's owner steps into view.

Bress.

Dennis fucking Bress.

He comes lumbering in with that slow sidestep he has, this quiet-stone way of moving that makes such assuring promises that are always just *lies*. That's what I hate most about Bress.

He was always this fatherly figure who made you believe you could trust him. He'd protect you, he'd do anything for his team.

In reality, he'd do anything *to* his team. Whatever it took to hide his secrets and preserve his own hide. Every ounce of fucking trust he's ever asked for was built on a lie.

I can't take my eyes away from him, this anger smoldering inside me.

He doesn't even look at me. Him and two men I don't recognize – reedy men in suits with the look of loan sharks, carnivorous and watching him intently – stride past and claim a table in the far corner. The fact that the fucker doesn't even glance in my direction, walking in here like I don't even exist after everything he did, pushes that slow, simmering anger into a fucking *boil*.

It's like someone just lit a fire under my ass and sent me shooting up with the pure force of heat exploding through me.

Because next thing I know, I'm on my feet and Blake's voice is distant, behind me through the white-hot roar of rage.

Warren don't, he's warning, *you don't want to do this.*

I know damn well that I *do*, and before I can let my good sense take over I shake off Blake's hand on my arm and stalk across the bar.

The whole room goes quiet.

It's no secret how I feel, never has been, but it's always been a look-the-other way thing because nobody knows the truth of what happened except me. So everybody kept their noses out of small town business for once, letting me avoid Bress and Bress avoid me.

Now it's like the calm before a tornado comes twisting down out of the sky. Every eye follows me across the room.

And when Bress looks up, the expression of resigned dread that crosses his face might as well be a confession of guilt.

It takes everything in me not to throw a punch. My fists

249

clench like I'm holding on to my own leash and dragging myself back from slamming full force into that hangdog face of his.

The fact that he looks like he's pleading with me for something.

Fuck him if he thinks he'll *ever* get absolution from me. If he thinks I'll let this go.

He should just be grateful I've let him live this long.

"Stay away from Wilma Ford," I bite off without an intro. "I've had enough of you fucking with my family."

And I can't stand it if Grandma turns up dead under suspicious circumstances.

Just like Jenna.

That's what happens to Ford women who get too close to Dennis Bress.

The suits facing him start to get up, but Bress calms them with a negligent wave of his hand, then rises, stepping closer to me. He looks at me long and thoughtful with a gaze mournful enough to make that raging boil turn into bubbling loathing. I can't believe he'd even *dare*.

"Look, I know you want to protect your grandmother, son," he says, reaching for my shoulder.

Son? Has he lost his fucking mind?

Snarling, I knock his hand away sharply, stepping backward.

"Don't ever call me that."

"Habit." He smiles wanly, weakly. "There was a time when you almost looked up to me like a father."

"That was before I knew what you were."

"Maybe so," he says quietly. "Or maybe you're confused."

I don't know what's happening.

He's trying to wind me up, or there's something he's not saying.

Something that makes me uneasy, but he could be trying to throw me off. Screwing with my head, playing on our past relationship, those old emotions of trust and friendship and camaraderie.

Especially when he continues. "I thought you might find me eventually. I know you're still angry. And I know this time of year brings those feelings up again. I'm proud that you've managed to hold it together this long. That every year you move a little closer to closure. But you're still eating yourself alive with fury, Warren. If you keep it up, there'll be nothing left."

I swear to God if we weren't in public, Dennis Bress would be dead right now.

How *dare* this twisted fuck.

How dare he take his fake, paternal tone with me.

How dare he act like he has the right to tell me how to handle my feelings, my loss, my pain – when every last one of those emotions comes down to *him* and his cowardly, self-serving –

I don't even realize I'm drawing my arm back with my fist clenched, all my rage bunched up and ready, until something catches on my shoulder.

It draws back on the tight-coiled spring of my bicep. *Blake.*

He's got me by the arm, dragging me back with my fist still raised, my face feeling like a frozen mask of hate with ridges of anger carved in my flesh, my teeth hurting from grinding them so hard.

Bress just stands there, looking at me with resigned calm, as if he'd *let* me punch him right in his droopy, evil face without even flinching if Blake wasn't holding me back.

"War," Blake says softly. "C'mon, man. He's not worth it. Not here. Not now."

Not here.

Not now.

Not in public, with all these people watching.

These people who don't have a fucking clue they're sharing air with a monster. These people who adore Bress, who buy into his quiet, patient image, who think he's just this father figure bringing fresh blood to our town.

I'd be the bad boy gone rogue, and suddenly everyone's talking about what I've been doing since I left, who I've been getting mixed up with, what kind of criminal I've turned into.

I'd be playing right into Bress' hands.

Because suddenly he'd be the martyr, and I'd be the villain going after my former mentor, my former team leader, my former friend.

Fuck.

Yeah. Whatever. I guess once I did see him as a father figure.

And that's why the betrayal hurts so goddamn much.

I let my arm drop, my hand goes lax, and I rake Bress with a once-over.

"We're going to talk," I promise, low and just between us. "Soon."

"Yeah. We probably should, s—Warren." Bress glances over his shoulder, then drops his voice. "There's something I need to tell you, anyway. But not here."

Christ, I don't want to hear it. I don't want to hear his secrets, his confessions, his excuses.

And before I can snap, before I can completely lose it, I turn and walk out. Blake hovers close by as if he's afraid I'll go rabid again and need to be put down for my own good.

He's not entirely wrong. I can't think straight.

My head buzzes with hornets, everything slashing

through me in stinging bites of emotion, making my skull swim and reverberate until everything's a blur.

Outside, I take several deep breaths of crisp evening air, letting it scour down inside me to clear my head and make the thump of my pulse calm down.

Breathe in, breathe out, breathe in, breathe out, curling and uncurling my fists in time. And all the while Blake just stands at my shoulder, looking up at the sky, letting me be.

It's a long time before I feel like I can speak without it being a pure animalistic growl, but when I do, I mutter grudgingly, "Sorry."

"Like I said," Blake says quietly, bumping his elbow to mine, "no shade. We all handle loss in different ways. I just didn't want you to get into trouble you couldn't get out of."

I smile grimly. "There's nothing Bress can do to me that I can't get out of."

Blake barks a laugh. "You're such an arrogant asshole."

"Some days, yeah. I can be." It's easier to breathe now, at least.

I hate how wrecked up this still gets me. It's like I'm frozen in time, and it only moves forward just enough to chase me every inch that I struggle free.

Yet the present catches up to me and pulls me back into the moment as my phone vibrates in my pocket. Just the sight of the little selfie Hay texted me yesterday for her icon, her mouth screwed up into a self-mocking smirk and one eye squinted, relaxes the ferocious thing howling inside me. I swipe my thumb across the screen and read her text, frowning.

Hey. Stewart texted me and said there's another problem with the car. Something about a gasket. Would you mind checking with him on your way back?

"That your girl?" Blake asks, leaning in.

"She's my something," I murmur absently and tap out a quick response.

No problem, Hay. Did you want me to pick anything up for dinner on the way?

There's a pause before she fires back, *Do you love mushrooms on anything besides that burger? Make or break question here.*

I grin. Somehow after all the mess, after all the rage and hate burning through me, I'm *grinning*.

Love. Does this mean we can or can't share a pizza?

My phone pings with another text from her a second later. *Just grab some mushroom caps. Or whole mushrooms and I'll just pluck the stems. Dumbass.*

It's followed by several heart emojis and a middle finger.

Yeah.

That's Hay.

"Damn, man. Haven't seen you smiling like that in a while," Blake murmurs. "Looks good on you."

"Haven't had much reason to," I answer, pocketing my phone. "I need to go. Sorry to cut this short."

"Yeah? Where to?"

"Just need to check on her car. Stewart's having some kind of problem with it." I smile wryly and offer Blake my hand. "Seriously, it's been way too long. We need to do something together soon."

"There's always summer fishing at the cabin, if you stick around." He clasps my hand and shakes firmly, warmly, with the comfort and strength of familiarity. Of old friendships, old bonds. "Doc always gets a laugh out of it."

"Because I can't fish for shit and they always slip the hook," I point out.

Blake snorts, but I don't feel much like laughing.

Because right now, with the way everything's going, I feel a little too much sympathy for the fish.

I feel like I'm being baited and left to dangle.

The only question is, by who?

* * *

PEP-PEP-GO IS dark when I get there, but Stewart's big old muscle truck is in the lot.

It's this massive thing on huge tires that looks like he stole it from a retired monster truck auction. It's big enough to practically crush my own truck and not even notice it.

I try not to wonder whether or not my friend's compensating for something.

Stew opens the door to the main shop just as I pull up. He's changed out of his usual coveralls into casual jeans and a t-shirt, and he raises his hand in greeting as I step out.

I don't see any sign of Haley's Mustang, but the garage section is rolled down and closed off for the night.

"Hey," I say, slamming the door of my truck. "What's up with Haley's car?"

"Nothing much, War," he says, and leans against the hood of my Dodge, folding his arms over his chest. "I just knew if I texted 'don't go to Brody's, Bress is on the way' you'd ignore me."

I narrow my eyes. "You fucking—you baited me to get me to leave?"

"More like tried to save your ass from a catastrophe, since you've been a live wire lately. I don't want to see you in jail," he replies flatly, lofting both brows and giving me a measuring look. "You were there?"

"Yeah."

"Did anything happen?"

Grunting, I look away, dragging a hand through my hair. "We had words. Blake dragged me outside."

"Good Blake. He did you a solid." Stewart sighs. "It's been thirteen years, Warren. You gotta let this go."

"I *can't*," I snarl. "He already took Jenna, and now he's after Grandma."

He blinks. "After Ms. Wilma? What the hell do you mean?"

"She's talking to him about investing. Partial ownership of Brody's and the inn after she retires," I grind out through my teeth. "He's doing it just to get at me. The fuck knows I'm onto him."

"War." Stew's voice is almost pitying, and I hate it. "You've got to stop with these conspiracy theories. Jenna's death was a mistake of wartime action. You want to blame someone, blame the bastard militias in those hills. Taliban never did fight fair."

"Wrong. There were no fucking enemy combatants on the field that day. And you *told* me you saw him standing over her. Just her and Bress and a whole baffled crew of minesweepers."

He frowns. "How'd you know that for sure? You were deployed a hundred miles away. Out on a scouting mission, weren't you?"

"Yeah," I growl. "Bress had witnesses other than you. He just doesn't know it yet. A few of those boys in the mine-sweeper saw Jenna when she went down."

"The sweepers? Nah, they didn't show up till–"

"The official report was wrong, Stew. Worse than wrong. I think somebody doctored up the whole damn chain of events and the timestamps on the testimonies."

Stewart's face drops. He's quiet for several moments. The look he gives me is thoughtful, concerned, and I'm starting to wonder if I need to be worried about him doing something drastic, like calling in the police. "War, what are you planning? You're not up to anything illegal, are you?"

"You don't need to know. It's better if you don't. I'm not gonna kill nobody, so don't worry."

Not unless I fucking have to, I think to myself, hoping it doesn't come to that.

I settle in against the truck bed, trying to soothe my hot rage, and glare down the darkened street. "Just trust me to get a confession. That's all I'm after. The truth from the horse's own damn mouth. I'll find out what really happened when she died—and he'll learn not to lie to me. No one in your old unit has his back anymore. Not after what he did."

"No one's gonna have your back, either, if you kill him."

"I'm not going to kill him," I snort. "Just going to make sure he suffers behind bars for the rest of his life. I'm doing this for Jenna, so I'll do it Jenna's way. By the book and by the law. If I had my choice..."

"Yeah. Thank God you don't." Stewart sighs. "You're still tangling yourself up in some dangerous shit. Maybe if no one's found anything after this long, there's a reason."

"Reason? It's called Bress' blood money. Plain and simple. Just leave it the fuck alone, Stew."

"And what about Haley and Tara?" he asks. "What happens with them when you go chasing after your man and get hurt or thrown in the slammer?"

"Won't happen," I point out. "Hay and Tara are my business. Why the hell does everybody need to weigh in about our relationship?"

"So there *is* a relationship?"

"There's...something," I grunt. "Fuck. I promised her I'd pick up mushrooms. I've gotta go."

"Aren't you the domestic," he retorts. "Tell her the car's fine, by the way. Turns out I found a working part in the back. Should have it back to her in a day or two."

My only answer is a middle finger tossed over my

257

shoulder as I climb back in my truck and floor it to the grocery store.

I can't believe Stewart used Hay to try to keep me away from Bress. I don't know what worries me more.

That Hay's got me on such a leash it almost worked? Or that Stew's starting to stick his nose in more and more?

Part of me wonders *why?*

And the rest of me is a little afraid to find out.

XV: HEAVEN AT HOME (HALEY)

I'm starting to think, when the time comes, I'm going to catch hell prying Tara away from Heart's Edge and sending her back home to her parents in Seattle.

I hadn't realized, when I first saw the main house at Charming Inn, that it was built around an atrium.

Ms. Wilma keeps a beautiful glassed-in courtyard that's only accessible from the side of the inn set apart for private family residency. The entire place is filled with life and light, with dripping honeysuckle vines festooned everywhere, a little pond, hanging trellises of fragrant jasmine, tall waving lilies and even cattails transplanted to line the edges of the glimmering pool.

Sunlight streams down in pale golden shafts, glinting off the jewel-toned shimmer of tiny hummingbirds that dart eagerly between the honeysuckle and jasmine blooms like they can't decide which sweet blossoms to feed on next.

And Tara's in heaven, kicking her feet on the little swing dangling from the low-hanging branch of a small but ancient gnarled oak. It was probably here even before the house.

NICOLE SNOW

It's so brilliant, so picturesque, and the dimming light of the sunset does nothing to dampen it.

I swear I could paint here for years and never capture it all, but part of me wants to try.

Right now, though, I'm content to sit on the little padded bench next to the pond and listen to Tara's laughter as she swings higher and higher, kicking her feet.

Next to me, Ms. Wilma watches too, her hands folded in her lap with a courtly grace I've noticed Tara's starting to emulate lately. "She's a darling girl, isn't she?" she says fondly. "You must be so proud."

"I am," I answer. "I'm just her aunt, but...ya know."

"Nonsense, dear. There's no such thing as *just* an aunt. Aunts are the mothers we wish we had when the ones we do have are being just a little unfair. They're our best friends, our heroes, our confidantes, and the women we often want to grow up to be."

I glance at her, lingering on the remote, warm look in her eyes. "Sounds like you had an aunt you idolized?"

"Oh, yes. My Aunt Nicolette. She was quite a fancy lady. A child of the Paris high life. She held these great balls that Gatsby would've envied, dressed up all in lace and entertaining in the finest hotels in New York."

I blink. "You're not from Heart's Edge?"

"No, dear." She flutters one slim hand to her throat, and that's when I realize there's a little old-fashioned silver locket nestled against the lace throat of her dress, so old it's been worn into a perfect polish from years of loving handling. "My Lawrence came from Heart's Edge. He swept through New York after the war and found me turning my ankles to the latest pretty tune, teasing all the boys. He decided right then and there he never wanted me to look at another man through my lashes but him."

260

I laugh softly. "Sounds like his grandson takes a bit after him. When he decides something, there's no swaying him."

"Warren is quite a bit like his grandfather, indeed." Her eyes soften. She reaches back to unclasp the locket, letting it spill into her palm, then gently opens it so I can see a handsome man in black and white.

His blunt jaw looks set just like Warren's, the same rough and ready expression on his face, his smile just as arrogant, his hair a slick of black swept back neatly to match his crisp, old-fashioned Air Force uniform. "They're both quite dapper, don't you think?"

"I do." I lean in, admiring Lawrence Ford. "Is it...okay to ask what happened?"

"Oh, it's been years, darling. It doesn't hurt to talk about it anymore." But there's a touch of loss, of heartbreak, in her voice, as she gazes down into that locket.

Then I wonder what it's like to love someone so much that they live inside your every gesture and word, even long after they're gone.

"My Lawrence was always a soldier. He couldn't seem to shake it, even after the war in Europe ended. Every time they called him back for one patrol or another, he was always on the front lines. One day, his plane malfunctioned over the Bering Strait during routine exercises to keep the Russians at bay." Her sigh is long and drawn, shaky. "They never found the wreckage, or his body."

It's not my story, not my loss...but my heart aches nevertheless, a sharp pang in my chest, both for her and for Warren. "I'm so sorry, Ms. Wilma."

"That's life. But I loved him while I had him, with everything in me—and that's all that matters." Her eyes gleam damp as she lifts her head, looking around the atrium with a smile that's so beautiful, it hurts to see. "We built this atrium together. Sometimes I feel like I can still feel him here.

Warren would come here so often as a boy, too. It's like he knew the energy without even being told."

"It's absolutely beautiful. I'd have never imagined, from the outside."

"We wanted it to be our secret place." She chuckles, closing the locket and slipping the chain around her neck again, fiddling with the clasp. "Now that we've made the manor into a hotel, guests can enjoy the view, but only family are allowed inside."

I wonder what it means that she's let me and Tara here.

It almost feels like Ms. Wilma has adopted us, and I'm not sure what to think of that in the context of my relationship with Warren.

Last night, he'd come home with four different varieties of mushroom, just because he hadn't known which one I wanted. And when I asked why he didn't just text me and ask, the look on his face and the dumbfounded confusion had us both dissolving into laughter, then falling into each other's arms.

Dinner was a bit late last night, but I don't think either of us minded.

I look over. Ms. Wilma's fumbling with the clasp, and I stand quickly, circling the bench.

"Let me," I say, and she murmurs her thanks while I take the delicate chain and slip the clasp so that it locks securely around her neck again. "Thank you for letting us see this place. And thank you for caring for Tara so much while I've been busy."

"You have no idea how happy it makes me to have a little girl around. It's been a very long time."

I know I shouldn't ask. I know. Because I can't get myself too wrapped up in this, can't tell myself this is anything other than what it is, and yet...

"Was Jenna here often?" I venture tentatively, curling my hands against the back of the bench.

Ms. Wilma turns to look over her shoulder, sharp and canny but not unkind. "Now where did you hear the name Jenna, hm?"

"Um, I guess I..." I duck my head, clearing my throat, shame washing through me and my entire body too hot with my pounding pulse. "Sorry. It's on his tattoo. And Stewart mentioned her name once or twice."

"Ah, the mechanic. Such a gossip. And naturally you'll be wondering who she is, and why Warren's still an open wound where she's concerned after all this time?"

Wincing, I nod. "I was just curious."

Smoothly, Ms. Wilma stands, straightening her skirt and calling out to Tara. "Run inside and wash up before supper, dear."

Tara immediately slows her kicking, bouncing off the swing with a nod, her pigtails swaying. "Yes, ma'am!"

I stare after her as she races off, disappearing into the house. "Wow. How'd you do that so easy? I have to beg, negotiate, and eventually bribe."

"Who says I don't bribe?" Ms. Wilma says with a merry wink. "Once you've tasted my cinnamon almond cookies, you'll understand." She inclines her head toward the door. "Come inside. I want to show you something."

Curious, I follow Ms. Wilma. I always feel small next to her, and not just because she's so tall while I'm the runt in the munchkin brigade. She's so graceful and stately and formidable, and I kind of think if I had an aunt I wanted to be when I grew up, it would've been Ms. Wilma.

The inside of the house is cool and shadowed compared to the greenhouse warmth of the atrium, and it takes a moment for my eyes to adjust as we make our way through hallways decorated in airy linens contrasted by dark carpets and the occasional tasteful painting here and there.

Maybe I should paint something for Ms. Wilma before I leave.

Put my all into it, make it my best, something I can be proud to offer her in gratitude.

But I'm distracted from my thoughts as she steps into the living room with its Victorian furniture that's been cared for so meticulously it looks almost brand new.

Several photos line the mantle, all of them in ornate gold frames that have been polished lovingly again and again, their shine soft in the bits of light glimmering through the curtains.

I realize this is what she wants me to see.

She stops at one end of the mantle, gazing fondly at a portrait of two kids that's been cropped so it's only the little boy and little girl, while the adults are just legs vanishing off into the frame.

It's Warren. I recognize those blue eyes, that fierce stare, even in a chubby, adorable little boy covered in mud.

And the girl next to him looks a lot like him.

That resemblance grows stronger, as they grow taller and older in one picture after another.

Photos of them laughing together.

Photos of them glowering at each other.

Photos of them glaring at a man and woman who must be their parents, as they sulk over apparently disappointing Christmas gifts, wrapping paper everywhere in glittery tufts.

I can't help but laugh. And it's a painful thing when I already know how this ends.

Because at the end of the line, past photos of Warren fresh out of training with his head shaved into a military buzz-cut and his uniform crisp like his grandfather's, past photos of Jenna – because she must be Jenna – in her own uniform with her hair knotted back and her posture straight and proud, there's tragedy.

A single framed, folded flag with another, smaller photo of Jenna tucked into the corner of the frame. That flag can only mean one thing. It's hard and hurtful to deal with even though I never even knew who she was.

I curl my knuckles against my mouth, staring at that photo, her eyes bright and determined; was this the last photo anyone ever took of her?

"She was his sister," I whisper. "He lost his sister."

"Yes. They were so close growing up. It took an absolutely devastating toll on him."

I shouldn't be getting emotional about this. Too bad the heart has a mind of its own.

And Ms. Wilma makes me feel so much like family that it almost feels like I somehow lost her, too – or maybe I'm just hurting for Warren. I suddenly understand all those angry, directionless prickles so much more.

He's just like me.

Life hit him so hard it sent him reeling, and he hasn't stopped spinning ever since, and it's making him furious that without this one thing that set his life in order, he still can't figure out up from down.

Oh, Warren...

"What happened?" I ask tentatively, fighting for words around my closing throat. "If...if it's okay to ask, I mean."

"An accident in the line of duty," she says sadly. "During her last tour. Apparently friendly fire during a confused ambush, but no one's entirely sure how it unfolded. The reports were...confusing. Of course, no one meant for her to get hurt."

I frown. Friendly fire? An ambush?

That doesn't really add up with what Stewart told me, but then I'm only getting fragments of the story. Maybe I'm just not piecing them together right. What do I know about war?

"Was Warren on deployment with her?"

"He was, but he was stationed elsewhere that day. A different unit." This time Ms. Wilma doesn't even try to stop the wetness in her eyes from spilling over. "One of my babies came home in a casket. The other came home a completely different man. Warren's never been the same since."

"Oh, Ms. Wilma..." For once I don't question my impulses.

I just go to her and wrap my arms around her and pull her in. She makes a startled, proud sound but then leans into me, her thin arms curling around me.

She's strong, and she hugs me so fiercely, so tightly, clinging to me. I'm glad I trusted my instincts. She's a proud, powerful woman, yes.

But even proud, powerful people need comfort now and then.

After a moment, though, she pulls back, smiling brightly despite her streaming eyes, then sniffs and wipes at her cheeks before gripping my shoulders. "Honestly, ever since you've come to Heart's Edge, he's been better. He's always had a temper. It's almost a relief to see him snapping off everywhere again instead of grim and brooding, bottling it up inside."

"Try being on the other end of his tantrums and say that," I say with a laugh.

"Oh, he wouldn't dare with me, darling," she says, her smile turning wicked. "And I dare say you've found your own ways to keep him in check?"

I don't know what to say to that. I don't know if I'm keeping Warren in check so much as we keep pushing and pulling on each other until the strings stretched between us are so taut, they're ready to snap.

But there's a look in Ms. Wilma's eye that's too much when she pats my shoulder.

"I did wonder if I'd ever have great-grandchildren. I'm not *that* old. It's not too late."

I choke, spluttering, somehow managing to gag myself on nothing but air.

But I'm saved from a dozen awkward denials by the sound of a car door slamming outside. It must be Warren, thank God.

He was supposed to be joining us for dinner, but he promised to stop by Stewart's shop to pick up my car first so I wouldn't be begging for rides to work tonight. Apparently, the Mustang will probably last another week with the short-term fix, but Stewart promised he'll do whatever he can to get the part in by then.

I called my sister to let her know, but she didn't answer.

Later, I got a terse text that she'd PayPal me the cost, but when I told her it was on the house thanks to small town hospitality, she didn't answer.

Ugh.

I guess Hawaii's not going so well.

It's that kind of cold splash though – the slow motion demolition of a real, loving marriage that's so closely connected to me – that pushes Ms. Wilma's starry-eyed daydreams of grandchildren and not-so-subtle hints from my head.

But I'm still breathless and nervous when the front door slams open and I hear Warren come thudding in. He's normally not this noisy.

He moves like the wild animal he is, this prowling beast of pure raw power so utterly in control of his body that he can move his massive bulk without making a single sound. But today he looks tired as he trails past the living room door out in the hallway, just a glimpse loping past as he calls

"Grandma? Haley?" before stopping and backtracking to lean on the living room door.

The oddest transformation passes over his face as he sees us standing in front of the mantel, Jenna's portraits lined up behind us, Ms. Wilma's face still damp from crying.

Underneath that swarthy tan, he goes pale, then red, before somehow going blank.

I hadn't realized how much he'd relaxed, the warmth in his eyes erasing the constant hostile tension that was always the norm at first – until suddenly that tension returns. It radiates out of him like sharp, jabbing spikes, ready to launch at me and Ms. Wilma at a second's notice. His jaw tightens, clenching, working back and forth, muscles slowly ticking underneath his beard.

"Your car's ready," he snaps off, his voice oddly toneless, before a quick flick of his wrist sends my keys sailing toward me.

Instinctively, I lurch forward to catch them, grasping them in both hands and clapping them together fast enough to make my palms sting as the edges of the keys cut into my skin.

"Warren?" I ask, but he's already turned away, broad shoulders rolling like moving mountains, an earthquake of silent anger.

Ms. Wilma clucks her tongue. "Oh, don't be that way, dear. I thought you were all going to stay for dinner?"

"Not hungry," he flings back over his shoulder, lifting a dismissive hand. "I'm sure you've got plenty to fucking talk about without me anyway."

"Swear jar," a tiny voice pipes up from the hallway.

But Warren's already sweeping out, and I hear the crash of the front door before his footsteps thud on the porch so violently it's like I can feel them kicking my heart.

Tara peeks around the door, her eyes wide, her face

drawn, her lip sucked in.

"Why's Mr. Warren so mad?" she whispers, a little crack in her voice, and Ms. Wilma sighs.

"He's not angry at you, darling dear," she says. "He's just hurting, and he doesn't know how to deal with it." She turns her gaze on me. "I'm so sorry, Haley. I don't mean for you to get caught up in our little family mess."

"It's fine," I promise, even if I don't know if I feel fine at all when I don't know what I'll find when I get back to the duplex. But I offer a brave smile and rest my hand lightly on her arm. "You're just trying to make me feel at home. And I can always take him a plate."

"Look at you, trying to take care of him." Ms. Wilma pats my cheek, her palm warm and smooth. "He needs that, even if he'll never admit it. Come. Let's enjoy our meal, even if we're short one snarling grizzly bear."

I only hold my smile wanly as I gather up Tara and follow Ms. Wilma to the dining room.

He needs that, she'd said. He needs someone to take care of him.

But that doesn't necessarily mean he needs *me*.

* * *

EVEN WITH THE stormclouds Warren left behind, dinner is still a warm, comfortable thing I want to hold on to for a while, maybe forever. Another memory to make up for the family memories I never had. I feel like this little sojourn in Heart's Edge is a chance to regain lost time.

It can't last forever, but it can help me capture a few moments worth keeping.

A still life with family, memory on neurons, painted by the strange emotions these new experiences make me feel.

I'm better by the time I wrap up a plate of steaming roast

turkey drenched in gravy, pasta casserole, and mashed potatoes to take back to Warren. Tara insists on carrying it, and I
just make sure she's got a good grip on the warm plate
without burning herself before we set out into the night to
enjoy the stroll back to the cabin.

This weird dread hovers over me the whole way, making
me feel like maybe this is the last calm I'll get for a while.

Warren almost looked *betrayed*, and I don't think I have to
guess what kind of reception I'll get.

Still, I can't help the little crush of disappointment when
we walk up the steps and I realize he's not waiting in our half
of the duplex.

I'd kind of gotten used to it over the last few days, him
spending more time on our side than on his, making himself
part of our lives while still keeping us distant from whatever
secrets he's locked away in his half of the cabin.

But our door is locked. His side is dark through the glass,
though I can see the faint light of his laptop from the
bedroom.

I sigh, closing my eyes, then make myself smile for Tara as
I reach for the plate. "Go wash up for bed, kit. I need to chat
with Warren before I send you right back to Ms. Wilma for
the night."

Tara wrinkles her nose. "Awww. Are you always gonna
work nights?"

"Only while I'm here, munchkin. I'll find a different job
when I move."

"I don't want you to move all the way to Chicago." She
relinquishes the plate only to fold her arms over her chest.
"It's too far. I'll never see you."

I want to tell her that's not true, promise her I'll see her
all the time...but then I'd be lying. I can only stare at her
softly, hating this.

I'm not ready to deal with that extra little stab of hurt on top of my chaotic feelings about Warren, but it's right there, staring me down.

Once I move, I might not see Tara for years.

Seattle and Chicago aren't neighbors, and the flights aren't always cheap.

We're not the kind of family who meets up for Christmas and Thanksgiving. We do phone calls on the important holidays. Sometimes there's a rough night on the anniversary of Dad's drunk driving death, and we'll call and make awkward noises at each other before we sit in silence, taking the comfort we need from just not being alone with so many conflicted emotions.

When did that stop being enough?

What the hell did this little small town do to me, where suddenly I'm wanting things I've never even thought about before?

Jesus. I'm standing out here on the porch clutching a plate for Warren, staring at my niece like she grew a second head. I don't know why my emotions are everywhere like this. You'd almost think I was—

No. Don't even think it.

Even if my birth control failed, it's way too soon for my body to start reacting to pregnancy hormones. I don't get an excuse that easy.

There's nothing but myself to blame for this mess.

"We'll talk about Chicago later, munchkin," I promise and put on my big girl britches to smile for her. "Go on in and wash up. Ms. Wilma promised you could stay up to watch TCM with her tonight."

Her eyes widen. "The King and I? Oh, wow! The dresses are so *pretty.*"

God, I hope I'm not doing something terrible when I say "Yes." I've never seen that movie. Ms. Wilma wouldn't show my niece anything too risqué, right?

...right?

But at least it sends Tara scampering off, disappearing into our half of the duplex. I turn back toward Warren's door.

A second later I yelp, stumbling back and nearly dropping the plate when I find him standing there, the door open, his bulk propped in it and his hard, forbidding gaze locked on me.

Shit. He's pissed. Or something.

I don't know what. I can't read him all of a sudden. I guess I wasn't supposed to know about Jenna because he's completely closed off.

We both say nothing, each of us waiting for the other to speak. But right when I open my mouth to find the words, he says, "You need something?"

"Dinner," I answer lamely, offering him the plate. "You missed it. Thought you'd want some while it was still nice and hot."

He drops his gaze to the plate, then back to me. His arms stay folded over his chest, leaving me awkwardly standing there with a plate outstretched. "Not hungry."

I frown, my temper snapping awake. "Jesus, Warren, what's your problem all of a sudden?"

"My problem is, people who won't let the dead lie," he throws back. "What did she tell you?"

"I..." Damn. I can't stay mad at him when we're talking about his dead sister and the pain he's so clearly carrying around like a boulder, fresh as the day it happened. "She told me Jenna was your sister, and there was an accident on deployment. Friendly fire."

"Nothing fucking *friendly* about it," he snarls, and it takes me a minute to grasp what he means.

He's not saying she was killed by an enemy combatant.

He's saying she was murdered, and – *oh, God.*

My free hand claps over my mouth, and I suck in a gasp. "Warren, I'm sorry."

"What else did she say?" he demands, his eyes flat azure chips, reflecting nothing, glassy and hard. "What else did she tell you?"

"Nothing." I shake my head quickly. "But Stewart said you came home to grieve. And that you need someone to keep you out of trouble."

"The only thing I need," he says, low and seething, "is for everyone to mind their damn business and let me mind mine. *Everyone.*"

I don't need to be told twice.

I'm torn between calling him every name in the book and shoving this plate of turkey right in his face, but I'm not one to stay where I'm not wanted.

And no matter where I am, I'm not going to beat up on a grieving man.

I didn't do anything wrong. Jenna was Ms. Wilma's granddaughter.

She had just as much right to tell me about her as anyone else, but for once I'm going to check my temper and respect Warren's space.

For once.

That doesn't mean I don't want to punch him just to get a real reaction.

Instead, I set the plate on the broad deck railing with a loud *thud*, leaving it there. "Enjoy your dinner," I whisper harshly. "Good night."

Nothing comes back.

Not even an acerbic answering *good night* whipped at my back.

Just the sound of Warren's door closing, while I bundle up my hurt and frustration and confusion and a guilt I shouldn't even be *feeling* to flee into the safe confines of my space.

XVI: NIGHTMARE BALM (WARREN)

*a*lmost every time I fall asleep, it's the same.

Maybe that's why I can't let go.

Because every night my brain yanks me back to the day she died like it was yesterday, playing out every graphic detail. I wasn't even there to see it, but my mind is happy to concoct scenes to make sure I know what suffering feels like whether I'm awake or I'm asleep.

BRIGHT DESERT SUNLIGHT.

It's a photograph – one I've seen tucked between the window and the dash in Bress' car, but this time the photograph's alive.

Jenna, Bress, and Stew, three musketeers geared up before deployment, grinning at the camera and holding up two fingers in peace signs like they were just heading out for a Sunday stroll.

They've been watching too many dark comedy flicks about Vietnam. Wrong place, wrong time, wrong war.

Every day in this place is a reminder how truly damn different the very meaning of the word can be.

They've been assigned to cover a mine removal crew doing clearance over an old dirt road. The Russians left a lot of presents behind in the eighties when they were here. We've had too many good people hurt twenty years later by old buried explosives from a war that's not even ours.

Stewart's cheesing it up for the camera, but Bress and Jenna only have eyes for each other.

Two lovers. One true and innocent, the other preparing a fucking knife.

Bress tries to look stoically forward, but it's not hard to see he's watching her from the corner of his eye.

Jenna's not even bothering to hide.

I'd teased her about it just that morning.

After a string of failed relationships with men who couldn't handle a military woman, Jenna swore she'd finally found The One in our own ranks. And goddamn I wouldn't be her big brother if I didn't give her shit about daddy issues with Bress being almost twenty years older than the lot of us.

But he makes her feel safe, makes her happy, and while I was gonna ride her ass about it at first and threatened to kick him up one sand dune and down another, in the end I was just glad they made each other smile.

Maybe there's a frozen moment. Some last peace caught in the glint of sunlight cast off smiling teeth and blue-eyed laughter.

One final bit of happiness, the tease of wind through messy bound hair, the blue of the Afghan sky so clean and clear it makes it seem like all's right with the world.

Until suddenly the sky splits apart.

The whole world breaks open, and the ground churns with bursting debris and shrapnel flying everywhere.

Mortars. Snipers. The same sneaky shit the pricks in the mountains always pull.

There's nowhere to run but straight, into the dust cloud kicked up by the big armored minesweeper.

Jenna races desperately ahead, then trips a mine the sweeper didn't catch.

Hell pops off in her wake like she's being chased by a thousand underground explosions.

Jenna keeps running, her eyes wide, her face determined, her fists clenched as she pumps her arms and races over the sand with no fear.

My Jenna, my sister, wouldn't have died sobbing and afraid. She'd be brave to her last breath.

But there's someone else there.

A familiar broad, heavy-set figure, familiar ash-blond hair, and the rifle in his hand is quick. He sees his chance to do something he's planned for too fucking long.

That rifle barks bullets after Jenna, masked by the hellish confusion and shrapnel the insurgents keep raining down.

A well-aimed hellfire strike from a drone in thirty seconds will take care of the assholes in the hills.

She doesn't last that long.

Jenna's a moving target. I don't know if she ever realizes her betrayal until the very end, she just knows someone is shooting at her.

She's ducking, weaving, handling this the smart way, but suddenly there's a thock *of a bullet piercing fabric, Kevlar, flesh, and a bloom of red.*

She windmills forward, her eyes huge with surprise.

The bright light leaves her eyes.

She's gone.

All because she trusted the wrong man, saw the wrong things, knew too much.

He pretended to love her to get fucking rid of her.

The worst part? She didn't even understand.

She knew she'd seen wrong, got in the middle of something. Maybe that 'drama' she told me about the last time we met was some asshole from their unit who'd mouthed off too much about the side gig shipping heroin back to the States. And maybe – fuck maybe, of course – he answered to Dennis Bress.

I want to wake up.

Every night I want to wake the hell up, but the dream won't let me. It's always relentless, forcing me to watch.

I'm the same helpless damn bystander who can't move, can't shout her name, can't do anything to save her. I just watch as she goes tumbling forward, slumping to the sand.

She's twitching, her mouth moving soundlessly, but I know the name she's saying.

I know because Bress thinks they're alone, but they're not.

Stew is there, watching horrified from behind one edge of the sweeper, too paralyzed to act and pinned down by enemy fire while Bress strides forward boldly and stands over my sister's gasping body.

Then I see what Stewart implied years later, the night we were drunk.

There's just a moment where her eyes roll back toward him before Bress puts the rifle to her forehead. And even though this is a dream, across the field of battle, Stew catches my eye, stares at me wretchedly, mouthing I'm sorry, War.

Then the sound of a single gunshot rings out over the battlefield as the drones sweep in, dropping a halo of hellfire.

It reverberates louder than a nuclear warhead, shattering my sleep and shoving me awake with all the violence of my own flesh and blood lost too soon.

* * *

"Jenna, fuck!"

I snap awake with my heart pounding and wild, my body drenched in the cold sweat of fear and loss. It's like every inch of me is crying to make up for my dry eyes, my parched throat.

It's not real, I tell myself. It's not real, *goddammit.*

What is real, though, is the woman lying in my bed, her soft fingers tracing my brow, bringing me back down to Earth.

Haley.

For a second, I'm confused. Then guilt swamps me.

I was a complete and utter shit to her tonight, so what's she doing here?

Why's she looking at me like she actually gives a damn, worry knitting her brow, instead of spitting at me for being a hulking jackass?

I just stare at her blankly, struggling to catch my ragged breath, that gentle touch of her fingertips seeming to mark rhythm and time until I can pace myself to her speed.

One breath at a time before I'm finally ready to speak.

"Hay? Shouldn't you be at work?"

She smiles faintly, sadly. "Really? That's the first thing you ask me?" Her touch stops, lingering at my temple. "I was worried about you. So I lied and said my car was still tanked and got someone to cover my shift."

"You didn't have to do that for me. Not after the way I lashed out."

"Well, I'll admit I thought about punching you in the mouth." Her smile strengthens, her fingers weaving into my hair. "But this time I understood what you were so upset about. Everyone gets a Mulligan in situations like this. Just don't take advantage."

Somehow, even with the awful chill of the nightmare still gripping me, she manages to make me smile anyway.

"Yes, ma'am," I murmur, curling my hand against her wrist.

I have this nightmare so often you'd think I'd be used to coming down from it, but no. It still leaves me raw and torched. Only this time, it doesn't hurt so much. I'm not so desolate, so alone.

Because for some unholy reason, this woman was willing to give me a little faith, and knew what I needed better than I knew myself.

Goddamn, I wish I'd met her in better circumstances. Without this obsession driving me, taking me over until I'm less of a man and more of a passion.

Not enough to make a woman like Hay happy forever.

I'm too broken. Too cold inside and out. Too many demons chasing for me to ever slow down.

There's no happy ending. Whoever leaves Heart's Edge first pulls the plug on this messy, beautiful thing we've got.

One day I'll have to let her go.

Tonight, though, I have her.

She's warm and soft and everything I need as I gather her close, fitting her body into my arms and against my chest like she belongs there. Even through my miserable haze, my dick goes hard the second her soft, supple flesh touches mine.

The weight of her holds me down, makes me stable and solid until nothing feels quite so shaky anymore. I sigh, burying my face in her sweet-smelling hair, and let my body go loose, the tension easing out of me.

"Thanks, darlin'," I murmur.

"Mm? What for?"

"Not letting me run you off like a wolverine." I close my eyes, still counting those slow, steadying breaths. "I'm sorry. When I saw you there, realized you knew about Jenna...I got too damn defensive for my own good."

She's silent. Then I feel those tender fingers on my arm.

I don't have to look. I know what she's tracing by the feel of her skin on mine, when I've followed those same lines over and over again.

Jenna's name.

"Why does it scare you so much?" she asks. "I know it hurts, Warren, but why do you keep everything about her a secret?"

I need a good long second to think. "Guess I'm afraid it'll happen again, Hay. If I tell other people the truth, they'll get sucked in, and I'll lose someone else."

"The truth?"

Fuck.

I take the deepest breath of my life and tense.

"You figured it out, darlin'. Sort of. I think my sis was murdered," I growl. "I *know* she was. Think she found out someone in her unit was into black market drug dealing with a little gunrunning on the side, and they killed her for it. I'm here to settle the score. Maybe I won't kill them...maybe I won't cross that line. But goddammit, they're gonna confess and serve time if it's the last thing I do."

Her hands curl against my chest, resting against me warmly as she looks up at me.

"Bress. You think Mr. Bress killed your sister."

"Yeah," I admit. "I have a witness I trust who saw it, and I can't let that asshole hurt Grandma, or you, or Tara. That's why I'm so worried. That you'll get caught up as collateral damage when he runs and tries to cover his tracks."

I expect her to reject it, deny it. She's becoming part of Heart's Edge so quickly, and maybe she's bought into that 'fatherly local businessman' act.

But she only frowns thoughtfully. "Mr. Bress owns a lot of businesses in town, doesn't he? Are those part of the drugs?"

"As far as I can tell," I answer, a little startled, numb that she's taking this seriously. "I just need to actually connect him to it. He's evasive. Good at covering his tracks with middlemen."

"And then what?" she asks, bright green eyes searching mine.

"Then, I hope I'm the man my sis would want me to be," I answer. "And that I can do this the right way."

I cover her slender hand against my chest with my own, rubbing gently.

"I know what you probably think of me, Hay. But I'm not here to murder a man in cold blood. Just to make sure justice gets served and the evil fuck stands trial."

"And what then?" she whispers. "When you've done that, what'll give your life meaning?"

I know she doesn't mean to put those thoughts in my head. Those wonderings about her, about what might be if I wasn't so wrecked.

But I can't shake them any more than I can throw off the heavy, needy feeling rushing through me.

"Don't know," I whisper, dipping my head toward her, drawn in by that sweet, earnest way she's watching me. "I haven't thought ahead that far."

She rises up to meet me halfway. What crashes between us barely resembles a kiss.

It's more like two rough forces colliding.

We're a firestorm of all the things we can't say, all the things that shouldn't be, this wrenching inside me that makes me feel like she'll destroy me from the inside out.

I've called her poison again and again, the sweetest venom, better than any booze. And she's soul-deep now, spreading through my veins, aiming to kill me with this raw, real emotion – and I'll go willingly.

That's when it hits me, stealing my breath.

It's not just some sappy bullshit.

I'd *die* for Haley.

Die to keep her safe, but I'd rather live to keep her with me.

Her arms around me.

Her body arching under mine when I roll on top of her. Then it's her wildness, her sweetness, and I'm like a madman, completely consumed by obsession as I kiss her, touch her, stroke her from head to toe and leave my mark on her throat with my teeth.

This woman's so fucking *mine*. Even if it's the last thing she ought to be.

And when she scurries out from under me and undoes my belt, her little fingers tugging down my zipper, I'm a goner. So gone I couldn't tell you what year it is to save my life.

I watch her little hand take my cock. So huge, so tense, throbbing like the end of the world in her hand.

There's a flash of green eyes, then she just engulfs my seething fullness.

"Sweet fuck, Hay!" I snarl, running my fingers through her hair.

I fist two-mock pigtails while she sucks me off. Her lips running up and down my cock, fighting to hold back my thrusts so I don't break her, this fury in my balls.

If she's an angel, her tongue is pure sin. She knows my body too damn well, probing up under my crown, taking me as deep as she can get. Her hand pumps the base of my cock, bringing it out, this flood of fucking magma I can't hold back for anything.

"Hay, fuck, gonna –"

Her eyes flash up for a second. There's no hesitation.

Do it, they say. *Come in my mouth, baby.*

It just tears out of me with a shearing groan. My hands are shaking, pulling at her hair, balls electric and pumping and overflowing her mouth.

She takes it like a good girl, everything she can, before it's finally too much and she has to back off.

Damn if I care. Her little hand keeps pumping, my seed spilling down her chin, a look in her eyes that says she's so fucking wet for me I can't even go soft.

Whoever said 'no rest for the wicked' must've never thought it'd mean sex.

I rip off her clothes and shrug out of mine a minute later. Then I'm just on her, in her, everywhere I can, ready to bring her off ten times as hard as what she did to me.

We're this wild meeting of locked lips and tangling bodies.

Her nails dig hard into my back, punishing me, and I give it back with bites raining over her shoulders, her breasts, her stomach, her inner thighs.

We make love like making war. I drive into her like a killing stroke as I lift her thighs up around my hips, spread her wide open, plunge inside that molten heat that makes my eyes roll back and consumes my entire body in fire.

Every muscle I own twitches something fierce the instant I claim her pink.

Fuck.

Then we're just one, this mass of thrusting, sweating, pumping.

I can't tell her voice from mine anymore as we shudder and moan and groan and cry, as we move in frantic rhythm, crashing together again and again. Two human waves hell-bent on finding release.

She feels so fucking good inside, better than ever, this slick burning wetness that licks over my cock and grips at me like she's trying to keep me here forever, joined to her, this writhing beast of two bodies but one mind, one heart, one driving need.

My thrusts come harder. I rock into her clit, bring her off once, almost lose it when her pussy sucks me off. But I keep fucking her straight through it, loving how she blows for me, and how she'll do it a couple more times before I fill her like mad.

It's incandescent.

It's perfect.

It's everything I've ever needed and never known I've wanted. *She's* someone who's wildness and desperation and broken edges and tentative, fragile hope. And she gives me two more whimpering Os before I can't hold mine in.

"Hay, come for me again."

"Warren..." She's gasping, her eyes telling me she can't, even if she's so damn close.

"Need you to come, darlin'. Need you to fucking come with me."

And just like that, we combust together. Bodies locked in straining, sweat-slicked heat as she convulses around me, tightening on my cock till I snap.

Everything rips out of me with enough force to make me snarl with the pain of it.

It's raw. Real. More alive than I've felt in years.

I'm only me, the me I'm *meant* to be, when I'm with her.

And maybe tonight I lay it on her so furious because I can't stand the ghost I'll become again after we finally go our separate ways.

As Hay nestles her damp, glistening body into mine, I press a kiss against her shoulder. "You should go away for a few days."

She chuckles drowsily, draping her arm over the one I've looped around her waist. "Go where? A vacation from my unintentional vacation?"

"Something like that. You've got to send Tara home soon, don't you?"

"Maybe. Her parents are being sketchy."

"They'll want their kid back eventually." I laugh, playing my fingers over the taut swell of her belly. "Just saying. Take off for a few days, see the sights, ship Tara home...and by the time you come back, I'll have handled Bress."

"Warren Ford." She smacks my arm lightly. "Are you trying to get me out of harm's way?"

"Might be. I'd rest easier knowing you were out of his reach."

"The way you make it sound, his reach extends far beyond Heart's Edge."

"Because it does." I don't say it lightly, tracing more and more kisses down her shoulder, her arm. "But in a bigger city, it's easy for you to slip away. And by the time you come back, Bress won't be able to hurt anyone ever again."

"Mm. Well..." With a drowsy sound, she snuggles deeper into me. "I'll see how plans go once I get in touch with Marie."

"All right." I give her a squeeze, then pull back. "Get some rest. You've been looking real tired after your shifts lately."

"Brody's keeps getting bigger crowds. Guess it's the summer wave." Reaching out, she catches my hand, and it'd take a much stronger man to resist the look that lingers on me. "Do you have to go?"

"I should work..."

I should. But fuck, it barely takes an ounce of pressure for her to pull me down onto the bed.

I'm not exactly fighting her, and with a laugh, I tumble down to sprawl next to her.

"Guess I could stay a little longer."

"Good." She burrows into me again. "Because your pillows suck, and you make a much better one."

"Ouch. Don't leave that on the feedback card when you check out."

She laughs. "I'd never say that to Ms. Wilma."

"She'd let you. I'm starting to think she likes you better than she likes me."

"Of course she does. I haven't disappointed her by not giving her grandchildren yet."

That saucy little minx's grin is back, sunny and bright, and I narrow my eyes with a growl. "I'm not planning on making any babies for a while, Hay," I say, tumbling her, squealing, back against the bed. "But I sure wouldn't mind demonstrating how they're made."

* * *

I ACTUALLY END up dozing off for a bit, after Haley and I rip each other apart one more time.

Deeper into the night, when it's quieter and everything around me goes still, I drift awake and linger on Hay's sleeping profile, the edge of moonlight making the faint peach fuzz of her cheek shine like silver.

Gently, I brush her hair back, then peel out of bed with careful steps, leaving her happily snuggled into the pillows she said suck so much.

Heading out into the living room, I snag my laptop and prop myself up on the couch, flicking through a few emails.

Nothing useful except a few potential leads for Bress' contacts on the other side of the swath of forests walling Heart's Edge off from the main roads into northern Idaho, that's my major stumbling point. He wouldn't keep anything damning here in Heart's Edge.

Still, I've got to find a reason to get to Spokane and trace the center of his distribution hub without being noticed. He's setting something up in Missoula, too, but Missoula's small-time.

Spokane's where I get him for crossing state lines with illegal distribution.

As much as I hate it, it won't be Jenna's death that takes him down. I've only got thirteen-year-old testimony from an unreliable eyewitness or two in the middle of pitched combat and uncertain circumstances. But the drug running, the money laundering?

I can have Bress locked away for life.

Doesn't matter how it happens.

It just has to happen.

An email with a large attachment stops me. It's from a contact in Spokane, a local who doesn't know why he's watching a vacant warehouse from his nearby apartment window. Just that I'm paying him sickening amounts to take discreet photos of any activity. He's done me one better.

He's sent me a video, starring none other than Dennis Bress.

It's shot at a distance, but there's another man and an exchange.

A briefcase opened, money counted.

A duffel bag, and inside...what looks like bricks of white powder. Bress looks around nervously, then gestures to one of the thugs flanking him. The man slits the end of a brick open, licks a line of powder from his fingers, sniffs, then nods tersely to Bress.

Fuck.

Considering the size of the distribution network I've sniffed out, there's no way in hell this is a full consignment. I'm guessing he's meeting with a new supplier for a trial run before they start moving larger quantities through his various businesses across the Pacific Northwest.

He's never gonna get to that trial run.

Gotcha, asshole.

NICOLE SNOW

* * *

It's almost dawn by the time Doc, Blake, and I convene outside the cabin.

I don't want to wake Hay, and I don't need their probing questions about the woman sleeping in my bed. We settle on the tailgate of my truck, drinking coffee from white ceramic cups and watching the video on my laptop.

"Well," Doc says in the slow, measured way he has that makes him seem like he's a wise old man of the mountain, considering every word and wasting none. "It's not hard evidence, but it's incriminating enough for a citizen's arrest."

"I don't know," Blake says. "You could get bagged just as easy for stalking."

"I'm not the one who took the video, and I paid my informant in cash. I'm just following up on a tip sent by a person in the know," I tell them. "Besides, bounty hunting and skip tracing are just licensed stalking anyway."

Blake smirks. "That why you're hiding the chick from us? Don't want her to overhear that you're basically a well-paid creep?"

Doc arches one sharp eyebrow. "What girl?"

"Her name is *Haley*, not 'the chick' or 'what girl,' and I'm hiding her so you mouthy assholes don't wake her up." I take a bracing sip of my coffee. "You in or not?"

With a snort, Blake smacks my shoulder. "I've got your back no matter what, bro."

Doc muses thoughtfully, then adds, "I suppose *someone* needs to be the cooler head to keep you two idiots out of trouble."

"Cooler head, my ass," Blake snorts. "Guess you were cool as a damn cucumber when you got yourself all mixed up with Nine."

Doc's normally serene expression tightens. "Truly? I

288

thought you knew me well enough not to fall for that *ridiculous* urban legend, Blake. Nine hasn't been seen around these parts in years. The man's probably long dead."

"Whatever, Doc. Give it another year or some shit. We're gonna have people out here hunting Nine instead of bigfoot over in Washington."

I roll my eyes as Doc just shakes his head. We don't have time to rehash whatever the latest crazy talk is around town about Doc and that scary-ass inmate he swears he never really met, even if they were both at the same hotel the night of the Great Heart's Edge Fire.

Sometimes, knowing how he sneaks around, I wonder...but today's hardly the place or time to poke at the truth.

"Guys, enough," I say dryly and take another pull off my coffee. "I'll have to map out a timeline. Figure out where and when we'll do it. You're still licensed for concealed carry?"

"Who do you think you're talking to, my man?" Blake asks, thumping his chest.

Doc counters with a more sedate, "Naturally."

"Then make sure you stay strapped just in case. We'll meet up again once I've got a game plan sketched out."

"Is it just us?" Blake asks. "What about Stewart?"

I hesitate. Blake's kept me from starting things I shouldn't, but Stewart's been pushing so hard for me to drop it, to move on, to act like a normal person and begin the healing process rather than pursuing this vendetta...damn.

He probably wouldn't want to be involved. But he's the one who told me, wasn't he? Who told me the truth, who exposed Bress for the snake he is, even if it took a night of hard drinking to pull it out of him.

I have to at least ask.

At this time of morning, he's usually up. Just to be on the safe side, I text him while Blake and Doc lose themselves in a conversation about the best bait to use for shallow water fishing.

Stew, I've got a lead and closing in. You want in?

Deliberately vague, just in case.

I'm not expecting my phone to light up in my hand seconds later with an inbound call and Stew's name. *What the fuck?*

When I answer, he doesn't even wait for me to say *hello* before he blurts, "What do you mean, a lead?"

"I mean...I've got Bress on camera in the middle of a transaction," I answer. "It's enough for me to bring him in, turn him over to the police for questioning, and drop the entire book of evidence I have in their laps. They can do the rest. So. We're planning a sting – me, Doc, and Blake. Citizen's arrest. You want in, or you still willing to sit back without ever doing right by Jenna?"

The phone shakes in my hand. I don't think I've realized how much his passive attitude has been eating at me till now.

He was the one who watched her die. He was in her platoon, covered her for several firefights, grew a bond almost like mine as her brother.

Yet while I've been eaten alive by grief, he's constantly been playing peacemaker. Trying to get me to drop it and move on.

He'll get his way once the score's settled.

He can either speed it along, or he can walk the fuck away.

"Stew? You there?"

"Yeah, and that's cold, Warren," he says after a long pause.

"So's spending years asking me to forget my sister was murdered."

"Goddamn. I was just trying to spare you more heartache, spare everybody, don't you get that?" He sighs deeply. "If this'll give you closure...yeah. I'll be there. Just clue me in on the plan when it's time."

I want to shout at him that it's about more than closure.

It's about doing the right thing, saving our town from this parasite crouched at its center, sucking it dry. But I don't have it in me, and even if Blake and Doc are still talking to each other, I can feel them watching, listening in. There's no point in starting a mess.

So I just say, "Thanks. I'll let you know."

Then I hang up, staring down at the phone, my palms clammy and my mouth dry.

It's happening. It's really happening. *Finally.*

I've got the key I need to unlock the door into Bress' world, and every criminal act that led him to the moment he decided he'd rather gun down the woman who loved him than let the world see him for who he really is.

He'll pay, Jenna. I promise you that.

God as my witness, you'll rest easy soon.

XVII: DON'T WAIT UP (HALEY)

*F*alling asleep in Warren's arms is getting to be a habit.

I shouldn't have even come to his place last night, but something about the way he'd looked when he'd walked away pulled on every last bit of me, leaving me scared and aching and just wanting to ease that torment inside him.

I've never been the kind of girl who needs to fix a broken man, but something about Warren makes me *care* that he's hurting. I can't fix him. Nobody can fix someone else's life.

But we wouldn't be human if we didn't want to offer.

And that's just it. I really *do* care about Warren Ford.

That's what got me in this mess in the first place, wanting to soothe him after that altercation with Flynn. Somehow, soothing turned into kissing, and kissing became a whole lot more.

The best sex of my life. The best rhythm my heart ever had.

I can't pretend I'm not deeply attracted to him for more than just a fling.

I also can't pretend I'm not disappointed to wake up alone

when the sound of heavy rapping on the door drags me from sleep.

I blink against the bright light of morning, squinting and rubbing at my eyes sleepily.

Warren's nowhere in sight in the bedroom. Yawning, I drag myself to my feet, hoisting up my jeans and stealing one of his t-shirts to wrap over myself before shuffling to the living room.

"I'm coming!" I mutter blearily, pushing my mussed hair back from my face. "I—"

"I've got it," Warren says tightly, already on a beeline from the kitchen to the door.

I stop in the middle of the living room, blinking at him.

I'm not really awake. Not really processing. The only things clicking are that Warren is clean and fully dressed as if he's been up for hours, vibrating with a restless energy.

And the person on the other side of the glass door is wearing muted tan. A sheriff's uniform.

Wait, what?

But the sense of dread and confusion doesn't congeal into something real enough to truly wake me up until Warren opens the door with a terse nod. "Morning, Sheriff Langley. What can I do for you?"

"You can tell me what you know about the murder of Dennis Bress," the short, stocky man on the other side of the door says. "And where you were last night."

All the sound, all the air gets sucked out of the room.

My stomach winds itself into a tight, sick coil.

I stare at Warren's tight, silently tense posture, at the man looking at him with flat, expectant eyes that say he's entirely serious. I want to scream, to say *stop this, you've got the wrong man!*

But I can tell where this is going already, helplessly rooted to the spot.

Warren remains calm, even if it's a grim, focused calm, like a soldier heading into a fight he knows he can't win.

"Well," he says slowly, "considering this is the first I'm hearing Bress is dead...that should tell you what I know. I was here last night. The entire night. What happened?"

"That's an interesting question." The sheriff hooks his thumbs in his belt loops, and I try not to stare at the gun on his hip, my lips dry. "Thing is, either you already know, or if you don't, I'm not at liberty to discuss the details of the case."

"Then why are you on my doorstep?" Warren asks flatly.

"Son, it's no secret that you almost went up on Bress at Brody's the other night. Way I heard it, you were ready to kill him then and there. And you left mad." The man sounds almost too casual, but those words are drilling, punching holes in my heart.

It's incredible they don't seem to have any effect on Warren. He's a wall of ice, never flinching.

"You're telling me I'm a suspect?"

"Maybe. Maybe you wait a bit, watch for your moment...and then you give Bress what you think he's got coming. Heard you've been stalking around him a bit. Working out some old grudge?"

"Not sure where you've been hearing things from, but you might want to check your facts, Sheriff." Warren heaves a deep sigh. "But let's do this the proper way. You want to cuff me, or you trust me to come along peacefully?"

As I realize what's happening, I jolt forward, my heart tripping and my breaths sharp. "You can't," I blurt out. "You can't arrest him! He didn't do anything—"

"Haley." Warren cuts me off quietly, but not angrily, turning a long look on me, blue eyes steady. "Go fetch Tara. Take her to Spokane. Send her home. Stay away from Heart's Edge for a while. I'll clear this up, darlin'. I promise." He shakes his head. "I've just got to do it right. Let the police follow proper procedure. Focus on you and Tara. It'll be okay."

But it doesn't feel okay. It doesn't feel okay at all.

And I feel like nothing will ever be okay again as I stand there in helpless silence, watching the sheriff lead Warren away.

* * *

Ms. Wilma is already waiting for me when I dress myself properly and trudge numbly up to the house to retrieve my niece. I find Tara ensconced in the atrium, staring with fascination at a dragonfly on a cattail stalk, forgetting even the jewel-colored green pencil hanging in her lax fingers.

Deep breath.

I settle on the bench next to Ms. Wilma, heaving a heavy sigh.

"My, you seem like you're carrying the weight of the world this morning, dear," she says. "I don't suppose it has something to do with why the police were parked in my drive this morning?"

God. I don't know how to say it the right way.

If there even *is* a right way to say something like this.

Darting an uncertain glance at Tara, I lower my voice. "Someone said, well...Mr. Bress is dead," I manage. As Ms. Wilma gasps, clutching her hands together, eyes widening and the color draining from her face, I continue reluctantly, "They think he was murdered. And they're questioning Warren."

"Pardon?" she asks faintly, before her lips set tightly. "Lord. I can't believe Dennis has been harmed, and that they think my Warren would—"

"I know." I reach over to cover her hands. "I'm sorry. I know Mr. Bress was your friend."

"He was, but I..." She shakes her head, eyes wide, turning her hand to clutch at mine. "I don't understand why they think Warren was involved."

What I don't understand is who else would kill Bress, when I know it wasn't Warren.

If Bress was the one who killed Jenna, it doesn't make sense.

It doesn't make sense that someone else would take him out. Not when he was the one making threats. He even told me he'd make sure I was taken care of, in that weird, ominous tone.

Unless? Unless he meant...

Someone else killed Jenna.

And he was offering to protect me before I got too deep in dirty secrets.

No. I've got to be imagining things, right?

I don't know the full story. I don't know anything anymore, but I do know it doesn't make sense for someone to eliminate Bress and conveniently leave Warren as the prime suspect.

But while I'm trying to make these pieces fit, Ms. Wilma watches me, waiting for an answer. I drag myself back to the present and smile faintly. "I guess they got into it at Brody's the other night, but I know Warren didn't do it. I was with him. He couldn't have."

Blood rushes to my cheeks. It's the first time I've even hinted out loud at what I know Ms. Wilma has already guessed.

Her eyes widen again before she smiles bravely as she looks away, blinking back tears and delicately rubbing at her nose.

"Well. With you in his corner, I know he'll be fine."

I swallow real heavy. *I hope.*

296

"How could someone do something so horrid to Dennis? *Murder?* In Heart's Edge, of all places."

"Warren will find out, Wilma," I promise. "But in the meantime, he made me promise to send Tara home to Seattle and stay out of town for a few days. Just until things are safe."

"You're driving to the Spokane airport? Will your car make it?"

"I think so. It's only a couple hours there and a couple back. And I've got my phone. I'll call if anything goes wrong." I squeeze her hand again, offering a smile. "I'll be back before you know it. It takes more than this to scare me out of town."

Her laugh is weak but genuine. And it warms something deep inside me, when she leans over and kisses my cheek. "You're a good girl, darling. I do hope you'll consider staying longer."

I can't really think about the implications of that right now, so I just squeeze her hand again and stand.

"Tara," I call, breaking my niece from her reverie. She blinks, lifting her head, fingers tightening on the pencil, and I smile. "C'mon. We need to talk."

Tara tenses, eyeing me warily. "Am I in trouble?"

"Nah." It's hard to smile, but for her I always find it in me. "I'll even take you for ice cream after. But give Ms. Wilma a hug first."

Tara gives me another long, suspicious look, then stands, smoothing her dress just like Ms. Wilma does. Then she launches herself at the woman like a little rocket and hugs her tight.

Those glimmering tears in Ms. Wilma's eyes bead heavier, threatening to spill over, as she hugs my niece fiercely.

"You're such a sweet girl," Ms. Wilma whispers. "Such a darling. Be nice to your aunt, and don't ever stop drawing your pretty pictures."

I don't think Tara realizes that's Ms. Wilma's way of saying goodbye. My heart feels like lead.

But finally they separate, and Tara tucks her art supplies under one arm before taking my hand, letting me lead her out into the light and toward the cabin. Her eyes glimmer with worry as she looks up at me.

"Auntie Hay?" she asks. "What's wrong?"

"Nothing, sweetie. It's just..." I squeeze her hand. "It's time for you to go home soon. Your Mom and Dad are coming back from Hawaii tomorrow, aren't they?"

Her face falls. "Oh, yeah. Guess so." She pouts. "But I don't want to go."

I stop on the grassy path, crouching down in front of her and looking up into her sullen, sad little face. "Hey. Talk to me, munchkin. Why don't you want to go home? Are things bad with your parental units?"

She shakes her head.

"No, no." She scuffs one foot. "I'm really having fun here. And Ms. Wilma doesn't make me go to bed by eight."

"I should probably have talked to Ms. Wilma about that," I say, ruffling her hair. "But that's really all it is?"

Tara blinks, looking confused. "I guess. I mean I miss my bed and my pool, but I'm gonna miss you more, Auntie Hay."

Dammit, this kid really knows how to rip up my heartstrings.

And when she flings herself at me, I grunt but catch her and hug her wholeheartedly, then lift her up and hold her against me as I turn to carry her into the cabin.

We cling to each other a minute longer before we separate so I can help her pack. But it's not long before I'm watching her zip around the house, run out to the car, run back into the cabin, then out again, digging and scowling with increasing frustration before she just stops in the middle of the living room and proclaims, "Oh, *shoot!*" with a little stomp of her foot.

"Swear jar," I remind her mildly, picking out a few pieces of her dirty laundry to wash before it gets packed up.

"Shoot isn't a swear!" she protests.

"It's a substitute for one, and you know quite well what it is." I pitch a shirt into the laundry hamper. "So what are you oh-shooting yourself over?"

"I left my new pencils in the car when it broke down," she says, "but they're not in there and I can't find them anywhere."

"Crap. Stewart must've taken them out at the shop."

"*Swear jar.*"

"I won't tell on yours if you won't tell on mine." I sigh. "I'll probably see Stewart at work tonight, so I'll ask if he can get them and bring them by when he has a chance, okay?"

"But I wanted to draw on the plane..."

"You can take my pencils."

Tara perks, eyes lighting up. "The good ones?"

I grin. "The *really* good ones."

She bounces and flings herself over to hug me. "Thank you!"

Chuckling, I give her a squeeze – then tense when my phone buzzes in my pocket. "Go find your flip-flops and wrap them up. I've got to take this."

I won't lie. Watching my niece race off, there's a desperate hope inside me that the call is Warren, telling me everything's all right and nothing has to change. But I'm surprised when I see my sister's name on the caller ID.

Uh-oh. Did she see something about Bress on the news, or does she just have really good timing? It's hard to believe a murder in a small town would make it all the way to Hawaii, but still...

I swipe the call as I step outside onto the sunny deck, then lift the phone to my ear. "Hey," I say awkwardly.

"Hey," she answers, quiet and oddly dull.

"Ready to take your kid back?" I ask. It's always flippant sarcasm with us, so I'm really not ready for her answer to be a choked sound that I realize is a sob, and then a single broken, sniffling word.

"*No.*"

Holy crap.

I can count on one hand how many times I've heard Marie cry since we grew up. On one *finger*.

Panic leaps through me, leaving me babbling, fumbling with the phone as if I could reach through it to push the off button and make her *stop*. "Oh—oh fuck, Marie, I'm sorry, it was just a joke, I—"

"No—no, it's not your fault," she says quickly, sucking in several loud gulps of air. "It's not your fault. I miss Tara. I just...I don't know how to tell her the news."

Oh. *Oh.*

I guess Hawaii's not going that well after all.

I go still, calming myself, listening to the faint little sounds on the other end of the line – the sounds of my sister trying to hold in her tears, and I suddenly wish she wouldn't.

We've never been good at being a family, but she's my *sister.*

And I want to be there for her.

"So tell me," I urge quietly. "Tell me, Marie."

"I don't want to impose..."

"It's not imposing," I promise. "It's *never* been imposing, and I don't know why we created this idea that it is. We're sisters. You can lean on me. I want you to lean on me."

I know Marie. I know this is the moment she shuts down, retreats behind a neutral comment, pretends to be unaffected. Instead, I just get another sniffle, then, "John. John and me, we..." She chokes out a bitter, humorless laugh. "It's over, and it's my fault."

"Oh, I doubt that. Sometimes two people just don't work, and it's not anyone's fault. What happened?"

She doesn't answer me until after several breaths there's a tentative whisper. "Haley?"

Leaning forward, I prop my elbows on the deck railing. "Yeah?"

Out of all the things I expect Marie to say, the last thing is "I...I think I'm gay."

Oh.

Huh.

While I stand there, blinking, trying to process that, Marie rushes on with a shaky laugh. "Oh, fuck. Or lesbian or whatever word I'm supposed to use. I can't believe I just said that out *loud* to someone besides John..." Her next breath is half laugh, half sob. "It's like I married him because I thought it would make me fit into who I'm supposed to be, and I *do* love him, just...not like that. And it's not fair to him that I did this to him and had a kid with him and used him—"

"Hey. Hey, slow down," I soothe. "Does he feel used?"

"That's the worst part. He was *so* understanding. He just smiled and hugged me and said, 'we had some good times, didn't we?' and then we both cried like idiots for like an hour, but...it was okay." There's a sound on the other end of the line, tissue paper ripping from a packet, then a sniffle. "And we both love Tara so much. We want to stay friends and be good parents to her. We don't want to split up her family."

"That's a good start," I say, and I don't know when I started smiling but somehow I'm crying, too. But they're happy tears even if I hate that my sister and brother-in-law had to struggle so much just to find what was right for them. "And just so you know, whoever you are, I'm always going to love the hell out of you."

As soon as I say it, we both go quiet. But she's the one to say what we're both thinking, a tentative, "Um, have we ever said that to each other before? That we love each other."

"Probably not for a long time." My smile widens even as I sniffle and wipe at my cheeks. "But I always knew. We're sisters. And you and John will work things out. You didn't use him. You just had work to do to figure yourselves out."

"And when did you get so smart about that?"

"When I fell out of my box and landed somewhere I never expected, I guess." My voice cracks, but I rein it in. "You're going to be okay. But I hope you know I'm going to give you shit every time I catch you looking at cute girls."

"Oh, *God*." I've never heard Marie sound so uncertain of herself before, but it's sweet. "That's...I've tried so much not to look, but I mean, just saying it out loud...now it's like I can't *stop*."

"It's new. That's going to be a bit shaky. But if it's who you are, be happy. I'm happy for you."

"Thank you," she says slowly, as if the words taste unfamiliar. "I wish I'd told you sooner. I've wanted to talk to you about it since high school." She lets out a dry, wistful laugh. "I had a crush on your idiot friend, Britney, before she went off in that dressing room with your ex..."

I snort. "You dodged a bullet there."

"Guess I did." She hesitates, then asks, "How are you? After Eddy, I never got a chance to ask. And we don't talk enough."

"I know. It's okay," I promise. "I'm okay. Doing better. It feels good to just wander without being lost for a while. No expectations." I tuck my hair back. "Losing Eddy and starting over may have been a blessing in disguise."

"You mean you're happy? Stranded out there in some nowhere town?"

"Yeah. Plenty to paint, fresh air, sweet mountains, good food..." I bite my lip. "Good sex..."

"Haley!" she gasps, but she's laughing. "Don't tell me you're shacking up with some farm boy?"

"I wouldn't call him a farm boy, exactly, but he's definitely down-home good." My smile fades. "But he's in some trouble with the locals, and he told me I should send Tara home and stay away for a few days."

"Have you gotten yourself into something? Do you need help?"

"No. No, it's not like that." I shake my head. "I don't think it's really going to turn into anything. And I love having Tara here. If you need more time to figure out how to have that conversation with her..." I look over my shoulder at Tara, watching through the glass door as she races around. "We'll just keep enjoying our little vacay together."

"If you could, for just a little longer, I'd appreciate it." It's not hard to tell Marie's not used to asking for things. It's always been hard for both of us, but it makes my chest hurt in the best way that she's willing to ask me. To *trust* me. "That's going to be a tough talk. John and I need to work together to figure out the right way to have it and what'll be best for Tara in the end. I'm sorry."

"No apologies. I love that little kit, and love having her around."

"Even when she calls you Auntie Hay?"

I smirk. "I love her a smidge less then."

"Idiot." She falters again, then asks more softly, "Hey, um, Haley?"

She stops. But I don't need her to say it. I know, and it's okay.

"I know, Marie," I murmur. "Can we try to talk like this more?"

There's a pause.

"Yeah," she says, relief audible in her voice. "I'd like that. A lot."

"Me too." This time, though, as Tara goes racing past, I open the door and lightly snag her arm, slowing her with a gentle tug. "Hey. Say hi to your kid," I say, offering my niece the phone.

Her eyes go wide, and if I was ever worried about how Tara was being treated at home, that worry vanishes when I see the clear *joy* in her face at the merest prospect of talking to her mother. No matter how our home life messed us up, made us weird about family, my sister loves her daughter enough that it doesn't matter, because she makes Tara so happy and is so good to her.

If Marie can do that, can start a family, no matter what missteps she took, and both give and receive that kind of love...maybe someday I can, too.

It's a breathless thought. I'm smiling uncontrollably as I hand the phone over.

"Mom?" Tara gasps into it, then *"Mom! Hi!"* before launching into a high-speed story of her drawings, of Ms. Wilma's garden, of all the pretty things she's found and kept, from shiny pebbles to bits of pink paper. It's nice to just sit back and listen while I slowly sort through these feelings inside me. I think I'm coming to a decision, and it's one that requires being brave.

But I've never backed down before.

I won't start now.

It's almost half an hour before Tara and Marie finish talking, but finally Tara says, "bye, Mom. I miss you. I love you!" before hanging up. As she hands it back to me, she asks, "Mom said I'm staying a little longer?"

"Yeah. I guess we both are." I pocket my phone and push away from the deck railing with a smile. "C'mon. Let's go tell Ms. Wilma she's not getting rid of us yet."

XVIII: DETOUR (WARREN)

*S*omething just isn't right here.

I'm no stranger to small town police work. In places like Heart's Edge, murder doesn't really happen.

When it does, it's always an obvious crime of passion with a clear perp.

My case doesn't qualify as that. One little argument in a bar, no one throwing hands, no one getting hurt, doesn't set up motive for enough rage to drive a crime of passion.

It's not enough to keep me here as a valid suspect, even if I'm the only option they've got right now.

So why am I still here, propped on the bench in the holding cell of the tiny local police station, pressing my knuckles into my mouth and asking myself – again and again – the only question that really, truly matters?

Who the hell killed Dennis Bress?

The most likely option is one of his drug associates. Maybe he crossed the wrong person.

Maybe he owed someone money.

Maybe they realized someone was onto him and got rid of him to tie up any loose ends.

Fuck maybe.

Something's eating at me. Doesn't feel right. I'm one bust away from bringing Bress in, and coincidentally, he dies.

Gunshot between the eyes, supposedly. I managed to get that much out of Sheriff Langley during my interrogation.

I doubt he was consumed with so much remorse and guilt that he took his own life over Jenna.

That doesn't mean someone didn't kill him because of my sister, and because I was getting too close.

Shit, what am I thinking? I can't possibly be implying – even just to myself – that Bress was *innocent,* and I've been after the wrong man all this time.

Stewart fucking *saw* him. Stew saw him, and the other members of the unit backed him up. I have only his word to go on, but his word's always been good.

And the only other person who could tell me the truth isn't around to testify about her own death.

Something's not adding up here.

I *have* to believe some rival in Bress' business took him out.

Because the other option, the *only* other option, is that Stew either lied to me, or got everything wrong and doesn't even know it himself.

PTSD has a way of doing that with traumatic events. It can rewire the whole damn memory until you see things that never happened and think they're real.

Christ. Have I been blaming Dennis Bress for an accident all this time? Just because I put blind faith in Stew's memory, when even he questioned it?

My face drops into my hands with a snarl. I look through my fingers at the scratches on the bench, mostly from years of other people locked up in here, wanting to leave their mark. Usually just for getting rowdy drunk or petty crimes.

There's a big etching in the corner, off in the shadows. A

large number nine next to a jagged heart, and the words, *Miss me? You will.*

I snort. There's one more little legend for Blake to give Doc a heaping pile of crap over. I'm starting to think Nine disappearing – the only real jailbreak in Heart's Edge history – might be easier to solve than figuring out what the fuck happened to Bress.

Think, dammit, I tell myself.

What about the other people on their team? Granted, they're more Stewart's people than mine, people he's served with, a few he still employs, but if he trusted them...

No. None of this fits together in my head. At least I have the cell to myself, though.

There's almost never any reason to use it, outside odd, scary cases like Nine, unless Flynn takes it too far here and there and gets thrown in the drunk tank till morning for his own good.

He's been staying more sober lately, so it's just me, myself, and my circling thoughts, trying to shove a square peg into a round hole when the edges won't line up. Sheriff Langley sits across from me in the single-room jailhouse, looking uncomfortable at his desk, trying to pretend I'm not in the room.

Neither of us can believe I'm here.

It'd be funny if I wasn't so damned pissed.

Did someone set me up?

I'm pulled from my thoughts by the door opening. I thought it'd be Grandma coming to raise hell as the town matriarch, if she didn't march straight to the mayor's office first.

What I'm not expecting is for Haley damn West to come strolling in.

Instead of her usual ragged cutoff shorts or the skimpier things she wears for work, she's done herself up in a pretty sleeveless dress in a summery blue. It's ladylike, clinging to her figure just enough to make my mind wander to my dick, the flare of her skirt adding a musical grace to those sweet fucking legs of hers.

Shame there's no conjugal visits in here.

She's skimmed her hair up in a deliberately messy twist, loose tendrils framing her face, her makeup subtly done until those wicked, snapping green eyes look innocent, beguiling.

It's almost like she's a whole different person.

She flashes me a quick glance, a secretive wink, before schooling her face to solemn as she approaches the desk. *Shit. She better not be about to do what I think she is.*

"Officer," she says pleasantly, offering her hand. "I didn't get a chance to introduce myself this morning. I'm—"

"Haley West," Langley says slowly, looking at her like she's some strange new creature he's never seen before, his brows drawn in a terse line. But he stands, taking his wide-brim hat off with a courteous bow before shaking her hand lightly. "Officer Wentworth Langley. Local sheriff and pretty much half the Heart's Edge police force. A pleasure, ma'am."

"The pleasure's mine." Hay dimples prettily.

Fuck me. I had no idea she had such manners and grace, and wonder if Grandma's been schooling her. Or if this is the face she puts on over that restless artist's spirit to survive in a world that doesn't get her kind of fire?

Soon she's on performance, moving smoothly, all charm and sweetness. "You caught me off guard this morning. I'm afraid I need to clear up a misunderstanding."

Langley sinks down in his chair with slow, thoughtful movements, watching her in puzzlement. "What's that, Miss?"

"Well, it's about Mr. Bress. I met him a few times. He seemed very nice, and I'm so sorry for the town's loss, but...he died last night, didn't he?" She watches him with liquid eyes, lashes fluttering, and Langley clears his throat, straightening his shoulders.

"Well, Miss, I can't give out details of a case still in progress to the general public, but I can confirm that time of death was at some point last night, yes."

"Then I'm afraid you have to let Mr. Ford go," Hay says with a simplicity that seems to assume it's just fact. Langley blinks.

"What?"

"Well, I...how do I put this?" She clears her throat, ducking her head, cheeks flushing beet red as she glances at me from under her lashes. "You see, I was with Warren all night. I promise you he didn't go anywhere or do anything to anyone. And if you need more testimony, then both my niece Tara and Warren's grandmother Wilma Ford can verify. Both his alibi and mine."

That's when it hits me.

Hay's here to spring me out of jail.

I'd told her to stay put and let me handle it, but this stubborn damn woman put herself out here to save my neck again.

She's a stranger here, with no good reason to think anyone in Heart's Edge would trust her with murder on the line.

And she risked it anyway.

For me.

My chest swells with something almost like pride. Fuck, Haley's something else.

Brave. Wonderful. Smart.

Tricky as hell, too. Because she's doing it, pulling the wool over Langley right now.

He looks uncomfortable, tugging at the collar of his shirt, adjusting his tie, and he can't quite look at her.

"Now, Miss, anyone can come in here and say they can

vouch for someone. Doesn't make it true."

"So you're calling Ms. Wilma a liar?" Haley asks sweetly. There's that touch of sugar-sweet poison I know so well. She's injected it in me so deep it practically burns in my veins. "Here's the thing, Sheriff Langley. I know the penalty for lying to an officer of the law. I'm out here on my own, no family but my niece, no money, and really the police could come up with any kind of charges and no one would be able to help me. But I'm willing to sign a sworn affidavit, admissible in a court of law, that I was with Warren Ford last night. Do you think I'd be willing to risk prosecution in my situation if I was lying?"

Langley doesn't stand a chance.

I'd say Hay's *definitely* been taking lessons from the Wilma Ford School of Kill 'Em With Kindness, but this is all her. And it's hard for me not to grin when Langley shoots me an irritated look before sighing and hefting himself to his feet, adjusting his belt.

"Wait here," he grunts, then eyes Haley. "No. Wait *outside*. I don't want you two colluding."

"No collusion here, sir," she says tartly, smiling up at him before turning in a flare of her skirt and sauntering out. She doesn't even *look* at me.

Little minx.

After the door closes, Langley gives me another sour look through the bars separating us. "You're lucky you got a woman who'll go to bat for you."

"I know."

I can't help grinning. I'm not mad. Langley's just doing his job.

With another irritable grunt, he adjusts his belt again and turns to stalk into the back room. I hear the sound of a copy machine before he emerges with a stack of papers and trudges outside, his shoulders bowed.

I don't envy him, honestly. Small town cops aren't cut out for murder investigations, and this case will probably be cold within twenty-four hours, even if the Feds descend and take control.

Good thing I'm an expert at picking up cold trails.

When he comes back, it's with those papers signed in dashes of blue ink. He rifles through the keys on his belt, then unlocks the cell and slides the bars open to let me out with a toss of his head. "Go on, then. Get."

I don't have to be told twice.

I'm out the door in a heartbeat, and I'm not going to lie: my heart does some damn weird shit when I step outside and see Haley leaning against her Mustang with her arms folded over her chest and her hair pulled loose in a windswept tumble.

She's so fucking gorgeous, and it's more than how she looks.

It's who she is.

And I may not know everything about her just yet, but I know plenty to realize she's really something special.

I rein myself in, just barely, as I draw closer. "I thought I told you to go, Hay," I rumble.

She cocks her head, looking at me sidelong. Even with that fresh-faced, dewy-eyed makeup, there's no hiding that the vixen is back in that catty little confident smirk.

"Yeah, well, I told me to stay," she retorts, then laughs and flicks her fingers against my stomach. "You could say thank you."

She's laughing. I'm not. I'm drawn in to her, leaning close.

"Thanks," I rumble. I'm fascinated by the play of the sun over her deep brown hair, bringing out whiskey and even red highlights, and I catch a lock to coil around my fingers. "Thank you for coming for me."

Her lashes sweep downward, and she shifts toward me –

only to break backward as Langley leans out the door, fixing me with a dire look.

"You're still a person of interest, Ford," he grunts. "If you try to leave town, I'll have to bring you back in."

I give him an exasperated look. "I'm not going anywhere."

I'm lying.

But I can't give that away, and I just toss my head to Hay as I round to the passenger side of the Mustang. "Come on."

She dips in a mockingly sweet curtsy to Langley, then slips behind the driver's side and sends the Mustang purring out onto the road toward Charming Inn. The engine sounds so good it's hard to believe it's running on duct tape, and I wonder what Stewart did to it.

Stewart. Fuck.

There goes my mind again. I prop my elbow against the open passenger side window, the warm, sluggish mid-afternoon breeze fingering my hair with the car's top down and the short miles between town proper and the inn rapidly vanishing.

"I'll need you to drop me off so I can get my truck," I tell her, watching the town's old ranch-style houses roll past and then fade into grassy fields.

Haley glances at me. "And where are you going?"

"Somewhere away from here."

"Warren! The sheriff just said—"

"I know what Langley said. But something's not right." I frown, grinding my knuckles against my lips. "Bress got killed just as I was closing in. He wanted to tell me something. What if Bress didn't kill Jenna after all?"

She breathes in sharply but doesn't sound very surprised. In fact, she almost sounds chagrined, a guilty look sliding toward me. "I...I'd wondered that when I heard the news. I just didn't want to say anything when you've been so *convinced.*"

"Not really much chance to say anything, either, when you'd been awake thirty seconds before I got hauled in."

"Yeah. That too," she says, then falls quiet as she eases the Mustang into the turnoff for the side lane flanking the inn. I don't say anything until she's pulled the car up behind my truck and killed the engine.

As we get out, I say, "So maybe my sister's death was an accident."

But that explanation feels too simple, too easy, and I shake my head as I slam the car door. "Or maybe there's more going on, and someone in Heart's Edge is watching me and doesn't want me to know the truth." I step closer to her, rounding the hood of the car. "So I need to leave Heart's Edge. Get out of sight so I can plot my next move."

She slips close to me, prettier than ever under the sun-dappled trees overhead.

Suddenly leaving seems like the last thing I want to do.

Reaching up, she curls her hands against my chest, fingers tangling lightly in my shirt. There's so much warmth in her eyes, so much more than I deserve, but it's enough to make me wonder if maybe, just maybe there's a man left underneath this broken wreck.

A man worth those worried looks, that warmth, the concern and gentleness she's shared. Totally at odds with every harsh word we ever spat at each other.

"For how long?' she asks.

"Not long," I promise. "Just long enough to plan my next move." I sweep an arm around her waist, pulling her against me, savoring the fit of her body against mine. I drink in her heat, that mix of delicate softness and toned, smooth skin hiding her strength. "I'll be back for you, darlin'. That's a vow."

With a soft catch of her breath, she turns her face away, that pretty sunset pink racing across her cheeks. I *love* seeing this. The softer side of her, the sweetness she hides behind the thorns.

"That's not what I was asking," she whispers.

Isn't it?

"Doesn't matter."

I trace my fingertips along her jaw, coax her back up to look at me – and to meet me as I dip, claiming her mouth with mine, tasting her. We kiss with parted lips and rushed breaths, this open and lingering thing that feels sweeter and dirtier than it should.

Conflicted, just like every day of my life since she tumbled in.

Just like it is now with how she trembles in my arms, how slowly our tongues twine together until there's intimacy in every deep, searching stroke; in every hitched and whispered sound; in every wet-hot locking of lips.

Fuck, this feels good. *She* feels good, right, in ways I hadn't thought I'd be able to sense again. I'm *alive*, for the first time in forever.

Because of Hay.

Bress may be dead, but my mission isn't over.

I *will* find the truth.

And then, just maybe, I'll find out what this could be with Hay.

When we break apart, her eyes are starlight seen through smoke. She clings to me for one last trace of my tongue against her upper lip, one last graze of her teeth against my tingling mouth.

"I'll be back for you," I promise again, then make myself pull away and stride toward my truck. I've got work to do.

Dead men don't wait for love.

XIX: LAST RUN (HALEY)

$\mathcal{I}$ don't like watching Warren drive away like this.

Not just because by that simple act, he's made himself a *fugitive* suspect in a murder investigation.

I miss him.

I miss him and he's only been gone for five damn minutes, but even worse...

I can't shake this terrible sense of foreboding that everything is about to go terribly wrong.

Letting myself into the cabin, I sink down on the couch, leaning forward and pressing my face into my palms.

"Man, Haley," I mutter, blowing out between my fingers heavily. "When you step in it, you really step in it."

Running away from my failed life, my cheating fiancé, and my best friend to get stranded in the prettiest little Podunk town I've ever seen.

Getting threatened with craft supplies.

Playing mom to my niece in ways that make me wonder when I'll ever get to settle down.

Meeting the most infuriating, sexy, idiotic, caring, ridiculously noble beast-man I've ever known.

Discovering what family means and rediscovering my sister all over again.

And now...the murder of a kind, older man who'd helped me one day just because he could, with nothing in it for him.

That escalated quickly. *My whole life.*

I'm so tired, spun in so many circles, it takes a few minutes for the silence to sink in. The cabin is empty. Tara promised me she was safe to stay on her own for an hour or so while I went to spring Warren, insisting that she was *ten* now and it was okay, and if she got scared, she'd go up to Ms. Wilma's.

But the cabin is empty.

There's no Tara in sight.

Oh, no.

Oh, *fuck* – I'm the shittiest, most irresponsible aunt ever!

I swallow something tight in my throat. Tell myself she's probably somewhere, maybe out back, chasing butterflies with Mozart or something.

"Tara?" I call tentatively, standing and peering through the house.

No sign of her in the bathroom, the bedroom, or out on the back deck. My heart sinks.

She hasn't snuck into Warren's place, either. It's locked down tight and dark, just as I left it when I let myself out this morning.

There's a sick, scared feeling in the pit of my stomach, but I won't panic just yet. If she's not with me, Tara's always with Ms. Wilma.

I'll probably find her in the atrium with her sketchbook in her lap, picking out the perfect colored pencil to capture a glimmering hummingbird's breast against the yellow of a daffodil.

But that sense of unease haunts me as I head up to the main house. Call it intuition, call it spidey sense, I don't care

– something's *wrong*. My palms are sweaty by the time I step inside the lobby and almost smack into Ms. Wilma.

I stumble and she catches my shoulders, steadying me and looking down with worried eyes. "Haley? Dearest, what's wrong? You look a fright."

"Tara," I say quickly, my mouth drying as I realize, before I can even get the words out, that I'm at a dead end. I slump. "She's...she's not with you."

Ms. Wilma's eyes widen, her mouth a startled O. "No, dear, I haven't seen her since last night. She—oh, *shit*."

Any other time I might have burst out laughing at prim, ladylike, elegant Wilma Ford gasping *shit*.

Now, though, all I can think about is my niece, suddenly MIA.

My pulse ramps up hot, and I rake my hair back, pacing back and forth. "She might still be in the house. We can split up, search—"

"Of course." Ms. Wilma nods decisively. "I'll get Flynn to help and call round to the staff." She clasps my hands warmly. "It'll be all right. We'll find her."

I nod, swallowing against the terror in my throat, and dash off down the hall.

I check the atrium first, but there's no sign that Tara had even been there today. The next twenty minutes dissolve into a frantic haze as I race from room to room and floor to floor, calling "Tara? Tara!" while other voices echo the same.

I'm going to throw up.

This is my fault.

I shouldn't have left her alone for even a minute. She's not here.

She's not here, and I don't know where to look for her.

When Ms. Wilma and I reconvene in the lobby, it's with grave faces. She squeezes my hand one more time, but her touch is no longer so certain. "I'll call Sheriff Langley and ask him to come out immediately," she promises, only to be cut off by the trill of my phone.

I fish it from the little hidden pocket inside my skirt, fighting the folds of fabric frantically when everything in me screams that it's Tara. It has to be, and then she'll laugh and say *gotcha, I've been hiding all this time* and everything will be okay.

"Hello?" I gasp into the phone, swiping without even looking.

"Hey, Haley," Stewart says cheerfully, and my stomach churns.

Frick, I don't have time for this.

Pinching the bridge of my nose, I pace toward the door. "Stewart, I can't talk right now, I'm looking for—"

"Tara?" he finishes without prompting. "She's right here at the shop."

Huh?

I stop in my tracks, rooted to the spot, darting a curiously watching Ms. Wilma a wide-eyed look. *It's Stewart*, I mouth. *He has Tara.*

Then out loud I manage, "What...how?"

"Aw, your little scamp walked all the way into town on her lonesome. Came to get her pencils, I guess."

I groan. *Goddammit.*

With Warren getting arrested and Bress' murder, I'd totally forgotten I'd promised to ask Stewart if he'd taken them out of the car. "Jesus, my bad. I'm really sorry."

"Don't fret. It's no problem. You want to drop by and pick her up?"

"Yeah. I'll be there in a few minutes." I flash Ms. Wilma the OK sign. She looks confused but smiles, though I'm already turning away, racing for the door. "Listen, Stewart...I'm sorry about your friend."

He sounds puzzled. "My friend?"

Crap. I'm just stepping in it everywhere. "You didn't hear about Bress? I'd thought you two were close."

There's such a long pause it makes me stop, frowning. There's that intuition, prickling like a cactus again.

Stewart's mournful voice sounds almost exaggerated as he says, "Yes, ma'am. I suppose I hadn't processed yet. It's still so new and...raw."

"I'm sorry if I was insensitive. Or if Tara intruded."

"You're fine. I promise. And honestly, it's nice to have a bright little distraction around this man-cave."

I smile faintly. "I need to hang up, but I'm getting in the car now. I'll take her off your hands real soon."

"No problem. But you might want to have a talk with the little doll about wandering off..."

"Oh, we'll *talk* all right. She scared the living crap out of me."

Stewart answers with an indulgent chuckle. "See you in a few, Haley."

"Sure." I hang up the phone, stopping at the driver's side door of the Mustang, just looking down at the screen.

Something still feels...weird.

If Tara walked all the way to Stewart's, why didn't I see her on the drive back with Warren?

Was it just bad timing?

Or is this warning call screaming in the back of my mind onto something?

But I have to go. I can't leave my niece in a freaking car shop alone.

So I jump into my Mustang and go careening out onto the highway toward town.

Only, I don't make it more than six or seven blocks before the Mustang abruptly sputters, coughs, and grinds to a halt so hard the entire thing shakes enough to rattle my teeth.

It's different from the other times it's died. That was

more like a sort of gentle tapering, as if it just slumped off to sleep. This feels like a death rattle.

"Damn you, not now!" I yell, banging my fist on the steering wheel.

There's barely enough momentum for me to get it off the road so I won't block what little traffic there is. Then, that's it. All she's got. The car just rolls to a stop.

Swearing myself blue, I slump forward and thunk my forehead against the steering wheel.

So much for that quick fix lasting for a week or two.

Fuck it. If Tara walked to Stewart's, I can walk the rest of the way, and I can ask Stewart for a ride and a tow back to Charming Inn.

But just as I'm getting out of the car, Stewart's massive monster truck comes rumbling toward me, the sun glimmering off it in heat waves as it appears out of nowhere. *What the...*

He eases up alongside the Mustang, leaning one arm outside of the window, offering me an almost sly half-smile. "Looks like you could use a ride. Lucky thing we're going to the same place, huh?"

Something about his disarming smile freezes my blood today.

I eye him, keeping the Mustang between us. "I don't get it. How'd you know?"

He shrugs, lightly slapping his hand against the side of the truck before pushing the door open and getting out. "Premonition, sugar. They always said my grandpa had it, and I guess it rubbed off."

I'm silent, almost trembling, wondering if this whole thing is a dream.

Then Stewart bursts out laughing. "Shit, girl, I'm just pulling your tail. Actually, I thought I'd head out to meet you partway. Damn good thing I did, considering the damage."

My brows press deeper against my skull. "Why, though? It's such a short distance..."

Stewart spreads his hands. His smile is a mask now, not quite reaching his flat, cold, brown eyes. "And yet here you are, stranded."

God, this definitely isn't adding up.

I peer past him, into the cab of the truck, but it's empty. "You didn't bring Tara?"

"She's safe at the garage. A few of my boys are keeping an eye on her," he answers too easily. "She's happy as a clam, just painting away. Did her one better than those pencils. We had some old poster paint lying around, and now she's got a pretty good start on a career as an impressionist."

Poster paint?

My breath goes cold and still. No.

No, I've got to be overthinking things after nearly losing my shit at the thought of Tara disappearing. Stewart couldn't be the one who left that blood-red threat slashed on my door. He couldn't.

But if Bress didn't do it, if Bress is dead...who did?

I curl my hands against the edge of the Mustang's door. It's the only thing keeping me from bolting. "What do you need poster paint for?" I ask warily.

And just like that, Stewart's smile vanishes.

He looks at me like a snake, flat and unmoving. "Get in the truck," he says tonelessly. "Got a tight schedule this evening, and I still need to get your 'stang hitched up."

Every instinct says no. Says to run.

But...but he's got Tara, and I can't leave my niece alone with this man who's making every alarm bell shriek inside my head right now.

I don't say anything, but I wish like hell I wasn't still wearing the heels from the prison trip this morning.

Maybe I can stomp on his foot if I need to, break a toe in self-defense.

Silently, I round the truck at the rear, keeping distance between us, and climb up the extremely high footboard to heft myself into the truck. It's so far off the ground I almost have to scramble.

I shouldn't be noticing things like that, but I'm already thinking about what if I have to throw myself out of the vehicle while it's moving at full speed?

Breathe, Haley.

I'm being ridiculous, I really am. It has to be the fear eating me up, but Tara's fine.

Everything's fine.

I still hold my tongue, smoothing my hands over my dress and my heaving stomach as Stewart gets in the truck, starts it up, and maneuvers it in front of the Mustang. We don't say a single word to each other as he hooks the Mustang up to the tow hitch on his truck, then eases onto the road, pulling my car behind us.

I keep myself as far away from him as I can, pressed against the car door and looking firmly out the window.

We'll be in town soon. I'll get my niece, and then I'll ask for help.

But if I call Warren, will he come? Especially when I don't know where he's hiding.

I can take Tara to the diner, call Warren or Ms. Wilma or even Flynn – he may be a drunk, but I think there's the core of a nice old man underneath.

I just *need* to be with people I can trust, right now.

And Stewart isn't one of them. Maybe I'm overreacting, but I know one thing.

Better safe than sorry.

Better safe than *wrong*. About everything.

Stewart pulls up outside Pep-Pep-Go. There's not one single car in the lot, and the garage is closed.

The lights inside the main shop are dark, and I can't see anyone through the windows.

Despite the bleary heat of the day, sweat chills on my skin. I lick my lips, curling my fingers in the edge of my skirt.

"Go on," he says, leaving the engine running. "She's waiting for you inside. I'll get your Mustang in the garage and have a looksie."

He's looking at me strangely, expectantly.

I'm trying not to look at him, but it's like we're playing this game of pretending we don't know something's wrong. I nod slowly, smoothing my skirt.

Really, I'm feeling for that inner pocket and making sure the shape of my phone is in it. It presses against my palm, and I breathe a bit easier as I get out of the truck – nearly falling that last drop to the ground – and push my way inside the shop, the bell jingling overhead.

It's so dark inside I can barely make out anything. I'm so nervous my entire body tingles.

Peering into the gloom barely lit by the light through the windows, I step in and let the door close behind me. It hits with an ominous *thump* and a jingling of the bell overhead, and my heart skips.

"Tara?"

There's no sign of her. No sign of anyone, and my stomach feels hollow as I turn slowly.

It's too familiar now. Like that girl in a horror movie who only realizes too late that she's walked into a trap – but she's beyond the point of no return and has no hope of turning back.

I can't turn back.

Not without Tara.

But I'm going to find her on my own terms, even if I have

to tear this whole garage apart. I'm not going to let Stewart scare or intimidate me, use my niece against me, or hurt Tara.

I'll *kill him* with my bare hands if he even tries.

Yet just as I'm turning back to the exit to head outside, a small voice at my back freezes my blood and rips at my soul.

"Auntie Hay?"

Oh, Jesus.

I don't want to turn around. As long as I don't turn around, it's not real.

The fear in Tara's voice. The soft, trembling plea.

But I can't stop myself. I stumble on my heels as I whip around, my heart nosediving, my breaths raw and thorny.

"Tara!" I cry.

Stewart pushes her through the rear door leading in from the garage – with a small jackknife peeking up over her head. She's dirty, greasy, like she's been pushed to the floor of the garage, her dress ripped, tears streaming down her smudged face as she moves forward shakily, her face white with fear.

White hot terror and rage ignite my blood.

I'll kill him. I'll kill him, and I start moving forward – only to freeze as Stewart swings the knife around and grabs her hair, pressing the tip against a single pigtail. Tara cringes, whimpering, holding perfectly still, her eyes so wide the whites show all around the dark, her begging look asking me to save her.

"Stay, Haley," Stewart warns. He's still smiling that unnervingly pleasant smile, bland and plastic. "Don't move, or this little girl might lose far more than her hair."

I make myself hold in my tracks, pulse pounding, fists clenched. "What do you want, you bastard?"

"Now, now. You don't want to put any coins in the swear jar, do you?" He clucks his tongue and pushes the knife through her hair. "Just listen to me. Cooperate for a little bit, and this will all be over like a bad dream. Step closer. Real slow. Keep your hands where I can see them."

Snarling under my breath, I take one halting step after another forward, spreading my hands to either side. It's a good excuse to get closer.

Maybe if I get closer, I'll spot a weakness, a vulnerability. He's a big man, but that's a small knife and if I can just get it away from Tara...

"Good girl," Stewart gushes. "Isn't your Auntie Hay a sweet, obedient thing, Tara-bug?"

"Don't you dare speak to her," I hiss, and he shrugs.

"Fine then. I'll speak to you, Ms. Mustang. Get on your knees and put your hands behind your head." When I don't comply, he narrows his eyes. "Do it."

I'm trapped.

If I don't comply, he'll hurt Tara.

Holding his eyes with all the hate I've ever had, I slowly drop down to my knees, lacing my hands together behind my head.

"Good girl," he purrs again, pulling away from Tara, but pointing the knife at her. "Don't move, little girl, or I'll snap your auntie's neck right in front of your eyes."

Tara holds perfectly still, except for her hands clapped over her mouth. She shakes her head, eyes streaming, sobs rising.

"Please! Please don't," she whispers, numb words muffled against her hands.

"It'll be okay, baby," I promise, even if I'm not sure of that at all.

Especially when Stewart stalks behind me and produces a pair of handcuffs from his back pocket.

He claps them around my wrists, cold metal against my skin, then uses them like a leash to drag me to my feet. I growl, struggling, jerking my shoulders, only to freeze as the edge of the blade kisses cool against my neck.

Better me than Tara, but it's not much consolation.

"Now you're gonna behave yourself, little missy," Stewart whispers, leaning over me. "You hear?"

Close, too close, making my skin crawl with the invasion of his sick heat, with his sickly-warm breaths against my ear. Very slowly, I nod, just once for the asshole.

"You're lucky I need you alive right now, but I might not always. If you keep on being a good girl, you might just walk away. Be a bad girl, though..." He leans into me, his hips pressed against my rear, and my stomach revolts, lurching. "And I'll make you very fucking sorry before I let War find your body."

I say nothing. I just start shaking. If I open my mouth, I'll vomit.

But I hold Tara's eyes as Stewart shoves me toward her, then catches her arm in a rough grip.

I need her to focus on me. To trust me to keep her safe. To trust me so I can trust *myself*.

Because one way or another, I'm going to get us out of this.

I just have to wait for my moment.

XX: ACROSS THE LINE (WARREN)

*C*oeur d'Alene isn't my best choice for a getaway, but right now it's the best I've got.

I need a city that's large enough to have adequate resources, and small enough not to be crawling with cops, but not so small that the locals would notice someone out of place, get suspicious, and find out I'm a person of interest who was ordered not to leave town because of an open murder investigation.

Damn it. I've become one of my own targets.

I'll just have to deal till I can sort out who killed Bress, clear my name, and find out the truth behind Jenna's death.

I'm in Doc's car, can't risk my license plate showing up on a traffic cam. Blake's in the back seat. I'd called Stewart so we'd have a solid four-man unit, but it must be a busy day at the shop because it went straight to voicemail.

We're currently parked outside a rent-by-the-hour motel where people think nothing of strange cars idling for a while, debating getting a room and setting up a command hub – if we'll even be here that long.

Reminds me a bit of the Ranger days, except transported to small town America.

Covert missions where we'd have to get in and out without being seen, often holing up in forgotten corners of strange cities and waiting for our moment or for the order to come through. Back then everybody in my unit thought we were invincible, treated it almost like some kind of damn video game.

We'd been young and stupid and high on the hype, but it stops being a game mighty fast when you put a bullet through someone's skull and realize you just took a human life, enemy or not.

I think that's what gets to me so much about Jenna's death.

Whoever the fuck did it, whoever shot her, they felt nothing when they pulled the trigger.

They didn't feel the moment of impact, the realness of what they did, the end of the life they cut too short. Wartime teaches you a certain respect for your opponents. You honor the fallen no matter who they are, because life's life and you're a goddamn human being with a soul.

But the demon who shot Jenna?

They couldn't have had a soul.

They sure as hell didn't honor her.

"I'm not hearing a plan," Blake says from the back seat. "This is fucked. How come you never told me, all this time, that you thought Bress killed Jenna?"

"You didn't need to know," I murmur, idly watching traffic pass through the passenger side window, rubbing my knuckles against my jaw. I'm spinning in circles, searching for a thread to pick up and trace to its source.

"Not to mention," Doc says coolly, "you can be rather indiscreet."

Blake scowls. "You knew?"

"Of course. Warren needed an informant in town, after all."

"And you're so good at being secretive, huh?" Blake says, eyeing Doc in the rearview mirror. "What with sneaking around everywhere like you own a damn strip club instead of an animal hospital..."

I slam my fist against the edge of the window. "Can we stop the playground sniping? We need a plan."

"Do we?" Doc asks. "Are you sure it's this urgent? You waited thirteen years to plan your move on Bress, Warren."

"And I don't want to have to start over and wait thirteen more," I point out. "So, yeah. I think we can rule out the most obvious question. Jenna's killer has to be in Heart's Edge."

"Yeah, but is it a townie?" Blake asks. "Or somebody who stalked you there because they knew you were looking?"

"I don't know. We may have a completely unknown actor," I growl. "Or we could be dealing with someone far too familiar."

"There's a problem with that theory," Doc says quietly, drumming his long, scarred hands against the steering wheel, his gaze remote as he glances over the parking lot.

"What's that?" I ask.

"If it's someone familiar, then...only five people in Heart's Edge have a history with Jenna in the army. One of them is dead. Three of them are here."

"So unless you're thinking it was me or Doc..." Blake adds uneasily, scrubbing a hand through his deep rust-brown hair.

I grimace. "Nah. You're too much of a damn puppy to pull off a murder plot and then frame Bress," I tell him, then eye Doc. "You, though..."

"Keep your wild conjectures to yourself, War. Or you might find out if I'm plenty capable of murder the next time you need my scalpel."

"Very funny." It's troubling, though.

Because I trust Doc. I trust Blake. There's only one other option...

"Fuck, this don't add up. It can't be. It can't be *him*."

I can't even say his name without my whole spine icing up.

"Yeah, Stew's our man," Blake says, picking up. "He wouldn't."

"Probably not," I say, but something's bothering me.

I can't quite put my finger on it. All the little things about the way Stew's been acting since I came back to town, strange and always misdirecting me.

Is it *really* misdirecting, though?

Or just a concerned friend trying to save me from myself?

"Besides," Blake adds. "Stewart always loved Jenna. He'd never—"

I snap my head up, staring at him in the rear-view mirror. "What the hell you mean 'loved?' She was with Bress."

Blake blinks. "You didn't know? Aw, man. He was hard-core into her once. Got real jealous when she went for Bress, but he took it pretty well in the end, said the better man won the girl. Part of the team and all."

I frown, my whole skull ringing with something like spiders tap-dancing inside it.

"Shit. What if that was his motive? For...for killing her."

The words are like ash on my tongue. Too insane. Too unbelievable.

"Please," Doc says, turning his nose up. "We're not in an Agatha Christie novel. Stewart wouldn't kill her out of jealousy and hide it for thirteen years, and if that had been the case then Bress would've told us himself. That's the pivotal point. If Stew's our murderer, why did Bress keep it quiet?"

"Whoa," Blake says, waving his hands, staring at us. "*Whoa, whoa, whoa.* How'd we get from 'Stew's the only one not here' to 'Stew probably killed your sister?' Think we ought to slow the fuck down."

"Maybe 'cause Stew's been trying to get me to drop this for years," I say grimly. "And since Stew's been acting damn funny since I came home."

Blake's face crumples, his eyes shifting like he's counting the awful possibilities. "But he's our friend. He couldn't possibly–"

"Surely even you've heard the saying 'keep your friends close, and your enemies closer,'" Doc whispers sternly. "We're not convicting Stewart. Merely ruling out possibilities. So if Stewart was involved, if he's responsible for Bress' death, the question remains – why? What's his motivation, other than petty jealousy? And what intel do we have that makes him the best suspect?"

"One, he's the only other man who was involved with Jenna and deployed with us," I say, counting off my fingers. "Two, he's been watching me damn close ever since I came home. Even caught me bugging Bress' car, trying like hell to divert me from him. Three, Bress is in some dirty business, proven, but something isn't adding up."

The whole car is quiet. My brain burns, hurts as it strings together the fucked up possibilities.

We hit the road, needing a distraction.

"I tracked him leaving town, going to the site where he was filmed with a supplier. Except at the time I thought I was tracking him, Stewart had my GPS unit. So it may have been Stew himself. But why was he going somewhere I know Bress has been seen? And four..." I take a deep breath. "He's the only one other than Haley I've confided my plans to. I haven't told him everything, but I had to explain the GPS, why I was stalking Bress."

"So what we have," Doc says thoughtfully, "is the only

person in Heart's Edge beyond us with complete insight into you, Warren. Your suspects, your plans, and movements."

Blake shakes his head ferociously. "I just...goddammit, we served together!"

His eyes bug out. I see Doc tense, the same as me.

We're all feeling the same hellish dagger tearing through our chests and reacting.

"You *sure* about this, War? You said Bress was into bad business. Thought he was for years and just proved it recently. So maybe he did kill Jenna. Maybe one of his criminal buddies took care of him before you could. That'd make a lot more sense than *Stew*."

I nod. "It's possible. That's why I'm tail-spinning so much right now. I don't want to pick up the wrong lead and spend another decade chasing a dead end. There are just too many damn open questions."

Doc rubs his chin. "Have you considered the possibility that Haley might be your missing key?"

"My key?" I shake my head. "What're you talking about?"

"Who's taken an interest in her since she showed up in town, joined at your hip, Warren? Who's been using her to get to you – or to throw you off?"

"*Don't*," I snarl with a vehemence that startles even me. "It's not fucking possible, so don't even try it."

I know the answer to his question. One person. But the possibility that's proof is so hideous it makes my guts wrench.

Blake whistles softly. "Somebody's head over heels."

"Yeah. I have feelings. And once I get this sorted, I'll get that fixed too. But let's take that option off the table right now. Hay made me a little distracted. She didn't make me stupid, blind, or deaf."

Doc holds up a hand in a peace offering. "My apologies."

With a frown, Blake leans back again. "Speaking of Hay...she gonna be okay with us gone?"

"Should be. I left her with Grandma, and nobody fucks with Wilma Ford. Let me call, though." I dig my phone from my pocket and tap Haley's number—the newest entry in my address book, that little selfie, and damn I *must* be in love when just her thumbnail makes my blood heat.

But not nearly as hot as it gets when I call her...and after five rings, it goes to voicemail.

What the hell? It's mid-afternoon. She wouldn't be at Brody's or asleep. I shake my head and pull up my Grandma's contact. "No answer."

"She may be busy," Doc offers neutrally. "A young lady has a life."

"So busy she can't pick up when she knows I'm a semi-wanted man?"

Doc arches a brow. "It might be to your distinct disadvantage to answer a call from you with Sheriff Langley no doubt grilling her."

"Fair point," I grunt, but then let out an explosive sigh of relief when, after a couple of rings, my grandmother picks up.

"Charming Inn," she says pleasantly, but there's something tight in her voice.

"Hey, Grandma," I say. "Is Haley around? Could you tell her to pick up her cell? It's urgent."

"Haley?" That tightness in her voice deepens. "Oh dear. I haven't seen her in hours, Warren. Her or Tara. I've looked, I've called...nothing."

That nothing hits me like a damn brick to the face.

"Why didn't you call *me?*"

"I wasn't certain I *could*. You're a person of interest," she says tartly. "But I was just getting into the car to go look for her."

333

"Don't! I mean, stay put."

"Don't you take that tone with me, young man."

"I'm sorry. Sorry, this is urgent, just—when was the last time you saw her?"

"She was off looking for Tara." Grandma Wilma's voice softens. "The poor girl went missing. We looked all over the grounds, inside the house, and she was nowhere. Then Stewart called, said the little imp walked all the way to the garage to pick up some pencils she'd left in the car during the last maintenance spree. Haley went to fetch her."

Stewart.

Again.

Goddamn. Just the sound of his name makes my entire body stiff. Sickness runs up and down my spine with diseased fingers, and my lungs fill with cement.

I know this feeling.

It's Jenna all over again, and I'm afraid the next time I see Hay, it'll be exactly the same.

Her, waxy and pale and broken. Lifeless. Nothing left of the person I knew, all her brightness *gone.*

"Warren?" Grandma asks, worry rising in her voice. "Are you there?"

Blake pipes up before I can answer. "Hey, uh, War, you don't look so good. What's wrong?"

"I have to go," I tell her quickly. "But I'll be back soon. Call me if Haley shows up. Immediately. *Please.*"

"I will. Would you like me to call the garage and talk to—"

"No. Don't do it. Things might not be right there. I can't explain, but I have to go."

"Of course, dear," Grandma says crisply.

She's always been one to read a room, and she actually hangs up before I do, sensing that I don't have time for pleasantries. I lift my head to find Blake and Doc watching me intently.

"I take it there's news?" Doc asks.

"Haley's missing," I say, my pulse pounding hard against my throat. "And she was last seen going to find her niece at Stew's garage. And now she's not answering her phone. It's hardly damning, but *fuck.*"

"Then let's be more safe than sorry," Doc says. "We'll worry about your potential inquiry with the police later."

As we tear down the highway, though, my phone rings again, vibrating in my hand.

Some wicked premonition makes it feel like it vibrates even harder than normal, jacking power up my arm, into my brain. Especially when I see the number on the caller ID.

Stew.

The beginning and the end of all this.

Yet there must be some part of me that's damn naïve. Because I still want to believe my friend – the man who consoled me through my grief, who made me have faith he'd told me what really happened to my sister – only has good intentions.

Even if all the signs point toward him.

The instinct, the unease, the fact that *he was the only other one there* and the autopsy showed Jenna was shot between the eyes with an Army-issued carbine, the bullet slug a match...

It's all wrong. Paranoia. The frustration of Bress slipping out of my hands and into the arms of death just when I nearly had him. My brain is rabbiting, looking for any correlation. Stew can't be dangerous.

He can't be.

Please.

I can't lose any more.

But I damn sure can't lose Hay.

I snap my thumb over the screen and lift the phone to my ear. "Stewart? Is Haley with you?"

He clucks his tongue. "Of course she's with me." His voice sounds strange, oily, cold. Knowing.

That sense of wrongness shrills up the back of my neck.

Then he speaks again, and I don't know who the hell I'm talking to. This is a different man.

"You knew. Why'd you wait, Warren? Why didn't you play your hand?"

My next breath just stops. I don't know what I'm feeling.

Fear. Rage. Disgust. Horror. It's all crushed up inside me into one hard knot that weighs a thousand pounds. "Because I trusted you, asshole! Because I thought...I wanted to believe...*fuck*. You killed Bress, didn't you?"

Stewart sighs deeply. "I wish you hadn't said that out loud. Now you're not giving me any choice."

"Choice in what?" I demand. He doesn't answer. "Any choice in *what?*"

Still no answer – until I hear a muffled feminine gasp, a ripping sound.

"*Stop!*" Haley yelps. "You vicious asshole—"

"It's just a little duct tape, girl. I didn't even take off any skin," Stewart snaps. "Not yet."

"Haley!" I roar, heart clenching.

"Warren?" she calls. "*Warren!* You have to be careful. Stewart framed Bress, he's been blackmailing him and—"

A sick smack of flesh crashing against flesh cuts her off.

I see red, slamming my fist against the dashboard, ignoring Doc's startled look. "Don't you fucking touch her!"

"I take it," Doc says calmly, "that I need to drive faster."

I can't answer him.

All my focus is on Stewart, that fucking traitor, as he speaks calmly into the phone. "I won't do anything to her," he says. "As long as you comply. This doesn't have to end badly, War. We can all walk away. You just have to learn to let go, but you've never been good at that. Why, if you'd just let Jenna go, it never would've had to come to this."

"Bullshit," I growl. "Liar."

It hurts. It burns all over again like the day I found out Jenna died, crushing down on me, only now the weight is three times as heavy when I know he could hurt Haley, too.

"Why? Why'd you kill her? Jenna was your *friend*. You cared for her!"

"And she got too nosy. This is what happens when you get nosy with me. You should've learned from Jenna's lesson." It's sneering, cruel, emotionless. I can't believe I ever thought that smiling, friendly face was real. "Now. Do you want to make arrangements, or shall I start with the little girl's precious pigtails before I slit your girlfriend's throat?"

"Fuck you," I bite off but force myself to rein it in. I'm miles out of town.

I have to play along until I can get within reach, until I can make sure the girls are safe.

"What the fuck do you want from me? Name your price."

"Simple," he says. "You're going to give me your truck to start. I can't have the police looking for mine, after all. It's quite distinctive. You'll leave it behind the billboard at the two mile marker outside of the north side of town with at least three handguns, double that many clips of ammo, and five hundred thousand dollars cash in the driver's seat. You won't be there when I come to pick it up. I'll leave the girls, and you can come fetch them in the morning. If you show up before then, no deal." I can almost hear the nonchalant shrug in his voice. "I'll kill them. And you'll never find me, and I'll just have to get my money elsewhere. So." Fuck, he sounds so cheerful I could murder him. "Why don't you just work with me, War? One more time? Best outcome for everyone."

I want to tell him to go fuck himself.

"Fine," I mutter. "I'll be back in town by afternoon. Make

the drop at midnight. Deal?"

"That sounds perfectly acceptable. Oh, and Warren?"

"What?" I snarl.

"Don't worry. I'll take good care of Haley for you. Keep her warmed up."

The bubbling rage in me blisters into an explosion, but before I can let out a furious bark, he ends the call. I fling my phone at the dashboard. The *crack* as it hits the windshield and the phone screen shatters is almost satisfying. Breathing hard, I dig my fingers into my hair, grinding the heels of my palms against my eyes.

"*Shit*. We're hosed, boys."

Blake's hand rests on my arm, reaching from the back, warm and firm and steady, reminding me I still have people I can trust. His goofiness is gone, leaving behind sober, sharp focus. "What's the rundown, man? Talk to us."

I take several rough breaths and make myself speak. "Short version: Stewart killed Jenna, lied about it as the only real eyewitness, framed Bress, and he's been blackmailing him all this time. Till I got too close and Stewart killed him."

"Fuck," Blake breathes. "Harsh. I can't believe I ever..."

"I know," I whisper, my voice a rasp. "But that's not all. He's got Hay and Tara. He wants a ransom of five hundred big, left at a drop point in exchange for the girls."

"Blind exchange?" Doc asks.

"Yeah."

"I take it we don't intend to trust that?"

"Not in the fucking slightest," I bite off. "Drive faster. Let's get back to the inn and grab my goddamn guns."

I'm coming, Tara.

I'm coming, *Haley*.

And when I get there, Stew will pay for betraying my trust. Our friendship. *Jenna.*

And one way or another, he'll pay for hurting Haley.

XXI: I SAY WHEN (HALEY)

$\mathcal{I}$ have a guilty confession to make.

I never much liked the movie *Pretty Woman*.

Don't ask why. Sure, the acting's good, but maybe I'm just the wrong generation to appreciate what it was for its time. One thing hasn't changed no matter how the movie aged, though.

That line after Philip Stuckey hit Vivian across the face, when Edward's icing her jaw.

She asks if they take boys aside in school and teach them how to hit a woman to make it hurt the most, and I'm starting to think they do – because the place where Stewart's fist crashes across my mouth throbs like a *bitch*, douses my entire face in flames, reaching up like stabbing daggers until I'm ready to scream.

I curl up on the floor with Tara next to me. I hate that she's here for this thanks to *my* mistake.

She's just frantic, clutching at me, starting to touch my face, then pulling away. "Auntie Haley," she whispers. I try to force a smile even though my mouth hurts like hell.

339

"It's okay," I murmur, keeping my voice low. "I'm okay, Tara. I'm okay."

I'm not okay.

But I have to keep a brave face on for her.

And watch for an opportunity.

Stewart hasn't bothered tying her up. The second I see an opening, I'm going to tell her to leave me and run. I'll create whatever diversion I have to.

She has to get away from this hell. Get help, but more importantly, be safe.

I don't matter, as long as Tara gets out of this.

Stewart hangs up his call with Warren. I hate that Warren has to go along with this, too, but I can't see any way out of it. I tried to tell him, to warn him.

The worst part is, this entire thing is going to end in heartbreak for him all over again.

My skin feels too tight, like it'll split and spill from my fear, when Stewart slowly turns to look at me.

I hold his eyes. I want his attention focused on me, not Tara, and it seems to be working.

He locks on with a sort of fixed intensity that makes me feel sick, as if he's looking for the easiest place to cut.

"You talk too much, you know that?" He sinks into a crouch in front of me. Too close.

I want to push away, but I don't dare risk any sudden movements. I'm still sprawled on the floor where he practically threw me with that backhanded punch, and my position right now doesn't offer me any advantages.

But I still manage a glare for him as he rattles on. "Now how'd you figure out I was blackmailing Bress? Did War tell you?"

"I'd like to think I'm a pretty good judge of character, and yours is lacking." I offer my sweetest, most venomous smile, even if moving my mouth at all stings like a desert wasp. "You've always seemed fake to me. Bress was kind." I shrug a little, and he tenses – does he think I'm testing the cuffs?

Good. Maybe that'll keep him nervous, paying attention to me, so I shift my wrists a little and keep talking. "So I thought, if Bress is this weird nice guy but he's running drugs like Warren thinks, why would he do that? Easy..." I can't keep the contempt I feel from showing as I glower at him. "You made him get involved. You used him as your cover. He's got connections all over Heart's Edge and beyond that you don't. It's your shitty drug network that's poisoning this town."

"Clever girl, piecing all that together from scraps. You'd make a better bounty hunter than Warren. He's so oblivious. So trusting. Brotherhood and all that shit." He tilts his head. It's an eerie, puppet-like movement, his eyes a little too wide and sharp. "His sister was smarter."

I gasp. Seeing how dark his eyes get when he mentions Jenna Ford sends a freezing current through my blood.

"What'd you do to her?" I whisper. "Why?"

"Because she had the guts to figure me out. Or maybe I got sloppy...me and Bress had ourselves a little dustup over her one fine Afghan evening. That boy was a big man, whipped my skinny ass good for talking shit, me saying he'd never know what to do with a woman like her."

Fricking creep. I wrinkle my nose. If only storytime was over...

"Jenna knew when he dragged himself back to her, probably saw the bruises I left. She came by my tent that night. Probably wanted to apologize, try to smooth things over, knowing one day we'd all be neighbors again in Heart's Edge. That's how she walked right in on the middle of me and my man from Army Intelligence talking about dividing up our cut of Afghan heroin, how we'd get it back to the States. That idiot got flustered, denied too much, tried to fold up our maps of the heartland a little too fast."

My heart stops beating. Stewart leans closer, a curl in his smile.

"Never knew how much she saw. Wasn't gonna find out the hard way. I'd heard there were assholes in those hills when we went out covering the sweeper crew. The ambush gave us cover. I did the rest. And then, years later, when it was all just a memory, I told Bress I'd frame his ass for killing her if he didn't let me borrow his sweet little empire for distribution."

"Bastard!" I hiss, kicking one leg. I'm too stunned to hit him, and he easily sidesteps.

"Quit your fussin'. You should be happy, Ms. Mustang. I'm finally leaving Heart's Edge and taking my poison with me. Gotta set up shop somewhere farther west and start over. So you'd better hope your man plays his cards right." He rolls forward onto his knees, leaning down, bringing his face in close to mine. His shadow envelops me. "Because you've got that shock in your eyes. You look a little too much like Jenna before she died."

I want to snap back in defiance, but my blood is too sick, too heavy, my tongue too frozen with fear.

I don't want to die. Don't want to leave Tara. I don't want to leave Warren, or this feeling like we could be something close to the family I've craved.

I'm scared for all of us, so scared, but I've got to push it down and remember to be brave for the little girl hugging her knees to her chest and silently crying.

But I won't get the chance.

Because Stewart reaches into his back pocket and pulls out a plastic-wrapped rag, then shakes it out. The moment the plastic falls away from the damply clinging cloth, the smell assaults me.

It's powerful, chemical, stinging my nose and my eyes. It hits me what it is a second too late, just as Stewart closes in, presses it against my mouth, giving me no choice but to breathe in.

Chloroform.

I try to struggle, to turn my face away, to hold my breath, but it's too late. I've already breathed it.

And his face is the last thing I see as I fade away in a cloud of heavy, bitterly drugging scent, my head swimming.

"Now," he says, a hollow voice resonating in the dark, chasing me into the blackness. "Let's make sure you don't give me more trouble like your dead fucking car."

XXII: FOXHOLES (WARREN)

*T*his *has* to work. There's too much at stake.

It's not a bad plan. I don't do bad plans.

Right now, I'm stashed in the back of my own truck with Doc. There's a false bottom in the truck bed that I've often used for concealing my perfectly legal weapons caches without dealing with questions from the cops.

Today it's the perfect size for two full-grown men lying in wait for a fucking snake of an asshole who kidnaps women and little girls.

Blake, disguised as me, dropped us off hours ago.

We threw a hat on his head and put him in some of my clothes, and he parked my Dodge behind the billboard as I was told, then ran back to town to change, grab his own car, and circle around the long way to take up a position on point a mile ahead, concealed behind some scrub brush at a turnoff, watching for Stewart through a pair of night vision binoculars.

We've been baking in here ever since the sun went down, holding perfectly still, a bag in the front seat containing the guns and a thin layer of money on top of dummy bricks.

It's not the plan that has me afraid.

It's Hay.

Fear that I won't be enough, just like I wasn't for Jenna.

Fear that Stewart will betray me yet again, outwit me somehow, and rip away another person I love.

Fear that I'll lose my redemption, the best thing that ever happened to me, my whole future.

And that fear amplifies into an adrenaline spike as the radio on my hip crackles. "Guys? I've got sight of him," Blake whispers. "He's coming in from town. Moving slow."

I don't dare move or signal, nothing to disrupt the false bottom acting as a roof over me and Doc, but Blake's been warned of that. His job is to relay info, ours is to stay silent.

In the darkness, Doc and I exchange glances. All I can see are the faint whites of his eyes. I can tell he's as grim and determined as I am.

Let's fucking do this.

Once Stewart drops off the girls and leaves in my truck, he'll have us with him. Blake will collect Hay and Tara and get them to safety.

Once we're sure the girls are out of the crossfire, we'll pop out and take this bastard down, drag him in, make sure he confesses every damn dirty thing he's done over the last thirty years to the police.

Including murdering my sister.

It's hard to miss the rumble, the growl of Stewart's engine in that souped-up monster truck of his.

I hear it coming long before it spills into an over-whelming thunder that echoes in my ears, the vibrations rattling through my Dodge, shaking me and Doc against the truck bed.

Then the engine cuts, and I hear the door of his truck open. Followed by his voice, hissing and harsh in a way I've never heard it.

345

"Out!" he snaps. "Pull anything funny and I'll shoot the kid."

"Then you'll have to shoot me too," Haley bites off, her voice muffled and distant through the wood and plastic over me – but so resolute, so brave, and even now I can't help but admire her. "Because I'm a witness. And I'll never forget."

"Don't get smart," Stewart snarls.

I don't hear Tara at all.

If I were her age in this situation, I'd be frozen into white-faced silence, not even crying. But her silence still worries me.

She must be alive, though. Or Stewart wouldn't be threatening to shoot her – and making my blood boil with rage – to keep Haley in line.

With Stewart so close, it takes every shred of willpower I have not to burst out the back of the truck right now and mow his ass down. Too soon.

I have to wait until the girls are safe.

So I pause and listen, sweat rolling down my spine, heart in my throat, as footsteps scuff in the loose dirt and grit behind the billboard. There's a door slamming – Stewart's truck.

Then the sound of my own truck opening. A small bounce ripples through me, and I can tell Doc feels it too.

Please, fuck. Please just let him leave the girls and drive off with us, none the wiser.

My radio crackles, and I tense, my gut plummeting, as Blake's voice whispers. "Something isn't right, War. I can't see—"

"What the hell?" Stewart snaps, and the truck shakes as the door slams shut again. "Get the fuck back in the truck."

"No," Haley bites off. "Warren? *Warr*—"

She cuts off in a crash of flesh on flesh and I see red.

Goddammit!

We're compromised.

He's going to run. Doc and I barely glance at each other before shoving upward, hurling the false bottom aside just in time to see Stewart flinging Tara, screaming, into his truck, grabbing Haley by the handcuffs around her wrists and lifting her up by the chain to throw her in after.

But as Doc and I stand, Stew whips around, snaring a pistol from the holster and firing quick shots. Doc and I both dive over the side of my truck, landing hard in the dirt but with the truck bed shielding us.

There's one more cry, another slam of the truck doors, and then a grinding, massive roar as Stewart starts the engine and peels out like a tornado.

Pulse pounding, I dart for the driver's side door of my Dodge and climb in, barely waiting for Doc to dive into the passenger side before I switch the ignition on and slam on the gas.

We spin out from behind the billboard in a haze of dust spraying from my tires, crashing onto the road after Stewart.

He's *not* getting away with my girls.

Blake comes over the radio. "Fuck, did I—"

"Doesn't matter now," I snap, grabbing the walkie off my belt loop and barking into it, keeping my eyes on the road. "We're going after him."

Stewart's a block ahead and charging on, ripping through town, that souped-up engine giving him an advantage in speed.

Not enough. He won't fucking shake me.

This asshole might have speed, but he's also got bulk, and that's going to slow him down in the long run. "Blake, listen – we're gonna do a pincer. There's only one road out of town that way, but you can take the highway intersection to meet him. Circle around and see if you can cut him off from the other side."

"Roger," Blake says before the radio cuts off.

I don't take my eyes off Stewart's truck for a nanosecond.

He goes barreling through town, swishing around a few people on their way to Brody's and sending their cars skidding off the road, tires squealing, horns honking, people leaning out of their windows and shouting.

They recoil in even more confusion as I dart past, gripping the steering wheel so hard it hurts my hands, teeth clenched and never looking away from those glowing red taillights in the dark, drawing me on like a demon's beckoning gaze.

I shift gears, grind down hard on the gas pedal, demand more and more speed from my Dodge, slowly closing the distance between us.

I've got to. Before he gets too far out of town, on the open highway, where he'll have the advantage and that beast of his can smoke us in the dust.

In the passenger seat, Doc calmly checks the clip in his Glock. "He'll have to slow down to turn at the edge of town where the road curves, Warren. I can try to shoot his tires out. At low speed he's less likely to flip if one blows."

"Too risky," I grind out, leaning into the steering wheel *hard*, like I can lend my own mass to make the truck go faster. "Not with the girls."

"Damn. You're right." Doc's eyes narrow and he nods.

But that turn's coming up, where Main curves around to become highway again, stretching out toward the Inn and then the main interstate. Stew has to slow down here, or he'll tumble, and that's my moment.

The smaller, more agile Dodge doesn't have to drop speed for the curves, and even as Stewart takes the turn gradually, I go tearing around in his wake and drop into the left lane to come up on him from the side.

Now! I'll shoot the fucker in the face through the driver's side window if I have to.

Ripping up next to him, straining to keep pace as he picks up speed with those massive tires churning so tall they're almost on a level with my head, I can see him in the driver's seat.

He's too calm, a tight, almost smirking grin on his lips. Past him, Tara looks bone-white and frozen and clinging to her aunt, Haley grim and silent with her mouth swollen and bruised and split.

I keep one hand on the steering wheel. The other reaches for my pistol.

But before I can draw and aim, Stew cuts a glance at me. His lip curls.

Then it happens.

He sends the monster truck whipping over to shove me like a pissed off quarterback ramming into an opposing team's player. Pure steel bulk slams into my Dodge, hard enough to make metal screech as the trucks tangle together.

Fuck!

Blood racing, I grapple at the wheel with both hands, wrenching over onto the shoulder and out of his reach before turning back and giving as good as I got.

"Hang on!" I roar.

Doc braces his hands on the dashboard as we hit.

The Dodge may not be the size of a monster truck, but when it catches one of Stewart's tires, the truck skews to the side, its tail jittering back and forth.

There's a long, low ditch on the side of the road. Hell, that's it.

If I can just make him tip into it, then it'll be like tipping a turtle on its goddamn back.

We'll stop this. We'll have him. We'll bring my girls back.

Stewart knows it too. Bastard flings me a vile look as he drags the truck back into line.

But I'm on him again, practically harrying him like a lion after an elephant, nipping at his heels and then darting away before he can use the monster truck's huge bulk to crush me.

Faster. *Faster.* We tumble in tandem down the highway, churning closer to Charming Inn.

Only for Blake to come roaring out from the feeder road up ahead in his beat-up old Chevy, intersecting the highway and careening into Stewart's path, using the entire car to block the road.

Hell, yeah. We've got the prick, he's trapped, there's nowhere for him to go –

Until he sees his chance and spins off the highway, onto the little dirt track running alongside Charming Inn.

It's the same place where me and Hay sometimes park, the place where I've stood under the sunlight drifting through the trees and watched lazy bees while we unloaded groceries from the trunk of her car.

The same place where I've walked hand in hand with her down the lane toward the cliff, quiet night memories that Stewart defiles with the vulgar roar of his truck as he goes slamming through, ripping up the dirt track in puffs of dust that blind me as I race on, following.

What the fuck? He can't. He can't take that road, it's a dead end, it doesn't go anywhere but *the cliff.*

Everything next happens in slow-motion.

I see movement, quick and frantic, through the rear window of the monster truck.

In the driver's side, Stewart jerks. The truck spins, careening in a top-heavy spiral, going completely out of control and skidding sideways on its tires toward the drop-off of the Heart's Edge cliff, digging up massive furrows in the dirt.

It hits something – a rock, a branch – and rolls.

Then goes careening right over the edge, taking my heart with it.

"*Haley!*" Her name explodes from my mouth as I slam the Dodge to a halt and tumble out, Doc on my heels. We race for the edge.

I'm nearly torn open, picturing the truck crushed down in the valley, Haley and Tara's bodies broken, only for a desperate call of "*Warren!*" to lift my heart with fear and hope and disbelief.

We hit the edge of the cliff hard and skid on our heels, looking down.

The truck's caught in the thick, gnarled tree roots that jut out from the cliff's wall, lying on its side against them like they've formed a safety net. A very *thin* one.

I swear to fuck I hear the roots groaning, bowing, threatening to snap under the truck's weight. It's so far down I don't know if we can reach them in time.

I see Stewart, unconscious behind the wheel, slumped and hanging by the seatbelt, his forehead bleeding. Then Tara and Haley, crushed against the passenger window, the glass damn near the only thing holding them up, keeping them from falling through.

I drop to my knees frantically, looking at Doc. "Hold me by the ankles."

He arches a brow. "Highly impractical. We need—"

"We don't have time," I snarl. "Ankles! I'll have to be the rope myself."

And then I go over the edge. There's not a second to spare, and I can't lose my girls.

There's one lurching moment of free fall and then Doc has me.

He's using all his strength to grip tight around my ankles,

holding me suspended as I lay my body against the cliff wall and stretch down, reaching my arms out.

"Haley!" I call. "Climb up!"

She looks up at me through the window of the truck, shaking her head. "I can't! I'm cuffed. I can't climb!"

Shit. My heart drops as she looks at me desperately, then turns a wan, shaky smile on her niece. "Baby, go. Go to Warren. Let him lift you."

"If we could hurry this up," Doc says, his hold on my ankles tightening. "I've no shortage of muscle, but my endurance can't last forever."

Tara shakes her head quickly, sobbing. "I don't want to leave you, Auntie Hay..."

"It'll be okay, kit," Hay promises with a watery smile, her eyes welling. "Go."

"Come on, Tara," I coax, stretching out my hands, while Tara climbs up the cab of the truck, squirming over Stewart's bulk to push herself out of the window. The truck sways, shaking, and she clutches with terror onto the rear-view mirror before tentatively stretching a hand out toward me. I strain, trying to reach her. It takes several passes before I finally grasp her wrist. "Gotcha!"

As quick as I can, I yank her up. She's light, at least, and I practically toss her up to where she can climb me, grabbing onto my jeans and my legs and clambering up, whimpering, until she's over the cliff.

But that leaves Hay, sweet Hay. She looks up at me determinedly.

"You're going to fall, Warren," she says, oddly calm. "I'm too heavy. It's...it's okay."

It's fucking not!

"No! I'm not leaving you, dammit. Haley, just try! Please."

There's a sickening *crack* – a root snapping – and the

truck jolts. Haley lets out a gasp, echoed by Tara's squeal from above.

I slip an inch, Doc swearing as he hauls himself back. "Warren...hurry."

"Just give me another second!" I yell, straining toward Haley. "Haley...Hay, come on!"

Swallowing, she nods, looking around before starting to squirm up using only her feet, her arms bound behind her back.

She stops, twisting, curling herself up in a ball and using the truck for leverage until she finds just the right angle. Then she loops the cuffs under her feet, pulls her arms out in front of her.

It's smart. It gives her some way to grab, to reach for me. The cost is precious seconds that actually take her farther away, leaving my guts dropping as the truck slips another inch.

"Hay!" I belt out her name again.

Determined, grunting under her breath, she climbs, wriggling past Stewart and catching the handle to throw the door open. She's out.

But she can't quite make it when she's not as small as Tara. With a soft cry, she reaches her cuffed hands toward me and – falls fucking short.

Damn!

I can't reach her. She can't reach me.

There's at least three inches of space between us, this tiny hellish gap that might as well be bigger than the space between the stars.

"Hold on. I'm coming," I whisper. "Doc, I'm going in!"

I lunge, only for Doc to cry out, pinning me down by one leg as my weight shifts.

Haley strains upward – and finally I catch the chain between her cuffs, pulling hard.

Big mistake.

There's a mighty *crack*, a shattering, and the truck goes tumbling down with Stewart still in it, a shining pinprick that slams into the valley below with a deafening crash.

Holy fuck.

Haley dangles from my grip, suspended over hundreds of feet of open air, the only thing holding us up is Doc's desperate, sliding weight on my leg.

"Warren," Doc says tightly. "I can't—"

"I'm here!" Blake cries behind him, dropping down next to Doc – and suddenly there's another pair of hands on me, grabbing me, holding tight and helping stabilize me while I grapple with my hold on Hay, my entire body iced over with fear for her.

"Come on, darlin'. Just a little more."

Managing to get her by one wrist, then the other, I throw everything I've got into it.

Then I'm dragging her against me, my poor girl sobbing as I loop her cuffed hands around my neck and yell up to Doc and Blake.

"Pull us up!"

It's another terrifying minute as they drag our combined weight into reach. It takes everything Blake has, I hear him grinding his teeth, his old war wound acting up something fierce.

Finally, they're both able to get two hands on me and haul us over the edge, and gravity no longer feels like a death sentence.

We're collapsing in the dirt, utterly drained.

Tara tumbles into us, clinging like a baby monkey, everybody crying or swearing – including me.

I can't fucking help myself. Wild, mad relief sweeps through me like a sword. We made it, and I'll never ask for anything else.

I kiss Haley's gorgeous face again and again, clutching at her to remind myself she's alive.

She's alive, and Stewart didn't take her away.

She's clinging to me just as furiously, whispering "Warren, Warren, oh my God."

She alternates between kissing me again and again and burying her face against Tara's hair. I need to find a key and get these cuffs off her, but right now?

I need to hold her. Know she's okay. Know I didn't lose her.

It's not long before we all hear sirens in the distance.

Good. The cops are coming, and maybe they can fish Stewart – dead or alive – out of the valley.

I don't care. My girls need medical help, not knowing what that prick did to them.

Whatever it is won't ruin this. We're gonna be okay.

"Don't ever leave," I whisper, not even wholly sure what I'm saying, as I clutch at Hay and bury my face in her shoulder. "You almost went too soon, darlin'. I love you. Love you so fucking much."

Hay swallows thickly, pulling back, her huge eyes sparkling.

Even bruised, even crying, she's still so beautiful, this pristine slice of woman I can't believe I nearly lost.

God, she's brave, smiling when she repeats shyly, "You...you love me?"

"Yeah. Tried to go over a cliff for you," I tell her, "isn't it obvious?"

"Maybe. But I think you'd go over a cliff for anyone. You're not nearly as bad as you pretend to be, Warren Ford." She leans into me, grinning through her tears. "Which is probably why I'm insane enough to love you, too. Get ready. I'm not going *anywhere.*"

It's too much. This volatile cocktail in my veins burns me the hell down when I hear her say those words.

This adrenaline, mingling with raw fear and rage at Stewart and then this sweet relief, this joy.

I capture her mouth, claim her again, sealing our love with a promise of what's to come.

I'll never let any asshole hurt her again.

Won't ever let anybody or anything take her away.

She's mine to hold, mine to keep happy, mine to fucking love.

Today, tomorrow, always.

Haley soon-to-be-Ford is my breath and my pulse and the reason I've finally realized why I'm on this wicked earth.

Smiling, I try to make her feel this glorious madness coursing through me with another brimstone kiss I dredge up from the deepest part of me, that dark secret place where I buried my heart till it could heal.

Till it was ready to love and to appreciate what she's given me.

By the time we break apart, we're both laughing, breathless and tired, and she leans her brow against mine. We smile, listening to Doc, Blake, and Tara chatter away behind us.

"Hey, man, give her some room. She's scared," Blake whispers.

"She's *relieved* in my considerable medical opinion." Doc squeezes Tara's arm, the soft space by her elbow. "Here, lovely lady, any pain?"

Tara shakes her head. He moves to the other arm, then both legs, checking her over.

"She's in good hands," I tell Hay. "This guy knows how to handle people."

Might be another five minutes before the paramedics

show up as the emergency vehicles rumble through the narrow mountain bends.

Blake snorts. "Aw, come on. Shouldn't we wait for a real doctor? You're just –"

"I'm *more* than a veterinarian, you clueless nugget. Let me do my job," Doc growls, pulling a giggle from Tara.

Blake backs away, his hands up, running a relieved hand through his hair. His whole expression says it. The same mad joy we all feel.

"Hey, Warren?" Hay asks softly, and I hold her tighter, breathing in the scent of her, savoring her warmth.

"Yeah?"

"Next time I get it in my head to kick the driver of a moving vehicle in the face..." She grins wryly, then winces, licking her split lip. "Remind me not to."

"Haley," I say, unable to help my own grin, "the first thing I learned when I met you is you're gonna do exactly what I tell you not to."

"Oh yeah?"

"Yeah."

"Then you should tell me not to kiss you."

I chuckle, leaning in close to her. "Don't kiss me, darlin'. Don't you dare."

With another soul-melting smile, she's on me, pressing her mouth to mine, fierce and hot and giving my promise back to me.

We're still like that when the EMTs and cops show up, tearing off to the sides and running out of their vehicles with a million questions.

I take my sweet time answering.

It's just me and Haley here.

And that's all I need.

XXIII: OVER THE EDGE (HALEY)

*S*o ends the longest month of my life.

Depositions. Witness interviews. Reliving our hell on Earth with Stewart hundreds of times.

I've retold our tale to lawyers, to cops, even to the FBI and DEA – and there's more to come.

Turns out, Stewart was crossing state lines with his drug operation, using undercover freight rentals parked on Dennis Bress' properties to move heroin to distributors who'd shuttle it all down the West Coast.

The asshole was even involved in tax fraud, and while he isn't here anymore for a confession, a few of the old guys from his unit who worked in his shop came clean about what they actually saw the day of Jenna Ford's death.

They'd been in Stew's pocket the entire time, generously bribed. Part of his operation, which he started overseas with pure Afghan heroin and turned into one of the most secretive drug pipelines from Wyoming through the Cascades.

The money was too good. They were happy to lie about a good woman's death when he executed her for finding him out.

Of course, they flipped pretty fast once their boss went down. A few tried to flee town and didn't get far. There's no money in prison for aiding and abetting, but there's some small benefit in plea deals.

It's not just Stewart we've been talking about, though.

I've been grilled repeatedly over what happened that day, the only witness to Stewart's total meltdown.

He didn't survive the crash, and everyone wants to know how he died, if there was any foul play involved. I know they're just covering their bases, making sure they can sign off on Warren's innocence without question.

But I *hate* feeling like I'm the guilty party here, even though they can't ask Stewart anything from the county morgue.

That's probably too morbid.

But I'm tired. I *get* to be a little morbid after this shitshow.

I miss Tara, too. I flat out told the cops they were getting one interview with her on video and nothing else.

She's a minor, and her parents aren't here to consent. And after how traumatized she was...no.

Hell no.

She might be my niece, but I've turned protective mama bear anyway. It broke my heart how every night she'd wake up screaming for the last week she stayed here, crawling into bed to take comfort, sandwiched between me and Warren so we could protect her from her nightmares of "the smiling man."

But she's home now.

Marie came out to get her, instead of having her fly back alone.

If I ever doubted the bond between my sister and her daughter, the way Tara lit up and a weight seemed to shrug off her erased those doubts. I know she'll be okay.

She's smart. She's resilient. She's strong.

She'll need some therapy, but Marie will take good care of her. So will John, as they ease into what they're doing.

The divorce won't make this any easier. But Jesus, I'm going to keep Tara my bright, sweet little girl.

I'll keep her happy no matter what it takes or how many times I have to fly out to Seattle.

And I think, now that everything's over, I can be happy too.

Especially since Warren's been *amazing.*

Before, I wondered if we were jumping the gun wanting everything from this brief, intense connection...but it's turned out to be everything.

All the love I never imagined and then some.

We still bicker, but it's just play. We challenge, giving each other crap. We push and pull until we fill each other's gaps and complement our differences as much as we highlight how we're alike.

And somehow, the sniping and the teasing always turn to kisses. Warmth. Touches.

Sometimes we're gentle and slow.

A lot of times it's rough and fast with the fury we play at in our mock arguments, turning into real, burning passion. He makes it easy to forget that scary feeling of dangling over the edge, moments away from dying, while he reached for me with so much naked fear on his face.

You never know how much you mean to a man until he's on the verge of losing you.

Then they react. With brutal indifference or total, heart-stomping love.

And Warren makes it easy to believe in a future here in Heart's Edge.

Screw Chicago. I'm not moving.

One little accident dumped me right where I needed to be and tested my soul. I know it now.

This is where I fit. It's perfect. It's right. It's beautiful.
It's home.

And it's also nearly midnight, marking the end of the first day of my wonky little exhibit in the small Heart's Edge gallery, featuring my first collection of paintings depicting Heart's Edge in traditional ukiyo-e style, capturing the town as though it's part of another world.

Which is why I'm giddy, leaning against the railing of the cabin that's become home for now, sipping champagne with Warren tucked against my back and Mozart draped on the deck railing a few feet away, the cat happily sprawled out, taking in the evening as much as we are.

"So, beautiful," Warren drawls, kissing my shoulder. "How do you feel about the whole town coming out to buy your work?"

"A little weird. I feel like they only did it because they wanted to support me," I answer with a dry laugh. "Not because they like my work. But, hey, it's a start. And I got a feature in the Spokane newspaper, so maybe I'll scale up to bigger galleries."

"Careful now. You're gonna get too big for Heart's Edge in a flash, and then you're going to leave us."

"Never," I promise. I don't know how to make him understand what that really means to me when I've been so tentatively skirting around these feelings. But I lean back into his grip, taking another sip of my champagne. "I like it here. For reasons."

"Reasons, huh?" He chuckles, a deep rumble pouring through me, this sound and sensation that makes me feel so warm and content. "How 'bout we pinky swear on that never?"

I laugh. "Do we still pinky swear at this age?"

"We could. Jenna always treated it like her religion," he says with a smile.

Something light and stingy pricks at my chest. I lace my fingers through his, grateful he's sharing something so intimate.

"Then let's do it. Pinky swear."

"Or on second thought...maybe I've got a better idea," he whispers, pulling away, then drawing me around to face him, reaching for my hand.

Underneath the starlight, those bright blue eyes of his are the same shade as night, looking down at me with glowing warmth that still, after all these months, makes my breath catch.

"Warren?" His name rolls off my tongue.

He captures my hand, tighter, tugging me gently toward the stairs down the back of the deck. "Come with me, darlin'."

I can't help being curious. So I set the champagne flute down on the deck railing and follow him to the grass that's been worn into pathways by too many feet.

He leads me across the field, toward the cliff that should be nightmare fuel after Stewart. And yet...somehow, I've never been able to shake the beauty and wonder I got the first time I saw the sun come up beyond its heart-shaped edge.

Not even a demon like Stewart can ruin that. We won't let him.

And the view is just as stunning tonight with the town's lights so dim they can't eclipse the blaze of the Milky Way overhead, the tiny glittering motes of lights and burning stardust so many light-years away. I wonder if the people in the light already lived out their stories eons before we ever saw them while we, down here, stand below with our stories just beginning.

I stop, looking up at the sky with my heart in my throat. Warren squeezes my hand, stroking his thumb over the edge of my palm. "Feel like tossing a few flowers?"

I laugh, but...he's serious.

Oh my God.

I tilt my head into the night breeze and squeeze his hand right back. "I thought you only did that when you wanted to make a promise? Isn't that how it goes?"

"Maybe I do tonight." For all my laughter, my playfulness, he's gravely serious.

I see it in his eyes, even if his warmth, his steadiness, never wavers.

Suddenly, I catch my breath, looking up at him as he bends to pluck up two pretty, waving peonies from the grass at our feet.

He offers me one, but he's holding it a little oddly, fingers pinched up just under the flower head.

The sweetness of it, the romanticism, distracts me as he rumbles, "Scatter one with me, Hay."

I can't help smiling, reaching out to take the flower, everything inside me feeling light.

But the flower is oddly heavy – and I realize *why* as I take it by the stem.

There's a ring perched in it.

Somehow, Warren freaking Ford has worked a delicate platinum and diamond engagement band over the head of a live flower, so that when he plucked it for me, it would dangle from the stem.

My heart flutters, my voice drying up into nothing as I let the ring slide off the stem and into my palm, my fingers shaking. "W-Warren?"

He smiles slowly. "I realize this might've been a backwards way to do this, but here we are."

Here. We. Are.

Then he sinks down on one knee, leaving no doubt what he intends as he gently takes my hand with the ring still cradled in my palm, the other hand still clutching the flower.

Those devastating, perfect eyes gaze up at me, dark with such devotion it's like he can't see anything else, the kind of attention that makes you feel stripped raw and bare. "Hay, you came crashing into my life like a gunshot," he says. "You struck me hard enough to spin me around. I've been dead for years. Stuck in limbo, in grief. But you make me ready to live again, and I can't imagine my second shot at life without you, woman. You're everything. The most funny, creative, fierce, loyal, smart, gorgeous chick I've ever met and—"

"Stop flattering me, you ass," I choke out, grinning from ear to ear, my throat tight and my eyes streaming. Warren blurs together in his muscle and ink and warmth. "Just ask me. Ask me so I can say yes."

"Hey now. Don't steal my thunder." But he's grinning, squeezing my hand warmly. "Okay, Haley West. Will you do me the honor of becoming my—"

"*Yes!*" I say before he can even finish, flinging myself at him. "God, yes, you gorgeous man."

He rises up to meet me halfway.

We crash together in a kiss like thunder meeting lightning, hot and salty as my tears. I was raised to hide them once, to never let anyone see my pain – but this is joy, and I wear it *proudly* as I kiss Warren like it's the first and last time. And a promise of many, many more.

That family I've longed for, that husband, that warmth, that togetherness...

I'm standing on the verge of it, looking out over this great cliff of Heart's Edge, ready to take the leap.

When we can't breathe anymore, when it's just a mess of us clinging together, we break apart...and I realize we're still clutching our flowers. His is crushed against his palm and my back, mine crumpled in my fingers. Leaning into him, unable to stop smiling, I nuzzle my nose to his.

364

"Hey," I whisper. "Let's make a memory."

We're holding hands when we do it.

Just me and him and the sky, plus the town that changed my life and made me who I want to be. Together, we send soft, pale pink petals streaming over the edge of the cliff.

We don't have to say anything.

The promise is in the ring on my finger, in the clasp of our hands.

And those petals flutter away, carrying wishes, hopes, and dreams, each one a whisper of what our future might be.

* * *

I WOULDN'T CALL our wedding a shotgun wedding, but it's close.

If only because the moment Ms. Wilma found out I was pregnant, barely months into our engagement, she practically threatened to *kill* Warren with a turkey baster if he didn't make me an honest woman quickly so the baby wouldn't be born halfway into our honeymoon.

I'm not sure I want to find out how she'd actually pull off murder by baster, but I know she'd do it.

So she's a little old-fashioned.

I don't really think she cares that we were definitely being indecent out of wedlock, but she'd like to at least pretend her great-grandchild wasn't conceived months before Warren actually put a ring on my finger.

I don't mind. I don't need a huge fancy wedding. I don't need bridesmaids dresses and fitting rooms and shitty grooms throwing money every which way just because they can.

I just need me. And Warren.

The light, wispy summer dress that makes me feel young

and sweet and fresh and new, as I step from my old life into my new one.

And my family all around me, gathered on the cliff at Heart's Edge where we made our promise, and where we'll now make our vows.

I don't just mean my blood family, either. Ms. Wilma is family to me now, and so are Warren's friends, Blake and Doc, who've already started treating me with familial warmth.

But my sister's here. John, too. They're still wearing their wedding rings, though they're not technically married. They hold hands anyway, and they look *happy*, and I'm so glad they found a way to stay a family both for their sakes and Tara's.

Tara's my flower girl, pretty and strewing petals all over the silk runner laid over the grass, but it's Marie who gives me away.

And the last thing I expect as she walks me down the aisle toward the priest is for her to burst into tears and give me a tight, fierce hug.

"I'm so glad for you," she whispers. "So *glad*. And I'm so glad you're my sister."

I feel myself tearing up, too, as I hug her close. "So am I," I choke out.

God, am I ever.

So many new beginnings, leading into the brightest future.

When I let her go, I have to wipe my eyes delicately, trying not to ruin my makeup, before I make my way up to what's less an altar and more huge stands of flowers gathered around, setting the backdrop for the priest, for Warren's friends as his best men, for all the waitresses from Brody's as my bridesmaids.

And for Warren himself, standing there waiting for me in

a crisply tailored, gorgeous suit that looks far better on his thick bulk than a stuffy tux ever could.

It works. It's us. We came together in this confused crazy jumble, and even our wedding's a patchwork of things thrown together. But what we made out of all these jagged pieces is so beautiful.

I wouldn't have it any other way.

And I wouldn't have anyone else, as I look up at Warren and the way he smiles just for me and only me.

His hands in mine.

The bouquet forgotten so we can clutch at each other so totally, fingers tangled, drawn in close.

The ceremony's short. We don't need the hour-long droning, the recitation, that's not us. It's as quick and crazy as we are, and as the priest makes his way through our vows, we're grinning, mouthing them along with him, almost racing him, until we get to that breathless moment.

I do.

We say it almost in tandem, and a chill sweeps through me.

Then it's laughter, music, the lock of our lips, the touch of hands made just a little heavier by rings that bind us with more than just a legal vow.

They bind us in heart's blood, in heart's promise, in heart's pain, and heart's soul.

In the future waiting here for us in Heart's Edge.

* * *

"CAREFUL! You're going to tear it if you –"

"Darlin', please. I've spent the last eight hours watching you prance around in the hottest fucking dress I've ever seen you wear. Excuse me for the hurry."

His rough fingers go to work. Somehow, he pushes my dress off intact a second later, without tearing it to shreds.

I step out in my ivory lace, into his arms, pulling on his tie. "Good things come to those who wait."

Warren smiles, all snarly promises in his eyes. "I'll show you good, Mrs. Ford. Turn the hell around."

How could I dream of saying no?

Three seconds later, he's got me bent over, tearing off my panties with his teeth. Warren's beard crisscrosses up my thighs as he kisses up, licking and biting, making me all too aware he was far from the only one suffering through the reception.

I've been wet and aching for hours. So damn ready to be under my husband.

Maybe it's the baby hormones making it worse. Whatever the case, the instant my legs tremble and a loud moan escapes my lips, I just know it's going to be one wild wedding night.

Warren pulls my legs apart, pushing his face deeper, kissing and stroking my slick folds with his tongue. I'm coming apart in a matter of seconds, slouched on the bed, arms stretched over my head and grabbing at the covers.

Holy hell.

"Oh, yeah. There!" I gasp as he finds my clit, smothering it with broad, tense licks that nearly burn me down. "Warren!"

He only slows down for a single sentence, pushing me onto his beard, making me ride his face. He might be smothered in my wetness, but there's no doubt at all who's large and in charge, who's guiding every bit of my pleasure I grind against him, my muscles so electrified it *hurts.*

"Fuckin' perfect pussy, Hay."

Perfect pussy. And he reminds me how perfectly talented he is at making it sing as he brings me off on his mouth, this clutching orgasm that shoots through my body like a meteor, douses my brain, and has my eyes rolling to the seventh heaven.

Oh, *hell.* If this is how married life begins, I wonder how it'll ever be better.

And I thought the night he planted his seed was the hottest.

Remembering how hot, how crazed, how furiously he slammed his body into mine just makes my O come harder. Warren was full beast mode that night, this feral thing, dark ink and seething muscles, pinning me down. His teeth sank into my shoulder as his balls let go, heaving his fire into my depths, too potent for the pill I took religiously.

God.

And now I'm thoroughly reminded how crazy he makes me as I force my eyes open, still shaking, turning to meet him. "Warren..."

"Yeah, yeah, I know. You see something you like." He's smirking, pulling off his suit, giving me the world's most eloquent strip tease.

It's a strange, wonderful thing, watching him peel off the most refined thing I've ever seen him wear, exposing the wild mountain man underneath.

There's no question. No matter how many times I see him get naked, I'll *never* get tired of this incredible, handsome, outrageous man.

Just like I'll never tire of how he's on me.

"Hay," he growls, his first kiss a gentle wave of heat.

Mush. That's what I am. Just soft, warm, feely, and horny as all Hades mush as my husband takes my mouth, and then takes me over.

The thing they never tell you about honeymoons is just how fast they blur by. Even when I'm sure I'm having the best sex of my life, it's all over in a breathless night that seems like an instant. But it belongs to me and him, man and wife, tonight and forever.

There's Warren, on my lips, his tongue chasing mine so deep, teasing ragged whimpers out of me.

Warren, on my nipples, teasing them until I'm just a shuddering mess.

And Warren, between my legs, taking me every which way.

His cock hammers against me so sweetly I'm shaken to my core. His thrusts are all power, quaking to my bones, this glorious strike of his steel on my molten heat. On me, in me, deeper and deeper.

The last time, I'm bent over, lost in total rapture. My lips are pursed, and my whole body trembles. I'm sure it's going to rip me apart when he comes inside me again, my pussy already on the edge, waiting for my husband.

"Warren," I whisper, sucking my bottom lip. "Warren, please!"

His fingers tighten on my ass. His thrusts quicken, deepen, so wickedly close to pushing me over. But I don't want to go alone.

"You really want this bad, darlin'?"

"No, *need!*"

I sense him smiling behind me. Cocky as hell, but of course I wouldn't have it any other way. If there's one thing Warren Ford delights in, it's sexing my soul out of my body and putting the pieces back together with his kiss.

"Fuck," I hear him growl, his voice an octave lower, the only warning I get. "Fuck, let's go! Come on this dick that's yours now forever."

And I'm gone.

My whole body arches as he lets out a groan like the world ending. Our bodies press together, tangled, and his cock swells in my depths. Then there's just my pussy clutching at his swelling hardness, wringing him dry, two bundles of nerves dipped in oneness and lit on *fire.*

Holy hell?

No, it's heaven. Nirvana. Paradise.

Just a white-hot wave that sweeps us up. He brings me off so hard, emptying himself in me, my legs shaking so hard my jaw pinches tight, muffling the screams working out of me.

Thank God.

Because the last thing we need are loud, angry complaints from the other cabins on Ms. Wilma's property the night before we take off for Cancun.

I'm still a mess of heat and twitching limbs and sweet memories when I fall into his arms, into his kiss. We taste each other for a good, long minute, savoring the afterglow.

"God. That was...I almost thought it might be our last night, Warren."

He grins. "Practice makes perfect, darlin'. We've got a whole life ahead to fuck each other's brains out."

I roll my eyes, swatting his chest. "Thanks, Shakespeare. How romantic."

"Needed a crappy opener, Hay. You'll get me when you see your wedding present."

My brows knit together. Still smiling, that's when he takes my hand, and then, leaning against the headboard, guides it to his chest.

"There, baby girl. I know it's dark but...there's enough moonlight."

It takes my eyes a few seconds to focus. Then I see it.

Right above the mess of flowers and US Army patchwork on his chest, there's fresh ink. *Surprise.*

The words HALEY ERICKA FORD and our wedding date. Next to a big FOREVER, stenciled in flames.

I'm so moved, so gushy, so touched I...I can't even speak.

"When? When did you find the time, you sweet, crazy, ridiculous man? I can't believe you—"

"Believe, darlin'. Your name's the second and last I'll ever honor on my skin. Today I made you part of me, Hay. Part of me forever, just like it says."

No words.

I have no words left to give this wonderful man.

So I just brush my fingers down his beard, loving the soft prickle, and kiss him until dawn.

EPILOGUE: NO PERFECT HUSBAND
(WARREN)

Years Later

IT DOESN'T HIT me till I've got my hand against the cold stone slab.

"No flowers today. Just came to talk," I mutter.

I need a moment. *Christ.*

It's never easy, but today? It's entirely brutal.

Because the words trying to force their way up my throat tear at me like hot tar dragged through a hornet's nest. Can it really be?

Can this shit finally – *finally* – be coming to an end?

"They got him, sis. Stew's last man is dead. Piece of shit got a blade across the throat last week while they were transferring him out to Susanville prison. Rival crew, men from some motorcycle gang or something Stew crossed moving his crap West of Spokane before we shut him down. But I guess you already knew, didn't you?"

Again, I need a moment.

The last dirty trace of my old friend, my demon, my sister's killer is actually *gone.*

Don't get me wrong.

Having Stew crashing to his end off the cliff took the danger away years ago. Seeing his whole crew of accomplices and henchmen put away behind bars was even better.

It did the whole town justice, every last person who'd ever been poisoned by the trash he brought in. It made my woman happier, knowing they were shut away where they'd never hurt her or Tara or anybody else ever again.

Honestly, having Stewart's entire operation dismembered let me sleep at night without wanting to fall to pieces or uproot the happy life I've had since Hay's world became mine.

Still, deep down, even through the best moments of my life, something in me *hated* every spare breath those bastards kept robbing from the air.

So I watched. I waited. I heard the stories about the first half dozen who were killed by the many enemies they'd made. The seventh asshole was the last to go, a big prick named Brice who'd hauled kilos of crap across several states and ruined countless lives.

Now Brice is six feet under with Stew and the rest of his scum, and they've got a bigger judge to answer to.

Sure, with everything that's happened the last couple years, Stew's own death feels like half a lifetime ago.

Mozart doesn't seem like the only one with a thousand lives anymore, considering the craziness that's come to our town since I had my big showdown at the edge of the cliff.

Doc and his goddamn secrets. Almost more to go around than the frigging zoo he runs at his clinic. That sneaky, tight-lipped Dr. Dolittle never would've made it as far as he has without me.

Blake and the hot mess he got into with his little girl. I

pitched in to pull him out of the fire like brothers always do. He taught me a thing or two about kids, maybe, and I'll never forget his advice about the teen years.

And Nine...Nine's a special kind of fuckery that nearly left Heart's Edge a smoldering crater. Hell no, we're *not* going there today.

Every person on this rock has got their own story.

Running my fingers across the name JENNA FORD, etched forever on stone, I know mine.

I know how bleak and horrific and gut wrenching some chapters get. Just like I know what a good woman did to save my soul, and how hard a man has to fight for his happy ending.

A chill breeze crisscrosses my back, forcing me to look up and sweep the hair out of my eyes.

Maybe I'm going a little lax the older I get, sometimes letting it creep down.

I'm lucky Hay just says it's hotter, tells me I should wear it this way damn near all the time.

It's a beautiful day, despite the fucked up turmoil in my veins, forming my hands into fists.

That wind's at my back and it'll stay there. Up ahead, I see the sun rising over the distant peaks, casting their shadows real pretty across the little cemetery sis calls home.

I don't realize I'm smiling till the urge to snort that smirk off my face shakes me something fierce.

"Yeah, yeah, things are just fine. I'm busy. Keeping the wife and our two munchkins happy, what more could a man ask for?" It's a question that has no answer. Truly. "You'd love 'em, Jenna. Hell, I think they've made Grandma a few years *younger* sometimes. Can't hardly keep up with her some days when she's got the kids. After she took one step into retirement, I worried..."

It's no lie. Thought the tough old bird would go stir crazy

after she hung up running the Inn one little piece at a time – assuming she didn't peck me to death for missing the little day-to-day details first.

Today, that place will be totally mine.

But the handover has been amazingly smooth. Gradual. And Grandma's taking to retirement with all the grace that's an elder Ford woman trademark.

There's a rustling in the trees when I look up again. "Yeah. You said it, sis. Nothing's ever gonna take Grandma down. Odds are you've got a good while before you'll see her again."

My hand crawls up the tombstone, grabs the edge, and squeezes something fierce.

"You already knew about Stew's man. That's not why I came. Well, not the only reason." I draw a harsh breath, sucking lungfuls of soft mountain air, each one cooler and more reviving than the last. "Doc got his hands on this last week – don't ask me how, or how the hell that man ever pulls off any of his weird shit. Here..."

Reaching into my pocket, I fumble around, searching. Then I drag it out, press the ice cold metal to my palm, lending a little of my heat before I lay it in the grass at the foot of her marker.

"That's the ring. Bress was gonna propose with it after you both came home. Before everything went sour, I mean. But you know that. You always do. Probably heard it from his own two lips, wherever you are." I pause, wishing I didn't sound like such an idiot.

Then again, the fact that I come here every season, talking to my long dead sister, says the line between sappy nostalgia and selfish foolery must be pretty damn thin.

"Figured you should have it anyway," I growl. "You deserved better. So did Dennis, even if he made his mistakes."

I mean every word.

I've thought long and hard about it over the years. I can't

blame Bress. He got boxed in by that freak everybody trusted, same as the rest of us.

I found out later he tried to set Stew up, even got a hit on him by the Grizzlies MC. Shame the piece of shit threatened his kid, leaving him to buckle and call it off.

"Eighteen years last week, Jenna. I'd say Rest in Peace like I always do," I say, my words slurring into a steaming roar. "But we know it didn't do a damn bit of good every time I'd come out here with those words. Not till Haley. Think you had something to do with bringing her into my life – or at least I hope you did. So let me just say thanks before I run. Thanks, sis. Thanks for everything. Rest easy like I know you will."

There's too much raw confusion rushing through my blood. I reach down, tearing gently at the grass in front of her stone, pulling at an inch or two of dirt, just enough to lay the ring in a little pit and shove the earth back over it.

Something cuts through me deeper than ever before as I stand, gripping her stone, and give the top of it a quick kiss.

Then, looking around to make sure nobody else caught that, I know it's time to go.

I'm a married man. A father. A business owner. A living, breathing creature trying to live every day like I know Jenna wants.

Sad to say, just her wanting the best for me wasn't ever enough.

But I found my *enough*, by God.

I found it the day that sweet, lush, all consuming whirlwind of a woman stepped out of her broken down Mustang and into the insanity that made us man and wife.

Every day since has been a blessing.

Every. Damn. Day.

Even when we were spitting nails at each other or were worried pale for our lives.

NICOLE SNOW

Because now these times where I find my way back to Jenna's grave are different. That's the ultimate proof the time's are a changin', as they say.

I'm not reminiscing about times gone by no more.

I'm telling her about the now, the future, every day I get to live in holy matrimony with sweet Hay.

And speaking of her, I'm gonna be late if I don't get moving. I've got to swing by the hardware store for some extra paint to finish up a little project we're doing.

She's expecting me. And these days, I'm never late for home.

* * *

I NEVER THOUGHT I'd see the day I'd be taking over Charming Inn without Grandma keeping one finger in.

Or that I'd be *happy* to, considering I never imagined this for my life.

Sometimes things happen. They just don't turn out the way you imagine, but that doesn't mean they don't turn out *exactly* the way they're meant to.

And it turns out what I needed was Hay to screw my fool head on straight.

This life, calm and settled, away from the roughnecks and the violence of bounty hunting, where my biggest problem every day is making sure the drunk vacationing college kids don't smash out our windows in between tallying up the daily cash.

It's been quieter on the home front, thank fuck.

Even old Flynn Bitters has gotten pretty helpful since I stepped into Grandma's boots.

Ever since he got into his program at church, he's been on the ball, helping keep this place running smoothly. Almost makes up for the years he spent creeping around, giving me crap, and hitting the bottle so hard it nearly got him canned more times than I can count.

Now? I see a new man. And he's hardly the only one.

Besides, chasing after rowdy college kids seems easy, and not just due to our little adventures with my friends.

Maybe it's because my own kids are little frigging *monsters*.

And having their older cousin Tara here is just goading them on. Hard to believe she was knee-high to a ladybug just a couple years ago. Now? I see a sweet, wiser, shy little thing who's coming into her own. Won't be more than a year or two before she's got boys beating down her door, and then I guess I'll have more trips to Seattle to look forward to so I can keep tabs on that. Her old man's a great guy, but too damn nice.

"Hey!" I hear Haley call out from the front foyer.

I'm on the upstairs balcony, touching up the paint on one of the little corner frescoes near the ceiling, balanced on the ladder. I grab hard onto one of the rafter beams as little Cody and Jenna come tearing through the lobby and race up the stairs, coming straight toward me.

Tara comes pattering after them, prim as ever in her preteens, but a glint of wickedness shines in her eyes that says *she's* the one who started this game, and she's not the slightest bit sorry.

The cat struts in behind them, orange tail in the air. Mozart pauses, glances at me dully, as if to say, *Please, War. I'm above all this – and how are you going to stop* me *from running, anyway?*

Haley's next, straggling out and brushing her hair back from her face, hands on her hips as she blows an exasperated huff through her lips.

She's dotted in paint everywhere, a look that's too familiar.

Must've been in her studio again. With the big show coming up in Portland, expecting a new showing next month, she's got to be ready to ship the paintings via special freight in two weeks.

And it's been mostly me and the kids with Mommy occasionally coming up for air every few days, blinking like the sunlight hurts her eyes.

She's doing it right now, though, squinting in that cute *is-this-the-real-world* way she has as she belts out, "Cody Michael Ford and Jenna Wilma Ford, you stop this instant!"

Our four-year-old boy and his three-year-old sister both freeze on the stairs, their eyes wide, lips thinning as they try not to giggle and flash each other guilty looks.

Tara, though, snickers without reservation, plopping down to sit on the stairs and crossing her ankles as she looks up at Hay.

"You didn't tell me to stop, Auntie Hay," she sing-songs, sticking out her tongue.

"Because you know better, young lady," Haley says, climbing up the stairs and settling to sit a few steps down from our kids. "These little creatures, though..."

Cody and Jenna plunk down with a giggle, exchanging one more mischievous look. "We were playing race to Daddy! Whoever wins gets hugs."

"Well," I say, "Daddy doesn't like it when you run when he's on a ladder, but since it's our game..." I drop down from the ladder, tossing my paintbrush into the waiting can and moving to the head of the stairs. Sinking down on one knee, I open my arms. "Everybody wins. Come get your hugs."

Next thing I know I've got an armful of kids who don't care that I'm as covered in paint as their ma.

Tara holds back, watching uncertainly, but I grin at her. "What the hell, girl? You think I didn't mean you too? Come give your uncle a goddamn hug."

"Swear jar, Uncle Warren," she says – some things never change – and then, with a grin, glues herself to me until it's like being tackled by a litter of puppies.

Laughing, I pretend I let myself get pushed back, wriggled over and snugged and hugged and buried in little hands.

Shit, look at me? Getting all torn up inside, this happy, sappy feeling so real it's a little bit like heartbreak.

Hard to believe this is my life in this town with the best woman on the planet.

Hard to believe everything once felt so empty, and now it's bursting full of light and love and life.

And I can feel that love, too, as I lift my head and catch my gorgeous wife watching us with this fondness in her eyes, pretty jade green soft and misted.

"Any room for me in there?" she asks.

"Always, Hay." I shift my armful of munchkins and hold one hand out for her. Haley immediately tucks herself into the crook of my arm, resting her head to my shoulder. I press a kiss to her hair. "All better."

Anything we might say is eclipsed by Cody and Jenna swarming to monkey-see, monkey-do what Daddy does, peppering kisses all over their mother's cheeks.

"We love you, Mommy," Jenna proclaims, blue eyes wide, and Cody nods emphatically.

"More'n anything."

Haley mock-gasps. "*No*. More than chocolate?"

"More than choc'lit!" Cody lisps.

"More than ice cream?" I add, and Jenna nods solemnly.

"More'n ice cream."

"Sorry, guys. I think I might like ice cream better," Tara proclaims, and everyone laughs.

"*You* just like to be contrary, kit. You'll grow out of it," Hay says, reaching over to poke her niece. "Speaking of chocolate and ice cream...who wants to go into town for a sundae?"

I lean down to murmur into her ear. "Do we have time?"

"For sure. This might be the last day we can get away before the summer rush hits," she answers, whispering against my ear, and even now the curl of her breath sends shivers through me. "We've got a whole bus of Japanese tourists coming tomorrow morning, remember?"

Shit, she's right. We'll even have to enlist Flynn to play tour guide around town so we can still get ready for Haley's show in Portland.

"Chocolate and ice cream and sundaes it is," I say and give the kids a nudge. "Up, up. Everybody go wash their hands."

As they scramble off, leaving me and Hay alone, we both watch after them, before Haley sighs, shaking her head with a smile. "Wow. They really are our kids. Sometimes it's hard to believe..."

"What? That they're full of trouble?" I grin.

"You're damn right." She leans into me, tucking her arm around my waist. "...we're both covered in paint and need to get cleaned up, too. So while we've got two seconds away from the kids, maybe we should make a little trouble ourselves."

I growl, and heat races over my skin.

We get so little time alone, and the thought of Haley in the shower, water beading on her flesh does terrible things to my dick.

"That's how we wound up with two kids, darlin'."

"I know." She grins, tangling her fingers in mine, and tugs. "Let's get a head start on making the third."

Shitfire. I don't need to hear it twice.

I run after her without hesitation as she drags me toward our bedroom suite and locks the door. We've got ten fiery minutes to ourselves before they'll realize we're gone and come looking.

Fuck.

Even after all these years, two adorable kids, settling down...she still kindles me into a raging flame with one look, one suggestion.

I can't imagine ever not wanting her. I can't imagine life any other way. We've paid our toll in hell for this heaven, and I'm gonna squeeze every sugary damn bit out of it.

Because I can't imagine my world without my Hay.

And there'll be no day without her for the rest of our lives.

ABOUT NICOLE SNOW

Nicole Snow is a *Wall Street Journal* and *USA Today* bestselling author. She found her love of writing by hashing out love scenes on lunch breaks and plotting her great escape from boardrooms. Her work roared onto the indie romance scene in 2014 with her Grizzlies MC series.

Since then Snow aims for the very best in growly, heart-of-gold alpha heroes, unbelievable suspense, and swoon storms aplenty.

Already hooked on her stuff? Visit nicolesnowbooks.com to sign up for her newsletter and connect on social media.

Got a question or comment on her work? Reach her anytime at nicole@nicolesnowbooks.com

Thanks for reading. And please remember to leave an honest review! Nothing helps an author more.

MORE BOOKS BY NICOLE

Stand Alone Novels

Accidental Hero

Accidental Protector

Accidental Romeo

Cinderella Undone

Man Enough

Surprise Daddy

Prince With Benefits

Marry Me Again

Love Scars

Recklessly His

Stepbrother UnSEALed

Stepbrother Charming

Heroes of Heart's Edge Books

No Perfect Hero

Enguard Protectors Books

Still Not Over You

Still Not Into You

Still Not Yours

Still Not Love

Baby Fever Books

Baby Fever Bride

Baby Fever Promise

Baby Fever Secrets

Only Pretend Books

Fiance on Paper

One Night Bride

Grizzlies MC Books

Outlaw's Kiss

Outlaw's Obsession

Outlaw's Bride

Outlaw's Vow

Deadly Pistols MC Books

Never Love an Outlaw

Never Kiss an Outlaw

Never Have an Outlaw's Baby

Never Wed an Outlaw

Prairie Devils MC Books

Outlaw Kind of Love

Nomad Kind of Love

Savage Kind of Love

Wicked Kind of Love

Bitter Kind of Love

Printed in Great Britain
by Amazon

54410652R20224